DUST OF THE LAND

303 -

44

8187

DUST OF THE LAND

J.H. FLETCHER

First Published 2014
Second Australian Paperback Edition 2015
ISBN 978 174369242 4

DUST OF THE LAND
© 2014 by John Fletcher
Australian Copyright 2014
New Zealand Copyright 2014

This is a work of fiction. Names, characters, places, and incidents are either the product of the author's imagination or are used fictitiously, and any resemblance to actual persons, living or dead, business establishments, events, or locales is entirely coincidental.

Published by
Harlequin Mira
An imprint of Harlequin Enterprises (Australia) Pty Ltd.
Level 13, 201 Elizabeth Street
SYDNEY NSW 2000
AUSTRALIA

® and TM are trademarks of Harlequin Enterprises Limited or its corporate affiliates. Trademarks indicated with ® are registered in Australia, New Zealand, and in other countries.

Printed and bound in Australia by McPherson's Printing Group

MIX
Paper from
responsible sources
FSC
www.fsc.org   FSC® C001695

To Selwa
Agent and friend
To whom I owe so much

I do not support Queen Elizabeth's nonsense about having a man's heart in a woman's body. I have a woman's body and a woman's heart, and together they make me a match for any man.

Bella Tucker

CHAPTER ONE

Bella Tucker woke at four-thirty, as she did every morning. As disciplined in mind as body, she never needed an alarm: this had been her time for getting up for as long as she could remember.

That it was a Sunday and her sixty-fifth birthday made no difference to her routine. She was one day older than yesterday, not one year, and the fuss made about such things always amazed her. Most women retired from work before they were sixty but Bella felt as young and vital as always. She had no plans to hand over the day-to-day management of the business any time soon; should she ever decide to do so, there was still a world beyond mining and iron ore. New challenges had always supplied the oxygen her spirit demanded and there were many projects out there to excite her. Retirement? Death? There was no room in her plans for either.

She got out of bed, feet sinking into the luxurious carpet, and headed for the bathroom. Twenty minutes later, after her customary workout, her mind already grappling with the challenges of the coming day, she went barefoot into the jarrah-panelled study next to her bedroom.

Unlike the downstairs office where Bella met staff and advisers, this was the place where she kept her personal mementos: photographs of her husband Garth and their two children, Peace and Richard; a snap of her mother taken forty-seven years earlier; and a more recent one of Maisie, the Aboriginal friend who had taught her so much about the bush and who had helped keep her sane during the bad times. On a side wall hung an oil painting of her grandfather, the earl, sitting on the terrace at Ripon Grange, his favourite gun dog at his feet.

This room was the thinking place where Bella planned her business strategies and the future. Apart from a leather-bound blotting pad and gold pen and pencil set, the desk was bare. She sat down, opened a drawer and took out a file containing the text of the speech she would be making that morning. Ten minutes later she put it to one side, satisfied she knew what she wanted to say and how to say it, and turned to the documents that Martin Dexter, her financial director, had sent over the night before. Sixty-fifth birthday or not, there was still work to be done.

For the next two hours she studied cash-flow projections, anticipated ore tonnages, details of the delivery of the last freight wagons, safety reports from the mine... Occasionally she jotted a note to remind her of a point that needed clarification, but in the main everything seemed in order.

At seven o'clock, half an hour after the first light had started stealing through the curtains, Bella locked the papers away and went into the bedroom to put on her riding gear. She pulled on her freshly polished boots, ran down the sweeping staircase to the marble-floored hallway and headed for the stables at the rear of the house.

She was wearing breeches, woollen shirt and heavy sweater: it was August, after all. She rode every morning she could manage; with two hundred and fifty acres of grounds, she had plenty of space. She saddled up, slapped on her hard hat and rode out as the sun rose in a festival of birdsong. She saw no one. The staff knew to keep out of her way; this was still her thinking time, and woe betide anyone who intruded on it.

Riding brought Bella closest to her husband and the days when they had mustered cattle together across the unfenced miles of the north. Dear Garth, who had given her so much. His death, twenty-one years earlier, was an enduring wound.

Riding also reminded her of her adolescence in Yorkshire, where she had first learnt about horses and the saddle. The memories returned every morning: childhood in the cottage with her unmarried mother; Ripon Grange and her wicked witch of a stepmother; her lost love; marriage to Garth Tucker; and the one-and-a-half-million-acre Miranda Downs in Australia's far north...

She welcomed them because they reminded her not only of how far she had come but how far she still had to go. It was the future that mattered and the future was glorious. Tomorrow she would sign the ten-year lease of a rail link owned by rival company BradMin. This would enable her to go on delivering ore to the Baoshan blast furnaces at Shanghai long and profitably enough to build her own railway and escape from reliance on a rival she did not trust. After all the years of struggle, the future of the company she had built from nothing and of her family would be secure.

It was a thought to bring music to her day.

She reached the gallop she'd had opened at the edge of the woodland so that both horse and rider could get the workout they craved. She leant forward to murmur in Caliph's ear. 'Let's go!'

She thumped her heels firmly against the gelding's flanks. At once they were flying, the cold air bringing tears to her eyes, the reins taut in her gloved hands. All too soon they reached the end of the ride and drew up, both panting. Bella patted Caliph's flank. 'Well done, boy.'

At one time she'd joined the breakfast gallops at Ascot, with its thousand-metre straight, but the media had got on to that and she had found she couldn't go out without some journo shouting inane questions at her.

'Mining, Ms Tucker? You reckon a woman's up to it?'

Darn right I do.

She walked Caliph more quietly, remembering how she had presented the draft agreement to the previous week's board meeting.
Martin Dexter apart, these were family gatherings – her children
Peace and Richard, daughter-in-law Su-Ying and herself – but Bella
insisted that meetings of the board be conducted formally, with her
in the chair.

'Of course we must sign,' said instant-action Peace. A top mining
engineer, she was as fiery as Vesuvius when the mood was on her.
'We can hardly carry the ore on our backs and pack mules went out
a century ago.'

Richard was an accountant, shrewd but cautious. 'Certainly we
need an agreement,' he said. 'But not this one.'

'Why not?' Bella said, to test him.

'I don't like the clause that says we can't build our own rail link
for five years after signing the agreement. It puts us too much in
their hands. They can close us down any time –'

'Typical accountant,' Peace interrupted. 'A problem for every
solution. Why should they do that? They'll be making good money
out of us. And in five years we'll have enough stashed away to fund
our own railway.'

'BradMin is not in the business of helping us deliver,' Richard
said. 'What they really want is our ore and our contracts. A typical
accountant can see that, even if a mining engineer can't.'

'I've convened this meeting to review our options,' Bella said
tartly. 'I am not interested in your childish bickering.'

She studied her two children.

Peace, face like flame, was in no doubt, but Peace was never in
doubt about anything. Thirty-nine years old and unmarried, she
was an honours graduate of the University of Western Australia
and the Camborne School of Mines, with an extraordinary nose
for land and minerals. Physically she resembled no one in the
family. She was five feet seven inches tall and broad-shouldered,
with brown hair and eyes. She was practical and intensely com-
petitive; faced with opposition, her instinct was to kick it to death.

Bella knew Peace would have dominated her, too, given half a chance: not that there was any likelihood of that.

Richard was a different proposition. Two years younger than his sister, just under six feet and slender, with Bella's dark good looks, he was a stiletto to Peace's battleaxe. Studious and reserved by nature, he was a financial whiz who was not only married to a Chinese woman but spoke fluent Mandarin, qualities that would be increasingly valuable to the group, with iron ore deliveries to China set to increase rapidly.

Brother and sister stood shoulder to shoulder against the outside world, yet in the privacy of the boardroom they were always picking on each other: Peace thought Richard not confrontational enough; he returned the compliment because she lacked subtlety.

Bella didn't let it worry her too much; it might present a problem down the track but for the moment she never let their conflicts get out of hand and their complementary skills were of huge value to the company.

Martin Dexter had been in favour of the deal. Bella had expected nothing else, because Martin had ambitions of his own. Not only did he want to remain financial director of the group; for years he had been sending her signals that he would like a personal relationship with her. In some ways she would have liked that, too. Sixty-five or not, she was by no means too old for a frolic if the opportunity arose. From time to time she indulged herself by imagining what such an affair would be like – Martin was almost the same age as she was but still a bundle of sexual promise, with good shoulders and a backside to die for – but she knew she would never allow it to happen. A woman in her position was often the target of ambitious men hoping to talk her into mixing business with pleasure but Bella was too much in control of her life to fall for that one, however charming the men might be.

She would go ahead, she told herself as she rode up the slope behind the house. Tomorrow she would sign. Delivery of ore to China's steel mills would continue far into the future: each of the especially commissioned locomotives drawing its load of two hundred wagons, eighty thousand dollars' worth of ore in each. Sixteen million dollars per trainload: it was a mind-boggling thought.

She reached the summit and reined in, looking down at the house she had named Desire. The grand building, white-painted, stood on a bluff overlooking Perth's Swan River. There was a five-acre garden around the house; the rest was scrub and eucalyptus bush with riding trails cut through it.

Garth had complained that the building, with its Corinthian pillars and portico, was ostentatious. He had been right. It was why Bella had bought the land in the first place. It was in the days when only a handful of people had known about the discoveries she and her husband had made in the far north, and she had intended the house to show the world that the Tuckers had arrived. At vast expense she had retained a world-famous architect to design the building in accordance with her wishes and a former curator of the Botanical Gardens to advise on the layout of the grounds. Even now it was a show place, demonstrating how far she – and Garth, before his death – had come from Miranda Downs, the property she still owned in the far north, home to snakes, dingoes, kangaroos, countless birds and approximately forty thousand head of cattle: no one knew exactly how many. Now she could foresee the time when Tucker Mining would be one of the wealthiest and most powerful operations in the country, because development of their open-cut mine in the Pilbara was only a beginning. With funds from the mine she would expand the company's operations to fifty times their present size. They would prospect for new ore deposits. They would diversify. They were already developing an open-cut coalmine in New South Wales. They were exporting live cattle to Indonesia, the construction company was doing good business and the engineering works was flat out satisfying the growing needs of the mining industry. Later there would be real estate, financial services and transportation. There was talk overseas of permanently renewable power, obtained from the sun and wind. Wouldn't that be something? she thought. There was a man in Denmark who was said to be an authority; she would get her London agent to contact him, confidentially. What about water? Australia was perennially short of water. Maybe they could resolve that, too, in time and with sufficient resources. Make the desert rejoice: wasn't that what the Bible said? They would fund hospitals, adventure schools, institutes of higher learning, medical research... Excitement swarmed through her as she rode. So many marvellous challenges lay ahead. And she would be equal to them. At that moment she was twenty again, the world at her feet. There was nothing she could not do. Once the lease was signed.

Back at the house she dismounted, casting her eye around the sky. It was cloudless – just as well, with two hundred guests for lunch. Bella handed Caliph's reins to a waiting groom and walked to the western side of the house where a large marquee had been erected on the lawn below the terrace. Teams of men were setting out tables and chairs; an electrician was running cables for the lights, microphones and band. The dais and lectern were in place and a bar had been set up along one of the canvas walls.

Deborah Smith, Bella's thirty-year-old assistant, was keeping an eye on things. She had been a member of the team for eleven years and Bella trusted her completely. Sunday or not, Bella expected her staff to work when required, although she always compensated them with extra pay and time off later. She walked over to her.

'Caterers?'

'Coming at eleven,' Deborah said. 'They'll bring their own cookers and portable barbecues but I told them they could also use our kitchens if they wanted.'

'Let me see the menu.' She studied it for a minute, pleased that her instructions had been carried out to the letter, then handed it back without comment. 'Flowers?'

'Within the hour.'

'The bar?'

'All the usual things plus soft drinks, tea and coffee. Twenty cases of champagne on ice.' Deborah smiled. 'Only domestic, but the premier won't be able to complain, will he? Not with us a wine-growing state.'

'Two hundred and forty bottles,' Bella said. 'Over one a head. Will they really drink that much?'

'Some will,' Deborah said. 'Especially the journos.'

Bella supposed she was right. She walked into the house and went upstairs to her bedroom. She stripped off and went into the bathroom, where Annie had prepared her bath. For much of her life such indulgence had been out of the question; mustering cattle in her Miranda Downs days even a simple sluice-down had often been impossible. She thought perhaps that was why she valued it so highly now. Whatever the reason, she regarded her daily bath as one of her most important rituals. It was not simply a question of cleansing her body: she had always believed that it cleansed her mind, too, leaving it free to concentrate on the problems and challenges of the day ahead. It had other benefits as well. Being rich and powerful had its dangers and she had known many who had let that sort of thing go to their heads. She was determined it would not happen to her. I may be an autocrat, she thought, because I know no other way to run my life, but I have always despised self-importance. Having her daily wallow was, absurdly, the best way she knew of keeping her feet on the ground.

She lay in the giant circular tub, letting her body soak in the scented water, while she considered the responsibility that she carried for the continuing success of the company. Upon that depended not only her legacy, what she had been able to achieve by a lifetime of struggle, but also the long-term well-being of the family. It was a glorious burden and she did not regret it for a moment. She was as fit as a flea, thank God, but her sixty-fifth birthday was an appropriate time to remind herself that the future would eventually lie in the hands of the next generation — Peace, Richard, Su-Ying and their children — and it was her duty to ensure they were ready to take over when the time came. It would not be easy — Peace and Richard had somehow to reconcile their differences — but somehow she must find a way. If she failed they could be looking not at triumph but disaster.

Pray God it will not come to that, she thought. If it does, all my life will have been in vain.

She allowed herself her usual ten minutes in the bath then climbed out, towelled herself dry and dressed in the same style of sober business suit that she wore every day of her working life. As she began putting on her make-up she rang the bell. Three minutes later Annie brought breakfast on a tray: a croissant with a miserly portion of imported cherry jam on the side, a thimble-sized helping of natural yoghurt and a pot of green tea, which Annie poured; this, too, was part of Bella's morning ritual.

'Breakfast is ready, Mrs Tucker.'

Annie left the room. Bella sat in the Hepplewhite chair, glancing at the morning paper as she ate and drank. Australia had beaten England in some football match. There was an article about the actor Richard Burton who had died a week ago in Geneva. Seven years younger than I am, Bella thought. And James Mason last month. At least he'd been in his seventies. It made you think, all the same.

There was a feature about Bella Tucker and her sixty-fifth birthday party. *THE NEW ALCHEMIST*, the headline read. *The woman who is turning iron into gold.*

The significance of the China connection had clearly sunk in. She put the paper aside, swallowed the last of her tea, collected her papers and headed downstairs to the office where nowadays the bulk of her business was conducted. This room was larger and more business-like than the study upstairs, with an adjoining boardroom where bigger meetings were held. The colours of the furnishings were vibrant, reds and yellows predominant. A lot of stainless steel and glass. The desk and chairs were Swedish, their design newer than tomorrow. Telephones provided direct lines to the mine, Miranda Downs and Martin Dexter.

She looked at the clock; there were three hours before she must get ready for the party. In the meantime she had time to get down to the neat piles of papers on her desk.

It was all so different from her old life. At Miranda Downs getting down to business had meant hours in the saddle, rounding up cattle and transporting them to the meatworks at Wyndham. It had meant dust, heat and the vastness of the unfenced bush. There were times when she missed the physical challenges of those days but it was impossible to go back; the future was now, and tomorrow, and the rest of her life.

By a quarter to twelve the sun was shining brightly. The day had warmed up and the guests were strolling around the grounds, suits and party hats much in evidence. There wasn't much to see in the flowerbeds, although here and there drifts of early-flowering narcissi were beginning to show their faces.

Bella watched from an upstairs window while Deborah chivvied the guests to their seats inside the marquee. The premier and his wife were there: good. Pete Bathurst, BradMin's belligerent CEO and Bella's long-time enemy, had brought Melanie, the young woman he called his executive assistant but whose duties extended beyond normal office routines. Or so said Bella's spy in BradMin's offices. Big-breasted Melanie looked thirty years younger than Pete and Bella wondered if she was worth it; she'd heard his last bimbo had cost him a packet.

The Australian representative of China's Baoshan smelting works had come alone, as had Mr Hong, the Chinese consul. Both wore well-cut lounge suits – only ten years back it would have been Mao jackets. But ten years back trade with China had been an impossible dream; only with Mao's death in 1976 had China begun to emerge into the light.

At last Deborah signalled that the guests were seated, the band ready to strike up. Bella walked downstairs. She paused at the top of the terrace steps. The guests could see her now and there was a murmur of applause but still she waited; she had always known the value of making an entrance.

She had decided on a Carla Zampatti outfit, striking without flamboyance: ivory silk brocade jacket, thigh length, with sculpted collar and cuffs; black silky pants and high-heeled ankle boots to show off her still-elegant legs. She was wearing the sapphire drop earrings that Garth had given her for their twentieth wedding anniversary and a sapphire and diamond sunburst brooch on her jacket. Her hair – dark, with barely a thread of grey – was glossy and impeccably fashioned, her perfume as fresh as summer roses, as expensive as her wardrobe. She had always believed that smelling good was as important as looking good and that both had to be suited to the occasion and her audience. Today she was looking for style, discreet glamour and an air of competence, and she thought she had pulled it off. Smiling, she walked down the steps to join her applauding guests.

An hour and a half later people had once again begun to circulate. Insofar as she ever was, Bella was content, knowing the occasion had been a success. Her eyes had been everywhere and she had made sure that her guests had eaten and drunk their fill. The lobsters had taken a caning, and the champagne. The tot who had been detailed to present orchids to the premier's wife had neither dropped them nor thrown up; Bella's speech, promising an era of increasing prosperity for the state and the nation, had been rapturously received. The premier had presented her with a plaque naming her the state's most prominent businesswoman. Everyone had joined in singing 'Happy Birthday'.

Pete Bathurst strolled past, Melanie hanging from his muscular arm. Bella gave him a big smile; she and Pete might detest each other, but this was not the place to show it. 'Glad you could make it,' she said.

'Hey, Bella, how're you goin'?' And continued without waiting for an answer. 'Great party. I mean it. That lobster... Wow!' He leered at Melanie. 'Bit of extra pep just where it's needed – ain't that right, sugar?'

Conversation with Pete Bathurst gave new meaning to the word gross, while Melanie eyed Bella curiously, no doubt wondering how anyone so old could still be alive.

'See you tomorrow,' Bella said.

Pete's expression became serious. He leant close, suddenly confidential. 'I don't want to spoil your party, but you might as well know. We got problems with the agreement, Bella.'

How sorrowful he looked! Yet Bella thought she detected a glimmer of triumph in the dark eyes. 'It has all been settled,' she said coldly.

He shook his head ruefully. 'You know these lawyers… I tell you frankly, Bella, I wonder sometimes why we have them.'

With a cheery wave he strolled on, leaving Bella's mind in turmoil.

Deborah, face drawn, was suddenly at her shoulder. Bella felt a flicker of concern. First Bathurst, and now?

'What's the problem?'

'A letter from the bank came an hour ago. Hand delivered. I had to sign for it.'

A letter from the bank? On a Sunday? Bella's concern deepened. 'What does it say?'

'I don't know. It was marked urgent and confidential so I didn't open it.'

'Why didn't you call me at once?'

'I didn't want to distract you. It was just before you started your speech.'

'When a bank letter has urgent and confidential on the envelope you let me know even if I'm in bed with my lover.'

Not, sadly, that she had one of those.

Bella opened the envelope, took out the letter and read it. She felt her lips go numb. Somehow she managed a smile.

'Everything all right, Ms Tucker?'

'Everything's fine. Why shouldn't it be?'

She returned to the party. The momentary wave of weakness had passed. Now was the time to circulate and she did so, smiling, gracious, while inside her head…

Dear God!

In phrases so convoluted as to be barely comprehensible, the letter advised that the directors of the bank had decided to rationalise Tuckers's loan situation. That was the phrase they used: to rationalise. As though there was anything rational about what followed.

The bank therefore advises that failure, within seven days of this letter, to return all balances to the agreed operating limits will necessitate calling in the entirety of the group's outstanding loans. Any inconvenience is regretted.

Inconvenience? Ruin, more like.

It made no sense. Halliburton, the bank's regional boss, had known they were way over their limit but had gone along because he had also known the situation would be rectified as soon as the money from the China contracts began to flow in. Now this.

Still Bella smiled, while congratulations and compliments buzzed about her like bees and questions blazed in her tortured brain.

Why today, of all days? When they were scheduled to sign the rail agreement tomorrow? All of a sudden both Pete Bathurst and the bank were on her case. It could not be coincidence. What was going on? If the agreement fell through, if the bank foreclosed…

She was ruined, and the family with her.

Bella checked her watch: half-past two; seven-thirty in the morning in London. She beckoned Deborah to her side.

'Find out whether there will be anything about the group in tomorrow's overseas papers. Check *The Wall Street Journal*, *Financial Times*, *Les Echos* in Paris, *Capital* in Hamburg, *The Rand Daily Mail* in Johannesburg. Be discreet, but I have to know what they're saying. Get on to it immediately. Okay?'

Deborah locked herself away in her office. Her phone ran hot. Within the hour she was back, her face a map of concern. She started to speak but Bella hushed her and took her to one side. When they were safe from eavesdroppers she stopped.

'Well?'

'*The Wall Street Journal* will be reporting a leading New York broking firm as cautioning its clients about our shares.'

'A selling signal?' Bella snapped.

'Not yet.'

Even so, a caution was bad enough.

'The other papers all have items questioning the group's viability. Are we all right, Ms Tucker? Is there anything I can do to help?'

Deborah was less than half Bella's age yet there were times when their roles seemed to be reversed, with Deborah anxious as always to protect and comfort her.

Bella laughed out loud for the benefit of the guests and gave Deborah her most radiant smile. 'Everything's fine.'

Why lie about it? Bella asked herself as Deborah walked away. Because it made sense to lie. The longer she could put off admitting anything the better, because the news was as bad as could be. Only rumours, admittedly, but rumours could kill. When the markets opened in Europe and the US, there would be a wave of selling. The predators would descend, scenting a victim. Thank goodness the family had a controlling interest.

Whoever had laid this ambush had done it well. To strike today, when she was surrounded by admirers who would run a mile if they knew what she knew now, when the future had seemed secure... It was a devastating blow that she would revenge when she could, but what mattered now was not so much who had done it but how to control the fallout. Delay would be fatal.

Owen Freeth, the group's long-time legal adviser, was talking to another guest. Smiling graciously this way and that, she made her way through the crush towards him.

'A word with you, Owen.'

He lifted a fastidious eyebrow. 'Now?'

Her smile did not falter. 'When the party winds up.'

CHAPTER TWO

Standing in the pale sunlight just outside the marquee, Peace Tucker watched her mother talking to Deborah Smith. Bella was holding a piece of paper in her hand, her face animated. Peace heard her laugh and felt the mixture of affection and resentment that had characterised their relationship for as long as Peace could remember.

Still boss of the sidewalk, Peace thought, and obviously planning to stay there for a long time yet. Which was all very well, but where did that leave Peace?

Not that she was planning to think about it for long. Not today, anyway. From the moment it began she had been itching for the party to be over so she could get back to work. She was well aware the rest of the world, her family included, called her a workaholic. She didn't deny it; it was a quality that had helped her get honours at uni and the Macalister gold medal for student of the year at the Camborne School of Mines in England, and on this occasion at least she knew her obsession was justified. New areas had been surveyed with promising results and at the last board meeting they had decided, subject to obtaining adequate finance, to go ahead. She had supported the decision and still did but there were time constraints. Once a company had indicated its intention to develop

16 J.H. FLETCHER

a claim the state government set a time limit within which extraction of the ore had to begin, so time was a horseman with his spurs set deep in Bella's flanks. In the circumstances Peace would have preferred not to be at the party at all but with such a big deal being made of her mother's birthday she had reluctantly accepted that she had no choice.

At least she had been able to rope in Bernie Thompson to help her out.

'I'd sooner it was you going to Mother's birthday bash than me,' she had told her assistant earlier that morning. 'But if I don't show my face I'll never hear the last of it.'

Bernie was young and enthusiastic. He had been invited to the party too but for the moment was happy to put work ahead of the dubious pleasure of socialising with his ultimate boss. He was also ambitious so Peace knew he might not always feel that way but that was a problem for another day and she had enough on her plate as it was.

'We'll need to construct a spur to connect with the main rail line,' she said. 'Otherwise we won't be able to get the ore out.'

'Judging by the contours that may mean some blasting,' Bernie said. 'Either that or go the long way round that incline. I'll look into it.'

'While I'm getting sloshed on vintage champagne,' Peace said.

'A tough job,' Bernie said, 'but somebody has to do it.'

Peace had promised she would be back with him as soon as she could make it and now, seeing Bella engulfed by well-wishers, she slipped away. Hopefully her departure would go unnoticed by anyone who mattered.

Bernie raised his eyebrows as she came into the office. 'I thought you'd be hours yet. What happened to the champagne?'

'It was domestic,' Peace said. 'How's it going?'

They discussed the work Bernie had been doing in her absence.

'It's like I thought,' he said. 'The gradient's too steep to go directly over that incline.'

'Then we shall have to blast,' Peace said. 'It's too far to go round.'

'I've got some figures here.'

An hour passed before they took a five-minute break for a coffee and a chat about how things were going.

'Finance fixed up?' Bernie asked.

'It had better be,' Peace said. 'Or we stand to lose the claim. But that's Martin's baby, not mine.'

'One thing you can guarantee,' Bernie said. 'It'll always come in over budget.'

'In the mega-millions, too,' Peace said. 'You're right. I'll have a word when I see him.'

They carried on with what they had been doing: good, productive work that warmed Peace's heart.

It was getting dark when the telephone rang. Peace, standing by it, picked it up.

'Peace Tucker…' She listened with dawning astonishment. Concern, too, although she took care to let none of her feelings show in her face. 'Can't it wait? We're flat out here.'

She waited, listening. 'Very well,' she said eventually. 'We'll get onto it straight away.'

Bernie watched her enquiringly as she put the phone down. 'Trouble?'

'I hope not. But Bella wants some figures and she wants them tonight.'

'On a Sunday evening? Must be something pretty important.'

'I guess we'll soon know,' said Peace.

'Interesting times,' Bernie said.

'They'd better not be too interesting,' Peace said.

It was late afternoon by the time Su-Ying and Richard got home from the party.

Richard said he had some work to do and went into his study while Su-Ying paid the babysitter. Adam, her number one son, was staying with friends but she settled down to spend what the stupid so-called experts called quality time with younger son James, aged seven. As if any time spent with your children could be anything but quality time, Su-Ying thought.

She should know if anyone did, because in her case she had often not seen her father for weeks on end. Of course things had been very different in Beijing in those days. Her father had been a high official in the communist party, an aide to Minister Deng Xiao-Ping, no less, and his responsibilities had meant that he had little time to spend with his family. Nevertheless it had been her choice as well as her filial duty to respect him highly and she still did, although it was a long time since she had last seen him.

Because of his position in the party she had been one of those sent to a school for the children of top officials. She had excelled at her studies and with Minister Deng's approval had been selected to go to Australia to improve her English and to learn the foreigners' ways in the hope that her knowledge might be used for China's benefit.

It had been a great honour to be selected to serve the party in this way but she had been horrified. All her life she had been taught that the people in the west were poor as well as ignorant and that starvation was rife – that living standards generally were far below those of China, which under the inspired guidance of Great Helmsman Mao enjoyed the highest quality of life in the world. She had also been taught that westerners hated the Chinese out of innate wickedness and because of their envy of China's great achievements.

She had pleaded with her father to be excused this responsibility. She had wept, offering to work as a labourer or a street cleaner if only she could be permitted to stay in China, but it had done no good. Her father had been adamant. She must obey or be driven out from the family, which was the most terrible punishment in the world. So she had come to Australia accompanied by men to instruct her and keep her safe and keep her father informed of her progress. She had discovered, first with surprise but later with a sense of betrayal, that things in the west were not as she had been taught. Living standards in Australia were far higher than in China, while the Australians she met did not hate Chinese people at all.

She had become friendly with a fellow student named Richard Tucker, but cautiously, knowing that her father would disapprove. Then had come the Cultural Revolution and the question of whether she should return to China to face the Red Guards or remain in Australia.

Su-Ying sighed, remembering those dangerous times. To distract herself from her memories she encouraged James to show her his latest drawings. The boy had talent and his teachers had spoken highly of his potential. She exclaimed over the work he showed her and then read to him until suppertime. After that she made him read to her, knowing how important study was and how his ability to read was vital to the success in life that she craved for him.

'A good education is the key to a good life,' she told him, as she did nearly every day. 'Therefore you must work hard and study hard. Hah?'

She had never lost her Chinese way of speaking, nor had she made any serious attempt to do so. Why should she? She was Chinese, after all.

Later, with James asleep, she and Richard went for a walk.

The mansion her mother-in-law had named Desire was easily big enough to accommodate all the family but two years ago they had moved out and bought a three-bedroom bungalow not far from the Swan River. It had seemed strange to Su-Ying that they should do this but it was the way things were done in the west and she had learnt to accept it, even though in her heart she did not agree.

They strolled along the footpath beside the water. The darkness was alive with cicadas. Water birds squawked sleepily in the reeds, the sky was full of stars and the surface of the stream was burnished with silver light.

They walked hand in hand, saying little, listening to the murmur of the water. In the bushes a dark shape took off in a thump of frightened feet.

Startled, Su-Ying's fingers tightened on her husband's hand.

'Only a wallaby,' Richard said.

'It made me jump,' she said.

'Leave jumping to the wallabies,' he told her, and kissed her on lips and eyes before they strolled on.

They walked for another five minutes before turning back. Su-Ying's being was suffused with warmth. Richard seldom kissed her outside the bedroom; what he had just done signalled affection rather than desire, yet affection was capable of kindling desire and she tightened her grip on his hand. Impulsively she stopped in mid-stride and turned to him. Starlight shone silver in his eyes as she put her arms around his neck, willing him to kiss her again. As he did. Willing him to place his hand on her breast, a portent of what was to come when they got home. As he did.

She knew she was beautiful tonight. When she was a child her grandmother had told her that love made all things beautiful; that knowledge gave her confidence, and her smile was radiant.

'Come on, then,' she said, tugging at his hand. 'Come on.'

They reached home to find the telephone ringing.

CHAPTER THREE

Bella crossed the rhododendron garden that in spring would be a wonderland of red, orange and white blooms and went into the house. It was a palatial entrance. From the glossy black front doors, fifteen feet high, the visitor had a view of a vast marble-floored hall with a sweeping staircase rising to the second level. It was a fairy-tale welcome to a fairy-tale palace. All was clean and ethereal, as though the hall and staircase were flying. The marble might have made it cold but the effect was softened by high windows rising to the second floor, through which the afternoon sunlight fell in slanting pillars of golden light. There were red and indigo silk carpets from China spread upon the floor and a Qianlong bowl in a display cabinet; Bella's taste had always favoured the Asian.

She climbed the stairs to her private study and sat at her desk. She studied the photographs of those who had loved her, those she had loved.

While she waited for Owen to join her she considered who might be behind the day's developments. Pete Bathurst was the obvious suspect. BradMin's boss had the most to gain if Tuckers failed yet he could not have done it alone. He might have tipped off the international press, but outside Tuckers's top management nobody knew their financial situation. It had to be an inside job. Who, beside herself, was in the know? Peace and Richard? They were her children, for God's sake! Richard's wife Su-Ying, whom she respected so much? Martin Dexter, her friend and would-be lover? Owen Freeth, the lawyer who had been with her for twenty-one years? It was unthinkable that any of them could have betrayed her, yet one of them must have done it. No alternative was possible.

Bella buried her head in her hands. Was there nobody she could trust?

The answer was stark and inescapable: there was not. She had always been alone; she had learnt that lesson as a child and repeatedly since, her memories of betrayal and abandonment as painful now as ever. Yet she had also benefitted from her experiences. She had learnt to fight, to be on her guard. No one got close to her without permission, while to be alone was also the burden and privilege of leadership. Now, in this hour of trial, that was doubly true. Betrayal was a blade, cutting deep. She could feel the hurt spreading through her body. Something else, too: a remorseless will to win, despite everything. And, in winning, to destroy the culprits. Whoever they might be.

She knew people called her ruthless. She preferred to think she was determined. Whichever it was, it stemmed from the time when she was six years old and had first discovered what it was like to possess, then lose, everything her heart desired.

CHAPTER FOUR

It was early morning, the blackbirds singing in the hedgerows, when Bella heard the horse in the lane. Mumma was sweeping out the sitting room and Bella saw her straighten her back as the gate clicked.

It's Daddy come to see us, thought Bella, clapping her hands, but then she remembered it couldn't be because Daddy had visited them only two days earlier and told them he would be away for two weeks with his father the earl visiting some of the family's estates in Devon.

The next thing Bella knew, this man, thickset and gaitered, was banging his clenched fist on the cottage's open door. He looked horrible, with a round, scarred head and close-set eyes. His shoulders filled the doorway. He smiled, showing broken teeth. 'Mornin', Missus.'

Mumma looked at him suspiciously. He was from the estate, Bella knew, but why he was here this sunny June morning she could not imagine.

'Nice place tha got 'ere,' the man said.

'It'll do,' Mumma said shortly. 'What can I do for you?'

'Name's Willis. Factor at Grange. 'Appen tha knows that.'

'I know who you are, yes.'

'Got bad news, Missus. Sorry 'bout it.'

He doesn't look sorry, Bella thought. His huge fist was holding a folded piece of paper, which he thrust under Mumma's nose.

Mumma looked without touching it. 'What is it?'

'Notice to quit. Twenty-four hours' notice.'

Watching, Bella saw Mumma's face go white. ''E's 'avin' us put out?'

'That I can't say. All I know is out tha must go, by this time termorrer. An' I'll be 'ere to make sure of it.'

'I can't believe it,' Mumma whispered. Her eyes were wet. ''Ow can 'e do this to us?'

'Thee an' thine,' Willis said. 'An' I've orders to check the furniture, an' all, to make sure tha don't tak' nuthin' that don't belong to yer.'

'But where will we go?'

'Where tha wants, as long as tes away from 'ere. 'Ere,' he said impatiently. 'Tha gunna tak' it, or mun I drop it on't floor?'

'It's a misunderstanding,' Mumma said desperately. 'I'll go to the Grange, talk to someone –'

'Tha'll not get past gate,' the man said.

'Who's to stop me?' she said with sudden fury.

'Orders. 'Ere, tak' it.'

He thrust the paper into her hand and walked away, heavy body swaying on his gaitered legs. At the gate he looked back at Mumma, still staring at him from the open doorway. 'This time termorrer, I'll be back.'

The latch clicked; he was gone.

Bella was scared, sensing trouble. Mumma stared at nothing, the tears running down her face.

''Ow could 'e 'ave done this to us?' Mumma said. 'When we loves 'im so much?'

She was talking to herself, or to the air, which frightened Bella even more. 'What did the man want?' she asked.

'They're gunna chuck us out.'

'Will Daddy be coming with us?'

'No, he won't.'

'But I like it here. I don't want to go.'

'You mustn't talk like that!' Mumma tried to put on a cheerful look but Bella was not fooled. 'We'll go back to London, jest the two of us. You'll like London. You 'n' me'll 'ave a great time together. What you think o' that, eh?'

Bella stared at the tears shining in Mumma's eyes. 'Why are you crying?'

'Excitement, that's what it is. A new adventure.'

But she put her arms around Bella and Bella felt the sobs she was trying to hide. Frightened and uncomprehending, she stood with eyes screwed tight, face pressed into Mumma's side, and felt the secure foundations of her world shake as she prayed with every ounce of her being that this nightmare, so terrible and unexpected, would go away.

Mumma found them a one-room flat in the slums of Rotherhithe, on the third floor of a dilapidated building not far from the church. Along the river the low tide exposed mud banks where gulls pecked at refuse brought down by the stream, and the air was foul with its stench. There was one bathroom and toilet per floor, shared by ten families. Usually it was filthy.

'This is a horrible place,' Bella wept. 'I want to go home.'

Home to the cottage, the apple tree, the blackbird singing in its branches.

'You'll just have to get used to it,' Mumma said.

Bella knew she never would. It was June yet the weather was cold and it never seemed to stop raining; after the neat Yorkshire cottage it was a nightmare. For weeks after their arrival Bella suffered from terrors that woke her every night, shaking and crying with fear. She couldn't understand how her world could have fallen apart so horribly or why Mumma didn't seem able to put things right.

Every morning Mumma went out, telling Bella she was going to look for work. Sometimes she came back smiling, saying she'd done some cleaning for a lady down the street. Those were the days she brought home something special for their tea – but it didn't happen very often. Most days when she came back Bella could tell from her expression that she'd had no luck. Then she would sit and stare out of the window and sigh and once Bella caught her in tears.

Bella ran and put her arms around her. 'Don't, Mumma!' She was so scared that she started to cry too. They clung sobbing to each other.

'Are we gunna die?' Bella asked.

Mumma choked and tried to smile as she wiped the tears off both their faces. 'Of course we're not gunna die!'

'There's only one thing for it,' she said the next day.

She polished Bella's boots, dressed them both in their best coats and hats and held her hand as they walked down the street to the bus stop.

'Where we goin', Mumma?'

'A house called Tankerton Manor, outside Whitstable. Your mumma was in service there before the war. That's where she met your daddy, when he was a guest of the family.'

'Why we goin' there?'

'To see if they'll give me a job.'

Tankerton Manor lay half a mile from the estuary and Bella saw the occasional glint of water as she and Mumma walked down the long drive beneath an avenue of elms warped by age and the wind. They went around to the back of the house and Mumma knocked on what she said was the kitchen door.

Bella knew how nervous Mumma was by the bright smile she gave her as they waited.

The door opened. A ferocious face, red and scabby, glared out at them. 'Yes?'

'Does Mrs Stubbs still work here?'

'Who wants to know?' the woman said.

'Tell her Jenny Tempest.'

The door closed in their faces.

'Who's Mrs Stubbs?'

'The housekeeper.'

They waited while Mumma jiggled her foot. Then the door opened again and the same woman confronted them.

'Mrs Stubbs ain't at 'ome to no Jenny Tempest.' A mean smile showed broken teeth. 'She says to tell you she wonders you got the nerve to show yer face.'

And the door slammed. Bella sneaked a sideways glance, saw Mumma's face as white as white. 'Why was she so nasty to us?'

'They didn' like me bein' friendly with your daddy,' Mumma said. 'That's why he took us to Yorkshire to live near 'im.'

'Why didn' they like you bein' friendly?'

'Never you mind.'

Sitting beside her in the bus Bella heard Mumma say: 'I'll 'ave to get 'old of 'im some'ow. What else can I do?'

And began writing a letter as soon as she got back to the flat.

'You writin' to Daddy?' Bella asked.

'No, dear. To my friend Mrs Grice.'

Wife of the Ripon Grange under-gardener. Bella remembered her; Mrs Grice was nice. And Ripon Grange was where Daddy lived, not far from their cottage. She'd been past it lots of times but never inside.

'Why don' you write to Daddy?'

''Cause I don't think he'd get the letter.'

Two weeks later a strange man – about fifty and tall, with grey hair and wearing a dark suit – knocked on the door.

''Elp you with sumfing?' Mumma said.

'My name is Rigby,' he said. 'I 'ave the honour to be in the service of Lord Richmond.'

Bella, watching from behind Mumma's shoulder, saw him look with distaste at the stained walls of the building. The way he spoke, he might have been a lord himself.

'I 'ave been instructed to locate Mrs Jenny Tempest,' he said.

'That's me,' Mumma said.

'Lord Richmond 'as sent me to bring you to him. At his town-house in Jermyn Street,' he added.

'Lord Richmond?' Mumma repeated uncertainly.

Mr Rigby had a beaked, haughty nose and used it.

'The Earl of Clapham,' he said.

Bella knew who that was. Daddy's father, which made him her grandfather.

'What's 'e want wiv me?'

'He did not confide in me. Come,' Mr Rigby said impatiently. 'Let us not keep his lordship waiting. There is a car downstairs.'

'I ain't goin' nowhere wivvout my daughter.'

'Lord Richmond did not mention a child,' Mr Rigby said.

'Too bad.'

They stared at each other but Mumma didn't budge.

Mr Rigby sighed. 'Bring her if you must,' he said.

Bella looked at the carved portico, the white pillars on either side of the granite steps leading to a door that was glossy with black enamel. 73 Jermyn Street was very different from Rotherhithe.

Mr Rigby led them into a side room and told them to wait. This they did, with Bella clutching Mumma's hand. They stood in the middle of the room and did not dare sit down. The door opened and a man came in. He was the tallest man Bella had ever seen, with grey hair, lined face and a big moustache.

He looked at them both, taking his time, before speaking to Mumma. 'So you are Jenny Tempest?'

'Yes, my Lord.' She gave him a curtsy.

'I find it hard to believe we are having this conversation,' Lord Richmond said, 'but there it is.' He crumpled his vast length into a chair and flapped his hand impatiently. 'Sit down, the pair of you.'

They did so, Bella's bottom perched on the very edge of the chair.

'I have seen the letter you sent my son.'

'I didn't mean to trouble you, my Lord –'

'I should tell you that neither my son nor I had any hand in your leaving the cottage. We had been away, as you no doubt know, and my son was shocked to find you had been evicted behind his back, and to have no means to contact you. It is fortunate that I had to come to town for the state opening of parliament just after your letter arrived. Tell me, how long had you been living in the cottage?'

'Six years, my Lord.'

'But you had known my son before that, of course.'

'Since just before the war, my Lord.'

'He has a very high regard for you,' the earl said. 'You know that?'

'I know it. Thank you, my Lord.'

'Don't thank me. I wish he'd never met you. But there it is. And now there is the question of the child. Your child. And his.' The beaky nose took aim at her. 'She is his, I take it?'

'Yes, my Lord. There's bin no one —'

'Quite. How old is the girl?'

'Seven come August.'

'Seven years. The same time that my son has been married.'

'Yes, my Lord.'

'Yet he and his wife have no children. The doctors insist there's nothing wrong but she remains childless. It seems probable,' said the earl, 'that this child will be the only grandchild I shall ever have. I have therefore decided to do something for her.'

Bella could feel Mumma quivering, her hands clenched tight in her lap.

The earl said, 'I intend her to come and live at the Grange and be raised as a member of my family. What do you think of that, eh?'

'I am sure it would be a great honour for her, my Lord,' Mumma said.

'Rigby tells me you are living in reduced circumstances. Being at Ripon Grange would give her chances she could not expect otherwise. She would meet people of a completely different class. It might be possible for me to arrange a suitable marriage for her when the time came. However…' The earl stared at Mumma severely. 'I am afraid there can be no question of your coming with her. My son's wife, you understand —'

'Perhaps I could move back into the cottage?' Mumma said.

The earl shook his head. 'I don't think that would be wise.'

'You want to take Bella away from me,' Mumma said.

Now Bella was more scared than ever. She whimpered, seeking the assurance of Mumma's hand.

'I don' want to go nowhere wivvout you,' she protested.

Neither Mumma nor the earl took any notice.

'I would be willing to pay you an annuity,' he said. 'Forty pounds a year, perhaps.'

'But Bella would no longer be part of my life,' she said.

He said nothing.

'My own daughter.'

'If you decide to reject my offer, I shall quite understand. It is a distressing business for a mother to be separated from her child. But, for the child's sake...'

'What about your daughter-in-law?'

'Charlotte will accept Bella into the household –'

''Ow can I be sure of that?'

'Because I shall require her to do so. As will my son. But there are limits. As I said, having you living in the Grange would be an impossibility. But you need have no fears for Bella's future, I promise you. That is her name, is it? Bella?'

'Yes, my Lord. Short for Arabella. Mr Anthony chose it. I would need to see her regular.'

'A meeting, let us say twice a year, would be perfectly acceptable.'

'I'll 'ave to think about it,' Mumma said.

'I understand. It is a big decision.'

The earl extracted himself from the chair and stood. 'Mrs Maud is my housekeeper here. You will let her know?'

'Yes, my Lord.'

He pressed the bell. A footman came.

'Show Mrs Tempest and Arabella out.' He turned to Mumma. 'Shall we say by the end of the week? Perhaps you could bring the child with you? If you decide to accept my offer?'

Six days later Mumma took Bella to have a final look at the river. A chilly wind was scything across the Thames and the river was running fast after all the rain they'd had. On the far bank, a barge was hoisting its tan sails.

Cheeks wet with tears, Mumma scared Bella afresh by crying aloud to the rushing water. 'Why do things 'ave to be like this?'

But the river did not know, or would not say.

'Not that I blame the earl,' she said. 'A real gent, 'e is.'

Bella did not understand Mumma's distress and fidgeted, wanting to escape, but could not, her hand held tight.

''Tes all that woman's fault,' Mumma cried. 'She was the one got us chucked out. Your daddy would never 'ave done such a thing: I knew it 'ad to be 'er, all along. I wish she was dead!'

'I wish she was dead, too, Mumma,' Bella said.

She'd said the same thing once about Beth Hardcastle, back at home, when Beth had trodden by mistake on a doll Daddy had given her. On that occasion Mumma had told her it was wicked to say such things but this time it must be all right, because Mumma had said it. If *that woman* had been the reason they'd been forced to come to this horrible place then Bella hoped she would die too. Daddy had never lived with them properly. Mumma had told her that had been *that woman's* fault, too. If she died maybe he would. Then they could be together like a proper family instead of him only coming to see them now and then.

Later, Mumma explained to her what was going to happen. She was crying when she said it.

'You'll be goin' to live at Ripon Grange with Daddy and your Grandpapa,' she said. 'It'll be a wonderful opportunity for you.'

'Are you comin' too?'

'No, I'll be stayin' 'ere.'

So Bella felt a growing sense of panic. 'I don' wanner go wivvout you!'

There was an empty, lonely place inside her heart. She could not believe Mumma was sending her away and her blue eyes were filled with terror. 'I ain't goin'!'

'It'll be a wonderful opportunity for you,' Mumma repeated. 'You'll grow up to be a real lady... I'll be that proud.'

Bella clutched Mumma's skirt. 'I don' wanner go! Don't make me, Mumma! Don't!'

Mumma's tears flowed faster than ever but she went on regardless. 'You'll be a member of one of the best families in England. You could become anything you like. Stay in London wi' me, what will you be then? Nuthun and nobody! I won't have it.'

A dredge hooted as it made its way downstream, its deck heaped with silt.

But Bella refused to listen. 'I'll be a good girl, Mumma! I promise I'll be good. Please, Mumma!'

Mumma clutched her, holding her tight against her, and Mumma's warm familiar smell made her cry all the harder.

'No! I won't go!'

Now they were both bawling as loudly as each other.

'You got to be a big girl, Bella,' Mumma sobbed. 'A brave girl for your mumma. I know you don't understand but I would never do nuthun to 'urt you. You knows that, don' yer?'

But Bella only wept. 'You don't love me no more!'

Mumma's hands pinched Bella's arms as she shook her. 'O' course I loves yer. But it ain't no good, see. I wants you to 'ave sumfing better in life than I did. That's why me an' your daddy got together in the first place. You'll 'ave sumfing I never 'ad: the chance to make a good life for yourself an' your kids.'

'I don' want a good life. I don' want kids. I wanner stay wiv you.'

Later, after they had gone back to the room and Bella had finally fallen into an exhausted sleep, Jenny stood at the window, looking down at the mean street three floors below. God help us both, she thought.

She'd not been brought up to think much about God. She couldn't remember the last time she'd been to church, but a French visitor to Tankerton Manor had told her once that God lived in the flowers.

'Ze flowers of fields and 'edgerows,' she had said. 'Zat is where you will find 'im.'

At the time Jenny had thought it a lot of Frenchy nonsense. But maybe the woman had been right. There were no flowers in Rotherhithe but maybe, if she thought about them hard enough, that would do.

She fixed her mind on the primroses that in spring used to flower in the cottage garden, and the memory of that place, where they had been so happy, was like a dagger in her breast.

'God, take care o' my darlin' Bella,' she said, face once again wet with tears. 'I'm doin' the right thing, God. You knows that. But don't never say it don't hurt, you 'ear me?'

She waited but there was nothing. Only pain, flowering like the primroses amid the summer's unseasonable cold.

CHAPTER FIVE

'Arabella Tempest,' said the stern lady. 'I have been instructed to welcome you to Ripon Grange.'

It didn't feel much of a welcome when Bella, terror in her heart, walked through the enormous entrance doors of a building that seemed to go on forever. Her face showed nothing but inside she was in tears, and inconsolable. She was thinking of Mumma, back in London; with all her heart she wanted those loving arms around her again, but the arms had failed her and the only way she could face that fact was to pretend none of this was happening.

I'll show 'em all. If she thought anything, it was that.

So, when the stern lady told Bella her name was Miss Hunnicut, she turned on her the same stony face with which she had left her mother.

Sulky little thing, Miss Hunnicut thought briskly. We shall see about that. There will be no sulks at Ripon Grange.

She looked at Bella with distaste, telling herself that the earl had taken leave of his senses, bringing this scruffy brat to live with them. All because the mother, who Miss Hunnicut understood had been in service at Tankerton Manor outside London – a *maid*,

I ask you, the daughter of a bait-digger! – claimed that Mr Anthony was the child's father. It might be true, but what of it? These things happened, as the earl should know better than most, and there had been a war on, which excused a great deal. Surely it would have been sufficient to pay the mother a small sum towards the child's education? To bring her here, just because the earl had decided she was his only grandchild... Miss Hunnicut thought it was ridiculous but supposed they should be thankful he hadn't brought the mother to live with them as well.

I can't imagine what Madam thinks about it, Miss Hunnicut thought.

Madam was Mr Anthony's wife. One of these days she would be the countess of Clapham and she was already very much in charge of the household, for Mr Anthony was a poor thing nowadays, a shadow of the gallant young man he had been before the war. Yet, in charge of the household or not, she had been unable to prevent the earl's latest lunacy.

Miss Hunnicut bled for her. How must it feel to have your husband's bastard thrust down your throat every day? Especially when it seemed Madam could have no children of her own.

It will cause trouble, Miss Hunnicut thought with a glow of satisfaction. She had also been young once. The earl had been known for his roving eye and there had been a time when she had thought...

No matter. Nothing had come of it and now, Miss Hunnicut told herself, she was glad. Because the old man had clearly lost his wits.

'Bates will take you to your room,' she told the child. 'She will unpack your clothes and give you a bath.'

The child astonished her by answering back. 'Don' need a bath.'

'Nevertheless you will have one.'

''ad one this morning.'

'Bates...' Miss Hunnicut turned to the maid, who all this time had been standing at her elbow. 'Scrub her thoroughly. You understand me? Thoroughly.'

Madam and Mr Anthony were staying with friends in Scotland. In their absence Miss Hunnicut was in charge. She was determined there would be neither sulks nor fleas at Ripon Grange.

That night Bella felt lonelier than ever before. The darkness of the vast room that she had been told was hers was full of terrors. Shadows stared. Unimaginable things crept in the darkness. She waited, only her nose showing above the blanket, eyes screwed tight. Mumma had gone; Miss Hunny-something was mean. The woman called Bates had tried to be friendly but Bella had locked up her sadly damaged heart and would neither smile nor talk, so that Bates, too, had eventually given up.

She had hoped she would at least see Daddy, who had visited them regularly when they were living at the cottage and who Mumma had said loved them both, but she had not. She had eaten her supper in a room that Miss Hunnicut called the nursery, where Bates had brought her food and Miss Hunnicut had sat and watched, correcting her manners from time to time.

'Arabella, you will not hold your fork like that.'

'Arabella, you will learn to eat quietly, with your lips closed.'

'Arabella, do you hear me?'

'Yes,' said Bella.

'You will not speak with your mouth full.'

'You asked –'

'Arabella!'

Silence.

I won't stay here, Bella thought mutinously. I shall run away.

But where?

Where was Mumma?

She would not cry. She was almost seven years old, a big girl, and would not cry. But later...

Sobbing, while formless fears watched her in the darkness.

'You'll live some grand life,' Mumma had said. 'Like a princess!'

I shall run away, Bella thought again.

The next day she got halfway down the drive before a gardener brought her back.

She got her bottom smacked for that but, if she expected tears, Miss Hunnicut was disappointed.

'You are a brazen child,' she said. 'But I shall tame you.'

The taming began with a visit to the Ripon Grange chapel where Miss Hunnicut said Bella would remain until she could recite the Lord's Prayer by heart.

'Madam has instructed me to teach you the Lord's Prayer. You have heard of it, I hope. Or is that too much to expect, given your background?'

Bella knew the words because Mumma had taught her, but would not admit it. She stood in the chapel, as instructed, and said nothing.

'Our Father, which art in heaven,' said Miss Hunnicut. And paused.

Bella said nothing.

'Repeat the words after me,' said Miss Hunnicut. 'Our Father…'

Bella said nothing.

'Are you stupid?' wondered Miss Hunnicut. 'Or stubborn? Or stupid *and* stubborn?'

Bella said nothing.

'Our Father…'

Bella said nothing.

'There will be no luncheon or supper until you say the words.'

For a long time Bella would not until, wearying of the game, she decided on a change of plan.

'OurFatherwhichartinheaven…'

And gabbled on until the end.

'…andthegloryforeverandeveramen.'

And stared, defiance in every inch of her.

'I see,' said Miss Hunnicut, and took her off to the nursery.

'Hold out your hand.'

The ruler descended three times, like a hot iron across her palm.

'There,' said Miss Hunnicut, breathing deeply, cheeks a dull red. 'Let that be a lesson to you. *I shall not have insolence.*'

Bella, every muscle tense, fought back tears. She said nothing.

'Badly behaved children get sent to bed without any supper,' said Miss Hunnicut.

Except that Bates, who had a miraculous ability to know what was happening even when she wasn't in the room, took pity on the poor motherless child and, at great risk to her own situation, smuggled a plate of goodies from the kitchen.

'I hope you have learnt your lesson,' said Miss Hunnicut the next morning.

While Bella, still stuffed from her evening feast of chips and jelly, did once again what had served her so well the previous day.

She said nothing.

CHAPTER SIX

Charlotte Richmond, back from Scotland, examined Bella as though she were a piece of furniture: novel, perhaps, but not to her taste. She talked about her as though she were a piece of furniture, too, incapable of hearing or understanding what was being said in her presence.

'What do we have here, Miss Hunnicut?'

'The child that his Lordship had brought from London, Madam.'

'And what sort of child is she? I will tell you. She is a bastard, Miss Hunnicut. A nasty, snivelling, filthy little bastard. That's what she is, Miss Hunnicut.'

She smiled at Bella, looking for some response, but Bella did not know the word and did not understand. Bella looked.

'How well behaved is she?'

Miss Hunnicut shook her head. 'Wilful, Madam.'

Madam stared Miss Hunnicut down. 'Then we shall have to do something about it, shall we not?'

'Indeed, Madam.'

The stare transferred to Bella. 'Wilfulness will not be tolerated. You hear me, Arabella?'

How could anyone not hear? Bella nodded.

'Well, miss?' said Charlotte Richmond.

Bella was unsure what was wanted so once again took refuge in silence. Which seemed to aggravate Mrs Richmond excessively.

'Wilful, you say?' she said to Miss Hunnicut. 'Insolent might fit the bill better.'

'You may well be right, Madam.'

'Insolent children are thrashed,' Mrs Richmond told Bella. 'You understand me?'

'Yes,' Bella said.

'Yes, Mrs Richmond.'

'Yes, Mrs Richmond.'

'Don't forget it.'

Bella wanted to ask where her father was and if she could speak to him, but did not dare.

'Well, miss?' said Mrs Richmond. 'What are you waiting for? Be off with you.'

So Bella left. Miss Hunnicut did not believe in allowing Bella freedom to wander, so it was the first time she had been loose in the castle. She explored this corridor and that, poked her nose into bedrooms, into rooms with leather armchairs and books in cases around the walls, into plain rooms and pretty rooms. She got lost.

She came across a staircase, very grand, sweeping up from the floor below. She stood, finger in mouth, staring at a gigantic painting on the wall opposite. The painting was of a lady with rosy skin and no clothes, with what looked like fat little dolls with wings fluttering about her head.

She studied it gravely until a voice made her jump.

'Like it, do you?'

She looked up at the very tall man who had come up behind her. It was the same man she had seen when Mumma had taken her to London. 'Why ain't she got no clothes on?'

He smiled. 'Because that was the way Raphael chose to paint her.'

She had no idea what he meant. 'She's fat,' she said.

'In those days they liked their women fat,' the man said. 'I'm partial to a bit of meat myself.'

'I'm not fat,' Bella said.

'Give you a few years and you will be,' he said. 'Bits of you, anyway.'

'The lady married to my daddy ain't fat,' Bella said.

'The lady married to your daddy is a spike,' the man said. He looked down at her from his great height. 'Do you know who I am?'

Bella shook her head.

'I am your grandpapa,' the man said. He held out his hand; cautiously, she put her hand in his. It felt knobbly and hard. 'Come with me. I want to show you something.'

She went with him obediently. She was still scared, but not very, because he had spoken to her kindly and was as different from Miss Hunnicut and Mrs Richmond as it was possible to be.

He took her into a room with books all around the walls. There was a long wooden table in the middle with chairs on both sides. He took down a big book, which he opened and put on the table. It was full of photographs. Bella stared, uncomprehending.

The knobby finger pointed at a picture of a man in a funny suit, with whiskers.

'That is my grandfather. Which makes him your great-great grandfather. He attended the coronation of Queen Victoria. He was a young man at the time, but this photo was taken when he was much older. Almost as old as me.' He laughed, and the child had no idea what he was on about. 'And this,' he said, turning the page, 'is my father, who died in Africa in a big battle with the savages.'

'Did they stick a spear in 'im?' asked Bella.

'I rather think they did.'

'Cor,' said Bella, and studied the photograph with heightened interest.

He showed Bella other photos, but they confused her more than ever, so that she soon stopped listening to what he was saying.

As the earl eventually saw. 'Has your father been to see you since he's been back?'

Bella shook her head.

There was a bell standing on the table. He picked it up and rang it. A man came.

'Ask Miss Hunnicut to come here.'

Within minutes: 'I beg your pardon, my Lord. Has she been troubling you?'

'On the contrary. I find her absolutely delightful. But she is in your charge, Miss Hunnicut. Why was she wandering around the castle unescorted?'

'She slipped away while Madam was giving me her instructions, my Lord.'

'I shall wish to see her every day from now on. Shall we say at eleven o'clock each morning?'

Miss Hunnicut hesitated. 'Perhaps I should speak to Madam –'

'I am the master of this household, Miss Hunnicut. Not my daughter-in-law.'

'Of course, sir. Sorry, sir.'

'Please tell my son I wish to see him here. Immediately. And one final thing…'

'Sir?'

'All these ain'ts and 'ims and 'ers… Teach her to speak the King's English, for heaven's sake.'

'You have been home two days and not been to see your daughter,' the earl said. 'May one ask why?'

'Charlotte felt that after Sunday chapel might be a better time.'

'What does Charlotte have to do with it? She is your daughter, man, not Charlotte's.'

'Bella needs time to adjust. We both decided it would be better from her point of view –'

'It didn't occur to you she might welcome a familiar face? A visit from her father, perhaps?'

From his expression Anthony Richmond felt himself wrongly accused. 'Charlotte thought, and I agreed –'

'Charlotte would have left her in London to rot. As you know very well.'

'We believe a child's place is with her mother,' Anthony said.

'I can arrange that, if you wish. Although what Charlotte would say if I brought the child's mother to live here I can't imagine.'

'Frankly, Father, we both feel it was a mistake to have brought Bella here at all. The previous arrangement –'

'Suited you very well, didn't it? All the home comforts and none of the responsibilities.'

'I hardly think you're in a position to talk about that,' said Anthony hotly. He might not be the man he'd been before the war but could still spark, if driven to it.

'You may be right,' the earl said. 'But she is my grandchild. My only grandchild,' he added spitefully.

Anthony flushed. 'That's really your problem with Charlotte, isn't it? That she hasn't given you a grandson?'

'She needs to produce an heir, damn it! Our family goes back to the fifteenth century. Do you *want* to be the last earl of Clapham?'

'You think Charlotte doesn't feel that too?' Anthony demanded.

'I don't understand it,' the earl grumbled. 'Her family's fertile. I had them checked out. Trust you to pick the only barren one.'

'I didn't pick her. You did.'

'And who would you have chosen? A bait-digger's daughter? Don't be ridiculous!'

'Charlotte may still have a son.'

'After this time? I doubt it. In the meantime I intend to raise my grandchild under my own roof and you and Charlotte had best get used to the idea. And go and see your daughter, man. Or are you afraid,' the earl asked sarcastically, 'that Charlotte may not approve?'

'Teach her to speak the King's English?' Charlotte said indignantly. 'The fact is he's as ashamed of her background as the rest of us.

But it will do no use, Miss Hunnicut. You cannot make a silk purse out of a sow's ear.'

Charlotte, forgetful of the sows' ears in her own lineage, prided herself on her originality of phrase.

'Should I engage a tutor?' ventured Miss Hunnicut.

Charlotte set her lips. You would have thought that bringing one hundred thousand pounds to the marriage would have given her the right to make her own arrangements, but since apparently it did not...

'Perhaps you should, Miss Hunnicut. If Lord Richmond is so set on the idea.' However, she was unwilling to let the earl have it all his own way. 'Make sure you teach her the catechism. Word-perfect, Miss Hunnicut! I shall examine her personally.'

Later, on Mrs Richmond's instructions, Mr Pearce, the local vicar, lectured Bella week after week on the unfailing power and love of God. As she grew older, Bella learnt to ask questions.

'Why are we rich and others poor?'

'Why did so many people die in the war?'

'Why are so many people starving?'

Although the most important questions she dared not ask.

Why did my mother send me away? Why does she never write? Why did she never answer the letters I sent her?

Because Bella had written as soon as she could and had waited weeks for replies that never came.

Mr Pearce told her these things were God's will, but surely a loving, all-powerful God would not have allowed them to happen? She began to doubt whether the words in her prayer book meant anything at all. She continued to recite them by rote, her mind busy with other matters. When Father and his wife were away she sang the hymns with full throat because she liked them, but when Madam was home there were none. Mrs Richmond did not approve of hymns. She had brought to Ripon Grange not only a fortune but a hard and glittering belief in a faith wedded to sin and retribution to which she demanded that all under her control must subscribe. So stern was she that burning at the stake might have been a possibility, had not that been associated with popery and therefore the work of Satan himself.

Arabella, as her stepmother insisted on calling her, or Bella, as she remained obstinately in her own mind, went through the motions; the sun continued to rise and set; the seasons came and went; the years passed. Bella's relations with her father remained uncomfortable, with her stepmother frosty, but with the earl she had become friends. She spent as much time with him as she could, learning from him the history of the family of which it seemed only he believed her a true member.

CHAPTER SEVEN

On the twentieth of March 1936, when Bella was sixteen and a half, she drove with the earl to visit the Hardys at Branksome, an estate five miles from Ripon Grange.

'Used to ride over,' the earl grumbled. 'Now have to use this wretched contraption instead.'

The earl's riding days were done; it was all he could do to climb into the back seat of the Delage.

Bella sat beside him. She didn't object to driving although she would have been happy to ride: something she had learnt to do very well during her years at Ripon Grange. She would have been happy to *walk*. She didn't care how she got there as long as she went, because she'd been in love with Charles Hardy for eight years now, ever since she had first set eyes on him at a Christmas party.

There were six months between them and their friendship had deepened with the passing years. As eight-year-olds they had played noisy games of hide-and-seek in the endless corridors of Ripon Grange until banned from doing so by Bella's stepmother, who would have prohibited the friendship altogether if she'd been able; they made rude faces at Miss Hunnicut behind her back and stole pastries – Cook's speciality – from the kitchen; they chased each other shrieking across the lawns of Branksome House.

A year passed. They hunted for newts in King Harold's Beck; Charles introduced her with limited success to cricket; they capsized Charles's dinghy in the freezing waters of Worsley Mere. There were no other children in Bella's life, nor did she feel the need for them.

When Charles went away to boarding school Bella thought her life had ended, yet when he came home for the holidays only the nature of their activities changed. With heavy boots and a rucksack containing sandwiches prepared in the Branksome kitchen they explored the moors that extended for miles around the two properties. They dared each other into standing on the very edge of the chasm called Gaping Gill. Their friendship was as strong as ever. It was as though Charles had never been away at all.

That changed when Bella was twelve and for the first time discovered what it meant to be a woman. It took her a while to adjust to her new feelings, her new body, and at first she was uncomfortable in Charles's presence. Then this, too, passed.

When they were both fifteen Charles came home for Christmas, with the first snows reflecting the brilliance of the winter sun. The air was as sharp as honed steel and Bella, coming into the Branksome drawing room and seeing Charles after months of separation, felt her life change. Before, they had been the best of friends, as children are friends with one another, but now she was a woman, Charles a man, and the foundations of their relationship had shifted. A log fire blazed in the huge grate; in front of the multipaned window an illuminated Christmas tree shone red, blue and gold. The combined light filled the room with a shifting radiance in which dark-haired Charles, walking forwards smiling to greet her, appeared to Bella as an enchanted being whose beauty kindled a wave of heat, as wonderful as it was unexpected, that stole the breath from her lungs.

When they were two yards apart they both stopped, as though compelled by the same instinct. Bella saw his dark eyes watching her and felt the pressure of his gaze. She was conscious of his physical presence, despite the distance between them. This new Charles was a stranger to her yet still familiar, the friend she had known all her life yet totally changed.

Bella's heart was a thunder in her body. She was overwhelmed by a sense of inevitability to which she surrendered without hesitation or fear. This, then, was to be her life. When she had thought of love – and what fifteen-year-old girl had not? – it had been as an abstraction, warm and much to be desired, but as something outside herself, to be accepted or denied as she chose. Now she knew it was a song that filled every particle of her being and that she could control no more than she could prevent the beating of her heart. It *was*, and she was captured by singing she knew would end only with the end of life itself.

'Welcome home,' she said, and was surprised to hear her voice so unchanged. Her eyes remained captive to his unwavering gaze. 'How was school?'

'It was okay. I'm in the under-sixteens now.'

Whatever that might mean. The words were useful only as a means to bridge the silence that engulfed them because Charles, she was convinced, was as aware of the change in their relationship as she was.

'Rugby,' he explained.

'Oh I see.'

Although she did not: rugby one of the masculine mysteries to which she accepted she would never be admitted. It was unimportant; what mattered was the harmony that love gave to the otherwise unchanging patterns of her normal life. The holidays, enriched by her new feelings, still followed the familiar routines, both of them aware of the change in their relationship yet unwilling, for the moment, to do anything about it.

That changed during the long summer break, beside the cascading waters of a beck flowing out of the high moors, when Charles first touched her as a man touches a woman and Bella, trembling, felt for the first time her flesh melt as a woman melts when touched by the man she loves.

The memory of that moment, when excitement had threatened to drown inhibition and was halted only by the unexpected passing of a man on horseback, now threatened to stifle her as the Delage sped along the road between hedgerows where the first spring flowers were beginning to appear.

'Warm family, the Hardys,' the earl said. 'Provided he don't fall out with his old man, young Charles stands to inherit three thousand acres when the time comes. No doubt a lot more besides; Will Hardy knows how to turn a penny even in this depression. Wish I could say the same, but I never could get my head around those damn shillings and pence.'

The Delage turned into the long drive leading to Branksome Hall. The drive was flanked by oak trees that had been there as long as the house, which was protected on either side by hills threaded with streams that Charles claimed were full of trout. They had supposedly been fishing for trout when the passing rider had saved Bella from what Miss Hunnicut would no doubt have called a fate worse than death. Bella had been startled to discover what little control she'd had over her feelings; now, as the car drew up before the entrance, she thought it was as well that the March weather ruled out any possibility of a repeat performance.

'Family's farmed these parts since the Middle Ages,' the earl said. 'Among the most substantial landowners in the county, don't you know. Not aristocrats, of course, but socially they'll do.'

And heaved himself laboriously out of the car's opened door.

Bella had brought a bag containing her riding breeches and later, while the earl settled down with William Hardy over a decanter of malt whisky to discuss the mess the recently defeated Macdonald government had left Mr Baldwin to sort out, and the rise of this feller Hitler whose troops had occupied the Rhineland two weeks before, Charles Hardy and Bella Richmond rode off into the hills side by side.

It was a crisp day and not fit for any outdoor sexual explorations. Charles thought he would give it a go anyway but Bella, skin cringing, laughed and told him to forget it.

'Don't you want to?' Charles said plaintively, that poor little boy.

'With the temperature around freezing?' Bella said. 'You must be out of your mind. I'll tell you what I will do, though. I'll race you back to the house.'

Because the shadows were already lengthening as the evening came down across the fells.

'What's the prize?' Charles wondered aloud.

'That would be telling,' Bella said.

She laughed joyously, dug her heels into the mare's flanks and within seconds was racing away with Charles in hot pursuit.

Across the tops she rode, blue eyes intent, black hair blowing in the wind. She leant forwards until her face was almost touching the mare's straining neck, while all the time she whispered in her ear, urging her onwards. 'Come on now, come on…'

As though her very life were at stake, and not simply the winning or losing of a race started on impulse. But that was Bella all over: in everything she ventured, winning was all. As to the prize Charles was hoping for… That would be awarded, or not, as she decided at the time. So Bella flew, the devil at her heels, and came to the steep descent at the bottom of which the first lights of Branksome were pricking out of the gathering dusk.

There were trees on the descent, hollows barely visible in the fading light, and juts of lichen-clad granite thrusting their way through the turf. Ahead of her, to the west, the first star hung above the horizon.

It was madness to ride like this in the half-light, on a broken slope that in places was nearer vertical than horizontal, but Charles was somewhere close behind her and he knew the land better than she: if she eased up he would win.

She was determined to prevent that.

The lights of Branksome grew nearer. Now she was halfway down the slope. A startled bird rose suddenly from under the mare's hooves. She swerved and Bella was hanging on by teeth and finger-nails, but the moment passed and still she had not slowed down.

Two-thirds of the slope was behind her now, a clump of trees dark with shadow ahead of her to the right. Still no sign of Charles and, although she dared not look over her shoulder, she had no sense of his being anywhere close behind her.

She was winning, adrenaline like fire in every vein of her body, when Charles, going hell for leather, rode out of the trees thirty yards in front of her and went pounding down the slope towards the lights that were suddenly too close for comfort. Taking advantage of his better knowledge of the countryside, Charles had found a short cut that had brought him out ahead of her. The house could not be more than quarter of a mile away; she had no hope of catching him.

Charles's horse appeared to stumble over a jutting rock in the semi-darkness and Bella saw him fly heels over head out of the saddle to end up on the slope with a thud that sent a bolt of terror through her heart.

The earl and William Hardy had finished putting the world to rights. Now they were discussing the subject that Mr Hardy suspected had been the reason for the earl's visit.

'I can't praise her highly enough,' the earl said. 'And of course they've been great chums all their lives.'

William had heard the old man eulogising his granddaughter before, but never so intensely. His nose, honed by years of negotiations with the most astute financiers in the City, sensed a deal. His first rule in such matters was to slow things down. Change the subject, if you had to. If they were keen, they would always come back to it. You learnt more that way.

He leant forwards and freshened their glasses. 'The Glenlivet has always been my favourite malt,' he said.

'It is excellent,' the earl said.

'I was able to pick up two dozen bottles when I was in London last week. Lassiters in Cheapside are selling up – victims of the times, I'm afraid, very sad – so I was able to do a deal at fourteen shillings a bottle. I could let you have half a dozen bottles, if you like. The same price I paid for them.'

'That is most kind. But I believe my cellar is adequately stocked. About Bella…'

'Oh yes?' said Mr Hardy, as though this were the first time her name had entered the conversation.

'I rather fancy she's taken a shine to that boy of yours.'

'Is that so?'

'I suspect he feels the same.'

So that's the way the wind is blowing, Mr Hardy thought. Well, a link between the families might be no bad thing, even if the girl was born on the wrong side of the blanket. Aloud he said: 'At that age they fall in and out of love all the time. I set no store by it.'

'My only grandchild,' the earl said. 'I daresay I'll be able to put something aside for her when she does decide to get hitched.'

'Land?' Mr Hardy wondered.

'Can't do that. Whole estate's entailed. But there'll be something, I daresay. Not sure it'll be needed, mind. Beautiful girl – have you seen her recently? – I don't fancy she'll be on the market long.'

'Planning to have her come out, are you?' asked Mr Hardy.

That was cruel; there could be no question of a court presentation for illegitimate Bella.

'Never did go for all that debutante rubbish,' said the earl. 'Waste of time and money, to my way of thinking.'

'I daresay you're right.' Mr Hardy, a victim of gout, shifted to a more comfortable position in his chair. 'What do you reckon to the shooting prospects this season?'

Bella's first thought was that Charles was dead. Overwhelmed by that dreadful prospect, her heart seemed to stop beating, while her mind was filled with silent screams of denial.

It could not be! It must not be! No!

She had hauled back sharply on the reins, skidded to a stop and was out of the saddle and running before she was aware of it. Now she cradled Charles's head in her lap and looked desperately at the

Branksome lights that a minute ago had been so close and now were so far. Too far to call for help. Too far to run for help, leaving Charles unconscious on the cold ground. And for her to lift him was clearly impossible.

She thought, If I hadn't suggested that stupid race...

Regrets were futile.

She leant over him. The light was almost gone but enough remained to see the closed eyes and clotted hair, the trickle of blood across his forehead. She couldn't tell if he was breathing or not. His arms and legs seemed all right, his head at the proper angle. Maybe he had just knocked himself out.

There were plenty of stars, now. She looked at them twinkling frostily in the sky; it was going to be a cold night.

I must get help, Bella thought. Otherwise he'll freeze to death.

But she was loath to leave him. Panic threatened to overwhelm her. She fought it down but was still in two minds what to do when she heard a faint sigh. She leant close, heart pounding.

'Charles?'

His eyes opened. Relief was sunlight amid darkness.

'Thank God!'

He said something: a jumble of sound, like marbles in his loose mouth.

'What did you say?'

He repeated himself; this time she heard it.

'Wha' happened?'

'You had a fall.'

'Is... is Diamond... all right?'

She hadn't given the horse a thought but now looked up and saw it standing nearby, reins hanging loose about its neck. 'Diamond is fine.'

Charles was smiling at her; only now, as the tears began to flow, did she realise it.

'I would have beaten you.'

She smiled back. It was crooked, although she gave it her best shot.

'Not a chance.'

She would have given him the win a thousand times for this not to have happened but would not admit it. Instead she raised his head, heavy in her cupped hands, and covered his face with kisses.

'What's my prize?' he said as soon as she gave him the chance to speak.

'I never promised you anything.'

He certainly seemed to be getting better: while she smiled at him, his eyes no longer wandering but clear and focused, he lifted his hand and caressed her breast through her riding coat.

'Dear Bella,' he said.

'If you're well enough to do that, you're well enough to walk,' she said briskly.

She helped him; it took a while. Eventually he was more or less upright but his scalp was still bleeding.

'How's your head?' she asked anxiously.

'Like hell,' he said.

'Let's get you indoors,' Bella said.

'What about the horses?'

'They can look after themselves for the moment.'

Bella's arm around him, they made their way down the hill to the stone wall enclosing the kitchen garden at the back of the house. The gate opened with a wail of hinges. The light from the windows fell in elongated rectangles on the dark ground. At last they reached the kitchen door.

'It's dark,' Mr Hardy said. 'Aren't those children home yet?'

Talking and drinking, the time had passed unnoticed. He rang a bell. A servant came.

'Is Master Charles back?'

'En't seen him, sir.'

'Where the devil can they be?'

There was a commotion from the kitchen. Mrs Simpson the housekeeper came running. 'Mr Hardy, sir! Mr Hardy!'

Gout notwithstanding, William Hardy was on his feet.

'What's happened?'

'There's been an accident, sir. Mr Charles has taken a fall.'

'Where is he? Is he all right?'

'He's cut his head. Miss Bella's with him. They're in the kitchen.'

'Is my granddaughter all right?' the earl asked.

'They both seem all right, sir.'

'Thank God,' said Mr Hardy.

Afterwards, having discovered how close he had come to losing his only son, Mr Hardy felt the need to blame someone. A widower who had never needed to guard his tongue in his own house, he spoke his mind about Bella's involvement in what had almost been a tragedy.

'Foolishness! Gross irresponsibility!'

'I don't think you can put all the blame on Bella,' the earl said.

'I blame them both.'

'I wouldn't worry about it,' the earl told Bella as they drove home in the darkness, the car's headlamps throwing tunnels of yellow light between the hedgerows ahead of them.

'He was right,' Bella said dolefully; there was nothing Mr Hardy could say that she had not told herself a dozen times. 'It was my idea.'

'Accidents happen. There is no point blaming yourself.'

'Mr Hardy does not agree with you.'

'He'll get over it.'

'I hope so.'

'My advice to you is pay young Charles a visit tomorrow. Go first thing.'

'Mr Hardy may not let me see him.'

The earl laughed. 'One thing you should know about Will Hardy. Good fellow, got all the money in the world, but money ain't everything. This family may not have the readies but it has something a good deal more valuable. Did I tell you a Richmond held Ripon Grange against Fairfax for three months in the Civil War? Lost everything when Cromwell won, of course, but got it all back again when Charles's son came to the throne. Got an earldom

out of it, too. The first earl of Clapham! Will Hardy would give his
back teeth for a pedigree like that. But he don't have it, you see, so
he settles for being friends. Makes him feel important. He's not the
sort to hold a grudge against this family, you may be sure of that.
No, ride over and see Charles tomorrow. I guarantee there'll be
no problem. You're a Richmond, you see. And that still counts for
something in this part of the world.'

Next morning was another fine day. The fells were white with frost
as Bella rode over to Branksome. Her heart was thundering as she
trotted up the drive beneath oak trees just showing the first hint of
green, but when she reached the house it was as the earl had said:
she was admitted without delay and Mrs Simpson herself escorted
her upstairs to Charles's room.

'Mr Charles?' said Mrs Simpson, knocking. 'You have a visitor.'

'Who is it?'

Well, Bella thought, he *sounds* all right.

'Me,' she said.

'Hold on a sec,' Charles said.

After a minute he opened the door. Bella had not known what to
expect; what she saw was a tall young man in a pair of shorts, chest
bare, head partly shaved and bandaged, with a smile that might
have set the Thames on fire. It had the same effect on Bella, who
was afraid her knees would not support her.

'Come in,' Charles said.

He sounded well; bandage apart, he looked well. He looked
wonderful.

Bella walked into Charles's room.

'Thank you, Mrs Simpson,' Charles said.

And shut the door.

Bella stood in the middle of the room and looked at him. Her
heart was having a busy day: all the way over it had been racing
because she had been scared of the reception that might be awaiting her; now it was doing the same thing for an entirely different

reason. She thought Charles must surely hear it but if he did he gave no sign. Instead he gave her a beaming smile, while his eyes ate her up.

'Am I glad to see you,' he said.

She thought: If he touches me now I shall melt. But when she answered she was pleased to hear not the faintest tremor in her voice.

'How are you feeling?'

'My head's sore. And I must've given my elbow one hell of a whack; I can hardly move my left arm. But not too bad, considering.'

'Your father blames me for what happened,' Bella said.

'That's nonsense. It was fun.'

'While it lasted.'

'Pity I didn't win, all the same. I would have done, wouldn't I?'

She smiled at him. 'We'll never know, will we?'

'A moral victory, then.'

'Funny choice of words,' she said.

Standing here unescorted, with a half-naked man in his bedroom? What would Miss Hunnicut have had to say about that? Of course Miss Hunnicut was a pensioner nowadays and had no real say in Bella's life. All the same...

'Why?' Charles asked.

'No reason,' she said, and smiled at him.

He had moved closer to her. His chest was so white. Strong, too; if she dared touch it, she was sure she would find it hard with muscle. Of course there was no question of anything like that but her heart was beating louder than ever.

He was really close now. Close enough to touch, which she did not; close enough for him to touch her, which was a different story. His right hand reached out. Very gently his fingers caressed the side of her face.

'Mrs Simpson seems very understanding,' Bella said.

It took quite an effort to sound cool, or get the words out at all, but she managed it.

'That is true.'

His hand continued to stroke her, so gently that she could barely feel it, while the tiny hairs on her body stirred as though an electric current were flowing through them.

'Mrs Simpson knows what's what,' Charles said. 'She likes you, too.'

His fingers had moved to the side of her throat. Their touch was so gentle; so confident.

'Which helps,' he said.

Bella's body was indeed melting as Charles's fingertips stroked her throat. The ear, which it explored so gently. Then down. And, gently, back again.

Bella's eyelids fluttered and closed while the fingers continued their exploration. Amid the darkness behind her closed lids, conscious of the increasing tumult of her ardent body, she heard him say:

'She knows how we feel about each other.'

'Does she?'

Now she was no longer cool; she could barely recognise her own voice.

'She knows we love each other,' Charles said.

It was the first time either of them had used that word.

'Do you love me?' Charles whispered.

His left arm, which he had said he could hardly move, was around her now while the right...

The fingers of his right hand were working at the buttons of her riding jacket.

That was all right. The jacket was all right. She helped him by shrugging it off and felt it fall to the floor. But now the fingers were playing with the buttons of her shirt. Playing with them, not undoing them. Not undoing them yet. Which might not be all right at all. He had touched her yesterday through her clothes; how clearly she remembered how her body had responded. How much more intensely would she feel it if he touched her bare flesh? Even the thought made her weak.

'Do you love me?' Charles whispered again.

Yes, she did. But if she said so, would those dangerous fingers not become bolder still?

Not that she wanted him to stop. Quite the opposite; but, without commitment on his part, that would not do at all. She opened her eyes. She stared at him.

'What about you?' she asked. 'Do you love me?'

She had never imagined having the courage to say such a thing but the words were out, now, and it had been easy. 'Do you love me, Charles?'

Charles's fingers were still. He looked back at her and she saw his soul in his eyes.

'Do you, Charles?'

'With all my heart,' he said.

It was what she had longed to hear but words were cheap. Did he mean it?

'Even though I'm a bastard?'

Bella chose the harsh word deliberately.

Charles laughed gently. 'You think I care about that?'

'Your father might,' she said.

'You're a Richmond. That's all that matters to my father.'

Exactly what Grandpapa had said.

'In any case, you're not planning to marry my father. I hope.'

And that was something else that had not been said. Instinctively she avoided the implications of his words. 'I am not planning to marry anybody.'

Now Charles was smiling. 'Is that so?'

'No one has asked me,' Bella said, staring at him boldly.

She was not the only one to be emboldened. His fingers were once again addressing the buttons of her shirt. One was undone; then a second one. She made no attempt to stop him as, his arm still about her, he led her to the tousled bed. As he pressed her backwards until she was lying across it. As he kissed her with renewed passion. She kissed him back, her arms about his neck.

* * *

They hadn't done it but it had been close. She had wanted him so much but in the end had had just enough willpower left to say no. No matter; there would be plenty of time for that later, when they were married.

Riding home, Bella was amazed how bright the colours were. The greenness of the springing leaves, the brown of the tilled earth, the cloudless sky, all shone in the spring sunshine. Everywhere were things she had never noticed before, or been so familiar that they had become invisible. Now she saw them all. A jay flew from a distant coppice in a rip of brilliant blue and she laughed with joy. Never had she felt so alive, because she was in love, and all this – the sky and meadows, the smoking chimneys of the cottages, the honey-coloured stone as she turned past the gatehouse and up the drive to Ripon Grange – was part of it. As was the music of Charles's voice asking her to marry him.

'They won't let us,' she'd said. 'They'll say we're too young.'

'They won't say that when we're eighteen.'

A year and a half's time. It felt like forever but Charles was right.

'All right, then,' she said. 'I'll marry you on my eighteenth birthday.'

'Not a second later,' he said.

Her joy was reflected in her expression, her laugh, the way she ran up the stairs to give Grandpapa her news.

She knew where to find him. He'd be in the archives room, poring, as he did every day, over the folders in which were preserved details of the family's past.

He was not there. The usual stack of folders was open on the long table but the room was empty. Bella thought he might be in the stables; even though he no longer rode, he had told her more than once that his best friends were not humans but horses. She would go and find him; she wanted him to be the first to hear her news.

She ran down the stairs, feet barely skimming the polished wood, and came face to face with Miss Hunnicut, old and tremulous now, who met her with tragic face.

'Oh, Arabella…'

Never would she be anything but Arabella to Miss Hunnicut but Bella sensed disaster in the broken words and did not think about that.

'What is it, Miss Hunnicut?'

Miss Hunnicut told her that at ten o'clock that morning one of the maids had heard the earl cry out and, going to investigate, had discovered him lying unconscious on the floor of the archives room.

It was a shock so terrible that Bella could barely comprehend it. She seized the old lady by the arm.

'Where is he?'

'In his bedroom. The doctor is with him. And Madam.'

'And my father?'

No, Mr Anthony had driven into town earlier that morning and was not back yet.

'I'll go to him now,' Bella said.

There had been a time when Miss Hunnicut would have been all teeth and snarl; now all she could manage was a bleat.

'Madam has issued instructions they are not to be disturbed.'

But Bella had the strength that came from knowing herself loved and was not to be deterred.

Achilles Richmond lay on his back in the great bed which had been the scene of so many of his less reputable skirmishes and would now witness his greatest adventure of all, for, at eighty-four, he no longer had the resilience to make a comeback from the stroke that had felled him.

Had he been conscious, he would no doubt have been sardonically amused to find himself the centre of such attention, watched silently by a daughter-in-law he disliked and a doctor whom he had once dismissed as a Hibernian quack. Hopefully he would have been quicker to appreciate the arrival of the granddaughter whom he had come to cherish above all other human beings.

If so, it was an appreciation not shared by Charlotte Richmond, who stared in annoyance at her stepdaughter.

'I gave instructions we were not to be disturbed.'

'Miss Hunnicut told me but I know it couldn't apply to me.' Bella smiled at her stepmother. 'I am a member of the family, after all.'

Charlotte's set mouth showed what she thought of that but this was no place for a row so she said nothing and Bella stayed.

Dr Grant shook his head lugubriously. He said: 'There is nae more I can do for his lordship at the moment. I have other calls I should be making but will be back again in an hour or two. If that is agreeable?' he appealed to Mrs Richmond.

'By all means,' Charlotte said. 'Tell me truthfully, doctor, what are his chances of a recovery?'

Grant hesitated. 'At his age I fear –'

'Thank you, doctor,' said Charlotte dismissively.

'Is there nothing you can do for him?' Bella asked.

Grant might have been less astonished had the bed spoken to him.

Charlotte intervened at once. 'Arabella, please don't waste Dr Grant's time. Did you not hear him say he has other calls to make?'

'I asked a simple question,' Bella said. 'Is there anything you can do for him or not?'

Grant was incapable of admitting there was anything he could not do. 'We must let nature take its course, young lady.'

'In other words,' Bella said, 'if he dies, he dies.'

'There is nae more any physician on this earth can do for his Lordship,' he declared. And stalked out, nose pointing indignantly at the ceiling.

Mrs Richmond gave Bella a baleful look. 'I shall speak to you later,' she said.

Bella cared nothing for her stepmother's outrage. She stared at the waxen features of the man who over the years had been her only friend and wished with all her heart that it might be possible to restore him to health.

'I feel so useless,' she said.

'We are in the hands of God,' said Mrs Richmond. 'I have sent for Mr Pearce.'

The earl had despised the minister even more than Dr Grant but Bella said nothing. In Mrs Richmond's eyes Mr Pearce was so close to God that she regarded even the mildest criticism of him as blasphemy.

They watched and waited and, twenty minutes later, Anthony Richmond arrived, followed closely by the minister. Bella and her father tried to smile at each other, but it was too hard; they had become strangers. Instead they stared at the dying man while Mr Pearce bleated a prayer.

Bella gave her father's hand a quick squeeze and left. She walked down the stairs and across the drawing room. She opened the French windows and stepped onto the terrace, which later in the year would be a wonderland of roses, before following the steps down to the courtyard. The ornamental ponds were pocked with raindrops but Bella did not care about that. She walked through what was no longer a shower until she reached the water. The ponds contained ornamental carp; she had read that in some countries they symbolised good luck so she waited, hoping to see one, but failing. Eventually, wet through and bedraggled, she walked back towards the house.

Bella had never been one for prayer, mainly because her stepmother set such store by it, but now she prayed that Achilles Richmond, seventh earl of Clapham, would make a full recovery. She prayed for him because she loved him. He had befriended her when she had been an abandoned child, lonely and lost, and Miss Hunnicut, her stepmother and even her father had treated her as though she had no business being at Ripon Grange at all. How many times in those early days had she wept herself to sleep? How often, as a six- or seven-year-old child, had she known the despair of someone who had lost the one being in the world who mattered to her? Without the earl she believed she might never have survived at all. Walking back to the house through the rain she prayed with all her strength for the two beings who mattered most in her life: that the earl would make a complete recovery and that, whatever happened to her grandfather, she would still be able to marry Charles, whom she loved more than life itself, because without these two men at her side she would be lost.

Charles will protect me, she thought. She remembered some words she had read long ago. Whatever happens to Grandpapa, Charles will be my sword and buckler.

She reached the house, where she did not have to wait long for an answer to her prayer.

She walked through the kitchen and down the flagged passage to the main part of the house, where she met Miss Hunnicut. The old lady was in such a state that she did not notice that Bella was soaked.

'Oh Arabella…'

Bella swayed, feeling the blood retreat from her cheeks. There was no need for Miss Hunnicut to say more, because Bella knew. Achilles Richmond, seventh earl of Clapham, was dead.

CHAPTER EIGHT

'We must do something about Arabella,' Charlotte told her husband two weeks after the funeral.

'If you mean marriage, she may have thoughts on that subject herself,' said Anthony.

Charlotte was aware of the attachment between Arabella and Charles Hardy, but it would never do. If they were married it would mean that the Hardys, husband and wife, would move in the same circle as the Earl and Countess of Clapham, and Charlotte was not prepared to accept the prospect of sitting at table with her husband's bastard.

'Surely you cannot mean the Hardy boy?' Charlotte's titter discarded that idea. 'A girl of Arabella's age needs a mature man, someone who knows the way of the world.'

'You are thinking of Hector Lacey,' Anthony said.

'I think the major would make an ideal husband.'

'He's certainly mature. I'm not sure about the major bit. Friend of your brother, isn't he?'

And, like Charlotte's brother and grandfather, making a name for himself in the City for all the wrong reasons.

'They are acquainted,' Charlotte said stiffly.

'I wouldn't have Lacey as a son-in-law if you paid me,' said Anthony. 'In any case Bella's too young.'

'Surely not? How old was her mother when you first became acquainted?'

Which informed Anthony that the knives were out in earnest.

'Many of the aristocracy marry young, do they not?' Charlotte enquired.

'Some may,' Anthony said. 'Lady Dutton did not get married until she was sixty-three.'

'Are you suggesting Bella should wait so long? Of course,' said Charlotte thoughtfully, 'many of the working classes also marry young, I hear. Those who marry at all.'

For years Anthony had thought his wife's titter would drive him to murder.

'It is strange, is it not,' Charlotte said, 'how so many of the upper classes enjoy slumming?'

'It is strange, is it not,' Anthony said, 'how so many of the upper classes have to go slumming in order to find affection?'

'If that is what you call it,' Charlotte said. And tittered. 'I have heard it called other names.'

'Then perhaps you should be more careful of the company you keep,' Anthony said.

'I see that becoming the eighth earl may have gone to your head.'

Perhaps Charlotte was right, Anthony thought. With the title had come responsibility: for the estate itself and all manner of things. For Bella most of all. He knew that Bella's presence was a constant aggravation to his wife. This for two reasons: that he had fathered a child by another woman and that Charlotte had proved incapable of having any of her own. Now her resentment had been fuelled by a further development. The old earl had left Bella ten thousand pounds in his will. Admittedly she would not get it until she was twenty-one but Charlotte still thought it outrageous.

'Perhaps we should challenge that clause,' she had said. 'I always suspected your father had been losing his mind and there's the proof of it.'

'We shall do no such thing,' Anthony had told her.

'But it is ridiculous! Ten thousand pounds? I am sure the courts would never support –'

'No!' Anthony spoke through his teeth. 'Let us hear no more of it.'

After the traumas of the war he had wanted a quiet life. Foreseeing problems, he had been against bringing Bella to Ripon Grange, but his father had as usual had his way. For this reason and because it was the easier option Anthony had left the nurturing of the child to his father. Now the old earl's death had woken his conscience to belated life. However deficient in care he might have been until now, he was no longer prepared to have his child sacrificed on the altar of his wife's resentment. The wife whom at that moment he did not like at all.

'Make sure becoming the countess doesn't go to yours,' he said.

Charlotte stuck her nose in the air but in truth her intentions were not affected by her husband's boorishness. Since the old earl's death Charlotte had observed Anthony and his daughter growing closer to each other. They had even begun to talk without the crippling sense of awkwardness she had done everything she could to encourage. On one occasion she had even overheard Arabella asking whether he was still in contact with her mother. What an outrageous suggestion! It reminded her of what Miss Hunnicut had told her many times in the early years, how Arabella had always been asking about her mother, whether anyone knew where she was and how it might be possible to get in touch with her. Miss Hunnicut had told her nothing, of course, as was only right. Arabella had been too sensible to ask Charlotte, who would have told her nothing as a matter of principle. All Charlotte knew was that her father-in-law had been paying the wretched woman a regular annuity, so presumably she was still alive. She had no wish to find out any more about her but naturally took steps to stop the annuity as soon as she was in a position to do so.

As for the growing intimacy between her husband and his daughter… That was something else she was not prepared to tolerate. The sooner Arabella was removed from the scene the better.

The next morning she had Horrocks bring round the Rolls – no Delage for the new Countess of Clapham! – and drove off to pay a social visit on Mr Hardy of Branksome Hall.

'I speak as a friend,' Charlotte said to Mr Hardy, who was better equipped than most to hear what was not being said in any conversation.

'I quite understand, ma'am.'

The coffee was delightful, the silver pot in which it was served brilliantly polished. Beyond the tall windows, a pale sun watered the extensive lawns that sloped to an ornamental pond.

'Are you acquainted with Major Hector Lacey?'

'I know the name. I have not met him.'

'A particular friend of mine. And – I tell you this in confidence – it is likely that very soon there will be the announcement of an understanding between the major and my husband's daughter.'

'Indeed?'

The countess watched closely but Mr Hardy might have been fashioned from stone.

'Such an arrangement would have our warmest approval,' she said.

Mr Hardy said nothing, while his eyes watched a family of ducks swimming on the pond.

'Our belief,' the countess said, 'is that it would be ideally suited to all parties. A young gel needs – I am sure you will agree with me, Mr Hardy – a mature hand to guide her through those first all-important weeks of marriage. In the circumstances my husband is of the view, and I agree with him, that any other friendship should not be encouraged.'

Now Mr Hardy looked her over thoughtfully. 'I appreciate your telling me.'

'However...' The countess smiled warmly.

'However?' Mr Hardy wondered.

'My husband and I value our relationship with your family and would like it maintained. If that is agreeable to you.'

Mr Hardy was willing to concede that it would be agreeable to him also. If he wondered what the battleaxe was getting at he hid it well.

'I cannot recall whether you have ever met my sister,' the countess said.

'I have not had that pleasure.'

'Then we must make arrangements. A most delightful girl. And,' as though it were of no consequence, 'several years younger than I. Still in her twenties. Would you believe it?'

'I would have said you were no older yourself, ma'am,' he said with a straight face.

'I understand that your son had been planning to go riding with Arabella tomorrow?'

Their eyes met.

'Unfortunately he will have to postpone that arrangement,' Mr Hardy said. 'I need him to go to London for me. Urgent family business. Regrettable, of course, but unavoidable.'

The countess was looking for her gloves.

'Would you like me to give her his apologies?'

'That would be most kind.'

'Will he be away long?'

'It could be several months, I'm afraid. It is an important matter.'

'Such a shame,' the countess said. 'But these things happen, do they not?'

And left, very pleased with herself and her morning's work. Poor Arabella, she thought complacently as she watched the fields flowing past. She will soon get over it. And the major will be much more suitable for her. I must invite Jane to stay. We are sisters, after all. And have been apart too long.

Charles was aghast. 'You're sending me to *Hackney*?'

'That boot manufacturer we took over last year,' his father told him. 'There's the possibility of a big contract, supplying boots to the German war department, but it will mean major modifications to the plant and I want you to be involved in it.'

'I know nothing about the plant. Or boots.'

'You will be working with Mr Griffiths, the manager, and he will instruct you. In any case you won't be there much of the time. Your main job will be to assist him in negotiations with the Germans, so you'll be spending a lot of time in Berlin. From what I hear, their government is very demanding.'

'I'm not sure my German is fluent enough for that.'

Charles, obsessed with Bella, did not want to go anywhere but his father had never learnt to take no for an answer.

'You studied German at Harrow, didn't you?'

'Yes. But –'

'Then do your best. Play your cards right, this could be a huge order for us.'

'Bella and I had been planning –'

Mr Hardy's eyes were like flint. 'You will have to forget about Bella Tempest.'

Charles had never learnt the knack of dealing with his domineering father yet for Bella's sake and his own was willing to try. 'At least let me tell her what's going on...'

'No time for that. You need to be on the three-fifteen train. Mr Griffiths is expecting you in London tonight.'

'Then I shall phone her from London,' Charles said.

'You would be wiser to forget her,' his father said.

Defiance took root. 'That I shall never do.'

But Mr Hardy's response was merciless, and devastating. 'You have no choice. Bella is engaged to be married.'

'*What?*'

Had the ceiling fallen on Charles's head it would have been a lesser shock.

'To a Major Lacey. A man, I may say, with a very bad reputation in the City of London.'

Blackness overwhelmed Charles. What his father was saying was impossible. Every atom of his being rejected it. Bella had been with him less than an hour earlier. She had told him she loved him.

She had permitted him to touch her. They had been happy, dreaming of a shared future.

'I don't believe it!' Charles said.

'The countess told me so herself.'

'She is lying…'

'Why should she do that?'

Because if she was not, Charles thought, there was no truth left in the world.

'Phone her from London, if you must,' Mr Hardy said. 'If it will put your mind at rest.'

As though a restful mind were possible after news like this!

'She is lying,' he said again.

CHAPTER NINE

Bella was up at dawn. After drinking a cup of coffee she saddled Lady, her chestnut mare, trotted down the drive and out through the lodge gates.

Above the moors the sky was streaked with green light and barred with cloud. The air was still, except for the occasional gust that came from nowhere and shivered the leaves of the trees before vanishing as quickly as it had come. Above the trees the rooks circled, cawing restlessly.

Bella eyed the sky as she rode. Overhead it was clear but in these parts the weather could change in minutes, and she sensed a storm brewing. It might pass, it might not, but it would take more than a storm to stop her because she was riding to meet her love, and her heart was singing in expectation.

She crested the rise and saw the massive elm tree beneath which they had arranged to meet, as they had every morning for weeks. Usually Charles was there first and she would wave and put heels to the mare, galloping down the lane to meet him, heart on fire with excitement and joy, but today there was no one. She had beaten him to it.

She trotted on sedately, expecting to see him appear at any moment, but by the time she reached the tree he was still not in sight. No matter; she reined in and waited.

Above the moors the clouds were winning. The streaks of green had disappeared and the sky was uniformly black, swallowing the light even where Bella was waiting. Lightning crackled, followed by a rumble of thunder. A gust of wind tore leaves from the trees and sent them tumbling along the lane, then all was still once more, save for the raucous circling of the uneasy rooks.

They were in for a drenching; no doubt about it. Once again Bella looked up the lane leading to Branksome but it remained empty.

What could have happened to Charles?

To pass the time her brain turned to her favourite fantasy: Mr and Mrs Charles Hardy riding side by side up the oak-fringed driveway to Branksome, the golden lamplight beckoning through the tall windows of the library and reflecting on the surface of the ornamental pond as light faded slowly from the landscape. She could hear Charles's voice and see his smile so clearly that it was a shock to return to reality and find herself still waiting beneath the elm tree's spreading branches, with the first drops of rain falling and Charles nowhere in sight.

He had never kept her waiting before. Now Bella began to worry. What if he'd been thrown? She still had vivid memories of his fall during their crazy downhill race. She had known she was in love with him before that but the accident had brought home to her what it would mean to lose him.

The rain was heavier now. The lane remained empty. A crackle of lightning, almost overhead, was followed within seconds by a bellow of thunder, and Lady stirred uneasily at her side.

'Steady, girl. Steady.'

She remembered her grandfather saying it was dangerous to shelter under a tall tree in a thunderstorm but the rain was falling in earnest now and beyond its shelter she would be soaked in minutes; already she could see rivulets running down the lane.

Still Charles did not come.

She had intended to wait out the storm but eventually her anxiety became too much and she set out, head hunched against the downpour, to ride to Branksome. The lane remained empty and when she breasted the final rise and saw the distant shape of the house she knew that something must have prevented his coming. It was still very early and by now she must look like a drowned rat but she didn't hesitate. Maybe he was sick; maybe something had delayed him. Whatever the reason, she had the right to find out what it was, and find out she would.

She cantered down the hill and up the drive to the house, the mare's hooves splashing through the puddles. Bella dismounted. Shoulders hunched against the rain, face running water, she marched to the front door and rang the bell.

A housemaid opened the door. Her startled eyes stretched wide.

'Oh! Morning, miss.'

She did not invite Bella into the house but stood blinking at her, seemingly at a loss what to say or do.

'Good morning, Katie. Is Mr Charles in?'

'Don't rightly know, miss. I'm not sure –'

Suddenly Mrs Simpson was there.

'Good morning,' she said, surprise in her voice.

She, too, did not invite Bella out of the rain.

'Is Mr Charles here?'

'Mr Charles is in London.'

'In London?' Bella was astonished.

'He went up last night. I thought you knew. It was all very sudden. Something to do with the Hackney factory. He was going to let you know but Mr Hardy said that you'd already been told.'

'Who would have told me?'

'I assume the countess.' Mrs Simpson was clearly floundering. 'As she was here yesterday morning…'

'I see,' said Bella. And did, only too clearly. 'When is he coming home?'

'I couldn't say,' said Mrs Simpson, more awkwardly than ever.

'Nobody told me anything,' Bella said. 'You say the countess was here?'

'That was my understanding. I'm sorry…'

'No need to apologise, Mrs Simpson. It's not your fault.'

She rode home, spurring Lady furiously up the hill, eyes narrowed against the rain that continued to fall. A drumbeat of mounting rage kept pace with the mare's hooves as she galloped down the drive to Ripon Grange. A stablehand took the reins. Drenched and not caring, Bella marched into the house and went to look for her stepmother, whom she found at her writing desk. And who turned to survey her with raised eyebrows and a disbelieving laugh.

'Arabella, you look like a ragamuffin.'

Bella's chin went up. 'Perhaps you mean bait-digger,' she said.

The countess waved the remark away. 'You are drenched,' she said.

'I've been waiting for Charles. We were going riding together.'

'In this weather?' Again the tinkling laugh. 'My dear child! What an extraordinary thing to do. Why don't you have a hot bath and put on something a little more respectable, while I finish this letter? Then I shall order us some hot chocolate and we can have a nice chat.'

Bella raised her voice. 'I was waiting for Charles but he didn't come.'

'I am sorry –'

'He didn't come because he's in London. As apparently you knew.'

'Of course I didn't know,' Charlotte said.

'You knew but didn't tell me,' Bella said. 'I wouldn't be surprised if you'd arranged the whole thing.'

'My dear, you're upset,' said the countess in a soothing voice. 'I assure you I knew nothing about it.'

'You were there.'

'I am positive nothing was said about Charles going away. You know, Arabella,' said the countess, 'I am not saying Charles Hardy is insincere, but young men can be very fickle. They fall out of love as quickly as they fall in. I am not suggesting Charles has fallen out of love with you, but should that unhappily prove the case,' the countess sighed, an older woman committed to helping her inexperienced stepdaughter, 'the only thing to be done, I am afraid, is to move on. Hearts mend, and who knows when other opportunities will arise? And you know, my dear,' Charlotte paused to give her words added weight, 'at your age, a mature man has a great deal to offer.'

All the way south, while the cinders flew back from the rushing locomotive and the darkness stole little by little out of a cloudy sky, Charles told himself the same thing over and over again. Bella could not be engaged. The countess was lying.

Yet the following day, when he phoned the Grange from London, Mrs Delport, the countess's new private secretary, confirmed what his father had told him.

'We are *so* excited,' she said.

'I want to speak to Bella,' he said.

Only if he heard the news directly from her would he believe. But Bella, it seemed, was unavailable.

He tried again the next day, with no better luck.

Mrs Delport said: 'I am sorry to have to say this, Mr Hardy, but we feel that in the circumstances it might be better if you did not try to speak to Arabella any more.'

'Is that Bella's opinion, too?'

'Hers most of all,' Mrs Delport said.

Darkness became a living presence. Three days later, he was in Berlin. But he would not give up. If they would not let him speak to her he would write.

And did so that very day.

Bella took no notice of her stepmother's warnings. Charles would come back; she knew that as certainly as she knew that day follows night. But he did not come back.

Now there were the beginnings of sickness in her heart. Swallowing her pride, she rang Branksome. The telephone was answered by a man whose rich and fruity voice she did not recognise.

'I wish to speak to Mr Charles,' she said.

'I am sorry but Mr Charles is out of the country.'

'Do you have an address for him?'

'Unfortunately not.'

'Do you know when he's coming back?'

'I'm afraid I don't. May I know –'

Bella set her teeth. 'Mrs Simpson, then.'

Surely she would help, if she could?

'I regret Mrs Simpson is also unavailable. May I know who is calling?'

Bella put down the phone.

She spoke to the staff at Ripon Grange: Mr Winchester the butler and Mrs Delport.

'Have there been no phone calls for me?'

'Nothing at all, Miss Arabella. Nothing.'

She asked the same question every morning for a week but each day the answer was the same. They told her there was neither phone call nor letter, and slowly the calamity took shape before her. Charles was not coming back to her. Not soon; not ever.

Each morning dawned in darkness, and inch by agonising inch she came to know the truth. Every romance she had read had spelt out the pain of heartbreak; now she experienced it for herself and it was worse than anything she could have imagined. Day after day she saddled up and rode out. Afterwards she remembered nothing but a blur of hedgerows and stone walls climbing the flank of the hill; gates to be opened and closed; open moors extending into a purple distance. As long as it was not back to Ripon Grange she did not care where she went. Even so, riding was hard: without warning tears would blind her, brought on by the sudden memory of Charles's voice, or the look of love in his eyes as he smiled at her.

One day she came to the chasm called Gaping Gill that she had visited so often with Charles. People said it was over three hundred feet deep, with a stream flowing into it. Driven by something outside herself, she dismounted and walked to the edge of the void. Below her the water poured, white-flecked, into the abyss. Its roar filled her, making thought impossible. She stood and waited for the nudge of an unseen hand. She closed her eyes and heard the uneasy beating of her heart.

No, she thought.

She stepped back from the drop. She remounted, face set, mouth determined, and rode away. Pain continued to claw her but life had the stronger claim. It posed a challenge, but the challenge would be met.

CHAPTER TEN

Sitting alone in her office in the house she had named Desire Bella thought, now I know what it must have felt like to be an aristocrat in the French Revolution, cowering in the tumbril with the mob screaming and Madame La Guillotine waiting in the Place de la Revolution. But this victim was not prepared to expose her neck meekly to the falling blade. She would leap out of the cart and launch a counter-attack. The bank's letter had been a shock but she was over the worst of it now. With all her labours of the last forty years trembling in the balance, Bella was determined to face the challenge head on. She picked up her private phone and dialled. At the other end of the line the receiver lifted.

'Gayle Hastings…'

The voice was cool and noncommittal. Discretion was Gayle's hallmark, and the discovery of concealed information.

'Gayle,' Bella said. 'We have a problem. Industrial espionage. I want you here as soon as you can make it.'

It was late Sunday afternoon but this couldn't wait.

'Good. Half an hour, then.'

She hung up. Gayle Hastings was the best enquiry agent in the business. She would uncover the culprit, if anyone could.

Next she tried to contact Martin Dexter, Peace and Richard. Martin had just got home; the babysitter said that Richard and Su-Ying were not back yet; Peace, predictably, was working.

She told Martin and Peace what she wanted from them but not why.

'I shall need the information tonight. As soon as you can get it to me.'

Peace tried to argue. 'Can't it wait? We're flat out here.'

'Just do it, okay?'

And put down the phone. I certainly got it wrong the day I named her Peace, Bella thought.

Almost at once the phone rang.

Never a dull moment, she thought. She picked it up.

'Yes?'

'Mr Hong of the Chinese Consulate.'

So soon? Well, it was to be expected.

'Put him on.' She heard the click. 'Mr Hong, I was glad to see you at the party. I am afraid the food was very poor, but I hope you can forgive me for that.'

'The food was excellent.' Mr Hong's English was excellent, too, with the faint twang of the Mandarin speaker. 'And your remarks, especially those relating to future co-operation between Australia and China... Inspirational, if I may say so. I have arranged for a transcript to be sent to my ambassador in Canberra. I am sure he will be equally impressed.'

'It is kind of you to say so, Mr Hong. And how can I help you?'

'My government believes that co-operation between our nations should be encouraged as a source of mutual benefit.'

'My sentiments entirely.'

'I would therefore like to suggest that we meet in my office to discuss certain practical measures that may help us achieve this objective.'

'I would welcome that opportunity,' Bella said. 'When did you have in mind?'

'Shall we say tomorrow morning at nine?'

Her appointment with BradMin was scheduled for eleven-thirty. Depending on what happened this afternoon, Owen Freeth was pencilled in for ten. Those meetings apart, her diary was clear.

Mr Hong has definitely heard something, Bella thought.

She said: 'I regret nine o'clock will not be convenient. However, I would welcome a meeting here, in my office, at eight. If that is not too early for you?'

Bella did not know what Mr Hong was planning to say but was determined that any meeting would be on her terms or not at all.

There was a pause; then Mr Hong said:

'Eight-thirty will be suitable.'

'I look forward to it.'

Bella put down the phone and walked into the vast reception room. Now this crisis had erupted, every step across the marble floor had a new significance. All this – the marble, the drapes, the building – was legally hers. Its treasures were hers also. But for how long?

She paused to examine the exquisite jade pieces presented to her on her first visit to China six years before; the Soong vase that she had bought at the same time and that experts told her was as fine as the specimen on display in the Beijing Art Museum; a pair of Hester Bateman candlesticks, with memories both loving and tragic; a Monet painting of water lilies in the artist's garden at Giverny. Each was worth a fortune in the world's terms, but to Bella they were valuable because they represented the highs and lows of her life: the births of her children and her husband's death; the near-fatal accident that might have destroyed her but miraculously had not; and now the business deal with China that all being well would be the foundation of the company's future wealth. The Monet had served a double purpose: she had bought it to console herself after Garth's death but also to demonstrate her confidence in the mine and the future. It was a challenge thrown in the teeth of fate, declaring that, in defiance of all odds, she would succeed in what she had committed herself to do.

The next few weeks, possibly even days, would determine whether they remained hers or not. Events were building to a climax that only that morning she could not have foreseen; now Mr Hong's phone call had made it obvious that China, no doubt concerned for its iron ore supplies, intended to get involved. She felt the edges of her mind, sharp and hard as tempered steel, turn to meet the challenge. Her brain knew it was possible to fail but her will would not accept it.

She walked restlessly around the room that, more than anywhere else, represented what had become her life. She might have remained happy as Garth Tucker's wife on Miranda Downs. She had loved the cattle station from the moment she first set eyes on it; she loved it still. Her life there had been years of work, hardship and suffering, but also of joy. Her children had spent their early years there. Even after she had started to develop the Perth property in 1953, it had remained her home. In a sense it still was: to this day she carried within her memories of the dry months, each day blurred by heat and dust; the intermittent floods of the wet; the humidity and emptiness; the people with whom she had shared her days and from whom she had learnt so many secrets of the sacred earth.

Fate had intervened. She had moved from the pastoral life into this palace, symbol of her dreams, and to the challenge of constructing a business with the potential to increase one hundredfold the wealth of this state and nation. It had become a sacred quest, absorbing her energy, intelligence and courage. She had battled the scepticism of a world that had not believed a woman capable of the task. She had fought banks, politicians and the law. Rivals had tried to destroy her. Somehow she had survived, yet now the edifice she had built was on the brink of collapse. If that happened, all would be lost; her sweat, tears and agony would have been in vain.

She stared up at the Monet, admiring its serenity even as she drew deep breaths of air into her lungs. She had put too much of her life into this venture to fail now. She would not fail. Again and again she repeated it, as a mantra. She would not, would not, would not fail...

Nor was she truly alone, because the past kept watch beside the present. Garth was beside her. She could sense the forceful masculinity that had first drawn her to him. He had been a true cattleman, and more than happy to let her take over the running of the mine, but he had always been there for her. He was there for her now, as were all those others who had been important to her over the years.

Even Charles Hardy, the Yorkshire boy she had loved and lost... Now, as the crisis threatened to sweep her away, the image of Charles as she had last seen him returned. He had been so young and brave, smiling as he had waved what she had believed was only a temporary goodbye. To this day she did not know what had happened, only that her stepmother must have been behind it. Whatever she might have felt in the days of her agony, she did not now believe that Charles had abandoned her. She did not blame him for marrying either, however much it had pained her when she heard the news; she had done the same thing herself, after all. He would have been here for her now, she thought. Had he known, and if he were still alive.

A click of heels on the marble floor as Deborah came looking for her.

'Is the media on to it yet?' Bella said.

'The phone never stops.'

'It's bound to be hectic for a while. Just tell them what I told you.'

'I shall.'

Most would have been flustered by the pressure but Deborah looked as calm as she always did. It was a great day when I took her on, Bella thought. 'You were looking for me?'

'Mr Freeth is here.'

'I'm coming,' Bella said. With all the artillery at my disposal, I am coming.

Deborah on her heels, Bella returned to her office and sat down.

'Shall I ask him to come in?' Deborah said.

'Give me a minute first.'

She sat with her hands flat on the desk while she considered what she was going to say to this man who had advised on her legal affairs for so many years.

Owen Freeth was over seventy but still fit. He was a bachelor who enjoyed parties and mixing with the movers and shakers of his world, yet as far as she knew had always taken care never to involve himself too closely with anyone. No doubt he would have said that distance aided sound judgement: the quality that his clients valued most in him and that over the years had made him both successful and rich.

He and Garth had met in the early thirties and formed a strong if unlikely friendship. Garth had seen in Owen a quality that he had perhaps wished he had himself: the dispassionate nature that her cattleman husband, living on the tiptoes of his life, would never have. For Bella's part, she respected both his opinions and his efficiency. When she wanted him to do something he did it quickly and well. They were friendly but not close friends: they were temperamentally too far apart for that. She knew he admired her courage and audacity, her unfailing instinct in matters of business and the law, but there were times when she suspected that her ruthlessness alarmed him.

She and Garth had attended meetings with him together. She remembered very clearly the first time she had met him and how he had started off by treating her as a decorative addition to her husband's life, someone whose function was to give style and support to her man. He had explained to her that a woman whose knowledge of life was confined to a cattle station was hardly qualified to compete with men whose natural milieu was the cut-throat world of business.

'Nevertheless I intend to do it,' she said.

He could not believe she was serious. 'It's a tough world out there with its own rules,' he said. 'Name me one woman who has made it to the top in industry, never mind in mining.'

'I know one who will,' she said.

After that they had got on better.

She picked up her phone. 'Please ask him to come in.'

She watched him as he closed the door carefully behind him: confidentiality might have been his middle name. She did not speak but gestured to the chair on the other side of the desk. Owen sat down and crossed his legs.

'A splendid party,' he said. 'Worthy of a special occasion –'

There were times when flowery compliments worked with Bella but this was not one of them; she cut him off in mid-sentence. 'You know this town better than anybody,' she said.

'I know a number of people,' he agreed cautiously.

'You have informers in many places.'

Owen smiled deprecatingly. 'Sources of information, perhaps.'

'You obtain information from informers,' she said impatiently. 'Let's not play games.' She sat back in her chair, pointed two fingers at him like a shotgun and gave him the news with both barrels. Pow! Pow!

'There will be reports in tomorrow's international press questioning this group's financial viability. The local media's on to it, too. Deborah is already fielding dozens of phone calls.'

Own was horrified by the news. He was a man who knew how to keep his thoughts hidden but after all these years Bella could read him like a paperback.

'What is she saying to them?'

A steely smile. 'What I have told her to say.'

'And that is?'

'That ore shipments are proceeding as planned.'

'And the rumours?'

'That it is not our policy to comment on rumour.'

'That sounds all right.'

'I've told Martin Dexter to prepare a report giving projected tonnages under our existing contracts, delivery dates to the Baoshan smelters, anticipated profits on shipments. When I can get hold of him I shall ask Richard to give him a hand. Peace is doing the same regarding our stockpiled ore and the mineral reserves in the unmined areas. I've told them I must have both reports tonight.'

Owen had taken out a pad and was writing notes with a gold pencil. 'Where do I come in?'

'I want you to vet both reports, consolidate them into one document and put them in the correct legal language. I shall need two versions: one showing the gross profit on each shipment, one excluding it. I shall need both documents from you by ten o'clock tomorrow morning. Four copies of each. Every statement must be one hundred per cent correct, but I want no mention of the Brad-Min rail agreement.'

Owen thought: It's possible, if only just. 'What do I do with the reports when they are finished?'

'Give them to me.'

She would need one copy for the bank, one for the Stock Exchange, one for herself and one spare. No others. No one to be informed. Everything to be kept absolutely confidential. She took a deep breath. She felt energised. Problems and challenges had always stimulated her; this one was no different. Nor had she finished with Owen.

'You have what you call sources of information. We need to find out who started these rumours. Do you agree?'

'We can try,' he said cautiously.

'I think we need to do better than try. We need to know. And soon.'

'How soon?'

'A week?'

He was shocked. 'That's impossible!'

'Let me help you. Who stands to gain from these stories?'

'Depress the market, buy at a lower price... Anyone; I could give you a dozen names in Australia alone.'

'And the timing?'

He did not understand.

Bella said: 'Tomorrow we are scheduled to sign that rental agreement. Yes?'

'Of course.'

'And today someone starts these rumours? Owen, this isn't some casual speculator looking for a quick buck. This is a plot to destroy me and my business.'

'Surely not...' His tone was indulgent.

'I've told you before not to patronise me, Owen.' Bella's blue eyes assessed him icily. 'You'd better read this.' She handed him the bank's letter.

Owen read it, then stared at her. 'That poses a problem.'

'How do we stand legally? Halliburton's known the situation for months.'

'The fact that Halliburton was aware has no bearing on the terms of the loans.'

'As I thought,' Bella said. 'They've given us seven days.'

'I'll speak to the bank. See if we can negotiate an extension –'

'I doubt that'll serve any purpose. There's more involved here than what we owe them.'

She told him of the warning shot Pete Bathurst had fired across her bows that afternoon. 'He's planning to spring something on us, I'm sure of it.'

'Without the railway all the China contracts will be at risk,' Owen said.

'And without them we're finished. Exactly.'

She debated whether to tell him about the next day's meeting with the Chinese consul but decided to say nothing at this stage. She did not know what Mr Hong was planning to say to her. In any case, if Owen thought the future of the company was at stake it might motivate him to get his informants moving more quickly than he might do otherwise.

'Now you see why we have to find out what's going on. You said it could be anybody. That is not quite true, is it? Excluding you, me and the bank, there are seven people who know the fine details of what is happening. It has to be one of them.'

'And they are?'

'Peace, Richard and Su-Ying –'

'Surely you don't suspect your own family?'

Her expression did not change. 'Until they are cleared, their names are on the list. Outside the family it could be Deborah Smith; someone in BradMin; someone in the Chinese government; Martin Dexter; someone in your office.'

That fired him up, as she had known it would.

'You cannot possibly think –'

'I think nothing. I suspect no one more than anyone else. But that leak has to have come from somewhere.'

'What about Pete Bathurst?'

'I have no doubt he's involved. But he must have had inside information. That's what I want you to find out: who on the list I've just given you has been talking.'

'I'll look into it right away,' Owen said.

'Meanwhile I'll get my own spies on to it.'

Owen looked affronted. Bella was always amused when people pretended a righteousness they did not possess. At least I am honest, she thought. With myself if no one else.

'I'm not as mealy-mouthed as you, Owen. I don't have sources of information; I have spies. Don't look so shocked; years ago you told me it's a tough world out there, with its own rules. I am playing by those rules. I intend to get to the bottom of this nonsense. And survive.'

The power and determination in the blue eyes transfixed him.

'I am sure you will,' he agreed hastily.

'One more thing. When you leave, you'll probably find a media presence outside the gates. I want you to be friendly and relaxed with them. Tell them the rumours are without foundation. Say everything is going to plan.'

'And that we anticipate no hiccups with the new rail agreement?'

'Better not say that,' Bella told him. 'I have a hunch there may be.'

The audience was at an end. Bella walked with him to the door of her office. Before he left she took his hand in both of hers and gave him the full benefit of her blue stare.

'Owen, I'm relying on you.'

She returned to her desk and eyed the closed door. And I'll be checking up on you too, she thought. Don't imagine I won't.

Deborah rang.

'Gayle Hastings is here.'

'Send her in.'

Time to get her own spies to work. After that she would have another go at getting hold of Richard.

Next morning Bella was in her office punctually at eight-thirty, but the consul was fifteen minutes late.

Bella had expected it. Mr Hong was playing the game according to Chinese rules, and being late sent a message that he believed he had the upper hand in whatever discussions he had planned. It was also a reproof for having changed his proposed timetable in the first place. She used the time to review the reports Martin and Peace had handed her last night, then asked Deborah to send him in.

Bella smiled cordially as she greeted him, hand outstretched. 'Good to see you, Mr Hong. Please sit down.'

She led him to two easy chairs placed on either side of an occasional table. They sat and smiled at each other. As always, Bella was wearing heels with a blue business suit, cut from a silky material that set off the colour of her eyes, though she had devoted more care than usual to her make-up. Mr Hong, neat and guarded, in his mid-forties, wore a double-breasted dark suit, white shirt and sober tie. His face gave nothing away; at the moment his smile was formal rather than warm, but Bella thought it was a good sign that he had agreed to meet her here, and at this hour.

'May I offer you coffee? Or would you prefer tea?'

'Coffee would be very agreeable.'

Deborah brought in a silver pot, milk jug and cups on a circular tray that she placed on the table between them. There was a plate of biscuits. Bella poured and Mr Hong accepted his cup but declined a biscuit. They sat and sipped coffee, smiling politely at one another, neither giving anything away.

'It is a little chilly this morning,' Bella said.

Mr Hong's smile did not falter.

'I apologise for asking you to come so early,' she said. 'Pressure of work, you understand.'

'The coffee is excellent,' Mr Hong said.

'Thank you. It is very ordinary.'

It was the best money could buy and both were aware of it. Mr Hong placed his empty cup on the tray.

'My government has received advance notice of the reports in this morning's foreign press,' he said. 'I am instructed to enquire whether there is any truth in them.'

'None,' Bella said.

'Beijing will be relieved to hear it. Beijing, you understand, is concerned that the questions raised may be used to delay shipment of the ore.'

'Not by us.'

'If I may be forgiven for pointing this out, it is not your attitude with which Beijing is principally concerned.'

'I cannot speak for others,' Bella said.

She remembered Richard's warning: *BradMin is not in the business of helping us deliver. What they really want is our ore and our contracts.*

'I am scheduled to sign the new railway agreement later today. Once that is done, I shall be in a position to continue delivering ore to the coast as at present. We have had no request for a delay,' Bella said.

Which was true, as far as it went.

'It is important that supplies should not be disrupted on account of temporary inconvenience,' Mr Hong said.

'Very important,' Bella agreed.

'Delay could jeopardise my government's arrangements with your company. The contracts contain a standard non-performance clause should delivery not be made in accordance with the agreed timetable.'

'I am aware of the clause,' Bella said.

'I am therefore instructed to enquire what arrangements you have in place to circumvent such difficulties, should they arise.'

This was getting tricky; Mr Hong obviously had sources of information better than hers.

'I have no reason to suppose any difficulties will arise. In this connection I am having a report prepared that will set out all salient information regarding production levels and ore reserves. If you wish I shall let you have a copy.'

'That will be most helpful. May I know your fall-back position if, contrary to your expectations, there should prove to be problems?'

She had to decide whether or not to tell the truth. She did not hesitate. 'There is no fall-back position.'

'Thank you for your candour,' said Mr Hong.

'People say honesty is the best policy,' Bella said.

Although not one to which she had always subscribed.

She thought Mr Hong's smile might be a shade warmer than it had been before.

'On the other hand,' he said, 'it is wise to have an alternative plan, in case of difficulties.'

'Very wise,' Bella agreed. 'When it is possible.'

'My government feels,' said Hong, 'that Mrs Tucker might care to consider another visit to Beijing. In order to explore what alternatives there may be.'

Bella tried to conceal her surprise; she had not expected such a summons. Because a summons was what it was, despite the delicate wording.

'Such a visit would need to be very soon,' Bella said.

'An embassy plane is flying to Beijing tomorrow.'

'And would be able to take me and any company directors I wish to accompany me?'

'It would be our pleasure.'

'It may not be necessary, if things go according to plan this morning,' Bella said.

'As you say, there is that possibility.'

He knows something I don't, Bella thought. It was embarrassing; he made her feel like an amateur. Once this was sorted out, she would make it her business to upgrade her intelligence arrangements, which were clearly inadequate. Gayle Hastings was the best in her field and Bella already had one informant inside BradMin but what she needed was someone with technical knowledge.

'I shall let you know about Beijing later this morning,' she said.

Yesterday Bella had left Owen Freeth to find his own way out; with Mr Hong she walked to the front door of the house and touched hands in what, with Mr Hong, passed for a handshake. She watched him go down the steps. A uniformed chauffeur opened the rear door of the gleaming black Mercedes. Hong climbed in and did not look back. She watched him drive away and returned to her office, summoning Deborah on the way.

'Phone Richard and Peace and say I want to see them right away.'

'To Beijing?' Richard stared at her. 'What does it mean?'

'It means the Chinese think we are going to have problems with BradMin.'

'What do you think?'

'I think they're right. Bathurst implied as much yesterday.'

'But going to Beijing…'

'Of course you won't go,' said Peace.

'Why not?'

'To jump just because they say so? They would see it as a sign of weakness.'

'Without the railway we have nothing.'

'It's all agreed –'

'But not signed.'

Peace looked mutinous, no doubt remembering their recent disagreement.

Bella looked at Richard. 'And you?'

'I said it before. Bathurst will do us down if he can.'

And at the moment was doing a good job of it, Bella thought. 'And Beijing?'

'Without the railway you'll have problems. Without China you're finished. You've no choice. You must go.'

'Weakness?'

'They might interpret it as strength.'

'To jump when they say jump?' Peace was derisive.

'To be willing to hear what they have to say. Sun Tzu said –'

'Spare us,' Peace said.

'They are Chinese. We need to think as they do.'

Bella thought briefly and made up her mind. 'If today's meeting with BradMin fails, I shall tell Mr Hong we accept his invitation.'

'We?' Peace said.

'Richard and Su-Ying will come with me –'

'Leaving me to guard the fort,' Peace said.

'Because you do it so well. I shall need Richard if we start talking figures. And Su-Ying because of her Mandarin.'

'And her father,' Richard said. 'Deng Xiao-ping rules China and my father-in-law is his protégé.'

'Maybe because of him, too,' Bella said.

CHAPTER ELEVEN

'We've got her, by God,' Pete Bathurst said, rubbing hands like shovels through his red hair. He stared around his palatial office on the twentieth floor of BradMin House, its walls decorated with aerial photos of the mine workings he had been involved in during his career. 'I've been waiting a long time for this.'

He was a giant of a man: fifty-five years old and six feet six in his socks, and his shoulders threatened to jam in every door he went through. He was accompanied by the two men he privately called his merinos. They were his senior executives, both polishing their asses on the chairs around BradMin's boardroom table, both of them suits who would not know an open-cut mine if they fell into one.

He looked at them now; company treasurer Amos Bellamy and legal counsel Sinclair Smythe. Their natural habitat is here, Pete thought contemptuously, on the executive floor surrounded by papers and files and deferential assistants, their only skill a political agility that has enabled them to climb as high as they have. Brad-Min for them was made up solely of financial statements and legal opinions, budgets, cash-flow projections, head office returns... No modern business could survive without the pen-pushers, but in his heart Pete despised them and all they represented.

His background was as different from theirs as they were different physically; he had started in mining as a fetch-and-carry boy in a blasting team on the floor of a huge open-cut working in Colorado; he had been no stranger to dust, flying stone and the ear-numbing crash of explosives. No stranger to fists and oaths, either. He had learnt to hit back, and the men he had hit had generally stayed down. Old man Bradford Gulliver had picked him out and put him through college at company expense, and he had emerged with degrees in both mining engineering and business administration, his feet set firmly on the promotion trail.

He had made enemies; this was a tough business and needed tough and ruthless men to run it. Pete Bathurst qualified on both counts. Success had brought him here in his early thirties, to the chief executive's office in BradMin's Australasian headquarters, but he had never forgotten his hard-drinking, hard-swearing beginnings and liked to think of himself as a wolf surrounded by sheep which knew to do his bidding, no questions asked.

'She's late,' Bellamy said, looking at his watch.

'Of course she's late.' Pete's grin opened a chasm in his granite face. 'She's a woman, ain't she?'

Not only a woman, but a woman who had presumed to trespass on a man's world. And one who over the years had caused him more trouble than a cartload of monkeys. He would enjoy cutting Bella Tucker off at the knees, to teach her a lesson.

It was Bellamy who had informed him of Tuckers's precarious cash situation; he had told Smythe, that arch-manipulator, who had passed the information to the banks. Acting on his instructions, Smythe had also fed the story to his tame journalist, with a list of the overseas newspapers that might be interested.

Talk about a self-fulfilling prophecy, Pete thought. Spook the banks by hinting at problems over the rail link; the banks stampede, exactly as you planned; you then use the negative publicity that you created to destroy the agreement.

As neat a trick as he had pulled in all his years.

Now here they were, at the death. Some disliked bloodsports, but to Pete Bathurst they were the breath of life. With Tuckers down, BradMin would not only pick up the mineral rights but have a monopoly on the China trade that Pete's nose told him was likely to be the biggest thing in mining for years to come.

What would that do for his reputation back in the States? Pete the Giant would become Pete the Giant-killer, with the near certainty of being invited back to Houston to take over the top spot as chief executive of the entire group.

It was a thought to warm the heart that many insisted he did not possess.

Melanie, the comely twenty-five-year-old who had accompanied him to Bella's party, poked her nose around the door. 'Mr Freeth is in reception.'

Owen Freeth; another suit. Pete frowned. 'Alone?'

'Yes.'

Maybe Bella had decided to do some shopping on the way.

'Send him up.' He gave Melanie a smile with messages in it. It was likely to be a warm night. After all, they would have something to celebrate.

He stepped forwards, hand outstretched, as Owen Freeth came through the door.

'Good to see you,' Pete said genially. 'Bella forgotten her handbag, has she?'

Owen Freeth gave him a cold smile; there was no love lost and both men knew it. 'Mrs Tucker will not be coming. She has asked me to come in her place, out of courtesy. While I'm here I might look at the latest draft of the agreement –'

Whatever else Pete had expected it was not this and, as always, the unexpected made him mad. 'You and Smythe prepared the goddamned thing, for Christ's sake.'

Exactly the wrong way to handle Owen Freeth.

'Yesterday you told Mrs Tucker you were unhappy about certain aspects of it. Naturally I have to satisfy myself that there have been no last-minute amendments.'

'Would I do that?' Pete grinned.

But there was one, and it didn't take Owen long to find it. 'Explain this clause to me.'

Pete gestured to the legal counsel hovering behind him. 'Sinclair will put you in the picture.'

And Sinclair did.

'We shall need time to consider the implications,' Owen said stiffly. 'When we are ready, we'll get back to you.'

'I doubt you need bother,' Pete said.

'The present agreement still has ten days to run –'

'Sure has. But we're talking a new agreement, right? And with all these reports in the papers… Hell, I'm not sure what Houston will have to say about them.'

'The rate of royalty has been agreed,' Bella said.

'It's not the rate per truck, it's the volume of traffic. When the original agreement was signed, no one anticipated there would be so much of it. There was no mention of it in the original agreement. Now BradMin is claiming there's too much, with Tuckers's loads on top of their own. Bathurst said they are concerned what it might be doing to the track –'

'Another of his excuses,' Bella said.

'He says they commissioned a new survey,' Owen said. 'The surveyors have come up with clay patches right in the middle of the run. He says we're more than welcome to read the report, if we want. He claims his hands are tied. His board has decided to limit us to a hundred trucks a day.'

'His board does nothing without his say-so,' Bella said scornfully. 'This is his idea, no one else's.'

'Perhaps. But that's what they're proposing. A hundred trucks will still enable you to shift up to four million tons a year,' Owen said.

'Four million. When we are committed to delivering twenty-five.'

* * *

'Wes-tern Pac-ific...' The operator chanted the bank's name.

'Mr Halliburton, please.'

'And who is call-ing?'

'Bella Tucker.'

'One mo-ment.'

'Bella...' Clive Halliburton's voice sounded grey and cautious, as well it might.

'I am flying to China,' Bella said. 'I expect to be away a week, maybe a little longer. When I come back I should have good news for you.'

'The bank has allowed you seven days only.' The banker's voice was a rustle of dead leaves.

'I need more. I am visiting Beijing at the request of the Chinese government and I cannot control their timetable. But a fortnight should be enough.'

'At the request of the Chinese government,' he repeated. 'Have they indicated the purpose of your visit?'

'To ensure supplies of ore are maintained. Why else?'

'And you expect to be back in two weeks?'

'Yes.'

'I can guarantee nothing –'

'An extra week, Clive.'

A long pause, Bella with her fingers and toes crossed. Finally:

'Two weeks, then. And the news had better be good.'

CHAPTER TWELVE

The following morning Bella, Richard and Su-Ying flew to Canberra, where the embassy plane was waiting for them. An hour later they were in the air, heading north.

This plane was very different from the one she had used on her previous visit to China seven years ago. That had been basic in the extreme; this was well equipped, the seats luxurious. The cabin attendant, a young and beautiful Chinese woman, was most attentive. Drinks were offered, and accepted.

'You want whisky?' the attendant asked.

'Orange juice,' Bella said.

Su-Ying followed her example; Richard had a beer. Bella knew he was dying to talk about the trip but she had cautioned them against discussing business during the flight.

'It's an embassy plane. It is certain to be bugged.'

Three hours into the flight the attendant brought them a meal. It was as far away as you could get from standard airline food and she told them it had been prepared especially for the embassy by the Lotus Flower restaurant in Beijing.

Afterwards Bella thought she would rest; there was no point preparing for a meeting when she did not know the agenda and for years she had been able to summon sleep at will. She closed her eyes.

She woke as the plane began its descent. She looked out of the cabin window; the early morning sun illuminated the city's buildings in golden light. Ten million people down there, she thought. Or so Su-Ying said. Ten million in a country of over a billion.

Say it again, slowly. One billion people. Think what it means.

It might have intimidated her once, but over the years she had grown resistant to intimidation. She smiled grimly as she watched the city grow larger beneath the plane's wings: now she was more in the business of intimidating others. Which was not to say the coming meetings would not be challenging but Bella had taught herself long ago to take each day as it came. Without that skill, she would never have survived the ups and downs that life had handed her.

'Heaven knows,' she said, 'there've been enough of them.'

Su-Ying shot her a questioning glance. 'I'm sorry?'

Bella had not realised she had spoken aloud. 'Nothing, dear. Just daydreaming.'

She knew the world, her family included, thought she had no nerves at all. If only, she thought. It would be a useful quality to possess now, but the truth was she was as apprehensive as the rest of them: just better at hiding the fact.

'How does it feel to be back?' she asked her daughter-in-law.

Su-Ying gave what Bella privately called her Chinese smile: a formal movement of the lips that revealed nothing. 'I am nervous,' she said. 'I do not have your strength.'

Bella patted her hand, saying nothing. China, she thought. The Middle Kingdom. The land of a million secrets. Of tyranny and hope, progress and repression. Name it, you got it. But, like it or hate it, the future. For Bella Tempest Tucker in particular.

Ripon Grange to Beijing. A long road, with many hurdles along the way. Somehow she had managed to surmount them all. Only one now remained, but it was the biggest of all. Fail here and her life would be in ruins. Everything she owned would be lost, swallowed up by the humungous debts, but she would not think of that. Failure was not on the agenda.

She smiled at her son, sitting beyond his wife on the other side of the aisle, as the runway reached up to embrace them.

Victory. She mouthed the word silently at him. It had been her slogan all her life. Nothing less would do. She thought again: I shall permit nothing – nothing! – to deprive me of it.

Brave words, but unenforceable. Unless China agreed.

The plane drew up on the apron. On her first visit there had been a guard of honour, immaculate and ramrod-stiff, but then the authorities had been hoping for something from her. There would be nothing like that now.

The landing steps were wheeled into place and secured. The cabin door opened. Followed by her son and daughter-in-law, Bella Tucker stepped into the freshness of an autumnal Beijing morning. Into her future.

A car was waiting. Middle of the range but at least a car. The driver held the door as Bella got in, followed by Richard and Su-Ying.

Bella watched the street as they sped into the city. There had been a lot of changes since she was last here. Few cars still but tens of thousands of bicycles. China was on the move at last.

High-rise buildings towered above the single-storey shopfronts of the past. Some were complete; many were not. Workmen swarmed like ants. Even inside the speeding car, the energy of what she was seeing was as stimulating as wine.

China had been far behind the rest of the world; now it was rushing to catch up. With over a billion people and such evident resolve, it would not take them long. Yet resolve would not be enough. They would need materials, too: cement, wood and in particular steel. Billions of tons of steel, smelted from iron ore shipped from the Tucker mine. And down the track maybe coal, too. From the Tucker mine.

Bella longed to see the ore flowing on and on into the future: freight trains conveying their precious loads from the mine to the coast; bulk carriers transporting it from Port Anthony to China. Behind her calm exterior she seethed with excitement.

Now BradMin was denying her access to its railway. Owen Freeth said that legally BradMin was within its rights. That being so, what could China do about it? Nothing, on the face of it, but the fact that she was here at all gave her hope. Negotiations would be tough but Bella was confident she would be equal to the task. She sighed contentedly, leaning back in the leather seat.

Richard looked at her anxiously. 'Tired?'

She was sixty-five, not ninety-five, yet sometimes he seemed to think she was verging on senility.

'I am fine.'

The car dropped them at their hotel. It was adequate and no doubt clean but a long way short of the best; in this land of symbolism, the authorities were sending her a message. She was the one seeking favours and would be treated accordingly.

Two hours later, showered and breakfasted, the same car deposited Bella at the ministry, one block from the Great Hall of the People. For this first meeting, she had decided to come alone. Eager for the fray, she followed the waiting officials inside.

The office was large, the furniture of the best quality, the floor covered with a luxurious green carpet. On the walls landscapes painted in the style of the old T'ang masters flanked photographs of Deng Xiao-ping, China's Paramount Leader, and State President Hu Yao-bang. Golden drapes of a silky material were drawn back from the windows through which Bella could see the emptiness of Tiananmen Square, where a huge portrait of the late Mao Ze-dong looked with spurious benevolence on a world that his successors were hurrying to change as quickly as they could.

Good news for us, Bella hoped.

The room combined elegance with a sense of purpose and authority. Bella took note; she would never know how high within the Chinese hierarchy was the person with whom she would be dealing but the room and its furnishings indicated someone of importance.

The official introduced himself as Comrade Fang. He was a burly, handsome man in early middle age and spoke through an interpreter: a young woman in a military-type uniform. Formally dressed in a western-style grey suit and tie, he began the courteous exchanges that might sweeten but not disguise the seriousness of the negotiations that would take place later.

'I hope you had a good journey. Australia is far away.'

'There is a saying,' Bella said. 'No journey is long if it enables us to meet a friend.'

'That is a true saying,' Mr Fang said.

'I would like to express our gratitude to the Chinese government for placing its aircraft at our disposal,' Bella said.

'Friends should help friends. Is that not so? You saw the new buildings being erected as you drove in from the airport?'

'Indeed I did. There have been many changes since I was here before. It is most impressive.'

Comrade Fang sat back with a pleased expression and rang a silver bell. The door opened and a uniformed man brought coffee on a silver tray.

'You like?' Mr Fang said, speaking English for the first time.

'I like very much,' Bella said.

Coffee was poured.

'I regret the cups are not of the best quality,' he said.

The cups were of fine porcelain.

'The cups are exquisite,' Bella said.

He smiled and drank his coffee noisily. Bella sipped more moderately.

'So much to do,' he said happily. 'For which we shall need the assistance of our friends.'

Bella returned her empty cup to its saucer. The waiter refilled it.

'I apologise for the poor quality of the coffee,' Fang said.

'The coffee is excellent,' said Bella.

Su-Ying had warned her: 'You must not expect any decisions to be made at the first meeting. Its purpose will be to set the basis for later talks.'

'Which will be when?' Bella had asked her.

'Today or tomorrow,' Su-Ying had said. 'Perhaps not for several days. It depends.'

'On what?'

'On how urgently they wish to reach a solution. Or how urgently they think you need one.'

'I see. So patience –'

'Is essential.'

Bella refocused her attention on Comrade Fang.

'China huge country, with huge problems,' he was saying. 'We need our friends. We also need to know they stand by us at all times. No deviation. No sudden changes of heart.'

'That is all-important,' Bella agreed. 'How else can there be trust?'

'I am happy to hear you say so.'

There was a knock on the door. The woman who came in was in her twenties, wearing an excellent quality blouse and knee-length skirt that hugged her slender frame. She addressed Fang in Chinese.

'*Hau!*' Comrade Fang made a show of looking at his watch before turning to Bella. He spoke in English. 'Our discussion is so interesting I quite forget I have other meeting. Mrs Tucker will have to excuse me. However, I believe good start has been made. Yes?'

'A very good start. And tomorrow, as they say, is another day.'

A blank look; he was clearly unfamiliar with the saying. Nor, it was obvious, was he committed to tomorrow. Or to any day. He said: 'I shall instruct driver to take you to your hotel. If Mrs Tucker wishes to go shopping or visit the open-air food market on Wang-fujing Street the car and driver are at her disposal.'

'And our next meeting?'

'One of my staff will contact you at the hotel.'

The car was waiting as Bella was escorted out of the building. The wide streets were mostly empty but that would change. The energy was unmistakable, the determination to move the economy forwards evident in everything Comrade Fang had said. The money and resources would be found. We are talking billions of tons of iron ore, Bella thought. Tucker Mining and BradMin were in the pound seats, but Pete Bathurst was not in the sharing business; he wanted it all.

The Chinese government undoubtedly had thoughts on that subject but what they were there was no knowing. Su-Ying had said patience was essential. Very well; she would wait.

Lying in bed that night, Bella once again went over her meeting with Comrade Fang. The atmosphere had been more amicable than she had dared hope. It was far too early to guess how the negotiations would work out but, whether they ended in success or catastrophe, one thing was certain. They marked the culmination of a journey that forty-eight years ago had begun with heartbreak, a series of events so painful that even now it hurt her to remember them, but which had resulted, for the first time in her life, in her taking charge of her own destiny.

CHAPTER THIRTEEN

Charlotte had made up her mind to marry Arabella off to her brother's friend Major Lacey, who had a small estate conveniently far away in the West Country. To that end she had invited him to spend a weekend at Ripon Grange, only to have Arabella turn him down flat.

Major Lacey departed, in high dudgeon at the loss not only of a nubile young woman whose figure had stirred his imagination but of the five thousand pounds the countess had promised him as a wedding gift.

'I cannot believe you could do such a thing!' Charlotte spat the words at Bella. She was not a woman who liked her plans thwarted.

More and more Bella suspected that her stepmother had been behind everything from Charles's disappearance to the major's proposal, so she was not in the best of moods, either. 'Such a ridiculous little man!'

'A gentleman with his own estate?' Charlotte said. 'As the granddaughter of a bait-digger, I would have expected you to jump at it.'

'I am also the granddaughter of an earl and the daughter of another one,' Bella pointed out. 'Both honest men, too, which is more than some can say of their ancestors.'

Charlotte discussed what she called the Arabella problem with her husband.

'That poor Major Lacey,' she said.

'Poor is right,' Anthony said. 'I have seldom seen a poorer example of a man.'

'But the owner of an estate.'

'Heavily mortgaged,' said Anthony, who had made some enquiries of his own.

'The question now is what is to be done about her. She was most distressed when Charles Hardy threw her over.'

'I never understood how that happened,' Anthony said. 'One minute I was thinking wedding bells, the next...'

'Young men and women fall in and out of love all the time,' said Charlotte, who had never fallen in love at all.

Anthony, who had fallen in love once but never out of it, was silent. Charlotte pressed her advantage.

'I feel for her but since it happened her behaviour has been intolerable. The things she has said...' She dabbed her eyes. 'You would think she hated me!'

'You never mentioned it before,' Anthony said.

He did not share her distress; he knew his wife better than she realised.

'I believe it would be in her best interests to go away for a while,' Charlotte said.

Anthony pondered. Charlotte was up to something, but a break might help Bella get over the Hardy boy.

'Where do you have in mind?' he asked.

'My brother Walter has an estate outside Sunbury-on-Thames. He tells me he is looking for a housekeeper and would be more than happy to offer Arabella the position.'

'A housekeeper?' Anthony frowned; he was not at all sure about Bella becoming a housekeeper. 'She is a lady, after all.'

Charlotte patted his arm. 'I would hardly call her that. She needs to make her way in the world. She doesn't get her grubby little claws on the money your father was foolish enough to leave her until she's twenty-one; she cannot expect us to support her in the meantime. At Sunbury she will have staff working under her and will soon make many friends. She cannot type and is too young to be a lady's companion. I would have said it was an ideal opportunity for her.'

Anthony was unconvinced, but the two women loathed each other and there would be no peace in the house while Bella remained. Perhaps Charlotte was right.

'Will you speak to her or shall I?'

'Arabella has taken such a dislike to me that she might be more willing to accept the suggestion if it came from you,' Charlotte said.

But when Anthony came to discuss the matter with Bella, he found he was too late.

Bella had never thought of going anywhere beyond Branksome Hall. Now Branksome was lost to her and everywhere she looked reminded her of the catastrophe that had destroyed her life. Convinced the countess was to blame, she would have seen her dead at her feet had it been feasible, but it was not. Consumed by bitterness, hatred and grief, she made up her mind to get as far away from her stepmother and Ripon Grange as she could.

If she had married Major Lacey she would have achieved that, but Major Lacey had been a friend of the countess and she would die before she accepted anything from that quarter. Fortunately he had proved such a vile man that turning him down had been easy.

She wanted her freedom but was determined to make the arrangements herself. On her next ride she stopped in the village, went to the post office and placed an advertisement in the *Morning Post*. Three days later she had a reply from a couple, conveniently located in York, who were emigrating to Australia. The Johnsons had lost a lot of money in the '29 crash and now, seven years later, had decided to give up the struggle in England and try their luck in Australia. Fortunately they still had enough money to buy a 20,000 acre property in Queensland in what the agent had assured them was ideal cattle country, in the ranges west of a town called Charters Towers. They had two young children and were looking for a governess to go with them.

The earl and countess were visiting friends in the Peak District so it was easy for Bella to get away with no questions asked. She took the train to York and later that day came back with everything arranged.

She went upstairs, changed her clothes and sat at the window of her room, staring out at the familiar view. It was particularly lovely today, the sunlight golden across the distant moors, the stream sparkling beneath willows as it flowed down the valley.

Now she was home she had time to be afraid. Her palms were damp, a taste like panic in her throat. What had she done? It was one thing to tell herself she would make her own way but now she had taken the first step she was scared stiff. To commit herself to two strangers and their children, to travel to the other side of the world: it was enough to scare anybody. She had not even liked slimy Mr Johnson; his wife, although a snob, had seemed harmless enough. And what did she know of the world outside Ripon Grange? She had hazy memories of a cottage with an apple tree in the garden, of the mother who had abandoned her, her voice a faint echo warning her to stand up for herself, but what did they have to do with her life now? To entrust herself to these strangers would be like throwing herself off a cliff, not knowing where or how hard she would land.

It was not too late. She had the Johnsons' telephone number. She could ring them and say she had changed her mind. And then? She would be a prisoner forever – of the countess and of her own cowardice.

She could not bear to contemplate that. She closed her eyes, drawing the cool air into her lungs. She would not think of the things that might go wrong. No harm would come to her. And, if it did… She would face up to it. She would see new, wonderful things. She would survive.

The next day, after his return from Derbyshire, her father put forward his wife's suggestion, pretending it was his own, but Bella was not fooled.

'I would not wish to do that,' she said.

It was a stiff way of talking but she could not help it: any mention of the countess or her family made her seize up.

'You'd be near London,' he said. 'You would make new friends –'

Bella had no interest in London or new friends. Most of all, she had no interest in working for the countess's brother.

'Don't you think it would be better if you could get away for a while?' Anthony wondered.

She watched his eyes roaming uneasily about the room, never meeting her own. Why, she thought, he dislikes the idea as much as I do. For a moment she felt embarrassed by his embarrassment, even though she was convinced he had no one to blame but himself. If he had to marry a fortune, she told herself, he should have been man enough to handle the woman who came with it.

'It's too late,' she said.

He looked at her. 'What do you mean?'

'You are right about my going away. I have already arranged it.'

'You are not marrying that fool Lacey?'

Bella laughed scornfully. 'I'd as soon marry a tinker as that man.'

'What, then?'

'I have taken a position with a family called Johnson,' she said. 'They are moving to Queensland, in Australia, and need a governess to help with their children.'

'*Australia*...?' He was taken aback; he was not sure about Australia. 'That was not at all what we had in mind for you,' he said.

Bella did not know what to say to that. Dig your heels in, she counselled herself. Don't let him talk you out of it.

Once again she took refuge in the ploy that had stood her in such good stead since her earliest days at Ripon Grange. She said nothing.

* * *

The day before joining the Johnsons in London, Bella summoned her courage and made one final effort to resurrect her past life.

The countess was visiting friends when Bella got the exchange operator to put her through to Branksome Hall. Her stomach was quaking as she waited, the telephone receiver clutched in her moist hand. She heard the phone ringing at the other end and took a deep breath, willing herself to be calm.

'Branksome Hall…'

It was the same man she had spoken to before.

'May I speak to Mr Charles Hardy?'

A pause.

'May I ask who is enquiring for him?'

'A friend,' Bella said.

'I am afraid Mr Charles is in Germany.'

Hope sank out of sight.

'Do you have any idea when he's expected back?'

'Unfortunately not. If you would care to leave a message…'

Bella put the phone down with a shaking hand. She had hoped, despite everything.

What a fool, she thought.

Later she saddled Lady and rode along the lane towards Branksome Hall. She had no intention of paying a visit but had ridden here the day Charles had first declared his love, seeing the world with fresh colours, bright with her deepest feelings.

How I loved him, she thought. She loved him still; it was no use but she knew she would love Charles Hardy until she died. That was her fate, but she would not let it destroy her life. For this reason she turned back before she reached the rise overlooking the house; the pain of seeing it might have been too much to bear.

On her way back to the Grange she looked for the last time at the line of the moors, the tree-shaded lanes, the emerald brilliance of the young corn. She would not be here to see the harvest but its beauty filled her heart. She was glad of that; it gave hope that somewhere, sometime, there might be an end to pain.

* * *

'The boat leaves from London,' Bella told her father that evening.

The two of them were sitting in the library, Father with a brandy decanter and glass on a side table convenient to his knee, Bella watching him from an easy chair on the other side of the fireplace. They had grown closer since the old earl's death but had still never sat and had a real talk. Tonight might be the last opportunity they would ever have.

The lights were low and the firelight cast shadows across the spines of the books around the walls. The shifting light created a warm atmosphere where confidences were more easily exchanged than in daylight.

'When I'm in London I shall see if I can find my mother,' Bella said. 'Do you really have no idea where she is?'

'I lost touch with her years ago,' he said. 'I did try but I never found out where she went after you came to us. I'm sorry.'

'She would have been sorry too,' Bella said. 'You know you've never told me anything about her?'

'Not much to tell, really.'

A log shifted in the fireplace, releasing a tongue of yellow flame.

'How did you meet?'

'At a place called Tankerton Manor shortly before the war. It was just outside Whitstable, on the Thames. She was one of the chambermaids. We fell for each other straight away. Once we knew you were on the way she had to leave, of course. I arranged for someone I knew on the Kent coast to look after her and after you were born I brought the pair of you up to live here, on the estate.'

'Until we got thrown out,' Bella said.

'That was not my doing,' Father said. He took a sip of brandy. 'But I have always felt I should have done more for her. For the pair of you.'

'You did what you could.'

'Got knocked about a bit in the war. Afterwards I never seemed to have the same spirit I had before. Not much of an excuse, I know, but that's the way it was.'

'One thing I'd like you to do for me…' she said.

'If I can.'

'That portrait Grandfather gave me. Will you hang on to it for me until I've got an address you can send it to?'

'Of course. And when your money from the estate comes due I shall send it to you as well.'

'If I find Mumma, shall I give her your love?'

Anthony hesitated, then shook his head. 'Better not.'

'If you still feel for her…'

'What good would it do?'

'Whatever you say,' said Bella. But knew she would do what seemed right to her at the time.

She had tried to reach Mumma so often over the years, always without success. Perhaps this time she would have better luck.

The boat was sailing in three days, which did not give her long to find someone in a place the size of London.

Bella didn't know where to start. Mumma might be anywhere – she might be dead. What Father had said about Tankerton Manor wasn't news; she had taken her there when they had been living in Rotherhithe and she had never forgotten how the kitchen door had been slammed in their faces. No matter; the daughter of the Earl of Clapham was likely to get more co-operation than they'd had on that occasion so she gave the owner a call anyway. It did no good. The lady of the house pointed out that it was many years ago and they kept no record of junior staff. However, if Jenny Tempest had indeed worked there, and if her father had been a bait-digger, she must have come from somewhere along the river.

Life had taught Bella that you had to persevere if you wanted anything. She caught the train to Whitstable. Unable to afford a taxicab, she set out to walk from one riverside village to the next. She did not know what she had expected, but what she found was poverty. Her earliest memories had been of the cottage. She had been brought up to think of herself as poor, but these tar-paper shacks… Had Mother really been raised in one of them?

Bella was dressed like the lady she had been brought up to be, which was a disadvantage here. Wherever she went, she was met by suspicious eyes and a reluctance to talk.

'Jenny Tempest? Anyone know Jenny Tempest?'

'Never 'eard of 'er.'

'I'm her daughter. I'm trying to find her.'

'Never 'eard of 'er.'

Until, on the afternoon of the second day, she walked along a jetty sticking out into the swirling tide and found a man, stocky and red-faced, brown hair turning grey, baiting long lines with large and hairy worms from a bucket at his feet.

In answer to her usual question, the man looked up at her thoughtfully. 'Who wants to know?'

'My name is Arabella Tempest Richmond,' Bella said slowly and clearly. 'And I am Jenny Tempest's daughter.'

'Then let me tell you something: there ain't no such person as Jenny Tempest.'

Bella's heart lurched. 'Are you saying she's dead?'

'I'm sayin' that ain't 'er name,' the man said. ''Asn't bin for nigh on ten year. Her name is Mrs Jenny Such, an' I'm her 'usband.'

Bella could not help it; she stared. Mumma married? How could she have turned her back on her past? On her love? But wasn't that what she was doing, and for the same reason? People lived their lives as best they could, and regrets were useless. So now she smiled at this stranger who, it seemed, was her stepfather.

'Where is she? I am so longing to see her.'

The fisherman's brown eyes continued to study her. 'But does she want to see you, I wonder?'

Bella had not considered that possibility. 'Why ever not?'

'Not a word, all these years, and now turnin' up, out of the blue... What you tryin' to do, break 'er 'eart all over again?'

Bella glared. 'I must have written a dozen times! And never a word in reply. I was six years old when she sent me off to live among strangers. I know she did it for the best but I've heard nothing from her ever since. Is that my fault?'

The man's expression changed. 'You sayin' you wrote to 'er?'

'The first day I was there; I remember it clearly. I don't suppose it was much of a letter at that age but I wrote it. I remember waiting, too, for an answer that never came.'

She had told herself she would not dwell on the past but the memories of those childhood days, when she had believed herself abandoned by the one person she had trusted and loved above all others, brought tears to her eyes. 'Never a word in all those years,' she cried. 'And you blame me for it?'

The man was on his feet. 'You'd best come wiv me,' he said.

They walked along the jetty side by side. Neither spoke. When they reached dry land Mr Such led the way through a tangle of shacks where women in sacking aprons stared and the rainwater lay in puddles along the rutted track. Eventually they reached higher ground and a brick cottage with views of the open country running south from the river. There was a paling fence, a vegie patch, a green-painted door that stood open, giving a glimpse of the room inside.

Bella's heart was beating fast.

Her companion stopped by the fence and called in a loud voice, 'Mrs Such! Visitor fer you!'

For a few moments, nothing. Then a woman appeared in the doorway. 'What you on about, Luke Such?'

She looked at Bella, puzzled.

'Mumma?' Bella said. And saw recognition dawn.

'My dear life!' Jenny said faintly.

Half an hour of wheres? and whos? and hows?, of broken explanations with both women talking at once, of tears and clutching hands, of joy miraculously erasing years of heartache.

Somehow – Bella never remembered how – mother and daughter were sitting in the little parlour, their eyes eating each other up, while Luke Such smiled fondly, his big shoulders almost filling the room.

'That dratted woman,' Jenny said. 'She was the one behind it, I'll guarantee.' She too had written a dozen times. 'More, but never no answers. The old earl: passed on now, I suppose?'

'In March,' Bella said. 'Father is the earl, now.'

'Which makes that woman the countess. What she always wanted. Much good may it do her.'

Jenny made tea for the three of them. Her offer to help turned down, Bella sat and watched her mother. She must be getting on for forty but still looked good, hair dark, skin unlined.

Jenny brought the tray: brown china teapot and milk jug, a slab of fruitcake.

'Cake?' Luke said. 'Now I know it's a special day.'

'An' why not?' Jenny said. 'Not every day your daughter comes back from the dead.'

They drank the tea and munched the cake.

'Ain't you supposed to be getting the lines ready?' Jenny said to her husband. 'The tide won't wait, you know.'

'You're right.' Luke winked at Bella. 'Hard life, being a married man.'

'Hard?' Jenny said. 'Let me tell you, you never had it so good.'

But there was warmth between them, and Bella was glad.

Luke finished his tea, swallowed the last morsel of cake and got to his feet. He took Bella's hand in his massive paw. 'You'll always be welcome 'ere,' he said.

He went out and they heard him whistling down the path.

'A good man,' Bella said.

'The best. I knew him long before I met your dad. He wanted to marry me but I told him no. Then, after you'd gone to live at Ripon Grange, he asked me again. Told me if I turned him down a second time that would be the end of it, so I said yes.' She smiled. 'The best thing I could do, the way things were.'

'Why did you send me away?' Bella asked.

It was a question she had asked herself a thousand times. Mumma took her hand. 'To give you a better chance in life than I 'ad,' she said. 'The hardest thing I ever done.'

So that Bella knew the truth and was comforted.

'I guessed the old man was gone,' Jenny said. 'He promised me an annuity when you moved to the Grange. Nothing in writing, but he paid it, regular as clockwork. Forty pound a year. It helped a lot, especially in the early days. But there was nuffin this year. He said I could visit you twice a year but they wouldn't let me past the gate. That woman must've given orders. Twice I tried but it weren't no use, so in the end I gave up. That woman got a lot to answer for. 'Ow did you get on wiv 'er?'

'Not at all.'

Bella told her about Charles Hardy and Major Lacey, and how she suspected her stepmother had been behind the whole catastrophe.

'If this Charles really cared he'd have tried to contact you some'ow,' Jenny said. 'Didn't he ever phone? Send you a letter?'

'I never heard from him again.'

'Maybe that woman pinched 'is letters. I wouldn't put it past her. You haven't thought to get 'old of 'im, now you're in London?'

'I phoned. They said he was still in Germany. I'll never believe he didn't love me, though. I think they sent him away, to get him away from me.'

'All the more reason to try and find 'im.'

'In Germany? I wouldn't know where to start. Besides, a girl has her pride,' Bella said.

'And pride goes before a fall. Ain't that what they say?'

'I wrote to him but never heard. I phoned, as I said, and that didn't work either. There was nothing else I could do.'

Mumma was obviously unconvinced but Bella was sure. Losing Charles was the worst thing that had ever happened to her but it did not stop her imagining something even worse: of sacrificing every last shred of pride and dignity, tracking him down somehow and finding that the countess had been right all along and that Charles no longer cared. She doubted she would be able to survive that.

'So now you're off to Australia?' Jenny said. 'I'll be that sorry to see you go, now we've just found each other again, but I'd say it's the best thing for you. You got no future at Ripon Grange with that woman in charge. There was a time your dad would've shown her who was boss, but the war put paid to that. He weren't never the same afterwards.'

'You have no other children?'

'There was one, but something went wrong. It was stillborn and the doctor said I couldn't have no more.' Mumma smiled and patted Bella's hand. 'You're the only one.'

'I'm sorry,' Bella said.

Mumma shrugged. 'Long time ago. I don't think on it no more.'

'Are you happy?'

Mumma looked at her for a minute before answering. 'I'm settled. Mr Such is a good man. And to find you again, after so long… All in all, I been very lucky.'

'Do you miss him?' No need to say whom she meant.

Jenny laughed. 'I'm a respectable married woman. What would I be doing, missing other men?'

'Not other men,' Bella said. 'My father.'

Jenny smiled a little sadly. 'I'll miss him till I die. But 'tweren't no good, see? We both knew that from the beginning. 'Twas me own fault. Thought if I could make him fall in love with me, it might set me up for the future. Only thing, I never reckoned on falling in love with him, and I did that, too. But it was worth it.' She stared proudly at her daughter. 'To see you a proper lady, with that posh accent… It does my 'eart good just to look at you.'

'I want a picture of you to take with me,' Bella said.

Jenny went ferreting around, came back with a photo.

'Mr Such took that of me with 'is Box Brownie when we was in Southend last year,' she said.

Bella studied it. It showed Mumma on a pier, laughing, hair blown by the wind.

'I'll take good care of it,' she said.

It was getting dark when Bella left. Before she left: 'He still loves you,' she said. 'He told me so.'

'Thank you, dear,' Mumma said.

That was all – the past was the past – but it was enough, and Bella was glad she had said it.

'Now remember,' Mumma said. 'You want to be 'appy, make sure you're a woman what does things rather than 'as things done to 'er. Never forget that.'

Inevitably there was sadness in the leaving but also a sense of joy that, against all the odds, they had found each other again. It was also good to know Mumma had found herself a good man to support her. Bella stared out the window as the train pulled out of Whitstable. Let's hope I'm so lucky, she thought.

CHAPTER FOURTEEN

One warm night, as *The Southern Star* ploughed its way down the Red Sea, there was a knock on Bella's cabin door.

She was almost asleep and the knock came a second time before she roused herself sufficiently to reply.

'Hullo?'

A man's voice answered her softly. 'May I come in?'

Mr Johnson's voice. Perhaps there was a problem with the children. Bella switched on the light, climbed out of her bunk and put on a robe. She opened the door. 'Is something wrong?'

He did not answer but slipped quickly into the cabin and closed the door behind him. Bella stepped back, drawing the top of the robe together. She had never taken to Mr Johnson; now he was in her cabin and she knew it had nothing to do with the children.

'Can I help you in some way, Mr Johnson?'

His smile made her skin creep and there was something wrong with his breath. She was frightened and put as much distance between them as she could, the backs of her knees pressing against her bunk.

'No need to be scared,' he said. There were spit bubbles on his lips. 'Just a chat.'

She knew he was lying but would go along with it for the moment, not knowing what else to do. Yet her knees were knocking, her body a-tremble.

'In that case you'd better sit down,' she said.

He did not but stood watching her, the same creepy half-smile on his face. He was looking at her breasts. The robe was gossamer-thin and concealed little. She crossed her arms in front of her body.

'You are very beautiful,' he said.

'Please, Mr Johnson –'

'I've been watching you,' he said jerkily. 'Ever since we came aboard.' His face was shiny with sweat. Bella was no longer frightened; she was terrified.

'Mr Johnson, please… Go back to your cabin. I am sure Mrs Johnson –'

The mention of his wife galvanised him. 'Mrs Johnson does not understand me,' he said. 'She finds me repulsive. Whereas you, dear Bella –'

She forced steel into her voice. 'If you don't leave this cabin immediately I shall scream. I mean it, Mr Johnson.'

She doubted anyone would hear above the engine noise but could think of no other way to stop him. It worked; she saw the tension leave him.

'I came to talk.' He was still breathless but spoke in a more normal voice. 'If I gave any other impression I am sorry.'

She stood watching him, her arms still crossed, waiting for him to leave.

He reached out – the cabin so small that he could touch her without moving – and patted her bare arm quickly. 'No harm,' he said.

Inside her skin Bella's flesh crawled.

He went out, treading softly. The door clicked shut behind him. Bella threw herself at the door, locked it after him and stood, gasping for air in the enclosed space, while the world spun and her frantic heart threatened to explode within her.

Later, tottering like an old woman, she climbed into her bunk and switched off the light. For a long time she lay staring at the darkness while the cabin continued to vibrate with the rhythmic thrust of the engines. She did not know what she should do. Complain? But to whom, and of what? He had barely touched her. Walk out as soon as they reached Sydney? She had no money and no friends. No, she would stay with the Johnsons and see how things developed. And remain – always! – on her guard.

CHAPTER FIFTEEN

In Sydney they boarded a train and headed north.

Bella had not known what to expect, so there was no way she could be disappointed. Nor was she. Sitting for long hours at the train window she saw space flowing endlessly past beneath a blue and shimmering sky; trees, grey rather than green, watching silently, leaves drooping. The wind blew dust in raging clouds across the distances, obliterating sight. That was the essence, Bella thought. The dust of the land. The wind died; the dust settled. Then the land was as it had been before: silent and watchful, as though it remembered the world long before the arrival of men, knowing it would still be here long after men had gone.

It would have intimidated many, but Bella was entranced, not by mountains or rushing rivers but the lack of them. Out there, in the emptiness, was a freedom she had never before imagined.

The smoke blew back from the pounding engine; in the distance dust devils were conjured by the wind. Everything was strange. Why, then, did she feel she had come home?

Mrs Johnson's reaction was very different. They had known that Charters Towers was a gold-mining town fallen on hard times, with nothing to show for its past but abandoned workings and mullock heaps on its outskirts, but she looked around her – flared nostrils and sour lips – as though tracking the source of a disagreeable smell.

'I never thought it would be like this,' she said. 'The place is derelict. I declare I believe the whole country is derelict.'

It was a view fuelled partly by weariness from the long journey but her mood did not improve when she saw the house in which they would be living. Bella could see nothing wrong with it – stone-built, with wide verandahs and a view that stretched forever – but it was not at all the sort of residence Mrs Johnson had expected when they had left dear England. There was another problem, too. Mrs Johnson was the proud possessor of a letter of introduction to the governor of Queensland. She had envisaged balls and entertainments in the company of people of her own class, only to find that the governor was based in Brisbane, at the other end of the earth from the unfortunates condemned to life in Charters Towers. Townsville, the nearest real town, was hours away, the road little better than a track. She had been warned that in wet weather even Charters Towers might be accessible only on horseback, and horses had formed no part of Mrs Johnson's rosy visions of life on the outskirts of the Empire.

'Distances in this country are too vast to be contemplated,' she said.

Something for which the people who lived here were naturally to be blamed.

Mrs Johnson's feelings about her new home made her an uncomfortable companion, but Bella didn't let that bother her. She was still determined to move on, the first opportunity she got. How that would happen it was difficult to see, but she watched the lean figures of the cattlemen in the streets of Charters Towers, their confident shoulders and eyes steady beneath their broad-brimmed hats, and sensed that self-reliance was needed for success in this land. She was comfortable with that notion; where she had acquired it she had no idea, but self-reliance was a quality she had in buckets. When an opportunity came, she would take it.

* * *

At three o'clock on a hot afternoon five months after their arrival, Bella stood on the verandah of the house with the two Johnson children – Jennifer, aged six, and Angela, two years younger – and watched the biplane circling overhead.

'I never seed an aeroplane before,' Jennifer said.

'I have never seen,' Bella corrected automatically. 'Neither have I.'

'Is it Mr Tucker? Is he going to land? Where will he land?'

Bella did not know the answers but assumed it was indeed Mr Tucker, because Mrs Johnson had told her he was expected and would be flying his own plane to get here.

'All the way from the Pilbara. Can you imagine it?'

'Where is the Pilbara?'

Mrs Johnson could not say but knew it was very, very far.

'Like everything else in Australia,' she sighed. 'No wonder people need aeroplanes to get about.'

'What do we do if he has a crash?' Jennifer asked.

'We rescue him.'

'And if we can't?'

Jennifer's endless questions would try the patience of a saint: something Bella had never claimed to be.

'We bury him,' she said.

Wide-eyed at the prospect of disaster, the children watched as the biplane banked before putting down, as smooth as silk, on a strip of ground on the far side of the creek that ran below the house.

'It looks as though we won't have to rescue him after all,' Bella told them.

The pilot leapt down from the open cockpit, did something to the wheels of the undercarriage, crossed the bridge spanning the creek and strode towards the house. Bella and the children came down the verandah steps to greet him.

He was older than Bella had expected: not far off forty, she judged, with dark hair, a sun-tanned face with deep blue laughing eyes and shoulders like a prize fighter. He was wearing disgraceful trousers, oil-stained and torn at one ankle, and a black leather jacket. A tangle of black hair showed in the opening of his checked shirt and a soft leather helmet and goggles swung from his right hand.

'I understand his wife died some years ago. They say he has a terrible reputation,' Mrs Johnson had said.

No need to say what reputation she meant. Looking at him now, Bella could well believe it.

'Mrs Johnson?' he said. His voice was firm, his accent flat as flat.

'I'm Bella Richmond, the children's governess. This is Jennifer,' Bella said, introducing them, 'and this is Angela.' She had always believed children should be treated as the people they were.

'How do you do?' said Jennifer.

While Angela, over-awed by the stranger from the sky, stared.

'And I am Garth Tucker,' the man said, and shook both children's hands solemnly.

Bella decided she liked him. 'Mrs Johnson is in town. We were not expecting you until later.'

'I picked up a tailwind,' he said.

Bella laughed. 'Is that supposed to mean something?'

'Only if you're a pilot.'

They walked up the verandah steps.

'Nice house,' Garth said, looking around at the vast living room. A Wilton carpet; an elegant chair here; a marquetry desk there.

'Mrs Johnson thinks it's a hovel,' Bella said.

She surprised herself, being so forthright with a stranger, but all of a sudden there the words were, unannounced.

Maybe I needed someone to confide in, she thought. I must have been more lonely than I knew.

'She should see my place,' Garth said.

'If it was mine, I would do it differently,' Bella said.

'Looks good to me,' Garth said. 'What would you change?'

'Mrs Johnson likes elegance,' Bella said. 'But this is not an elegant house.'

'Not an elegant country,' Garth said.

'So I would furnish it for comfort, not sophistication.'

'Spit it out,' Garth said.

She hadn't expected to be put on the spot like this but guessed that was Garth's way. What was the saying? Put up or shut up. Very well, then.

'I'd have rugs, not this carpet. They wouldn't need to be valuable, as long as they were colourful; I wouldn't want it to be a house where people had to kick off their boots every time they walked through the door. I'd have big, comfortable chairs, with good cushions.'

'Somewhere to relax after a hard day,' Garth said. 'I like it.'

'Shelves overflowing with books.' She gestured to the long wall facing the window. 'A huge fireplace; winter nights up here can be cold enough for frost.'

'In other words, comfort,' Garth said.

'A home and not just a house,' Bella said. 'Anyway, that's how I would do it. But it's Mrs Johnson's house.'

'Very interesting,' Garth said.

'As part of the comfort campaign, I can offer you tea,' Bella said. 'Or whisky, if you'd rather.'

'One followed by the other sounds good,' said Garth Tucker.

Forty or not, his smile was enough to devastate a whole regiment of women. Not that Bella planned to be one of them.

She joined him in the tea and brought orange squash for the children, who sat staring like wide-eyed mice at the stranger.

Garth sipped his whisky, then said, 'What the hell,' and tipped it down in one gulp. 'My first for a week,' he said.

'Then I'm sure you can manage another one.'

'I wouldn't say no.'

'Your first for a week,' Bella repeated. 'Why's that?'

'Whisky and flying don't mix,' he said. 'It's taken me the best part of a week to get here.'

'From the Pilbara.'

'Right.'

'Wherever that may be,' Bella said.

'Past the black stump and keep going,' he said.

'Am I supposed to know what that means? I'm English, remember.'

'It means to hell and gone. Head northwest from here. Just before you fall into the Timor Sea, stop. That's the Pilbara. I got a cattle station there.'

Classical Greek might have been easier.

'The Johnsons have twenty thousand acres,' Bella said.

She saw that Garth Tucker did not look too devastated by the news.

'Mrs Johnson thought it would make them big landowners. But it doesn't, does it? Not in this part of the world?'

'Not real big.'

'Your place bigger?'

'Properties tend to be bigger up there,' Garth said.

'How big?'

'Miranda Downs is a million and a half.'

Bella stared. 'Acres?'

'Two thousand square miles, give or take.'

'You own two thousand square miles of Australia?'

It was hard to get her head around it.

'Doesn't mean much; it's the cattle make the difference. Cash on the hoof, the cattle.' He laughed. 'That's what I tell the bank, anyway.'

'And how many cattle do you have?'

'Hard to say. No fences, see, and the bush is pretty dense. I'd guess about forty thousand head.'

'Give or take,' Bella said.

His trademark grin stirred her like a spoon; God, he was an attractive man.

'Right,' he said.

'So you're a millionaire,' she said, to tease him.

'For what it's worth.' Again the smile, like a slow-burning fuse. 'Cue for you to say I'm the first you've met.'

'Is that so?'

She enjoyed fencing with this man. In truth there was a great deal she was enjoying about him.

'Her father's an earl,' Jennifer said.

Garth began to laugh, then saw the confirmation in Bella's face. 'Bloody hell!'

'But she's nice, all the same. When you get to know her.' Jennifer was obviously enjoying the impact of the news on her audience.

'Am I supposed to call you Princess, or something?'

'Can if you like,' Bella said.

'But seriously?'

'Seriously, no. I don't have a title. I wouldn't have, even if my parents had been married.'

'And they weren't?'

Bella shook her head slowly, watching him and smiling.

'Thank God for that,' Garth said with feeling. 'Aussies aren't much for titles and such.'

'And marriage?'

'My mother used to say it was the biggest mistake she made in her life.'

'Did she mean it?'

'The old man could be a bastard, at times.'

'So am I,' Bella said.

'That was your parents' doing. My dad managed it on his own. Mind you, he was the one made the money originally.'

'How did he do that?'

'Had a lucky strike at Halls Creek.'

Bella looked blank.

'Halls Creek was the site of a gold rush in 1880,' Garth explained. 'Dad was one of the lucky ones.'

'He found gold?'

'Enough to buy Miranda Downs and stock it.'

'And you've carried on the good work.'

'Something like that.'

'And what brings you to Charters Towers, Mr Tucker?'

'The name's Garth. Gold brought me here, Bella. I'm a cattleman at heart and always will be, but I'm interested in mining, too. Got the itch from Dad, I suppose. I thought I'd take a look at the mines here, see if any of them are worth reopening. I doubt anything will come of it, but it's worth a look. In any case I wanted to look up the Johnsons. A mate of mine sold them the property and I told him I'd see how they're settling in.'

'You came all this way for that?'

'It's what people do in the Outback.'

Where everything, it seemed, was larger than life, men included.

'I'll show you your room,' she said.

Garth fetched his bag from the plane. The children had lost interest and wandered off during their conversation but Bella went with him.

'What sort of plane is it?'

'A Tiger Moth. I call her Minnie.'

It had two wings, one above the other, held in place by a complication of struts and wires; the open cockpit had room for the pilot and one passenger.

It was difficult to think of questions when you did not understand what you were seeing, but Bella did her best. 'Does she go fast?'

'Hundred miles an hour. Three-hundred-mile range. It's the transport of the future, especially for people in the Outback.'

'I haven't seen any around here,' she said.

'Not dinkum Outback.' He grinned. 'Back home there's not even roads.'

To be somewhere even more remote than this... It was hard to imagine.

'It sounds wonderful.'

The words were out before she knew it.

Garth looked at her quizzically. 'It's not for everyone.'

He grabbed his case from the cockpit.

'There's oil around the propeller,' Bella said.

'Shh! You'll hurt her feelings.'

Heaven help us, Bella thought. Yet it was encouraging to find a man who was such a far cry from Mr Johnson, someone not only physically attractive but with a quirky sense of humour, too. He was about as different from Charles Hardy as it was possible to be, too, yet perhaps that was a good thing: already, within an hour of meeting him, she had discovered she fancied him a lot. It was the first time since Charles that she had felt even the slightest interest in a man and she welcomed it, hoping it was a sign that she was beginning to get over her loss.

She thought she was attracted to Garth Tucker not only physically but by the unfamiliar. Charles had been a true man, in his way, but still boyish and answerable to his father. Garth Tucker was also a man, strong and intensely masculine, and he was answerable to no one. She couldn't imagine why that thought should excite her but it did.

They walked back to the house.

'It must be wonderful to be up there with the countryside spread out below you,' Bella said.

'Take you for a spin while I'm here,' he said. 'If you like.'

'You sure it wouldn't be too much bother?'

'I would like it.' He grinned, his blue eyes appraising her frankly. 'It would be a new experience. Not many earls' daughters in the Pilbara.'

'I believe it would be very interesting,' she said.

Now there's a word, Bella thought. Interesting in what way? And did not seek an answer.

She left him to unpack, walked on to the verandah and looked out at the bush flowing back until it reached the foothills of the Great Dividing Range. It was empty country, still at the moment, but as she'd seen in their journey north a sudden wind could raise dust storms in seconds. They seldom lasted long but, when it happened, Bella could taste the dust for days. Tasting the land, she thought. It gave her a sense of belonging: as though, with the dust, she was breathing in the essence of the country.

Yet Garth had said this was not the true Outback. To be so far away, dependent on yourself for everything... It gave Bella the shivers – of excitement, fear? – even to think about it.

A vehicle had crested the distant ridge. Trailing dust, it headed down the track towards the house. She went into the house and knocked on Garth's door.

'Mr and Mrs Johnson are coming,' she said.

Garth Tucker stayed a week. At mealtimes and in the evenings he talked with the Johnsons, although for the most part he watched and said little. At other times he focused his attention on Bella.

He took her up for a flight, as he had promised. Bella, who had expected to be terrified, enjoyed it.

He took her with him when he borrowed the car to drive into Charters Towers. They went three times, checking mining records in the Town Hall, poking about what remained of the old workings. Once he took her into what he called an adit: a tunnel slanting deep into the earth that would connect somewhere, he told her, with the main shaft.

It was as black as death inside the tunnel, the roof so low they had to bend double to make any progress at all. The beam from Garth's torch emphasised rather than dispelled the blackness, and Bella was glad when they turned back. When they emerged the sunlight was like a blow.

Thank goodness, she thought.

'And will you be digging up lots of lovely gold?' she said.

Garth shook his head. 'At present prices it would cost too much to get out. I knew that the first time I looked at it.'

'So why did you keep coming back?'

'Coming back with you,' he corrected her. 'There's a difference.'

'Devious,' she said.

'My speciality.'

'I shall have to remember that.'

'There's gold in the Pilbara,' he told her. 'Not much. Iron, too, somewhere. The experts say I'm wrong but I can smell it.'

'Mrs Johnson said you're a widower. Do you have any children?'

'A son. Colin. He's nineteen.'

A year older than she was.

On his final day Bella walked with him to his plane.

Garth said: 'I wanted to ask you something.'

'So ask.'

'You were saying your father's an earl back in England.'

'That's right.'

'Yet you seem so adaptable. I mean, this life's got to be a lot different from what you're used to.'

'My mother was a chambermaid and is married to a fisherman. Her father dug bait for a living. Maybe that's where I get it from.'

A flock of small birds with bright yellow wings came swooping. They settled on the grass and began pecking at seeds. Bella watched them, conscious that Garth was inspecting her.

He said: 'You remember when I arrived, telling me how you'd make the house more comfortable if it was yours?'

'I hope you haven't been quoting me to Mrs Johnson.'

'My place is like a tip.'

Bella's heart went thump.

'Staying out there, you forget what it's like to live in a civilised way. It's only after seeing this place that I realise how much my son and I need a housekeeper and I liked what you said about making a house into a home.'

'You want me to be your housekeeper?'

'You like the country. You relate to it: I can feel it. We get on well together. And I've watched you and Mrs Johnson. I'm not convinced she'll stick it out. Even if she does, you are very different people, so I am offering you the chance to move on.'

She had told herself repeatedly she would leave the Johnsons the first opportunity she got. But she also remembered Mrs Johnson's words. *They say he has a terrible reputation.* She remembered the panic she had felt on the boat when Mr Johnson had come into her cabin. The Pilbara was the ends of the earth: Garth had said so himself. What would she do if he tried a Johnson on her?

She was a modern girl; no more than her mother was she unduly concerned about what Mrs Johnson would have called her virtue, but she and no one else would decide whom she would take into her bed. She wasn't afraid he would attack her but she could well imagine his propositioning her. The way she was feeling at the moment she might well be happy with that, but what if she wasn't? At the very least it would be awkward. And if she said no and he chucked her out, where would she go?

She was tempted by his invitation and was certainly drawn to him but physical attraction was a long way from love. To go to the Pilbara with this man would be to risk her entire future, and that was something that for the moment she was not prepared to do.

'I'll leave it for now,' she said. 'But thank you for offering.'

He seemed unconcerned. 'Change your mind, drop me a line care of the Wyndham post office.'

She patted Minnie's side. 'Take care of him for me,' she said, surprising herself once again.

He took off. She watched while the plane dwindled to a speck and disappeared. The sound of the engine lingered but eventually that too was gone. She walked back to the house, asking herself whether she had made the right decision or not. Either way, it was too late now.

Charters Towers was dead, or close to it. With the gold mines working it would have been a busy place but now even the idea of prosperity had flown. Unemployed men polished their shoulders against the walls of buildings and the few women Bella saw wore furtive expressions and shuttered eyes.

She had brought the two girls into town to buy something for their mother's birthday. She doubted there would be much choice but that didn't matter; the only present that would have lifted Mrs Johnson's spirits was a return ticket to England.

The general store smelt of kerosene and sold everything from farm equipment and seed to clothing and trinkets for the home, all piled in heaps with no attempt to display them properly. There was one other customer in the shop, a tall, lean man in a broad-brimmed hat. Even he was not buying anything but talking to

Mr Wright the shop owner, a man with a big belly and a mean mouth.

'Mate, I can't help it if the goods haven't got to Townsville yet. Soon as they arrive I'll get 'em out to you. I can't say fairer than that.'

'It's not good enough,' the shopkeeper said.

'You got a gripe,' the tall man said, 'take it up with Sydney.'

'How'm I supposed to keep my customers happy?'

'I can see 'em rioting,' the tall man said, looking around the deserted shop.

Bella found a framed picture of an Alpine snow scene that she thought Mrs Johnson might like, also a cheap pink paper parasol that Angela fancied but that Mrs Johnson would probably never use. Never mind, Bella thought; it was the thought that counted.

She paid from the money Mrs Johnson had given her. The two items were double the price she'd expected but she said nothing. They left the shop at the same time as the tall man.

'Mean as snake's piss,' he said, and touched the brim of his hat to Bella. 'Pardon my French.'

'I've heard worse,' she said, smiling.

He looked at her, head cocked, eyes questioning. He had an interesting face.

'New in town?'

'I'm with the Johnsons. They bought the old Macdonald place. Mr Johnson is planning to run sheep on it.'

'He'd be better off with cattle. You a relation of theirs?'

'I'm the governess.'

'Paul McNab,' he said, extending a horny hand. 'McNab's Hauliers. Anything needs hauling, I'm your man.'

She laughed. 'I'll remember that.'

She saw him again, once or twice, over the next three months. They exchanged smiles and the occasional word. He was always cheerful. Quite an achievement, given the state of the world, and she liked him in a casual way, thinking nothing of it.

CHAPTER SIXTEEN

The Johnsons had gone to a party. They had been invited by a farming family on the other side of town and had driven over in their motor, warning they would probably stay overnight.

It was a chilly evening. The stars were crackling and there would be frost later. Bella had put the children to bed at eight o'clock and an hour later was thinking of following them when she felt a breath of cold air as the kitchen door opened. At once she was rigid, listening. The light was still on out there but she hadn't thought to lock the door; in the months they'd been here Garth Tucker had been their only visitor. There was a gun in the Johnsons' bedroom but it was locked up. There were knives in the kitchen but that was where the intruder was. She was helpless.

Footsteps, a stumble, a soft curse. Bella listened, the sweat cold on her back. A shadow in the doorway. A man entered, bringing darkness.

'Well, well, the lovely Bella…'

It was Johnson, but relief changed rapidly to alarm as Bella realised he was drunk. She remembered *The Southern Star* and a shiver ran down her spine.

Swaying, Johnson made his way to the settee and fell into it. He smiled owlishly and patted the cushion beside him. 'Come and sit with me,' he said.

Apart from the children, they were alone in the house. A nerve pulsed in Bella's stomach. She did not move. 'I didn't expect you back tonight,' she said. 'Is Mrs Johnson with you?'

'Mrs Johnson is unavoidably delayed,' he said.

Bella didn't like this at all but was determined not to let him see her feelings. 'I didn't hear the car,' she said.

He placed a crafty finger alongside his nose. 'Because I did not want to disturb the beautiful Bella. In case she was asleep in her lonely bed.' He shook his head sadly, as though at a profound truth. 'It makes no sense.'

She pressed her knees together. She had no idea what he was talking about but had no plans to ask.

'You in your cold bed, me in mine,' he said. 'When we could be warming each other.'

'I don't like you talking like this,' she said. 'I think you should go to bed.'

'An excellent idea. Let's go together.'

She would not allow panic to get the better of her. 'Stop it, Mr Johnson! Stop it this minute!'

'Give me a kiss first.'

Fear changed to anger and anger gave her strength. She stood up. 'You're talking nonsense, Mr Johnson. I don't want to hear any more of it.'

She saw her words strike home.

'Good God, girl, I was only teasing.' Johnson tried to repair his tattered dignity. 'Where's your sense of humour?'

He stood, staggered, and made his way laboriously to the corridor leading to the bedrooms. 'Since we cannot talk like civilised people I shall go to bed.'

There was an edge of damaged pride in his voice and Bella remained rigid until she heard his bedroom door click. Only then did she collapse into her chair. She drew a deep breath and closed her eyes, her body shaking. For the moment the crisis had passed but she knew it was not the end of it. This was the second time. Sooner or later Johnson would try his luck again.

She had to get away, she told herself. If only she'd accepted Garth Tucker's offer!

For several minutes she stayed where she was; she could not have stood if she'd tried. There was no sound from Johnson's bedroom but she could not relax, knowing that the rest of the night remained. Finally she managed to drag herself out of her chair. She switched off the lights. Heart in her mouth, she tiptoed to her room.

Her door had no key. She thought of blocking it in some way but the back of the only chair was not high enough to reach the handle and the chest of drawers, a relic of the previous owner, was too heavy to shift. She normally slept naked despite the cold, but tonight she put on a nightdress and buttoned it to the neck. For a long time she lay unsleeping, nerves wound tight, but heard nothing. Eventually she drifted into a troubled sleep.

Some time later, her bedroom door whispered open.

At once she was awake, hands clenched, nerves screaming.

'Are you asleep?' Johnson said softly.

She did not speak. She was so afraid, praying silently that he would go away again. She could feel him waiting. Listening. The door closed but she sensed he was still in the room. She could barely breathe, her body sour with terror. She sensed him standing beside the bed and could keep quiet no longer. 'What are you doing, Mr Johnson?'

She spoke reasonably, hoping to shame him, but her words had the opposite effect. He was on her at once, growling like an animal as he ripped at her nightdress. She tried to fight him off but he was too much for her. A jet of pain, white-hot, speared as his fingers wrenched at her breast.

'Stop it! Stop it!'

He took no notice.

'You want it. You know you want it…'

Pain, terror and outrage combined as she fought him. She screamed as loudly as she could, shocking even herself, but he took no notice. His knee forced her legs apart. He was moving on top of her and instinct took over. She smashed her knee into his groin. A strangled scream as she did it again, kneeing him with all her might.

She felt his strength run away like water. He fell off her and lay moaning and sobbing, knees tight to his chest. She inched away from him, her face a mask of horror and disbelief. Her breath came unevenly; her heart threatened to explode in her chest. She was crying, the darkness spinning in a whirligig of coloured lights, every part of her being spastic with shock.

She closed her eyes, still panting. The night was still. Miraculously, the children in their room at the end of the corridor seemed to have slept through it all. She drew a deep breath. Slowly control returned. She staggered to the door and turned on the light. She turned, hating even to look at him, and saw him lying there weeping, eyes blind to anything but pain. The bed… a battlefield.

Rage rose like the tide. She crossed to the bed and glared down at him. His eyes were open yet he seemed unaware of her.

'Get out.' Her voice was jagged with fury.

He did not move.

She was loath to touch him but forced herself, dragging him off the bed and dumping him on the floor. She bent over him, eyes and mouth taut with horror, and whispered in his ear.

'Come near me again and I'll kill you.'

She meant it; at that moment she could have killed him without a thought.

Still he did not move.

'I'll drag you if I have to,' she threatened.

He whimpered, but inch by inch gathered himself and began to crawl away from her. When he reached the door he clawed his way up far enough to open it. Still hunched, he dragged himself out of sight. She slammed the door behind him.

Now weakness returned. She was shaking so much she could barely walk. Somehow she reached the bed and fell across it. So cold… Arms tight about her body, eyes open, she saw only images of the frenzied battle in the dark. Tears poured down her cheeks. The night seemed without end.

The morning came with a bone-white sky and frost in the hollows. Bella, defiled, sat on the verandah and stared out at an empty land. The sun was still hidden and there were no shadows. She hugged herself against the frost, against despair.

She had to leave, that much was clear. But go where? There was nowhere. Behind her in the house the children were sleeping. Mr Johnson? She would not think of him. Yet he was there, too, a presence and a threat. In the chilly light of morning it was hard to believe all that had happened last night, yet it had. A darkness heavier than the darkest night, it lay upon her spirit and she did not know what to do.

A blink of brilliant light appeared above the rim of the distant hills. The shadows leapt across the pale land as the sun rose. A flock of ravens stirred the air. Raucous-voiced, wings black against a sky that to the east was now flushed with golden light, they flew eastwards towards the sun.

The movement of the birds, the distant curve of the hill's dark shoulder, meant nothing. The air was cold but Bella did not move. After the traumas of the night shock remained, preventing thought or movement.

She remained motionless as an hour later she heard the first cough of the car's engine. It appeared around the side of the house, crossed the bridge and drove away up the road in a smear of dust. Mr Johnson was going to collect his wife. Soon they would be back.

What had happened the night before had left a stain on her mind. Perhaps also on her life. If she could, she would have left already, would even now be striding along the road to somewhere.

But where? It was a question she could not answer, so she stayed. Besides, there was a question of wages owing to her.

Presently she got up and went to the kitchen. She made herself a cup of coffee. She came back and sat down, warming her hands on the hot cup and staring once again at the empty landscape flowing away from the house. Soon the Johnsons would be back. She had injured him, perhaps badly. It was unlikely that he could hide it from his wife. Would not want to, perhaps. After what had happened he was probably as eager to get rid of her as she was to go. In which case he would say something to his wife. If he did that, Bella thought, he was bound to lie.

She sat unmoving, the empty cup clutched in her hands, until she saw the sunlight flashing on the approaching car as the Johnsons returned.

'After your conduct last night there is no place for you in this house,' Mrs Johnson said.

Bella, exhausted by lack of sleep, was not prepared to be dismissed like an insolent housemaid. She felt anger and an overwhelming sense of injustice. 'Do you have the slightest idea what happened last night?'

'My husband has told me what happened.'

'Did he tell you why he decided to rush home and leave you behind, Mrs Johnson?'

'He was feeling unwell. He had to leave early.'

'That wasn't the reason. I'll tell you why he did it. To make a pass at me. Did he tell you why he can't stand up straight this morning? Why he can't walk without limping? Did he tell you that, Mrs Johnson?'

Bella had been brought up a lady and ladies did not talk of such things, but this lady had been forced to fight off a would-be rapist only a few hours earlier and now, it seemed, was to be dismissed for the crime of defending herself. That made for plain speaking. 'Did your husband tell you that he tried to *rape* me last night, Mrs Johnson?'

Mrs Johnson flinched as though Bella had struck her. Mouth set, lips white, she said: 'You will pack your things immediately. I shall take you into Charters Towers in one hour's time.'

Bella was furious. It was one thing to hand in her notice and leave with a suitable reference, quite another to be driven out like this. 'And if I refuse?'

'Then I shall contact the police and have you put out. I shall not tolerate home wreckers in my house.'

'Your husband attacked me in my bed –'

'I refuse to listen –'

But Bella shouted over the top of her. 'I had to fight him off the only way a woman can. I kneed him in the *groin*, Mrs Johnson. That is why he's limping. What do you have to say about that?'

Mrs Johnson's hands were over her ears. 'I refuse to listen to such wicked lies –'

'Perhaps I'm the one who should be going to the police.'

Bella's voice might have knocked the paint off the ceiling but Mrs Johnson, face contorted, screamed louder still. 'Wicked woman! Wicked! Wicked! I won't listen to another word.'

It was hopeless. To Bella, raised from the age of six in a household of power and privilege, it was a nightmare beyond imagining, but she knew she would be blamed whatever she said. She saw from her expression that Mrs Johnson suspected what had really happened. Perhaps she'd experienced the same thing in the past. However that might be, it was clear that she was now determined to get Bella out of the house. If Bella complained to the police they would not believe her; no one would believe her.

She could not imagine what would happen to her now. She had neither job nor prospects; there were few enough jobs for men out there, for women they were virtually non-existent, and once people heard Mrs Johnson's version of what had happened there would be no chance for her at all. She would starve in the gutter and no one would lift a finger. Yet she had no choice. Go she must, and now.

If I'd let him do it I wouldn't be out of a job, she thought bitterly. One last spark of defiance: 'You owe me for the months I've been here,' she said.

But that, too, was doomed to failure. Bella saw madness in Mrs Johnson's eyes.

'Pay you?' She laughed hysterically. 'After what you've done?'

'Without money I can go nowhere,' Bella said.

'Not one penny!' There was froth on Mrs Johnson's lips. 'You hear me? Not one penny!'

It was useless to persist. No matter, Bella told herself. She would survive.

An hour later, Mrs Johnson drove Bella into town. Neither spoke. Dropped off at the bus station, Bella barely had time to grab her bag before the car door slammed behind her. A clash of gears and Mrs Johnson was gone.

Mrs Johnson went into the newsagents, where Miss Wickes the proprietor greeted her.

'I need your help,' Mrs Johnson said. 'I need a new nanny for the children.'

Miss Wickes pricked up her ears; gossip was good for the soul. 'Is Miss Richmond leaving you?'

Mrs Johnson allowed her distress to show. 'Speaking in the strictest confidence, Miss Wickes, I had to let her go. She proved completely unsuitable to live in the same house with a married man.'

'Oh?' Miss Wickes was agog. 'Is that how it was?'

'I do not believe in spreading tales, Miss Wickes, but I would not want others to be deceived, as I have been deceived.'

'Certainly not,' said Miss Wickes.

Her mission accomplished, Mrs Johnson bought a newspaper and went out. Miss Wickes picked up the phone; she was not only a news vendor; she was a news purveyor and news like this, in a town like Charters Towers, spread like wildfire.

* * *

Dumped in the shadow of the mullock heaps beneath which she
and Garth Tucker had explored the potential of the town's abandoned mines, Bella thought: God knows how, but somehow I have
to get to the Pilbara. Garth offered me a job. I turned him down
but what choice do I have now?

Getting there was as close to impossible as made no difference. It
was a district of which she had only the vaguest knowledge, thousands of miles away on the far side of the continent, and she had
no money. Even if she did somehow manage to get there, she had no
idea what her reception would be. Yet what other options did she
have? She answered her own question.

'The fact is,' she said to the deserted street, 'I have no choice.'

Charters Towers was a ghost town; there would be no jobs here.
She had to get to Townsville, find work, save her money, take a
passage to Wyndham. How she would then get to Garth Tucker's
property she had no idea, but at least she would be in the district.

Walking into town, Bella saw Paul McNab's van outside the general store, with Paul and another man carrying cartons into the
shop.

When he saw her expression, his smile of greeting changed to
concern. 'What's up, darl?'

'The Johnsons have thrown me out.'

'Want to talk about it?'

She hesitated. 'You're busy.'

'This can wait. Come and have a cup of tea, tell me what's biting
you.'

There was a café across the road.

Paul ordered two teas. The café owner – middle-aged, grey hair
pulled savagely back, tight mouth – shook her head.

'I ain't servin' that one with yer.'

'Don' be like that, Myrtle.'

'I mean it.'

Paul set his shoulders. 'You will, Myrtle. If you want to keep my
trade.'

'Askin' for trouble, you are,' said Myrtle.

She poured the two cups, all the same, and shoved them across the counter. Even the most ordinary customer was worth keeping, in the Charters Towers of 1937.

Bella and Paul went and sat at a table.

'Tell me,' Paul said.

Bella was exhausted. The night's traumas; the way Mrs Johnson had behaved that morning... The memories beat like hammers in her head. She could have put her head on the table and howled. She did not, nor could she tell him exactly what had happened; he was a relative stranger still, and a man, and at the moment she found it hard even to look at a man. But he was kind, and she needed a friend. She said: 'Mr Johnson... He...'

It was no use; she could not tell him.

'What did he do?'

She opened her mouth to say, but no sound came.

'I can't talk about it.' Tears flowed without warning. 'I am sorry,' she sobbed. 'Sorry...'

Paul McNab had not come down in the last shower of rain. 'Do something to you, did he?'

'He tried.' More tears. 'I stopped him but now I've lost my job.'

Her hand, lying on the table beside her cup, clenched. She hid it in her lap. The world was an aching void, herself alone in the middle of it.

'Mrs Johnson didn't believe you?'

'She did believe me,' Bella said. 'That's why she got rid of me.'

'Bastards,' he said. 'What you gunna do?'

'I have to get to Townsville. I'll never get a job here.'

'Ain't that the truth?' he said. 'Tell you what I'll do. I'll take you home with me when we finish up here. Have a word with the wife, put you in the spare room tonight, run you into Townsville in the morning. How does that sound?'

It sounded wonderful but, when Paul took her home, his wife had other ideas.

'We're Christian folk in this town, miss. We don't want your sort here.'

Bella could not believe what was happening to her. 'I have done nothing –'

Trix McNab glared at her husband.

'I heard about it. I'm telling you I won't have her in the house.'

'Stay where you are, Bella,' said Paul.

No job, no money, now this… Despair threatened, but pride prevailed.

'I'll start walking,' she said to Paul. 'I've caused you enough trouble.'

'You're going nowhere,' Paul said. 'And you can quit your maggin',' he said when his wife tried to interrupt. 'You talk about Christian principles? What you expect her to do? Walk all the way to Townsville? Sixty miles alone, in the dark? Is that how a Christian behaves? I'll tell you something else, too: I don't believe a word that Johnson cow's been saying. Not a word.' He turned to Bella. 'Sleep in my truck tonight,' he told her. 'Like I said, I'll run you into Townsville in the morning.'

Trix glared but eventually turned away with a look of disgust. 'Do what you want.' She threw the words over her shoulder. 'You always do, anyway.' She went back into the house.

Paul winked at Bella. 'I'll get you a blanket.'

'I'm causing you trouble.'

'I'll talk to her. She'll be right.'

Paul brought her two blankets and some cushions. Bella stretched out in the back of the truck and pulled the blankets over her. It was cold and would become more so but she knew how fortunate she was to be sleeping here and not by the roadside, covered in frost. Although sleep, when it came, was riven by nightmares.

Archibald Johnson ripped at her like a maniac.

'No! No!'

She came awake, heart pounding, frightened eyes staring into the darkness.

Mrs Johnson's screams echoed in the cold night. 'Wicked woman! Wicked, wicked woman!'

Accusing faces swung in a cacophony of accusing voices.

'I ain't servin' that one with yer!'

'I won't have her in the house…'

Bella lay, despair like acid in her mouth. What was she to do? What would happen to her?

Light came by inches. Bella was stiff and cold, apprehension a weight on her chest. She looked around the yard in which the truck was parked. Lights shone through a window in the McNab house. The world, which yesterday had turned its back, was returning to life.

And today?

She wanted to get moving, to face down the worst. Anything, however terrible, was better than what she could imagine.

Lying in an alleyway, or beside a lonely road… Lying dead…

She climbed out of the truck, swinging her arms to get warm, and walked out of the gate and down the road, then back. She did it three times, putting all her effort into it, until the blood was singing in her veins and the night-time terrors had slipped away. For the moment, at any rate.

Paul came out of the house. 'You'll want the bathroom,' he said.

She certainly did. But…

'Not if it causes you trouble.'

'It won't. I talked to her last night.'

Bella used the bathroom and afterwards tucked into the fried breakfast that Paul had prepared. She felt strength flowing back into her and, with strength, hope. Today, as Paul would have said, she'd be right.

'Thank your wife for her kindness.'

'You're a good Pom,' Paul said. 'That Johnson cow's a whinger. It makes a difference.'

'Thank her anyway.'

They walked out into the sunshine and he drove her to Townsville. He dropped her in the centre of town.

'Port's that way. Shops down there.' He hesitated, looking at her searchingly. 'Got any money?'

'You've been so kind,' she said. 'I'll not take your money as well.'

He fished some notes out of his pocket.

'Coupla quid. Pay me back when you're right.'

The wicked cruelty of some; the kindness of others. Bella was in tears.

'I'll never forget.'

'Yeah, right.' She'd embarrassed him. He rammed the transmission into gear. 'See ya.'

He was gone.

CHAPTER SEVENTEEN

Bella walked the town flat, looking for work. She went into the three hotels in the main street. When they asked what she wanted she said a job. She was willing to do anything, she told them. Work in the kitchen, clean the floors and bars, serve at table. Anything. There was nothing. As the shadows lengthened she found a lodging house near the docks. The proprietor – sour face, eyes that had seen it all – gave her a look but took her money anyway.

The room was up a steep flight of uncarpeted stairs. It was frowsty, redolent of dust and what Mrs Johnson would no doubt have called sin. The smeared window looked out on the blank wall of a warehouse.

She looked around her. She would sleep and tomorrow she would find work and risk the expense of moving to a better place. But for tonight it would have to do.

She went out to a café. She had a bowl of watery soup to warm her and a bread roll and went back to the lodging house. There were lights from the port and the shapes of moored vessels, and shadowy figures walking to and fro. Somewhere a whistle sounded, echoing off the walls of buildings, and it was a lonely sound.

She went into the lodging house and the man said:

'Interested in makin' a quid?'

'I beg your pardon?'

'I asked if you was interested in makin' a quid. I got blokes willing to oblige, if you are. Men off the freighters. If you're willin'.'

A slap in the face would have been less shocking.

'No. No, thank you.'

She scurried up the stairs, heels clattering on the boards. Even to be *asked* such a thing... Was it possible?

She went into the room, closed the door and leant against it.

Yes, she thought. It was possible. More than possible, if she found no work. Her mind would not accept it, yet that might be the future, if all else failed. I'll kill myself first, she thought. But life was strong in her, and she doubted that she would.

Tomorrow I'll get a job, she thought. Then I'll be able to smile at all this. But the next day was no better than the first. By evening she was exhausted and in despair. The lodging keeper's suggestion no longer seemed ridiculous; it began to seem inevitable. She examined a mental image of herself with a man. With men. She could not, would not believe it. She would not accept it. But if it was that or starve...

What have I come to? she thought.

The man looked up as she came in. 'There was a sheila lookin' for you. Said she'd be back.'

She knew no one in Townsville. She went wearily up the stairs. Her stomach was growling; she felt weak. It seemed years since she'd eaten her fried breakfast in Paul McNab's house. She had to have a proper meal soon.

Who was this sheila? What did she want?

She didn't have long to wait. There was a knock on the door. When Bella opened it, a woman was standing there. She was about forty years old, blonde and pleasant, seemingly respectable, although Bella, on her guard at the woman's so timely arrival, had her doubts.

'May I come in?'

Inside the room, the woman looked around without comment. 'My name is Moira Higgins,' she said. 'I may have a job for you, if you're interested.'

'How did you know about me?'

'The word gets around.'

It had to be the man at reception. Who had suggested she might like to make a quid entertaining men off the freighters. Bella's suspicions were on high alert but, with no other jobs on the horizon, who was she to complain?

'What sort of job are you talking about?'

'Have you heard of the Cockatoo Club?'

'No.'

'I work in the office. It's a club patronised by businessmen and their wives, mostly. They go there for a drink, a meal, meet their friends. There might be a vacancy, if I think you're suitable.'

'As what?'

'Hostess. We have several on the books, but are always in the market for more.'

'What does a hostess do?'

'Welcome guests when they arrive. Serve drinks. Sit with the customers, if asked. All highly respectable, I promise you.'

'How much would I be paid?'

'You'll get tips, of course. Some of these sugar magnates can be most generous. Plus a basic. You're a beginner, so you start at the lower grade. The manager, Mr Henry, will discuss all that with you once you've got started.'

'You said you *might* have a job.'

Moira Higgins smiled. 'We'll expect you at six o'clock,' she said.

It was dark; the clack of Bella's heels rebounded from the shuttered buildings as she walked. The Cockatoo Club was in Cable Street, between the high street and the harbour, in an area where muddy lanes ran back between the buildings. Tugs hooted eerily and the salty air was ripe with the smell of mangrove and mud.

Bella had accepted the offer without a second thought. It was not a real job but would do until something better turned up. When Moira had spoken to her she'd had fifteen shillings and four pence left; she couldn't be too particular when a job was offered.

'Don't forget your things,' the man at the reception desk had warned. 'We're not responsible for stuff left behind.'

'I've left everything,' Bella had said. 'I'll be back.'

She was not ready to move on yet, this club opportunity not being a real job.

The Cockatoo was located in a double-fronted house set back from the street, with steps climbing to the entrance and a sign creaking on a metal pole outside. Both house and sign were in darkness but a light shone from a window at the side of the building. Bella followed a concrete path and came to a door standing ajar; she pushed it open and went inside. The small room was empty, brightly lit, with what looked like a storeroom off to one side. There were four stick-back chairs, a padlocked cupboard and a table top running around the walls with mirrors above it. The air smelt of talcum powder and sweat.

'Hullo?' Bella said.

Nothing.

A second door led to a larger room. At this end was a bar, with bottles on glass shelves, at the other a small stage. In between there were perhaps a dozen tables, each with four chairs and a pottery ashtray advertising a brand of beer. The room smelt of tobacco smoke and the stale memory of last night's liquor.

She had not known what to expect, but it was nowhere near as smart as she had hoped. Perhaps it would look better with the lights up.

A door behind the bar opened and a man came through. He was in his twenties, middle-sized but strong-looking. He wore a Clark Gable moustache, a muslin shirt – yellow, with a pattern of purple palm trees – that fitted tightly across his chest, and black, oiled hair combed back.

'Help you?' he said.

'I'm looking for Mr Henry,' she said.

'And you are?'

'Bella Tempest.'

'Moira mentioned you. Tempest your professional name?'

'My real name.'

He whistled and winked. 'You musta been born to the job. Done mucha this work, have you?'

'Never.'

'You'll soon get the hang of it.'

'Moira told me to see Mr Henry.'

'Mr Henry's away,' the man said. 'He asked me to fix you up instead.' He came from behind the bar and stood in front of her. 'Name's Joe. Let's have a look at you.'

He walked around, looking her over, then smiled at her with sparkling, sassy eyes. 'Very nice,' he said.

Bella didn't like this at all but it was a job in a town where there were no other jobs to be had, so she said nothing.

'Where are your things?' he said.

'At the hotel.'

'Hostesses sleep on the premises. Moira shoulda told you. No sweat; I'll send someone to collect them. She explained the set-up, right?'

'She said something about serving drinks and entertaining the customers.'

'Yeah, right.' He laughed at a private joke, and again winked at her. 'Service before self: the Cockatoo's motto. I can see you'll be right at home here.'

'How much do I get paid?'

'Mr Henry will sort all that out when he gets back. You sleep upstairs with the other girls. I'll get one of them to show you later. In the meantime let's fix you up with something to wear.'

Bella looked at him.

'Can't let the customers see you like that,' Joe said. 'Long dress, that's what you'll be wearing. This is a classy joint: didn't Moira tell you?'

'I don't have a long dress.'

'We'll find something for you. What size are you, anyway?' But lifted his hand before she could answer. 'Don't tell me. Let me guess.'

He found a dress in the storeroom. 'That should be about right. Put it on, let's have a look at you.'

The dress was black, with sequins and crimson highlights across the bodice. It was made of some harsh material and smelt faintly of sweat.

'Where's the changing room?' Bella asked.

'Right here.' He did not move. 'Let's get on with it, darling.'

'Do you mind not watching me?' Bella said.

'Forgive me,' he said with mock humility. 'I wasn't thinking.'

He turned his back. Bella was down to her underwear before she realised he was watching her in one of the mirrors. It made her mad.

'Get out!'

'Whatever you say, sweetheart.'

He strolled out, smiling and taking his time.

She put on the dress, pulling it this way and that. It was tight over the bust and showed an awful lot of cleavage, but otherwise fitted her well; whatever else, Joe had a good eye for women's sizes.

She went to show it to him.

'V-e-r-y nice,' he said. 'Just one thing.'

Before she could move, his hands were beneath her breasts, lifting them until they were halfway out of the dress.

She leapt back. 'Take your hands off me!'

'Got 'em, show 'em: that's what my old granny used to say.' He looked at her, the laughter wiped off his face. 'Get used to it. You'll have worse from some of the customers. Especially boozed up on a Saturday night.'

'Anyone tries it, I'll slap his face for him,' said Bella.

'Service before self, remember?'

The grin was back, and the wink. And Moira Higgins had said it was a respectable club.

* * *

Bella wondered how she would get on but the first few days weren't too bad. There were wives, or women at least; the tips came on schedule; and apart from the odd stroke and squeeze, the customers left her alone. But tomorrow was another day, and the weekend was coming.

'How you going?'

Stephanie was one of the girls but spent most of her time serving behind the bar.

'So far so good,' Bella said.

She knew the other girls were talking about her behind her back. What could she expect? She came from a different background and they were suspicious of someone who, as she had overheard one of them saying, might turn out to be a la-di-da galah.

'I was you,' Stephanie said, 'I'd keep your tits out of sight. Some blokes might take it as an invite, the way you're showing 'em now.'

'That was Joe's idea,' Bella said.

'That Joe,' Stephanie said. 'If it was up to him he'd have us topless.'

Mr Henry came back Saturday. He had a white face and black, glittering eyes. He was not a big man and was wearing an unremarkable black suit and sharply pointed shoes, yet there was something about him that said watch out. He wore a chunky ring of yellow metal on the middle finger of his right hand and was smoking a cigarette.

He spoke to her in his office, just before the club opened. 'How you doing?'

'All right so far.'

His black eyes dissected her, inch by inch. 'I been hearing good things about you. A bit shy, but that'll change. You'll want to know about pay, I suppose?'

He waited, a man who would always expect people to come to him.

'Yes,' Bella said.

'Two quid a week and board,' he said. 'How does that sound?'

'That's not much,' Bella said.

'It's all you're going to get,' Mr Henry told her. 'There's ten per cent out of work, or hadn't you heard?'

'I heard.'

'It was much higher last year and people are saying it could easily go up again. I reckon two quid a week is better than starving in the street. Isn't that so?'

He was right, of course.

'There are tips on top,' Mr Henry said. 'And some of the girls earn extra on the side. Know what I mean? The ones who go upstairs with the customers? We keep twenty per cent for overheads but the rest is theirs. Looks like yours, it would soon add up.'

'I wouldn't want that,' she said.

'Your choice.' He looked at her neckline and at what it did not quite conceal. 'Enticing but not crude,' he said. 'I like it.'

Saturday was a rough night, as expected: lots of booze, loud voices in an atmosphere so blue with smoke that it was hard to see across the room. There was a three-piece band, with half-drunk customers shoving each other unsteadily around the tiny dance floor. No doubt Bella's was not the only backside to get felt up that night.

'Lookit the knockers on that one.'

A young bloke leering. She ignored him.

A customer's booze-red eyes regarded her over the top of his glass. 'In the trade, are you, darling?'

She had already seen two of the girls taking customers upstairs.

'Yes,' Bella said. 'In the carry-around-drinks-for-the-customers trade.'

'If you change your mind...'

'You'll be top of my list.'

She was learning; a few days earlier she would not have had the courage to say such a thing.

All in all, she thought, she should be able to survive. Stay here two months and, with tips, she should have twenty-five pounds.

Enough to get her to the Pilbara. She would not think what might happen after that.

But at the end of a month there was a problem.

'What do you mean, you don't owe me anything?'

'Hire of the dress,' Joe said. 'Rent of the room. Food…'

'Board and lodging was part of the deal.'

'So they are. For the girls who take customers upstairs.'

'That was never the agreement,' Bella said.

'So sue me,' Joe said.

'Let me get this straight,' Bella said. 'I work for you but only get paid if I take customers upstairs?'

'Got it in one,' Joe said. 'Basic principle of business. Money comes in, money goes out. I'm not seeing any money coming in from you. Or have I missed something?'

'But –'

'Looks like yours, you'd have a queue. Then we'd be sweet.'

They were cheating her and it made her mad. All right, she thought, if that was the way they wanted it…

She could walk out, but that would leave her with only seven pounds in tips to show for four weeks' work. And Mr Henry was not a man to cross.

She had to think.

It was close on midnight, the club as full as ever, when Stephanie said: 'I got to have a pee. Watch the till while I'm gone.'

One of the girls came with a drinks order. Bella dealt with it, then there was a gap. She looked around. No sign of Joe or Mr Henry; no one was watching her. She opened the till drawer and pulled out a roll of notes. No time to look at them; she closed the drawer again, leant down so that the bar concealed her, lifted her skirt and slipped the notes into the waistband of her knickers. She let the skirt fall back about her ankles and smiled as another girl came with an order.

Her heart was thundering fit to burst. They would check the till first thing in the morning yet would certainly see her if she walked out now.

The only thing to do was wait until the club was closed and slip out then. She refused to think what they might do to her if they caught her.

It was three o'clock when Bella came tiptoeing down the wooden stairs. She was wearing a sweater and carried her shoes and suitcase in her hand.

The bar was still. The motionless air remembered the rowdiness but only the staleness of booze and tobacco smoke remained. Every creak of the staircase made her heart stop. Behind the bar the line of bottles gleamed in the solitary light.

The main entrance would be locked and barred. The side door should be a different story, with the key hanging from a hook in the storeroom. It was dark but she found it all right. She slipped the key into the lock and turned. It clicked back. She put on her shoes, drew a deep breath and inched open the door.

The clamour of an alarm shattered the night.

CHAPTER EIGHTEEN

She was running, frantic in the dark street. Behind her...
Commotion.

Within seconds, she thought, they would be after her. Mr Henry
was not the sort to let anyone walk out on him in the middle of the
night. Worse, he would guess she would never do it without raiding
the till, because that was what he would do himself.

Cable Street was endless, full of shadows but no shelter anywhere.

She came to a side lane running down to the sea. Instinctively
she turned into it, realised when she was halfway down that it was
the worst thing she could have done. They would see the empty
street and know she must have turned this way. They would follow
her to the shore. Exposed on the beach, they would soon catch her.

She rounded a corner. An overhead light cast a wan glow over the
muddy ground and the walls rising high on either side. Beneath the
light, a side lane opened its jaws. Bella swerved into it, feet pounding, breath aflame in her chest. The lane ran into darkness. The
buildings hemmed her in.

A streetlight was shining ahead of her, a warehouse wall beyond
it, and she realised that the lane was leading her back into Cable
Street. She looked about her, panic stirring, knowing that whatever

she did would be fraught with danger. She glanced behind her, terrified she might see her pursuers racing towards her, but there was no one.

She had to find somewhere to hide until daylight, then see whether there were any vessels in port that might take her to Darwin and beyond.

Whatever else, she could not stay here; anyone coming down the lane would be sure to see her. Warily she retraced her footsteps, looking for an opening that might offer shelter. The after-effect of the evening's traumas began to weigh her down.

Eyes grown used to the darkness, she saw something she had missed before: an opening between two walls on the seaward side of the lane. It was narrow, and might be a dead end. Blacker than the pit, too. God knew what might be hiding in there, but at least it offered a possibility of escape. While she hesitated she looked back and saw the dark shapes of two figures standing beneath the street lamp at the point where she had first entered the lane. The darkness concealed her but if they came this way…

They did. The lamp threw their shadows ahead of them, gulping and swaying upon the walls. It made the men seem huge and doubly menacing and made up her mind for her. Heart pounding, barely able to breathe, she forced her way into the opening.

If there had ever been a path it had not been used for a long time. It sloped steeply; every step dislodged a clatter of stones yet doggedly she went on, stumbling and groping, while branches of unseen bushes caught in her hair and cobwebs brushed her face. Once past the buildings, the path – if that was what it was – plunged downhill. The smell and sound of the sea surrounded her. The slope ahead lay thick in shadow, with broken rocks and puddles left from the last rains. Mosquitoes whined. At last the ground levelled. Her nostrils full of the rancid mangrove stink, she edged forwards and found herself facing a quagmire of mud and mangrove stems growing so closely together that they almost touched; there was no way out in that direction. She looked first left, then right. Going left would bring her up against a vertical rock face; no chance of escape there, either, but progress might be possible in the other direction. She took a deep breath and headed that way.

If she had thought the gully was hard going she soon realised it had been nothing compared with what faced her now. The tough bushes yielded only reluctantly to her efforts to force a way through them. Thorns snagged her clothes and scored bloody streaks down her cheeks. Occasionally she stepped ankle-deep into stinking mud. Several times she became so entangled that escape seemed impossible, yet somehow she managed to free herself. She had no choice if she did not wish to leave her bones in this hellish place.

At last, after what seemed a lifetime, she was out of it, exhausted but safe for the moment. The harbour lay before her, its complement of fishing boats and freighters dark and silent. A solitary light cast a wan glow at the end of the jetty.

She was about to step on to the shelving beach when she froze. Not twenty yards away a man was standing, his outline almost lost in the shadow of the jetty. Was he from the Cockatoo? It seemed likely. She dared not let him see her. It was difficult to tell in the shadows, but she thought he was looking away from her, up the empty road leading to the town centre. Bella eased back into the shadows.

It was still dark. Get another twenty yards away without drawing his attention and there was a fair chance he would not see her at all; she sank to the ground and crawled as stealthily as she could across the dark-ribbed sand. The waves ran up in a froth of bubbles and retreated; beyond the harbour wall the riding lights of a passing steamer shone as it headed north inside the reef; little by little she distanced herself from the waiting man.

Now she could hardly see him. She stood cautiously, avoiding any sudden movement that might attract his attention. But where was she going? In the starlight she could see a headland a hundred yards away. Whether it was possible to go beyond the headland she had no way to know. A dark patch on the sand proved to be an upturned dinghy; she considered sheltering beneath it for what remained of the night. That way she would be under cover, but if

162   J.H. FLETCHER

anyone came looking for her it was one place they would be certain
to check.

Bella looked around her. Once they failed to find her in the town
the beach was the obvious choice. Wherever she chose, it would
have to be somewhere not only secure but inconspicuous. She
found it in a hollow beneath a low hedge that divided the beach
from the buildings at this end of the town. It was cramped but as
safe as anywhere could be. Exhausted after all that had happened,
she had to rest. She settled with her back against the stem of a bush,
her presence hidden by a screen of leaves.

Eyes gritty with weariness, skin stinging from the scratches and
bruises she had received during her escape, Bella leant back. The
leaves murmured softly, the waves lulled upon the beach, and she
closed her eyes.

It was light when she woke. She came to suddenly and for a moment
did not know what had disturbed her. Then she heard the growl of
men's voices close by her hiding place. She froze but through the
bushes could see the expanse of sand in front of her and two men
examining the upturned boat. They were not thirty yards away.
If they decided to search the hedge they could not miss her. She
clamped her chattering teeth into silence but could not still the
shakes that had invaded her body. She was so cold, so frightened,
and the men were so close...

Why were they so determined to get her back? She was nobody.
She had taken cash from the till, certainly, but there was a good
chance they did not even know that yet. Even if they did, a pound
or two – she had still not counted it – hardly warranted the effort
they were making to hunt her down.

As though to answer her unspoken question, a gust of wind from
the sea brought clearly to her what the men were saying as they
peered beneath the upturned boat.

'I never seen him so mad,' said the shorter of the two men.

'What you expect? He's made up his mind she's a virgin –'

'In the Cockatoo?' The short man laughed.

'Imagine what he could sell her for, if he's right. No wonder he wants her back.'

'Well, she ain't here,' the short man said.

'Not anywhere, seems like. Searching all night, I'm fair buggered. But if we don't find her, he'll go ape.'

'Maybe we should try the town again.'

Their boots crunched on the sand. They came right past Bella's hiding place while she sat with clenched hands, eyes squeezed shut, and waited. But they passed. The sound of their voices faded. She took a succession of deep breaths.

Thank God!

She did not stir until mid-morning. The town would be busy now, and safer; there was obviously less chance of their snatching her with other people about. Even so, she walked cautiously as she headed into the town, because now she had discovered another reason why Mr Henry was so determined to get her back. While she had waited in her hideout, with the sun rising and the sea extending in patterns of green and blue to the horizon, she had counted the money she had taken from the till.

The notes had been in a roll, with a rubber band around them. She flattened them and counted them one by one. When she had finished she leant back against the bush, her heart pounding once again: not this time from fear but disbelief. Fifty pounds. She checked it again to be sure. No wonder Mr Henry was so upset.

His own fault, she thought. If he had not tried to cheat her... It was not as though she could take any of it back.

She found a public toilet where she washed off the worst of the dirt and did what she could to tidy herself. Her face looked like she'd been in the Battle of the Marne but it would have to do. She went into the ladies' department of a clothing store in the high street and bought a new outfit, as different as possible from the one she was wearing: a dress of emerald and gold, a straw hat with a wide brim and artificial roses in the velvet band. Anything to blend in with what most of the women in town seemed to be wearing.

The assistant looked askance when Bella said she would buy the
clothes and put them on at once but her attitude changed when
Bella pulled out her roll of notes. Having money made the difference, no matter how you got it. She packed her old clothes into her
case and with renewed confidence went into the hotel across the
street and ordered breakfast in the dining room: steak, eggs, grease.
She wolfed the lot, feeling energy pouring back into her.

After she had paid Bella walked down the street, still keeping
a wary eye open, until she came to the office of a shipping agent.
Garth had said if she wanted to get in touch with him to drop him
a line care of the Wyndham post office. There was obviously no
time for that now. But if she could get to Wyndham and ask, someone would surely be able to tell her how to find him.

Once again, what choice did she have?

She pushed open the door and went inside. There was a counter
in brown wood, a fly-specked photograph of a steamer with a red
and blue striped funnel and a fat youth wearing a white shirt, not
too clean, and a tightly knotted black tie. Beyond a door behind the
counter a typewriter was hammering.

'I want to book a passage to Wyndham,' Bella said.

The youth reached out a languid hand and drew a book of forms
towards him. He placed his hand flat on the closed book and looked
at her.

'Seven quid,' he said.

She paid him. He scrawled something on a form, tore it out of
the book and handed it to her.

'You're in luck,' he told her.

'In what way?'

'Lucky there's a spare cabin. Lucky she'll be leaving on the tide.
One hour's time. Miss it, you'll have to wait a week.'

'Can you ring for a taxi?'

The taxi came; Bella climbed in as quickly as she could; now
she was so close to escape her nervousness had returned. She leant
forwards to speak to the driver as he drove down the street towards
the harbour.

'Drop me close to the gangway.'

She doubted whether any watcher would recognise her in her new outfit and it would take less than a minute to get aboard. They could hardly kidnap her from there.

The driver did as she asked. She thrust a note into his hand and was out of the cab, leaving him staring open-mouthed at the pound she had given him for a two-shilling fare. She had not asked for change, afraid even so close to safety that they might grab her before she could get up the gangway.

A blue-jerseyed sailor checked her ticket and carried her bag down the corridor to her cabin. There was the expectant air of a vessel about to put to sea, the faint rumble and vibration of the engines. Bella went into the cabin and closed and locked the door behind her before looking around.

It was small but clean, with a single bed covered in a candlewick quilt, a corner cupboard for her belongings and a brass-rimmed porthole. Through the porthole she had a view of the jetty, where a crane was swinging last-minute cargo aboard. She heard the thump of hatches being closed and a number of men in blue coats and trilby hats went ashore and watched as the gangway was drawn in. Longshoremen stood ready to cast off. A steam whistle peeped briefly, the hawsers were thrown into the water and hauled in, the vibration of the engines increased and the boat began to move. Relief drew the strength from Bella's legs and she sat down on the edge of the bunk.

Safe at last.

CHAPTER NINETEEN

A week later Bella stood on the dock at Wyndham and thought: What now?

There was no telephone contact with the interior, no roads, no way of getting to Miranda Downs except on horseback or foot. It was too far to walk, there were no horses she could hire and she did not know the way. There was radio contact of a sort, but it was unreliable and in any case the harbour master told her that Garth Tucker often left his set switched off.

'Him and his son,' he said. 'Not much for the outside world, either of them. The camel traders are your best bet.'

They called them Afghans, he told her, although many came from India. Several times a year they travelled through the bush with goods that they sold to the stations of the interior.

'Only way to keep places like Miranda Downs supplied,' he said. 'The government is always promising roads but nothing ever happens.'

'How long shall I have to wait?'

Again she was in luck; the harbour master told her the next camel train was being prepared as they spoke.

'They'll be on their way in two, three days,' he said.

'Will they take me?'
'Of course.'
It was part of the service that the Afghans provided.

It was a different world, governed by the slow, swaying gait of the camels. They were traversing a range of hills and every morning Bella woke to a vista of mixed scrub and forest bisected at intervals by meandering streams. Their progress seemed infinitesimal beneath a sky whose vastness dominated the earth; every sunset brought a display of crimsons, purples and greens the like of which she had never seen; every dawn showed no change from the day before.

She remembered lines from a poem she had learnt as a child:
We were the first that ever burst
Into that silent sea.

It was cattle country but she saw no cattle. From time to time she spotted kangaroos that watched the passing humans with curious eyes, or raced away with giant bounds that seemed to devour the earth. The camel drivers uttered harsh cries, goading their charges with sharpened sticks, which the camels haughtily ignored, swaying under loads draped in cloths whose lurid colours struck an exotic note in an otherwise green landscape. Beneath the cloths the supplies were mundane: bolts of calico, pots and pans, tins of paint, items of clothing, rifle and shotgun ammunition...

Running a remote station was a practical business; there was no room for the exotic in the operators' lonely lives.

Three days after leaving Wyndham they came to the first station on their circuit. Even before the camels arrived at the homestead, the caravan was surrounded by the welcoming black faces of the Aborigines: tall, long-limbed and smiling, yet with their own intense dignity. The children and many of the women cast curious eyes at Bella but the men ignored her as they bought penny packets of tobacco and snuff. The station owner's wife and daughter, faces bleached by heat and humidity, picked over what the traders had brought.

'Where you headed?' the wife asked Bella.

'Miranda Downs.'

It was only by good fortune that she had remembered the name of Garth Tucker's place.

'Good luck.'

Was it a casual remark, or was she suggesting Bella might need it?

The women selected the items they wanted, money changed hands and the train moved on. The solitude of the bush enfolded them.

Slowly the countryside became less hilly; the trees and scrub pressed closer about them. *The bush is pretty thick there*, Garth had said, and so it was. When he had told her he had forty thousand head of cattle, give or take, no way to know exactly how many, it had sounded a tall story. How was it possible not to know how many cattle you possessed? But now, seeing the countryside, she understood. The trick must be finding the creatures at all, she thought.

No doubt all would be revealed in time. Even if she landed the job of housekeeper it would have nothing to do with the day-to-day operations of the station but she already knew she would want to take a hand in that as well, if Garth Tucker would let her. Why not? She hadn't come all this way to be stuck indoors forever.

Ten days after leaving Wyndham, they arrived at Miranda Downs.

Bella stared. She had travelled thousands of miles to get here; she had escaped abuse and danger, she felt she had lived ten years in two months. It was entirely possible that Garth Tucker would not want a bar of her, yet she was beyond caring about that. She was here and for the moment that was enough.

All the same, her first impression of Miranda Downs was disappointing. Several buildings of grey, weathered planks were built around an open square of almost bare earth. A paddock, enclosed by a wire fence, held horses that kicked up their heels as the camels strutted past. A creek with sandbars, fifty yards wide, ran away between trees. The house was the biggest of the buildings. It had a corrugated iron roof, rusted in patches, and a partly roofed verandah that ran around two sides. Empty crates and pieces of lumber were piled up; an airstrip had been hacked through the undergrowth and a windsock hung limply from a leaning mast near its edge.

All in all it didn't look much but a closer inspection would have to wait, because once again they were surrounded by an excited group of Aborigines, the children racing and staring at Bella with huge eyes, the adults observing her less obviously, while behind them, mounted on a black stallion of eighteen hands, came the station owner.

He saw Bella and she saw him frown. Her heart sank.

He walked the stallion over, taking his time about it, and looked down at her. 'What are you doing here?'

She sensed that on his own turf boldness was the only way with this man. She gave him a merry smile. 'You offered me a job. I've decided to take you up on it.'

He grunted. 'As I recall, you turned it down.'

'I changed my mind. A woman's prerogative, right?' she said, fishing for the smile she did not get.

'How did you get here?'

'Long story.'

'You'd better go into the house. You can tell me about it when I've finished here.'

He turned away from her and spoke to the Afghans' leader. 'You got horse shoes?'

She might have ceased to exist.

She walked slowly towards the house. At close range it looked more of a wreck than ever.

His shout stopped her.

'Hey!'

She turned. Still with the Afghans, he was staring after her.

'You got any baggage?'

'One small case.'

'Take it with you. It's self-service here.'

Good luck, the station owner's wife had said.

'I'll leave it where it is,' she shouted back at him. 'Until I decide whether I'm staying or not.'

She turned on her heel without waiting for a reply. She walked on, climbed the steps to the dilapidated verandah and went into the house.

CHAPTER TWENTY

The house was a wreck. Bella's first impression was not so much of dirt, although there was plenty of that, but neglect. It was as far from being a home as you could get, yet she already knew she wanted to stay. Was it the bush? The challenge? The fact that she had nowhere else to go? Or had Garth Tucker something to do with it? She had come here looking for a bolt-hole, a refuge after the terrors of the Cockatoo Club. Her feelings for Garth had been very low on her list of priorities but now she was here she thought that despite his unfriendly welcome it would not take long to reawaken the heat she had felt for him in Charters Towers.

He had not renewed his offer of a job, but if she showed she was willing to work she thought she might have a better chance of persuading him to do so.

She made a start by seeing what she had to contend with. It was an eye-opener, and a depressing one. The building's basic structure was sound: outer walls of timber beams pegged horizontally to uprights set in the earth. The beams were weathered and looked as though they had never been painted in history, but they must be sturdy enough to withstand the cyclones that back

in Charters Towers Garth had told her hit the area from time
to time.

That was the end of the good news. The interior of the house
was a disaster. The concrete floor must have been laid by a drunk
because it was pitted and uneven and tilted – even the naked eye
could see it – towards the door. Only two of the window spaces had
glass in them. There were no ceilings; the whole house was open to
the iron roof. The interior walls were also of iron. In hot weather it
would be an oven, in winter they would freeze, in the wet the sound
of rain on the roof would deafen them.

There were three bedrooms and a kitchen. The kitchen contained
a kerosene stove, a wood-burning cooker and a banquet of black-
ened pots. It looked as though the whole camp had cooked up in
it and forgotten to clean it afterwards. An adjoining section had
a dining table and chairs that were deep in dust. Piled with old
magazines and papers, they were obviously never used. The bathroom and lavatory were ten feet away, with a door that would not
close properly. No doubt, with the corrugated iron walls, the sound
effects would be horrendous.

And Mrs Johnson had thought she was roughing it at Charters
Towers.

'Quite a change from Ripon Grange, too,' Bella said to what she
had already christened Tucker's Horrendous House.

Where to start was the question.

She settled on the kitchen. Luckily it had its own door that
led out into a fenced yard. The door would not stay open so she
jammed it with a baulk of wood, carried out everything she could
lift and dumped it in the yard.

At least now there was space to move.

'And room to appreciate the filth,' Bella said.

It was hot and humid. Sweat was running off her in streams and
she was just beginning to get an idea of the task that confronted her
when she felt someone behind her and turned.

A tall, black-haired man of about her age stood in the doorway.
Sturdy shoulders, strong arms, shorts. A cheesecloth shirt, arms

sheared off. He was scowling, obviously unwelcoming, but said nothing. She knew at once who he was because he was the spitting image of his dad.

'You are Colin,' Bella said.

Garth had mentioned him back at the Johnson place, saying that his son was a year older than she was. He looked older than that; no doubt the life in the wilds accounted for it. The likeness to his father was unmistakable and she remembered Garth saying that Colin was all he had left of the wife who had died twelve years before.

'He's an ornery bastard, when he wants to be,' he had said, grinning. 'Just like me. But he's an okay bloke, mostly; not that I tell him. We aren't the sort to make a song and dance about our feelings.'

Colin's eyes went past her to the emptied kitchen.

'What's going on?'

'I'm cleaning it up. I'm Bella.'

He ignored her outstretched hand. 'The latest in a long line,' he said. 'And how long do you plan on staying?'

'As long as I can put up with your dad. And you,' she added.

She was sending him a message. *Don't mess with me*. If it registered she saw no sign of it.

'What's a bloke gotta do to get a cuppa tea around here?'

Like father, like son.

'Make it himself,' said Bella. 'Your dad told me it was self-service.'

'That right?'

She saw he had a matchstick in his hand. He made a show of picking his teeth with it.

'With that attitude I give you twenty-four hours,' he said. 'Tops.'

'We'll see,' Bella said.

'Too bloody right,' Colin said.

He made himself tea on the kerosene stove. Nothing for her, though.

Bella was busy with the rickety cupboard, digging out cloths and even – miracle! – some steel wool and a tin of Brasso.

'I'll have a cup, too, if you're making,' she said.

'Self-service. Remember?'

'I'll do a deal with you,' Bella said. 'Make me a cup, I'll let you off scrubbing the pots.'

'You should be so lucky,' Colin said.

But made her a cup, after all. Things were looking up.

She dragged out a couple of dining chairs. They sat and drank their tea together, staring at the bush that grew close to the house: a sight familiar to Colin, no doubt, but new to Bella. The tea was as strong as tar and they did not speak, but it was a start.

Striding fast, Garth came round the corner of the building. He saw them sitting and stopped.

'Two ladies of leisure,' he said. 'What's this, smoko time?'

Local jargon for a tea break; Bella had heard the expression in Charters Towers.

'Something like that,' she said.

Garth saw the emptied kitchen. 'What the hell's going on?'

'Says she's tidying up,' Colin said.

'I haven't even said you can stay yet.'

'I'm here now,' Bella told him. 'And it needs doing. You told me so yourself.'

'I was thinking of employing you to keep house,' Garth said. 'Not wreck house.'

'Comes with the territory,' Bella said.

Garth grunted and switched his attention to his son.

'I want to head up towards the Tait River country, soon as we can make it.'

'O'Malley's not gunna like it,' Colin warned.

'O'Malley can take a jump,' said Garth. 'It's our property right up to the Archer Ridge.'

'Sure is,' Colin said. 'But not beyond it.'

'There's a mob of cleanskins up there. Best part of two thousand head, I'd guess. Flew over them the other day. You think I'm gunna let them go begging?'

'From the air, you can't tell if they got brands on them or not,' Colin objected.

'Maybe you can't. I can smell them,' Garth said.

'You go anywhere near O'Malley's place?'

Garth grinned. 'Right over his roof.'

'Did he see you?'

'He even shook his fist at me. Right neighbourly, I thought.'

'Lucky he didn't have a gun,' Colin said. 'Now he knows you're back, he'll have his boys out, for sure.'

Teeth gleamed as again Garth grinned. 'The day I can't handle O'Malley and his boys is the day I retire.'

Bella watched them together. Father and son, yet they spoke as equals. No doubt the way they lived explained that, too. As for her, she might have been a fence post, the attention they paid her. She looked at Garth.

'Will someone please explain what you're talking about?'

'No time now. I want to leave first light tomorrow,' he said to Colin. 'We've the coaches and horses to get ready, so let's get moving. There's work to be done.'

And both men were gone without another word.

At least it gave her time to get on with sorting out the kitchen. Scrubbing and scraping, she thought: how the countess would gloat. The bait-digger coming out: that's what she would say, the bitch. All that was past, mostly; ever since leaving England she had known nights without number when she had lain awake, aching for Charles's touch, his smile, his presence, and could have wept for missing him so much. She felt his absence now, most keenly, in this strange and unfamiliar place. It is loneliness, she thought, and the darkness of the unknown. But Charles was gone, in reality if not in her heart. She would never forget him, nor would she wish to. He had been the governing light of her life and there was no doubt her memories of him would influence her future, especially where men were concerned. Always she would remember him with love and great fondness but now it was time to move on. Back in Yorkshire, standing on the lip of the chasm called Gaping Gill, she had for a few brief moments believed that life without Charles was impossible. She knew better now.

Forget him, she told herself sternly. What mattered was the future. She must concentrate only on that. The work confronted her and she would deal with it.

As she worked, she prepared in her head a list of what she would need. New cupboards in place of the rickety antique they had now; new pots also: most of the existing ones were rusty and some even had holes in them.

By the time she'd finished everything was clean but she was exhausted, thinking there had to be a better way to do things. She dragged everything back indoors and turned her mind to what to prepare for supper. She'd come across a meat safe with a large joint of beef in it. The beef was green around the edges but she could cut off the worst bits and thought it would do. It would have to; apparently it was the only piece of meat in the house. There was a sack of potatoes, half of them sprouting, another of onions and one of flour. There were no green vegetables. She'd learnt how to make damper at Charters Towers.

She had no idea when the two men would be back but decided to roast the meat, anyway, with potatoes, fresh damper on the side, and hope she got the timing right.

She didn't; not quite. She had it ready, with no sign of them, so she raked out the stove and left the dish of meat to keep warm. She walked outside to catch the evening breeze that was now swaying the branches of the trees. She was unbelievably tired, which was hardly surprising. She sat on the chair, legs stretched out and eyes closed, the breeze pleasant on her hot face, and suddenly Garth and Colin had caught her off-guard, their faces vexed with the problems of a day that had obviously not gone according to plan.

'Three horses with walkabout,' Garth was snarling. 'Three! At this time of year! How did that happen?'

It was not a question with any useful answer. He was frustrated, wanting a target for his feelings: and there, on cue, was Bella taking her ease, with not a care in the world.

Garth exploded. 'What the hell you think you're playing at, Duchess?'

She opened her eyes, then her mouth, but before she had a chance to answer him he had turned to his son.

'You and me slaving our guts out and this one too ladylike to lift a finger.' He looked back at Bella, eyes furious. 'I didn't take you on to sit around, Duchess.'

Bella's weariness was replaced by rage. After fighting off Archibald Johnson, escaping from the Cockatoo Club and spending days with the Afghan traders just to get to this *slum*, hours labouring in that abominable kitchen, even going to the trouble of preparing supper for them, to be spoken to like this? No way would she put up with it!

'I am not a duchess. As you know very well. My father's an earl and one of my grandfathers was an earl, but my other grandfather dug bait for a living and my mother is married to a fisherman. *As you also know very well.*' She was blazing; had she been six inches taller her nose would have had his eye out. She was shouting, too, more fishwife than aristocrat. 'You think I'm so useless, why did you hire me?'

She saw the derisive grin vanish; his face darkened. 'I haven't,' he said.

'Yes you have. You just don't know it yet.'

Garth stiffened and opened his mouth, no doubt planning to give her a blast, but Bella beat him to it.

'You told me you wanted me to turn this rubbish tip into a home. If you still mean it, I can do it. But I shall need help to clean it up. I shall need money to buy what's needed. And I shall need no more clever remarks about duchesses! You hear me?'

It was touch and go. Colin's mouth hung open; it was likely he had never heard anyone speak to his father like that before. As for Garth: she could feel him quivering. But she dared him, mouth set, eyes fixed on his.

Another word and I'm out of here.

And Garth buckled. The blood receded from his face and he took a deep breath. He opened his mouth, closed it again, and finally said: 'I'll have a word with Tommy, he's my overseer. Get some lubras to give you a hand. Tell him what you want, he'll make sure they do it. And let me have a list of what you need; next time someone goes into town we'll see what we can do.'

Success left Bella drained. She was careful not to show triumph because it wasn't over; there would be other challenges. It was probably the first time in Garth's life that anyone had questioned his authority in such a way. She knew he wouldn't yield one inch without a fight, but at least she was still here and had learnt one thing that would be useful in the future. In the bush nothing came free. If you wanted respect you had to earn it. Perhaps she had taken the first step towards achieving that; hopefully things would be better from now on.

'Come and eat your tea,' she said.

The first sign of an improvement came that night when Garth turned up unannounced in the closet he had called her bedroom. There was nothing much in the way of furniture; she supposed she should be thankful there was a bed.

Nerves still raw from the Johnson episode, Bella watched him cautiously but he had come only to talk.

'You didn't understand what Col and I were talking about earlier.'

'About O'Malley and cleanskins? You might have been talking Greek. And you mentioned coaches, too. What are they?'

'The properties up here are too big for fences,' Garth said. 'The cattle are wild and go where they like. Until they're branded there's no saying who they belong to, so cleanskins – ones without a brand or ear tag – can be claimed by whoever gets to them first.'

'Provided they're on your property,' Bella said.

'Right.' There was a world of devilment in Garth's grin. 'Of course, it's thick bush out there. Sometimes it's hard to tell where you are. On your own spread or –'

'Or O'Malley's,' Bella finished for him.

'Precisely,' Garth said.

Some would call it rustling. Well, she'd had Garth Tucker down as part pirate as soon as she clapped eyes on him; that was what made him so attractive.

'And the coaches?'

'Oxen. Tame animals. You spread them out, run the wild cattle into them and they help calm them down. It makes the round-up easier. When they're settled you drive them to Galloway's meatworks at Wyndham. Then you go back for more.'

'All the year round?'

'Only in the dry,' Garth said. 'No one can move in the wet. Besides, that's when the crotalaria becomes a problem. Horses eat too much of it, it drives them crazy.'

'Is that what happened this afternoon?'

'Yes. By rights it's too early in the year but these things happen.'

'So you're off in the morning,' Bella said. 'When can I expect you back?'

'When you see us.'

Garth paused in the doorway before leaving her. 'I'm sorry I was a bit toey when you arrived. It was one hell of a morning and when I saw you I thought more trouble. But from what I've seen so far I think you're gunna fit in right well.'

Bella didn't think apologies came easily to Garth Tucker, so that was quite a compliment.

'And the meal tonight was a treat,' he said.

No doubt about it, things were looking up.

Weeks passed. Bella's eighteenth birthday came and went unannounced and therefore unnoticed by anyone but herself. Even she had a problem remembering, every day a carbon copy of every other day at Miranda Downs. The next camel train brought the things she needed. With her band of helpers recruited by Tommy from the Aboriginal camp, Bella transformed the house. It would never be a Macdonald's Place but at least it was clean, with two new cupboards and half a dozen new pots in the kitchen, new chairs in the sitting room. Garth had drawn the line at curtains for the windows or rugs for the floor, but at least it was more homely than it had been.

'And the new pots will mean we're less likely to die of food poisoning,' Bella said.

Her relationship with Garth was still very much on and off; he agreed with much she did but was very protective of his own turf and quick to lash out when he thought she was trespassing She had not forgotten Colin saying she was the latest in a long line; once or twice she thought Garth might be looking at her in the way a man looks at a woman he desires. She liked the thought; it woke tentative flutters in her body even as she told herself to be careful, but nothing came of it. Probably she had imagined it; at other times he seemed less interested in her than in the mineral samples he had on a trestle table in his bedroom.

One day he showed them to her. The table was covered in pieces of rock that he said he'd picked up in the course of his travels. He showed her one piece of reddish stone that weighed heavy in her hand.

'Hematite,' he said. 'Iron ore.'

'You mentioned it in Charters Towers,' she said. 'You've never found any?'

'Not yet. But it's here somewhere.'

At the beginning of September there was a change.

'We're having a round-up next week,' Garth said. 'Now you got the house sorted I suppose you might as well come with us.'

Colin was less than thrilled when he heard. 'The old man's never taken one of his women on a muster before,' he said.

'I am not one of his women,' Bella said.

'Stay here long enough you will be,' Colin said.

Bella ignored him. She had not forgotten Charles and never would; his loss was a living ache. Just after she arrived at Miranda Downs she had told herself she had to put the past behind her and move on. She still said so; it just hadn't happened yet. If and when that time came, she believed she could do a lot worse than Garth Tucker. Once again she felt the faint butterfly flutter of desire as she watched the slow, devilish grin with which he raked her emotions so effortlessly whenever he directed it at her.

One of his women? No way. But Garth Tucker's woman, wedded and – of course! – bedded: that was beginning to look an entirely different proposition. She was determined there would be none of this nonsense of sleeping with her and then pitching her out, like he had her predecessors. If he wasn't prepared to marry her he could forget the rest of it.

There were fifteen of them when they rode out: Tommy in charge of the stockmen, Wallaby the horse minder, Sarah the camp cook, Garth, Colin and Bella. Bella was on Lucas, a grey gelding that Garth had said she could ride. He had checked her riding skills first: more proof that respect, in this country, had to be earned.

'The Aborigines you've got working with you,' Bella said. 'What arrangement do you have with them? About wages and so on?'

'We pay them a wage. Not a huge sum but better than most other stations. O'Malley doesn't pay his people anything. We give them rations, too, of course. If they're crook I'm always willing to fly them to the hospital in Wyndham. Not that they often want it, mind you.'

'Why's that?'

'Most of them aren't keen on going up in Minnie. Why do you want to know, anyway?'

The real reason was that Bella had decided Miranda Downs was going to be her home and she wanted to know everything there was to know about the place. But if she told him that she was afraid Garth might think she was being presumptuous, so she didn't.

'Just wondered, that's all.'

'Now you know,' he said. 'So let's get this show on the road, shall we?'

There was a bite in the air, the tame cattle bellowing as they were herded along, the dozen or so working dogs circling them or rushing off with excited yelps to explore the thousand intriguing smells of the bush. The main party was followed by the camp wagon, driven by Wallaby's brother Dave and stacked with supplies, from food and tobacco to baling wire and a first aid kit.

They were heading towards the furthest border of Miranda
Downs, on the far side of the Tait River country. Two days out from
the homestead they reached it.

A saddle extended across the valley, with a narrow draw down
the middle of it. Garth had halted, reins hanging loose as he lifted
his binoculars and inspected the higher ground ahead of them. The
Miranda land ended just this side of the ridge; beyond was Limerick. It was the one open stretch along the border of the two properties and Garth stared at the area just below the ridge where a rolling
cloud of grey dust was heading down the slope towards them.

Garth licked his lips. 'I don't believe it,' he muttered.

He wheeled, reins taut, kicking his heels into the horse's flanks.

'Get the coaches spread out,' he shouted.

Instant action as the stockmen ran.

With no idea what to do and knowing better than ask, Bella did
what she could to keep out of the way.

The cloud was much nearer now. She heard the thunder of hooves
and made out the shapes of the stampeding animals, barely visible
in the dust. They were bellowing, their horns tossing in a confusion
that stole her breath. It looked like half the cattle in creation were
racing down the draw towards them.

Instead of going after the cattle, the cattle were coming after
them. But why?

No time to ask; no time for anything as the frontrunners reached
them. Bella's world became a frenzy of mounted men, thundering
hooves and the fleeting shapes of cattle, of danger emerging suddenly from billowing clouds of cinnamon-coloured dust. Then, as
suddenly as it had come, it was over.

'Reckon there were a thousand cleanskins in that mob,' Garth
Tucker said exultantly. 'And we got the lot.'

There were nowhere near a thousand animals tossing their horns
amid the placidly circling coaches: more like four hundred. Bella
looked the question.

'The rest are somewhere on Miranda, now,' Garth said. 'We'll get
all of them in time. And won't O'Malley be mad!'

'Why did they charge down the valley like that?' Bella asked.

'That's the best joke of all. His boys were up on the ridge. They were trying to turn the mob but somehow they sent them the wrong way.' He chuckled. 'I wouldn't be in the boss boy's shoes for quids when O'Malley gets hold of him.'

'But, if they started from his land, aren't they his?'

'Without a brand they're ours now,' Garth said. 'And not a thing he can do about it.'

He was almost dancing in the saddle. Bella had never seen him so exuberant. It wasn't gaining the extra cattle that had fired him up, she thought, it was winning. For a man like Garth Tucker, that was the most potent drug of all. She could relate to that. Winning had always been all-important to her, even before seeing off the vile Major Lacey. Maiming Mr Johnson, emptying the till at the Cockatoo Club and evading her pursuers had all been part of the pattern. Life offered its rewards to winners, not losers, and she was determined to have her share of them.

There were other trophies besides a few rustled cattle and out-smarting the neighbours. Back at the house, two days later, Garth obviously decided there was another one he wanted. The time had come to get into Bella's bed.

CHAPTER TWENTY-ONE

It was ten o'clock at night and as black as pitch. In Bella's bedroom – in Bella's *bed*! – Garth was laying siege to her.

'No!' Bella said.

'Come on, Duchess. Don't be like that,' Garth said. He put his hands on her breasts.

She pushed them away. 'I said no!'

'You let me in,' he said. 'What did you expect?'

It was true; she had let him in.

'I thought you wanted to talk.'

A lie: she had known exactly what he wanted. Despite what she'd told herself during the muster, she had wanted it, too. She had wanted to feel his strong hands caressing her but at the last moment memories of the Johnson nightmare had overwhelmed her and she had found herself physically incapable of going through with it.

It would infuriate Garth but there was nothing she could do about it. Perhaps it was just as well. What had she told Colin? I am not one of his women. If she did not stop him she would be and that, she thought, could be fatal.

'No!' she said again, with greater vigour. 'Stop it, Garth! I mean it. *Stop it*!'

She could feel how worked up he was and wondered if she'd left it too late, but no. He fell off her and lay on his back. She dared not speak or move but lay until his breath had returned to normal.

Only then was she willing to sound penitent. 'I'm sorry, darling. I want you, too, but I don't want to be just another of your women.'

It was risky; playing hard to get never made a woman popular yet, but for Garth to want her now was not enough. He had to go on wanting her. And to achieve that...

She had to make him love her. 'Humour me? Please?'

They lay quietly, hand in hand. They talked a little but not for long. Finally: 'If there's nothing doing here I'd best get to bed,' Garth said.

A chaste kiss; he was gone. The door creaked shut behind him. Alone, Bella contemplated what had happened between them, as well as what had so nearly happened but had not. She knew she would have to be very careful. She wanted him; there was no doubt about that. Once she had managed to put the Johnson business behind her she would want him more than ever. When that time came she thought she might find it very difficult to resist him. Yet the problem remained. To give too much, or not enough: how was a girl to know where to draw the line?

Early the next morning Bella saddled up and rode out. She wanted to be alone. Now Garth had given her the gelding she was determined to take every opportunity there was to explore the tract that was Miranda Downs. She had been here only a few short months yet already the land had taken hold of her. To explore it would be to pay court to its vastness, its inscrutability, the power and glory of which the Bible spoke, the manifestation of a creative energy that had formed the land and that she could sense still in its almost limitless space. This was majesty, a place of humility and pride where, in a way she could not articulate, she could reach out and touch the beginning of all things. A beginning and a continuation. All that had been, still was and would be forever until that time, unimaginable aeons into the future, when past and present and future would become one, consumed in the vast conflagration of the exploding sun.

Mrs Johnson had owned a book about what it called the creation myths of the Aboriginal people. As far as she knew Mrs Johnson had not read it but Bella had. Knowing nothing, she had learnt a little but would like to learn much more. She knew that what the book had said could of course have been wrong and would certainly have been incomplete. She had watched the faces of the women who had gone with them on the muster and knew that when she had given them time to know her better she would seek from them whatever they might be willing to reveal of their version of the truth of things.

So Bella Tempest rode, a speck of dust on the landscape, and the landscape swallowed her. She was open to the sounds and silences of the land, the clopping hooves of the horse, the mystery of trees, the wonder of the hills that stretched away. The screech of a cockatoo attacked the stillness, deriding the futility of the woman whose heart longed to understand.

As she rode, she thought. She had no regrets about the previous night. She had done the right thing and Garth's reaction gave her hope that he must care for her, at least a little. That was good news, because she had fallen in love: not yet with the man, but completely and absolutely with the place.

She rode up a steep incline to a stretch of open ground from which it was possible to look out across the countryside. Broken only by the lines of creeks, the bush was partly obscured by mist but in her mind she could see it: the pattern of hills and plains that was Miranda Downs. She was excited by the sense of adventure that came from knowing that all around her were areas where no human foot had ever trod. She had loved England and still did, but there you could not take a step without standing on soil that had been trodden by a thousand generations before. Here it was still possible. Miranda Downs had become vital to her. She could not bear the thought that one day Garth might get rid of her, as he had those before her. There was only one way she could guarantee her future here and she knew, watching a cockatoo flying, its sulphur-coloured crest bright in the sunlight, that she would take it.

She rode back. Garth gave her a curious look but did not ask what she'd been doing. Perhaps, as someone else who loved this land, he knew.

It was a fortnight later. So far, miraculously, all was well. When they were with others Garth was as he had always been, but alone he was both tender and considerate. He paid her no more night-time visits, leaving Bella wondering how she would react if he did.

They went on another muster, Bella quite the old hand now. Immersed in clouds of red and amber dust, they drove their cattle to the meatworks at Wyndham. Life in the bush had become second nature and she loved it. The living remained spartan but Miranda Downs was now her home, and it was obvious from the way the hands treated her that she and Garth were regarded as an item. It led to problems that Bella supposed she should have foreseen. Colin had been taciturn from the first. Now he became even more wary, watching her with resentful eyes. Later, after an evening when she heard voices raised between him and his father, they became hostile. Never chatty, he hardly spoke to her at all but she felt his scowl everywhere she went. Finally she'd had enough.

'What's wrong?'

'That's what I admire about you,' Colin said. 'You want something, you go for it. To hell with everyone else. And then you ask what's wrong.'

'I have no idea what you're talking about.'

Except she thought she might. In this house you could hardly *breathe* without everyone knowing: witness the argument she'd overheard between Colin and his father. It was highly probable, Bella thought, that Colin had heard at least something of what had happened in her room that night. No doubt he would have misinterpreted it, too. But so what? He had already told her that she wouldn't be the first visitor to have Garth Tucker in her bed, so why should he care? She asked Garth about it.

'He'll get over it.'

So that she felt shut out by the unwillingness of both father and son to explain or even talk to her about it.

That night as it was getting dark, wearing shirts buttoned to the wrists against mosquitoes, she and Garth strolled down to the creek together. The dying light formed puddles of silver and gold on the surface of the water but the blackness of the undergrowth on either bank was impenetrable. Like the people of the land, Bella thought. A few shafts of light, revealing little, and surrounded by the darkness of what could not be told. A land of mystery, indeed, but there were some mysteries she was not prepared to tolerate.

'I want you to tell me why Colin is so anti,' she said.

She watched the profile of Garth's features as he stared at the water: the defiant beak of nose, the forceful thrust of jaw. Now he rubbed the back of his neck.

'I guess, Bella, because he's scared of you.'

'*Scared*? Why on earth should he be scared?'

He glanced at her and there was just enough light for her to see his wry smile. 'Thing is,' he said, 'there've been one or two here before you.'

Bella laughed. 'I never doubted it. So what?'

'I guess Colin's grown up with the idea that they come and they go and nothing changes.'

Bella had the feeling they were on the edge of something that might prove important, if she wanted to stay. She sensed that Garth was exploring his own feelings and knew she must not hurry the pace of the conversation or intrude in any way. Once again she followed the pattern that had worked so well for her in the past. She said nothing.

'And now it has changed,' Garth said.

Bella's mouth was so dry. 'In what way?' she said.

'Because you're still here.'

'And plan to stay, as well,' she said. 'If you don't kick me out.'

'Why?' he asked. 'No night life. No fun –'

'Because I love this place.'

His eyes glinted as he looked at her. It was too dark to see his expression but she would have swallowed her words, had it been possible. Again she wondered whether he might think it presumptuous that someone who hadn't even been here twelve months should lay claim to such feelings. He might even think she was lying to curry favour. But it was the truth and she stood firm, looking back at him.

'I had a feeling you did,' he said. 'That is good.'

Warmth flowed through her. It was much better than good. It was wonderful that he should understand and accept what she had told him. But… 'That doesn't explain why Colin should be scared of me.'

'Because he loves Miranda Downs too. It has been his whole life. Since he left school – what? – five years ago, he's been nowhere else. He *knows* nowhere else. He's grown up to think of this place as his heritage. I've encouraged him to think so. Now he's afraid you may take Miranda Downs away from him.'

'I wouldn't be able to do that even if I wanted. Miranda Downs is yours.'

'He probably thinks you might talk me round. Seeing you love the place so much.'

She saw he was testing her, too, trying to sense whether Colin's doubts might be justified. 'I might,' she agreed. 'But I wouldn't. I would never do anything like that.'

'I believe you,' he said. 'But you can understand how he feels.'

Now even the silvery light upon the waters of the creek was almost gone. A mosquito sang.

'I must talk to him,' Bella said.

'Leave him be,' Garth said. 'Like I said, he'll get over it.'

Bella had her doubts but let it go for the moment.

Unfortunately, as she had feared, Garth proved to be wrong. Colin remained hostile: to her, mostly, but to his father also and as the months passed she learnt to ignore the atmosphere; it seemed you could get used to anything, given time. But learning to ignore it did not mean it had gone away.

It was July 1939 and the storm clouds were gathering in far away Europe. On Miranda Downs Colin had long ago stopped thinking that Dad and Bella were sleeping together but that didn't make him feel better. On the contrary, it meant that Garth had changed his behaviour from how it had been with Bella's predecessors and that was a worry. Taking her mustering was a case in point. Colin had given up hoping she would make a fool of herself; from the beginning she had never put a foot wrong. She had not complained about the discomfort; she had lent a hand where she could; she had not panicked when the stampede had brought the cattle within yards of her.

It was twenty-two months since her first muster and she seemed more at home than ever, which to Colin was not good news. She was proving to be one tough lady and tough, Colin knew well, was the road to his father's heart.

What was going on? Nearly two years she'd been there, far longer than any of her predecessors. Surely she wasn't planning to marry the old man? She was way too young, younger even than he was! Yet Dad was smitten with her; blind Freddy could see that.

'Isn't she marvellous?' Garth had said, with a fond expression that did not suit his hard features. 'A real gem.'

If they did get married and she had a son, where would that leave Colin?

He had played with the idea of coming on to her himself, to see how she reacted, but it was too risky; the last thing he wanted was to fight Dad over a girl. Instead he thought he'd try something else. Dad had met her at the Johnsons' place, in Charters Towers. As far as he knew, she had never said why she had left them. He would write to the Johnsons and find out.

The post took forever in this part of the world but halfway through August a letter came.

Colin read it and took it to his father, who was working on the plane.

'What's this?'

'A letter. I think you should read it.'

Garth gave him a sharp look but took it, handling it gingerly with oily hands. He read it through, then looked at his son. 'How come we've got this?'

'I wrote to them.'

'Without a word to me?'

The look that Dad gave him! Colin quaked but it was too late to change tack; he would have to tough it out. 'I thought we owed it to ourselves to find out about her.'

It was plain that Dad, face darkening with rage, did not see it like that. 'You went to the Johnsons behind my back? Mate, I ought to knock your block off!'

Fists clenched the way they were, he might just try it, too. Colin was as big as his father and probably as strong but he wasn't game to fight him; a lifetime of respect made sure of that. So he did not respond but stood with unclenched hands at his side.

Seeing it, Garth regained control of his temper.

'Clear off,' he said in a dull voice. 'Before I do something I might regret.'

'And the letter?'

'I'll deal with it.'

Bella read the letter to the end, put it on the table and walked to the kitchen door, while Garth stood watching her.

The chooks were kicking up a racket in the run that Bella had persuaded Garth to have built so they could enjoy fresh eggs. She liked the warm, homely smell of their feathers; it awoke a childhood memory of the cottage and carrying the precious eggs indoors in hands barely large enough to hold them. Now these hens represented all she valued about the past and how much she had lost over the years. The memories were especially important now, alone in an uncertain world.

She turned. Garth was watching her.

He had come in with a face like thunder. Busy preparing tea, she had turned to greet him and he had thrust the letter into her hands.

'Read it.'

Since then he had neither moved nor spoken. She read his silence as an accusation and it made her angry.

Anger was good; anger might save her. 'You wrote to the Johnsons without a word to me? How could you?'

'Never mind that. Is it true? What she says there?'

She would not dignify his question by giving him a straight answer. 'That I'm a home-wrecker who tried to seduce her husband? You think I'd admit it, if it was true?'

'I don't think so,' he said. 'I just wonder why she's saying it.'

'Because her husband tried to rape me and I fought him off.' The words were out of her mouth before she knew they were coming.

'*Rape?*' His eyes went round. 'You never said.'

Snake-quick, she struck back. 'You think it's something I like to talk about?'

'How did you stop him?'

'I kneed him in the crutch. Twice.' She spoke with satisfaction, remembering how Johnson had collapsed after she'd done it. 'That took the steam out of him,' she said.

'Lucky I didn't know that before I tried my luck with you,' Garth said, making a joke of it.

'You're different.'

'What happened afterwards?'

'He must have spun Mrs Johnson some yarn about how I'd come on to him and she threw me out.' She shuddered. 'As though I would! That slimy little man!'

'What did you do then?'

'I tried to get a job in Townsville but there was nothing doing. So I remembered what you'd said and came here.' She spoke as though crossing the continent was nothing.

'You took one hell of a chance,' he said.

'No choice.' She lifted her chin and looked at him challengingly. 'Are you going to chuck me out, too?' she said.

'Not unless you want to go.'

'I want to stay,' Bella said. 'But I need you to trust me.'

'I do.'

'And you want me to stay?'

'Forever, if you like.'

So all that had seemed lost was regained. Now, conscious of victory, impulse drove her.

'I don't want to be another of your women. I want us to do it properly.'

She would not think of Charles Hardy. Because the letter had contained a cutting from the society page of the Yorkshire newspaper that Mrs Johnson received every week.

It is rumoured that an engagement will shortly be announced between Charles, only son of Mr and the late Mrs William Hardy and heir to the extensive Hardy estates, and Jane, younger sister of the Countess of Clapham.

There was also a note for Bella's benefit, written with such glee that Bella could almost see the venom glistening on the page.

When we engaged Miss Tempest she mentioned that she had been a close friend of the Hardy family, so she may find this of interest.

I want us to do it properly… There could be no mistaking Bella's meaning. But Garth said: 'Colin is my son. I would like him to be friends with you before we take things further.'

Neither of them had mentioned love.

'I'll try,' said Bella. 'But you should speak to him, too.'

After Garth had left her Bella walked out into the air. How she needed the air!

The sky was darkening; leaves rattled in the breeze and the creek glowed with sombre fire as the night came down. In the chook house, all was quiet.

Charles and Charlotte's sister, she thought.

The world was indeed a lonely place.

* * *

It was Sunday, the third of September. She had decided she would speak to Colin the following morning but that night the wireless broadcast an announcement that put everything else out of their heads.

'War?' Garth said. 'Bloody hell!'

Bella remembered what Jenny had told her about the last war and how she had waited, week after week, to find out whether Father was alive or dead. She thought: not again. Let us pray that no one we know becomes involved.

The next morning Colin informed his father he intended to join up. Within seconds Garth was shouting.

'Not without my say-so you won't.'

If he'd thought about it for a week he couldn't have come up with a worse way to handle his son.

'I'm twenty-one years old, Dad. I'm gunna do it. Get used to the idea.'

Within the week he was gone. Before he left, he spoke to Bella, but it was not a friendly parting.

'With me out of the way, you'll have a free run,' he said. 'The old man will marry you now.'

'There was nothing to stop him marrying me before, if that was what we wanted,' Bella said. 'Even if it happens you'll never lose Miranda Downs. Neither your dad nor I would want that.'

But she could not reach him. It saddened her, but she told herself he must think what he liked; it would make no difference in the end.

CHAPTER TWENTY-TWO

Perhaps it was inevitable; within two days of Colin leaving, Garth made another move on her. As before, it went nowhere. Once again Garth accepted her rejection, returning to his own room without too much of a fuss, but this time he didn't hide his exasperation.

'This is hard yakka for a bloke,' he grumbled.

Not only for a bloke. Bella was twenty years old, healthy and very much aware of her own sexuality, but she was also scared. She wanted Garth, all right, but say yes and down the track he might lose interest in her. She wanted to stay on at Miranda Downs and keeping him at arm's length was the only way she knew to make it happen. Even that might not work; say no too often and he might chuck her out anyway.

She got off the crumpled bed, hearing the faint whistle of the kerosene lantern as she walked naked to stare at herself in the wall mirror. She checked out the blue eyes, tousled black curls, the smooth skin of her shoulders, the firm breasts that no one but Charles Hardy had kissed.

Not bad, she thought. No wonder Garth fancied her. She fancied him, too, increasingly. She knew she had been eyeing him more and more over the last weeks, the hard chest and muscled back.

Against all her inclinations she had rejected him again tonight but she could not go on saying no forever. Do that and she would lose him for sure.

Garth said: 'How about taking a trip?'

Bella stared at him. 'At this time of year?'

It was the third week of September, dry weather with loads of sunshine and temperatures in the mid-twenties. It was cattle round-up season and Garth was not given to taking time off when there was work to be done but he said he was edgy about the war.

'The air force will take Minnie any day now. And I heard the other day they're gunna cut out petrol for private use. So I was thinking, why not make the most of it while we still can?'

'I'm game,' Bella said.

She was not only getting used to the country but to the lingo, too.

She had thought Derby, or maybe even Perth, but Garth had never been one for the city and had other ideas. He took her into the emptiness.

On the evening of their fourth day they put down on an open stretch of country beside the Carlisle River. At this point the river flowed through a rugged gorge out of the unknown country to the southwest, but there was no time to explore. By the time they had anchored Minnie against any wind that might come up in the night, fetched their swags from the cockpit and made a fire, it was too dark to see much, anyway.

Bella chewed on salt beef and yesterday's damper, looking at the stars like a million fireflies in the black sky, and was overwhelmed by wonder. She felt close to the roots not merely of the land but of the universe. She wanted to share her feelings with Garth but knew better than try. Garth loved this country, too, without seeing any reason to say so. He was a practical man; flights of fancy never got off the ground with him.

No matter. She looked at him in the flickering firelight and took perhaps the biggest gamble of her life.

'Do you think we should get married?' she said.

It was against every rule in the book and Garth, forthright but deeply conservative, might run a mile. Or be offended that she had usurped what by tradition was his prerogative.

She risked a glance; Garth was staring at her, open-mouthed, across the flames.

'Stone the crows!' he said.

Her smile might have quivered, had she let it. 'Does that mean yes?' she enquired.

'If I marry you, does that make me a duke?'

'I'll call you Duke every morning before breakfast, if that's what you want. Particularly out in the bush. The boys would love it.'

'My oath they would. What about Colin?' he asked.

'Garth, please… Say yes or no. If it's yes, we can work out the details in the morning.'

'And if it's no?'

'Turn down being a duke? Not you,' Bella said.

Silence, while Garth chewed on it.

'You're serious, aren't you?'

'Deadly serious.'

'All right then. Yes,' Garth said. 'We'll give it a go.'

What happened next… Afterwards Bella never quite worked it out, but there she was on Garth's swag, naked beneath the firefly stars, and now there were no inhibitions and her arms went around his neck. Something else she remembered: waking during the night, loins stinging, thinking drowsily that now at least she wouldn't die wondering. Thinking, too, that what had happened was right, every bit of it right. The future stretched before her; she saw it clearly in the moments before she fell asleep again, and it was glorious.

It was barely light when Bella woke. She yawned and stretched and only then became aware of something different in herself and the texture of the morning. She opened her eyes, remembering. She was astonished that she had dared do what she had done. A woman proposing to a man? And being accepted? It was unheard of, surely?

She almost laughed but did not, not wishing to disturb the man sleeping beside her. What would the countess think of such behaviour? As if she gave a damn what that old bitch might think.

Careful not to wake him, she eased her body away from Garth and stood up. The air was fresh in the half-light and she took her discarded shirt and slipped it on. She could hear the river running in the pre-dawn stillness and walked to the edge of the gorge. Far below the river was lost in shadow, with only an occasional flicker of light to show the presence of rapids. The air was still. There was no cloud and along the horizon the eastern sky glowed apricot with the approaching sun. Old Sarah the camp cook had told her of ceremonies that the traditional people held every morning to welcome the sun's return. Bella, half-naked on the brink of the gorge, could relate to that. She took off the unbuttoned shirt and let it fall. Rock still, she stood and waited for the dawn.

A new sunrise; a new future. So strange… Only yesterday it had been impossible; today it had happened and nothing could change it. It was a gamble; Garth might go back on his word. There might be delays, excuses, but nothing she couldn't handle. Because it had happened.

The sun broke the horizon. The apricot sky had turned to a blue so pale as to be almost no colour at all. Within the instant, the level plain was flooded with light. Every rock and blade of grass shone yellow but Bella, naked on the gorge's rim, stood as white as alabaster in the stillness of the dawn.

She waited, skin puckering in the chill air, until the sun had cleared the horizon, then put on her shirt, buttoned it and returned to the camp and the remains of the dead fire, black now and wet with dew. Garth still slept, black hair tousled, one arm thrown out. She pulled on her breeches and knelt to remake the fire.

Breakfast was black tea, very strong, and more of the chewy beef. At least the damper was fresh, mixed and cooking on the coals of the new fire while Garth still slept. That was something else she had learnt: how to live in the wild. The Mrs Johnsons and countesses of the world might think themselves superior but in reality were as helpless as lambs, and it was the quality in her they would have most despised – the blood of her grandfather, Nate Tempest the bait-digger – that had made her able to handle the challenges of her life.

She was tough and knew when to make a stand. Knew when not to, as well, which was just as important.

'Where does the river come from?' she asked.

Garth poured himself more tea from the kettle.

'Through the mountains some place. There will be gorges and white water up there, but where it rises I've no idea. Upstream from here is all unknown country.'

It was exciting to be on the edge of the unknown. Like her life, she thought. The challenge of an unknown future. Perhaps a little better known than it had been yesterday, but still a mystery. She would not have had it any other way.

'When do you want us to get married?' she said.

'I must speak to Colin first.'

'We don't need Colin's permission.'

'Of course not. But he's got it into his head that we're planning to cut him out –'

'That's nonsense.'

'But what will he think if we get married as soon as his back's turned? I want the three of us to be friends. No, I'll tell him about it, face to face. I want him at the wedding, too, if he'll come.'

'When will he get leave?'

'No idea. Couple of months, maybe.'

Don't go getting cold feet on me.

But she would never allow herself to say such a thing to him or permit herself to think it, except occasionally.

Colin came home for Christmas. He was polite, smiling and even shook Bella's hand, so that she dared hope his resentment was behind him. Unfortunately it didn't last.

In Europe Poland had been carved up between Germany and the Soviet Union and at Miranda Downs Garth told Colin he was marrying Bella Tempest. Oh dear. Colin stormed out of the house, grabbed a horse from the paddock and rode off. He was not seen again that evening.

It grew late and Bella, concerned for Colin's safety, wanted Garth to go looking for him, but Garth refused.

'Never find him in the dark,' he said. 'Besides, he's got to get used to the idea.'

'And if he doesn't?'

'I told you. I would like youse to be friends. But if he won't come round...'

'Then what?' Bella asked.

'Like it or lump it,' Garth said.

On Christmas Eve, Garth and Bella flew to Wyndham in a torrential downpour as the Wet tightened its grip on the land. They came back with all the Christmas goodies they could lay their hands on. It was a hairy ride but they made it without incident, spray exploding around the wheels as they landed. The engine died and Bella heard the rain drumming on the wings above her. The ground was the colour of blood and awash with water. In the air, the plane's design had protected them from the worst of the weather but it would be no use now. Laughing like children, they ran for the shelter of the house; it was not more than twenty yards, yet they were soaked by the time they got there.

'How do we get everything indoors?' Bella wondered.

'Maybe we could persuade the turkey to swim for it,' Garth suggested.

Bella shook her head. 'This is Christmas,' she said. 'Easter's the time for resurrection.'

The rain stopped within the hour. At this time of year the break wouldn't last long but it gave them time to get everything unpacked and indoors. By the time they had finished they were in mud halfway to their thighs, but it didn't matter. Nothing mattered; Christmas was here; the world, Poland excepted, was peaceful if not at peace; and, most miraculous of all, Colin seemed to have put his temper tantrums behind him. After his outburst on the night of his arrival he had been unfailingly polite to Bella. No signs of any great affection, admittedly, but there was plenty of time for that. One step at a time, she thought. That is how we must handle it.

They'd brought back a fair bit of booze and by Christmas afternoon the three of them were comprehensively liquored up before they were halfway through the turkey. And that was only the start of it, with a plum pudding and mince pies to follow. And brandy to sit warmly on top of the beer and champagne and red wine and whisky they'd already drunk.

'I tried to make a trifle,' Bella said owlishly. 'But it didn't work.'

She had been dreading Christmas, fearing animosity might ruin things, but everything had worked out fine. They were all loving each other before they were through, and if from time to time Bella caught Colin eyeing her as though he knew something she didn't, what of it? They were a family, weren't they? Or would be soon enough.

Later Garth hoped to love Bella in a different way, but, three-quarters drunk though she was, with Colin in the house she was having none of it.

'You can wait,' she told him. 'Not long now.'

Colin was due back in the army on the tenth of January, so they had fixed the wedding for Saturday the sixth.

'Just my luck,' said Bella. 'This time of year, I'll be half-drowned by the time I get to the church.'

'We can always put it off until the dry weather,' Garth pointed out.

'With you most likely chasing cows the day of the wedding? I'll stick with what I've got, thanks very much.'

Garth and Bella flew to Wyndham the day before the wedding. Colin had ridden up the day before and they had arranged to have dinner together that evening.

'Do you mind if I bring a guest?' Colin asked Bella.

'Colin's bringing someone with him,' she told Garth later. 'Maybe somebody he met in the army.'

'Or a beautiful woman,' Garth said.

'What a shame you're booked,' Bella said.

'Not too late yet,' Garth told her.

'Would you prefer I had dinner in my room?'

The Cow and Bucket was a roast-and-vegie type of hotel but to honour the occasion Garth had ordered a couple of additional courses: oysters, prawns and asparagus as well as the beef, with champagne and malt whisky. Having checked everything was in order, he and Bella were sitting in the dining room when Colin arrived with his guest.

'Good God,' Garth said. 'It's Billy Gould.'

His tone was hostile, but Bella had never heard of Billy Gould. 'Who is he?'

'I'll tell you later.'

Bella saw a weedy man in his mid-twenties, with chewed nails, a chalk-white face and a petulant mouth. She looked at him, wondering why his face seemed to nudge faintly at her memory. His hand when she shook it was moist and cold.

They sat down and began to eat.

'What are you doing here?' Garth asked Billy.

'To celebrate his uncle's wedding,' Colin said. 'What else?'

'I'm not his uncle. And guests normally wait for an invitation,' Garth said.

'But we've never been a family to stand on ceremony,' Colin said easily.

'Billy is the grandson of Josh Gould, my father's mining partner,' Garth explained to Bella. 'Still poisoning your workers at Van Damm Siding?' he asked.

Billy Gould looked at Garth with indifferent eyes. 'Something like that,' he said and reached for another prawn.

'Billy has an asbestos mine,' Garth said. 'The state medical officer says it's a health hazard and wants it closed but Billy won't do it.'

'I certainly won't. The profits are good and the dangers grossly exaggerated.'

'Maybe,' Garth said.

Bella felt uncomfortable; there were currents here she did not understand. It angered her that Colin should have brought this man – the evening before her wedding, too – when Garth obviously disliked him. She also didn't like the way Billy watched her throughout the meal, or the way Colin sat, observing what was happening with the same crafty smile he had worn at Christmas.

There was something going on and it was not well meant. Later that night she found out what it was.

She was sitting in her room. Billy Gould's presence had made her uncomfortable but she was thinking not of him but of the next day and what it would bring. This time tomorrow she would be a married woman. It was a strange thought. Was her heart having palpitations? No. Was she short of breath? No. Did she have a hollow feeling in her stomach? No. She respected Garth, trusted him, desired him, was fond of him, but would it be enough? She had none of the half-pain, half-joy she had known with Charles. None of the sense of being both possessor and possessed; of being one, body and soul, with another human being. But she was older now, more – dare she say it? – more mature. Less impulsive. Her feelings for Garth, less starry-eyed, perhaps, might provide a better basis for married life than the romantic images of the past.

Give it time, she told herself, and love will come.

When Garth came into her room she wondered what he wanted. He wasted no time telling her. 'Billy Gould has been talking to me. Colin brought him here for a reason.'

'I guessed,' said Bella.

'Billy owns a half-share in a sugar plantation outside Ayr. That's on the coast near –'

'Near Townsville,' Bella said. 'I know.'

'He said you were a hostess at the Cockatoo Club near the Townsville docks. He said he recognised you from the times he's been there himself.'

That was where she had seen him. Of course. She remembered him now.

Lookit the knockers on that one.

Oh yes, she remembered him well.

Garth paused but Bella did not speak. She watched him, her face showing nothing.

'He said it calls itself a club but it's really a brothel.'

Still she said nothing. She stood facing him and his face showed no emotion.

'Is it true?' Garth asked.

'Yes,' she said. 'It's true.'

Garth closed his eyes for a moment. 'You want to tell me about it?'

At that moment Bella knew that love would indeed come. Because he had neither judged nor condemned her.

You want to tell me about it?

For that, whatever happened now, she would be forever in his debt.

She went and sat on the bed. 'Come and sit with me,' she said.

He did so cautiously and sat down. He did not move as she told him everything that had happened, leaving nothing out.

'I never told you,' she said, 'because of the Cockatoo's reputation. I did not want you to know. But I never went upstairs with anyone. Does he say I did?'

For the first time she dared look at him.

'He implied it, yes, but did not say it.' He sighed heavily. 'I am sad and disappointed,' he said.

'I understand,' she said.

He looked at her then.

'No, you don't. You have told me and I believe you. It is Colin I am disappointed in. My own son. I would not have believed it.' His fists clenched. 'I could kill him,' he said furiously, 'for treating you so badly.'

She raised her fingers to his lips. 'You don't mean it. I don't want you to fight him. Especially not just before our wedding. I want it to be a joyous occasion, not a time of hatred. I want him there. And so do you.'

Garth stared at her. 'But what do I say to him?'

'Say nothing,' Bella said. 'That is the best way.'

The day turned out fine.

'Happy is the bride whom the sun shines on,' quoted Bella in the white dress she had decided would do as a wedding gown.

The rector was an old buffer who cautioned them against vice while casting a surreptitious eye over Bella's stomach to see how far along she was: old buffer or not, he knew the habits of most of his parishioners when it came to the wedding ceremony. But Bella, despite Garth's most vigorous efforts, remained as slender as a reed.

Colin attended, which pleased his father. Bella never knew what Garth had said to him but he had the grace to look embarrassed and after the ceremony congratulated them both.

'I hope you'll be very happy.'

Billy did not come, which suited Bella fine; if she never saw him again it would be too soon.

Man and wife – Bella still could not quite get her head around that – Garth and Bella Tucker spent the night in the local hotel, where they were serenaded by the spasmodic bellowing of drunks still drinking their Christmas, and the normal rituals of a wedding night passed off to their mutual satisfaction.

The next day they flew back to Miranda Downs. On the ninth of January Colin left to return to the army and the newly married couple was alone.

'Thank God,' Garth said.

He picked up his wife and carried her into the bedroom.

For two days they were hardly out of bed. Bella was twenty years old, Garth thirty-nine. They both had stamina to spare. She was certainly not complaining, although there were times when she wondered whether she would ever be able to straighten her legs again.

CHAPTER TWENTY-THREE

Months passed.

The Dry returned; Garth exchanged one saddle for another when the Tuckers went back to the bush for the first cattle muster of the season.

The old war with O'Malley was resumed with a dispute over more unbranded cattle that might, or might not, have originated on Limerick Downs, while in Europe the real war remained stalled.

Not for long. In June 1940, what people had been calling the Phoney War became phoney no longer. The Germans attacked with appalling savagery and within weeks the whole of Europe from the Pyrenees to the Danube was overrun. With the United States still trying to stay out of it, only Britain and the Empire stood firm against the Nazis.

Minnie was requisitioned, as Garth had expected. Petrol was rationed. A generation that had taken the use of trucks and motor-cars for granted rediscovered the importance of the horse. In the Indian Ocean, the *Sydney* was sunk with all hands. Colin was not among the Australian troops who fought and died in Crete and Africa but there was talk of another threat closer to home.

With so much catastrophe in the world Bella's inheritance seemed too trivial to worry about but to her it was not trivial at all. It was due on her twenty-first birthday and with the war on she worried whether she would ever get it but it seemed Australia was in what they called the sterling area so it was all right. She had opened an account at the bank in Wyndham back in 1938 and notified the executors of the earl's estate and the money turned up on schedule: a minor miracle, in the midst of war. She wrote to them to confirm receipt, in the same way she sent Christmas cards every year to her father and mother, but she never heard from any of them. With the state of the world she supposed that was hardly surprising and what she would do with the money now she had it she had no idea.

With the news consistently bad, Garth and Bella shut their ears to what was happening and got on with their lives. Cattle and the weather: cool, then hot and humid, the air like a damp sponge.

Making love in the Wet, Bella felt like a damp sponge herself. There was still pleasure and a deep fulfilment in the act but no sign of a baby. It bothered Garth more than Bella.

'Getting old,' he said. 'That's the problem.'

'You could have fooled me,' Bella said.

'We're not talking about sex,' he said. 'I guess my fertility's shot.'

'You're forty, so stop talking nonsense,' Bella told him. 'You're a young man still.'

She didn't care one way or the other, but it was what Garth wanted to hear, so she said it. As for her own feelings... She supposed she wanted a child, but it didn't fret her. What was the point? It would come or it would not. In the meantime life, and death, went on.

There was no shortage of death. The Japanese were in the war now. Even the United States had joined in, courtesy of the attack on Pearl Harbor. The war was getting closer. Hong Kong fell. Malaya. Singapore. The Dutch East Indies.

They rode into Wyndham for supplies: what they could get, with rationing now in force. They stopped off at the pub for a beer, if you could call it that.

'More piss than hops, I reckon,' said Garth.

Not that it stopped him swilling it down.

They chatted with the locals: no joy there.

'Some o' them islands is only a few hundred miles from Australia, for God's sake,' said Old Man McMurtrie. He was over eighty but knew his subject: he had spent years on a trading schooner in the archipelago.

They did not talk about the war on the way home, but each was wondering.

Japanese forces landed in New Guinea and pushed south. Soon the only obstacles between them and the Australian mainland were the Owen Stanley Range and a bunch of Aussie conscripts, poorly trained and armed, at the end of an excruciating jungle path called the Kokoda Track. There was talk of evacuating the northern part of Australia.

'Over my dead body,' Garth said.

Bella supposed it might come to that for both of them, if the Nips gained a toehold.

Colin was overseas somewhere; they didn't know where. At least he hadn't been swept up in the debacle of Singapore.

A Japanese submarine penetrated the defences of Sydney Harbour. It was sunk, but for it to have got so far south made you think. The war teetered on a knife's edge.

And then a miracle. Against all odds, the Aussie heroes of Kokoda held firm. The half-starved Japanese retreated. Between one day and the next the shadow of invasion was lifted from the land.

'Now we got 'em,' Garth exulted. 'There'll be no stopping us now.'

He was right. Where before there had been nothing but catastrophe, now the news was good and getting better by the day.

Victories in New Guinea, El Alamein, Stalingrad. All over the world, Japanese and German forces were in retreat. Things were looking up.

On the fourth of September 1943, troops of the Australian Ninth Division landed east of Lae, one of the last Japanese strongholds in New Guinea, and were attacked by Japanese aircraft.

* * *

Garth had been away three days on round-up. Bella had a stomach bug and stayed at home. She was repainting the kitchen when she heard the toot of a horn.

One of the side effects of the war was that the government had at last driven roads through the bush. Built so that troops could be rushed into the area if the Japanese invaded, they remained in use even after that threat had receded. The maintenance was kept to a minimum and in the Wet they were always having problems with wash-aways, but the locals had discovered the benefits of having the roads and joined together to keep them patched up.

It meant they could now look forward to a regular mail service. The red van fought its way through to Miranda Downs once a fortnight.

'Never brings anything but bills,' Garth complained.

Today, however, it brought something else.

Bella went out with the cup of tea she always had ready for Syd the postie when he arrived.

It was a beautiful spring morning, with the cry of a kookaburra bubbling in the distance and sunlight dappling the ground beneath the trees. Mitch, her bull terrier, looked up from his favoured resting spot beneath the pomelo tree and wagged his apology of a tail.

'What a lovely day!' Bella cried.

Then she saw the expression on Syd's face.

'What is it?'

Silently he held out the brown envelope. She looked at it and everything stopped. The kookaburra was silent; the creek was frozen in its bed; even Mitch's tail was still.

Envelopes like that contained telegrams, and they both knew what telegrams meant.

Movement returned to the world. The kookaburra's call tailed off. Bella's hand went unconsciously to her throat. She looked at Syd's troubled eyes.

'Come three days ago,' Syd said. 'I'm that sorry, Bella.'

The envelope in Bella's hand, so light a gust of wind could have blown it away, was heavy with the sorrows of the world.

'Best open it, I suppose,' she said.

Syd stood helplessly. There was nothing he or anyone could do.

The envelope was addressed to Garth but Bella had always believed that trouble must be confronted head on. If she left the envelope for her husband it would make no difference to the contents, but its unspeaking presence would haunt her unbearably until he came home.

She took a deep breath. With an abrupt jerk of her hand she tore the envelope open. She pulled out the telegram.

Her mind snatched at anything, however implausible, that might offer a reprieve from the news she dreaded. Perhaps the message was to say that Colin had been wounded. Or was unexpectedly on his way home. Perhaps it was about something else entirely.

Mouth dry, she unfolded the flimsy sheet and read the message printed on it.

We regret to inform you…

She looked up with stricken eyes. Syd was watching her apprehensively. Of course he knew; from the first, they had both known.

'Colin has been killed,' she said.

'I'm sorry,' he said.

So was she. She was devastated: as though she had lost a child, even though he'd been a year older than she was. Far worse than her pain was her dread of the impact it would have on Garth. To lose his only son…

For the first time she wished they had a child of their own. Not to compensate, nothing could do that, but at least it would be *something*.

'They say where?' Syd asked.

'It says Lae. Wherever that is.'

He shook his head; he had never heard of it, either. It made the news even more terrible, that Colin should have died in a place of which neither of them had heard.

'It'll hit Garth hard,' Syd said. 'Tell him I'm sorry, eh.'

After he had gone she took the empty teacup into the house and put it in the sink. The house seemed twice as empty as a quarter of an hour ago. She walked into Colin's room, looked at the few books, a photograph of his mother on the shelf. A piece of pink crystal. A penknife and other odds and ends: not much to show for twenty-five years of life.

And now someone or something had killed him. In Lae. A place of which she had never heard.

How do I tell his father? she thought. How do I comfort him?

Garth came home three days later. It had been hard going but they had brought in three hundred head and he was in good spirits. Until he saw her expression.

'What is it, Duchess?'

Silently she held out the open telegram. He took in what it was and she saw the blood leave his face.

He read it and let it drop to the floor. For a minute he stood in silence, shoulders hunched, staring at nothing, then turned abruptly and went out of the house. Bella almost went after him but at the last moment did not. She was there for him, would give him whatever comfort she could, but until he turned to her... She had come to love him, she believed, which made it doubly hard to do nothing, but this was something Garth must deal with himself.

She watched him through the window. He walked like a blind man, groping, then disappeared into the shed where they kept their spare harness. Blue, his heeler-cross and the only dog truly personal to him, came around the corner of the shed and went in after him. She wondered how dogs could sense these things but hoped with all her heart that the animal would be able to provide the man with some measure of comfort.

Garth stayed in the shed for the rest of the day and all that night. Bella was beginning to wonder whether she should go to him, after all, when he emerged and came back to the house. He was calm but the news had aged him and for the first time Bella saw what he would look like when he was truly old.

He looked at her silently. She did not speak but went and put her arms around him. He did not reject her, neither did he respond. He stood. Presently he said:

'I think we might squeeze in one more muster before the Wet.'

'May I come with you?'

'I was hoping you would.'

'The man who died…' In accordance with custom, Maisie did not speak Colin's name. 'You got a shirt you can let us have?'

Bella looked at her: wrinkled, black and old.

'Why do you want it?'

'You'll see.'

That night the Miranda Downs people came to pay their respects. The whole camp, men, women and children, sat in a half-circle on the ground in front of the house. Bella watched through the window as they placed the shirt on the ground and lay on it, one by one, before returning to their circle.

'What are they doing?'

'Custom,' Garth told her. 'If he had died here they would lie on the body, showing they wished they could bring it back to life.' He sighed. 'I had better get out there.'

'Should I come, too?'

'You stay here.'

She obeyed because of the gravity of the ceremony and the fear that she might inadvertently damage it in some way. She knew that much knowledge of their beliefs and customs would always be denied her because she was a woman, or outside the kinship system, but insofar as it was possible she was resolved that this would be last time she would be shut out from whatever it was permitted for her to see.

Garth went out and sat with them as they buried the shirt in the dirt. Afterwards they placed the cut branches of trees in a circle around the spot, to signify that Colin had died as a warrior. A little later, without sound or ceremony, they went away.

Respect had been paid.

Two days later they rode out. Everyone in the district knew about Colin; even O'Malley had ridden over to pay his respects. Garth barely spoke. To begin with the team took their lead from him and

for the first two days were uncharacteristically quiet, hardly a word
between the lot of them. The dogs foraged as always; the cattle were
as full of fire. Dust clouds, gold-glinting in the spring sunlight,
rolled across them as they wrestled recalcitrant bulls to the ground,
branding irons were heated and thrust home in an acrid stink of
burnt hair and hide, and the ground shook with the thunder of
stampeding hooves, yet for those first days the muster had more the
feeling of a wake than a round-up.

That is what it is, Bella thought: the affirmation of the life and
future of Miranda Downs, which Colin would have inherited. Now
Colin was gone yet the land, with its dust and droughts, violent
downpours and floods, its times of coolness and breathless heat, was
eternal, as life was eternal. That was what this unscheduled muster
was about: the reaffirmation of life in the face of tragedy, the refusal,
always, to admit defeat. And she knew that slowly, as perhaps Garth
had foreseen, the land would reassert its power. The sense of loss
would never disappear but now the first shock was past it became
easier to bear and, by the time they returned to the station, things –
at least on the surface – were more or less back to normal.

'And we gave ourselves another two hundred and fifty head,'
Garth said. 'A bonus!'

It wasn't much, perhaps, but a start. And in the awakening of
new hope Bella did something she had not dared do for the eight
days of the muster: she went to her husband, put her arms around
him as she had when he had first received the news, and kissed him.

He had been smiling as he watched Blue roll in the dust to celebrate his return home. Now his smile faded and he kissed her in
return. 'Dear Bella. You are a true wonder to me. I dunno where I'd
be without you.'

'I love you,' she said.

Her smile was radiant, because it was true. She had married him
out of desire and a need for security, knowing no other way to
guarantee her future in this place she had come to love. They had
been married almost four years, and they had been good years. He
had satisfied her physically; she had been able to put her stamp on

the house and perhaps the property; she had become able to think of it truly as her home: but Garth – this belligerent, piratical man of furies and unexpected tenderness – had remained her friend and partner, a companion of whom she had been fond, but no more. Now she realised that the tragedy had changed that, that what had been expedient had become sincere, that artifice had become reality, that in sharing her husband's suffering she had discovered a new depth to their relationship, a truth and beauty whose existence she had never before suspected, containing in its heart a promise of fulfilment beyond anything she had imagined.

Two weeks later Miranda Downs had an unexpected visitor.

Billy Gould was one of the first outsiders to use the new road. He did not come into the house but stood and talked to Garth for ten minutes before heading out again.

Garth came indoors and threw himself down in an easy chair.

The homestead was vastly different from what it had been when Bella had first arrived. The concrete floor had been covered with pine planking, stripped and pegged to fit snugly around the walls and then polished. In one of the sheds she had discovered a side table that had belonged to Garth's father and that she suspected might be a real antique: even Chippendale, perhaps, like much of the furniture at Ripon Grange. This table, glossy with polish, now had pride of place against the wall facing the entrance. There were curtains in the windows and pictures on the walls. Much remained to be done but it was now at least half-civilised. As Bella said, the fact that they lived in the bush did not mean they had to live in a tip.

Garth never said much but didn't object, either, which Bella knew was probably as close to approval as she would get.

Now she looked at him. 'What did he want?'

'You should have come out to speak to him,' Garth said. 'He's close to being family, after all.'

'I was busy.'

Billy Gould was certainly not family but an enemy who without provocation had tried to destroy her marriage.

'He came to say how sorry he was to hear the news about Colin,' Garth said.

'He drove all this way to tell you that?'

'He said he knew we hadn't always seen eye to eye in the past. He said he was sorry for it.'

'He tried to ruin our marriage.'

'Forgive and forget,' Garth said. 'What's the point in having enemies?'

Bella was not in the business of forgiving or forgetting.

'Hold your friends close but your enemies closer,' she quoted. 'He came for a reason.'

'Because of Colin's death.'

'Another reason.'

Billy Gould, she told herself, was a man to watch.

There were times when Garth fell silent, and once she surprised him sitting quietly on the bed in what had been Colin's room.

'You all right?'

'I'm fine,' he told her, although his expression told a different story.

On the whole, though, he came to terms with it pretty well. It hit Bella, too: harder than she would have expected. Colin had never been a mate but his death had left her diminished, all the same. She felt such sorrow for a young life cruelly extinguished – for Garth – even for herself. No man is an island... How true that old saying was.

She walked around the horse paddock, up and down the landing strip, but found no consolation. War, she thought. How can men be so foolish?

It was in those dark days that she found a friend.

Old Maisie, who had asked her for one of Colin's shirts, had been born in the Pilbara, as had her ancestors for thousands of years. She was illiterate and her eyes contained all the sorrow and wisdom of the world. She said little but held Bella in her skinny arms until Bella's sense of futility and loss turned slowly to acceptance.

CHAPTER TWENTY-FOUR

It was August 1944 and Bella was reading the paper when Garth came into the house.

'Anything interesting?'

'Mostly stuff about the war.'

'Spare me.'

These days the war news was uniformly good but by now everyone was sick of the endless bloodshed, wanted only to hear that it was over at last.

'There is one interesting item, though. It says Doug Galloway is closing his meatworks.'

Garth scratched his chin; they had dealt with Galloway's, strategically located on the Wyndham waterfront, for years. 'I don't like the sound of that. If it closes, the Wyndham works will have a monopoly. That'll push down prices, for sure. Does it say why they're closing?'

'He's seventy next month and has no one to leave it to.'

Because Doug's son Angus had been another victim of the war.

'What'll happen to his workers?' Bella wondered.

'They'll have to make the best of it, like us,' Garth said. 'Could be a good little business for the right bloke, though.'

Bella watched through the window where Winifred, the tame wallaby that the year before she had rescued from her dead mother's pouch, was playing a violent game of pounce with Mitch. 'I sometimes wonder how those two don't kill each other,' she said.

'Talking of Wyndham,' Garth said, 'I've a list of things I need for the workshop, next time you go in.'

'I'll go tomorrow,' Bella said. 'I need to buy stuff for the kitchen, anyway.'

Restricted by rationing, she did what shopping she could; restricted by supply shortages, she bought Garth's appliances for him; she went to see the accountant who handled their tax assessments; and she paid her regular monthly visit to the bank. Finally, after one more visit, she drove home.

Garth was hammering away in the workshop. She did not want to disturb him so waited until he had come in and washed the muck off his hands before she sat him down at the kitchen table with a cup of tea and a large envelope full of papers.

He looked at the envelope, then at her. 'What you got there?'

'Galloway's accounts for the last three years.'

'Galloway's accounts... What are you up to, Duchess?'

'I've spoken to the accountant and the bank manager,' she said. 'I've been to see Doug Galloway at the meatworks.'

'Why?'

'It occurred to me,' she said, smiling sweetly at her lord and master, 'that you might want to put in an offer for Galloway's business. Only if you think it's a good idea, of course.'

'I don't know anything about running a meatworks. Neither do you.'

'Doug's foreman has been with him twenty years. He knows everything there is to know about it. Most of the others are long-time workers, as well.'

'Doug Galloway's a tough old bastard,' Garth said. 'He'll want an arm and a leg for that plant.'

'I know what he wants,' Bella said.

Garth stared. 'You mean he *told* you?'

'Of course he didn't tell me.'

'Then how can you possibly know –?'

'He's an old man, alone in the world. His wife's dead; his son's dead. He wants out. He's put out a few feelers, the accountant says, but no one's interested, the market being what it is.'

'So why should we get involved?'

'Because once this war is over meat prices will go through the roof. Everywhere people are starving, Garth! And we can afford it, which the majority can't.'

'We can afford it, you say?' Garth smiled ironically. 'How did you work that out?'

'Own the works, we get our beef processed for nothing. That's a massive saving, right there.'

Garth was willing to listen, which was more than he would have done once, but Bella knew she still had to cosy up to him if she wanted him to agree.

'When you first mentioned it, I thought it was a brilliant idea,' she said. 'So, as I was going to town anyway, I thought I might as well poke around, see what I could find out. It's your plan,' she said earnestly. 'I wouldn't dream of interfering, but I thought it wouldn't hurt to make some enquiries.' She gave him an anxious look. 'I hope that was all right?'

'My plan? Where did you get that idea?'

'Oh yes, Garth, it was definitely your plan. I remember you saying what a good business it would be, for the right bloke.'

He went to interrupt but she put her finger to his lips.

'Your very words, Garth! A good business for the right bloke. I would never have thought of it, but when you said that, I thought how right you were –'

'Spare me your nonsense,' Garth said. 'It never entered my head and you know it.'

'But now that it has,' Bella said, 'what do you think about it?'

'I think we should forget all about it and stick to what we know.'

Such a demure smile! 'Whatever you say, dear,' Bella said.

That night, as they lay side by side in bed, Bella flopped on to her side, then back again. She sighed.

'Are you restless?' Garth asked.

'I was just thinking…'

'Thinking what?'

'What you would consider a fair price for the meatworks.'

It was Garth's turn to sigh. 'I haven't given it a thought, girl.'

'Because, if someone else bought it, might we not end up having to pay more to have our animals slaughtered? Instead of getting them done for nothing?'

'I also think it might be a good idea to sleep on it,' Garth said.

'You're right,' she said, smiling in the darkness. 'As always.'

Having set the hook, Bella slept.

The next day, with the early morning sun puddling the ground outside the window, she found Garth studying the copies of Galloway's balance sheets on the kitchen table. She said nothing but busied herself getting breakfast with Mary, the young Aboriginal woman who gave her a hand about the house.

'You say he definitely wants to sell up?' Garth said, chewing on his morning steak.

'I only know what it said in the paper. Plus what he told me, of course.'

'But you think –'

'He wants out? Yes, Garth, I do.'

'If it was your decision, what would you offer him?'

She was shocked. 'It's not my decision. It's yours.'

'I said if. Theoretically speaking?'

'I'd pay him a lump sum for the buildings and equipment – not much, mind – and a lifetime annuity, based on last year's results.'

'Last year's figures are way down.'

'I know,' Bella said.

Half-frown, half-smile, as he studied her across the breakfast table. Bella nibbled a piece of toast.

'I'm beginning to think I've underestimated you, all these years,' Garth said.

She agreed with him but knew better than say so. 'I'll be happy to give you moral support, but I think you should do the negotiations. Don't you agree?'

Garth looked uncertain: an unfamiliar look, for Garth.

'Perhaps you're right –'

'What I could do,' she said quickly, 'is draw his fire, so to speak. If I talk to him first, we've always got a let-out, haven't we? Because naturally I'll need your okay on any agreement. He'll expect that.'

'Naturally it has to be my decision,' he agreed. 'But he's not going to give it to us, is he? What do we use for money?'

'There's my inheritance,' Bella said.

They talked first to the bank manager, then to Anderson the accountant. The plan had then been to go together to beard old Doug Galloway in his lair at the meatworks he had run for forty-seven years, but at the last minute Garth remembered a meeting he positively had to have with Mike Rogers the vet.

'An hour?' he said.

'Should be ample. Then you can say yea or nay.'

Bella walked into Galloway's office.

He gave her a keen-eyed look from beneath sandy eyebrows. 'Your husband no' with you?'

'I'm so sorry. It was a last-minute thing, but he had to speak to the vet about something. He'll be along later.'

Galloway looked relieved. Not surprising; he'd probably never had to deal with a woman before.

She had thought she might be nervous, but was not. Far from it; she relished the challenge. Perhaps Garth is not the only one to have underestimated me, she thought.

'If it's all right with you, Doug, I thought we could have a chat while we're waiting? If that's agreeable? To establish the guidelines?'

'We can always talk.' A Hibernian smile. 'Talk's free, ye ken.'

'So it is,' Bella said. 'I was wondering what you felt would be a realistic price for the equipment?'

'Ye'll find the value set out in the latest balance sheet. If you're no' familiar with accounts, perhaps I can explain the figures –'

Bella chuckled: all mates together. 'Those are tax figures, are they not? I was thinking of their true value.'

'That is their true value to me,' he said.

'But not to us,' Bella said.

'Which is?'

Such an apologetic smile! She named a price. Diffidently.

'Ridiculous!' he said.

'Well, of course,' she said. 'Naturally, if he thinks my price is too low, my husband may over-rule me.'

'Nae doot,' Galloway said.

'Or if he thinks it's too high.'

'Too high?' A stuck pig could not have screamed more shrilly.

'The market value depends on the market, does it not? And for the moment we are your only market.'

'I could never accept such a figure,' Doug said.

'What figure might you accept? Theoretically speaking?'

'The figures are in the balance sheet.'

'Oh dear.' Bella stood up. 'If I hurry, I may be able to catch Garth before he leaves the vet, save him having to traipse up here.'

'Or mebbe a little lower,' Doug Galloway said.

'I suppose we might be able to squeeze another thousand,' Bella said. 'Though I don't know what Garth will say. He's not that keen, you see.'

'Make it fifteen hundred.'

Such an apologetic smile! 'I daren't go one penny over twelve fifty. My husband, you see...'

'Then there's the goodwill,' Galloway said.

'I was thinking perhaps an annuity?'

By the time Garth arrived, twenty minutes later, there was nothing for him to do except say yes. Naturally he would not do that.

'It's a matter of principle, you see,' he told Doug Galloway. 'Mate, I think you'll have to shave your price on the equipment. By say two fifty?'

Bella congratulated him all the way home.

'I'm feeling pretty smug about it myself,' he confessed.

Such an admiring smile! 'A masterstroke! Two fifty off the price? I would never have dared suggest it,' she said.

'It takes a man,' Garth said.

In October, a month after they had finalised the deal on the meatworks Garth came into the house one morning and found Bella standing stark-naked in the bedroom and examining herself in the mirror.

'What the hell you playin' at?'

She grabbed her shirt and put it on.

'Just looking.'

Garth had become philosophical about his wife's crazy ways. He put his hands on her shoulders.

'Take it off, then. Let's all have a look.'

'In the middle of the day? Oh no, Garth, I couldn't do that.'

'You weren't so particular once.'

He tried to remove the shirt but she resisted him, protesting loudly until at last he gave up. He stared at her as she buttoned the shirt, hiding her nakedness.

'I've never known you prudish before,' he said.

'I'm not! Truly I'm not!'

'Could've fooled me,' said Garth.

'It's just that –'

'What?'

'I suppose I'm just not in the mood,' she said lamely.

'And my mood has nothing to do with it?'

But smiled as he said it, so Bella saw that it was all right. Emboldened, she laughed, too.

'Nothing to do with it at all!' she said.

'I am too easily bullied,' he said sadly.

She laughed again, in part at the idea of anyone bullying her husband, but also because inside she was overflowing with joy.

She decided not to tell him yet. He might be the sort to expect her to sit around all day doing nothing, and she couldn't bear the thought of that. But there was another and more important reason. Events after Colin's death had brought home to her the reality of her love for her husband, but it was too soon for her to have grown into full acceptance of it. She wondered sometimes whether *his* feelings for *her* were as strong. With Garth, not a man to parade his emotions, it was hard to tell. How would he react to his wife waddling round, blowing out like a barrage balloon, for the best part of a year?

Plenty wouldn't like it, she thought. And Garth, praise be, was a lusty man. Perhaps he would think the baby an intrusion, so soon after Colin's death. Or welcome it, for the same reason.

No, she thought, I'll not tell him. Not yet. But supposed she ought to think of some excuse to get into Wyndham, to see the doctor.

That night, as though to make up for her reluctance that morning, she sent the unspoken signals common where there is true affection between wife and husband and he responded, taking off her clothes with a queer, stilted gallantry so unlike his normal ways, while she waited unmoving, closed eyes and thundering heart, until at last the final garment fell to the floor and she embraced him with a ferocity that he had not known in her for several months.

The war in Europe ended in May 1945. Bella was delighted – who wouldn't be? – but had more immediate concerns. Her baby was due on the ninth of June, or so said Doctor Page at the Wyndham hospital. Garth had acquired a second-hand truck and their petrol ration would just about get them there so, on the first of the month, Bella found herself bouncing along the deeply rutted track into town where she would stay until the baby was born.

They had considered alternatives.

Doctor Page, an enthusiast for new techniques, had mentioned induction, a new and so far seldom-tried procedure. Garth had

vetoed it; no one was going to use his wife as a guinea pig to check
out untested theories.

Bella favoured having the baby at home.

Garth stared. 'You crazy?'

'Old Maisie will take care of me.'

'She's not a midwife!'

'She's had nine of her own. She knows what to do.'

'She might not be willing.'

'She is. She told me so.'

During the years since her arrival at Miranda Downs Bella, step by
cautious step, had grown close to Maisie and several of the other
women. In that time they had travelled from a state of mutual sus-
picion through a period of appraisal to the final stage, the acceptance of the good faith of each other.

'First time any white woman want to study our ways,' Maisie
had said.

'You are of the land,' Bella had told her. 'As one day I hope I shall
be also. I am glad to be taught what I am permitted to know.'

When acceptance came it did so with a rush. She sat with them
as they laughed with her and joked. She often did not understand
the detail of what they were saying but the sense of welcome and of
being a part of the whole was unmistakable and suffused her spirit
with light.

The high point came when Maisie invited Bella to observe the
ceremonial greeting of the ochre-painted young men, the *marlulu*,
when they returned from their travels during the first and public
stage of their initiation process.

'It is permitted?'

'The greeting stage, yes. The boys have been to gather a mob to
help in the initiation. Now they come back to say farewell to the
grieving families, the *karnku*. This all can see. But afterwards boys go
away to private place to learn secrets. No woman permitted there.'

So Bella watched as the young men returned, ochre-painted, each
with a wooden club in hand. She saw how the initiates sat briefly in

the laps of those to whom they were saying farewell and what might have been ridiculous became a moment of reverence and mutual respect. With every moment Bella felt more and more strongly that she was indeed standing with one foot in the unknown. This was mystery and at the same time awareness. Awareness of the earth, the sacred earth, and of the people of the earth. It was a privilege to be there and to be instructed in a way of living that had been old when the Pharaohs ruled in Egypt.

It was an experience that united Bella not only with the people of the ceremony but with the land itself, and she knew she had been changed thereby. She bent and gathered dust that she rubbed into the palm of her hand. This she had come to late but it was part of her now as she was part of it. She and the land had become one. Maisie was watching her and Bella saw that she understood how the ceremony had affirmed her place in Miranda Downs, that this country was no longer merely the place where Bella lived but had become, now and forever, her home.

'Of course Maisie can handle it,' Bella said.

But Garth was not persuaded. 'And if anything goes wrong?'

'There's the Flying Doctor Service.'

Garth would not hear of it. He was not going to hazard the lives of his wife and unborn child to flatter the ego of an old Aboriginal woman, no matter how many kids she claimed to have had. The hospital it was. For once Bella let him over-rule her.

'Now we've got the road, it's a pity not to use it,' Garth said. 'I'll tell you something else. Once petrol rationing ends, we'll be trucking the cattle to the meatworks instead of driving them. Think of the time that'll save.'

Even with Bella ready to pop, work and cattle were never far from Garth's mind.

Bella was feeling like a load of cattle herself by the time they reached town. Granted the state of the track, it was a mercy they had gone in when they did.

'Any later,' Bella said, 'I'd probably have dropped it on your feet.'

As it was, she had to wait. And wait.

The ninth came. The tenth. The eleventh.

Garth, back at Miranda Downs, was on the wireless and getting more frantic by the minute.

'What's going on?'

His voice was barely audible through the static.

'Not a lot,' Bella told him.

'How're you feeling, Duchess?'

'Like an elephant.'

'I'm beginning to think that Doc Page don't know what he's on about.'

Bella smiled apologetically at the doctor, who was listening from the other side of the table.

'He knows exactly what he's on about.'

'And when she's had it,' said the doctor, just to show Garth he had overheard his last remark, 'I'll patch her up as good as new, no worries.'

'Make sure you do. And you,' Garth said, presumably to Bella, 'look after my boy, you hear?'

The static took over.

It began that night.

To start with it was nothing but the hours passed and the pain grew worse.

You will not cry out, Bella told herself. You will not make a fuss. But in time she couldn't manage it.

There was a nurse, and the doctor. And the pain, circling her and periodically...

'Oh,' Bella gasped. 'Oh dear God...'

'There's my brave girl,' said the nurse.

Bella did not feel in the least brave. She felt helpless, a prisoner of a body whose endless contractions she should somehow control but could not. 'Is this going on forever?' she cried.

'There's my brave girl,' said the nurse.

The nurse's round, red face came and went, came and went. The pain savaged Bella, eased, only to savage her again. Each spasm was worse than the last. Excruciating pain owned a world in which Bella was alone.

The nurse's face peered down at her. She was smiling, caring, concerned. Yet could not know what I am feeling, Bella thought.

She was crying out now, no longer caring if the birth *killed* her as long as it was over. As long as there could be an end to pain.

Until at last the nurse began to move with greater purpose, grasping Bella's sweating hands, and Bella, panting, knew things must be coming to a head. Jaw set, teeth locked, every atom of her being combined to expel this *thing* that was waiting, poised. Because everything was flowing at last, and with a supreme effort she felt herself victorious, overcoming both pain and herself as the child slipped away from her.

Look after my boy. You hear?

That had been Garth's last message. Well, Bella thought some hours later, cradling the new arrival with wonder and apprehension, you can't win them all. Because the baby was a girl.

She had a round face, wispy brown hair and her unfocused eyes were the palest blue. She looked like no one Bella knew; no doubt that would change as she grew older.

She named her Peace. It seemed appropriate, with the war over at last. Who could say what real peace she would know in her life? Not too much, Bella hoped. She wanted no more fighting and killing – who did? – but there would be challenges in the baby's life, as there were in everyone's, and she must be up to handling them. Bella's hope was that Peace would have the guts to fight for what she wanted. To fight and win, as Bella had done. As she planned to do all her life.

'Life is a great adventure,' Bella told her daughter, 'and we have a lot of living to do.'

Her body was still sore but she felt exhilaration as she looked down at the baby's head peeping out from the shawl in which the nurse had swathed her. She was sure there would be many problems ahead but did not care; she welcomed them with open arms.

'We shall fight them together,' she told Peace. 'We shall fight and we shall win. Because life is fighting.'

Yes, she thought, to fight and win... How could it be anything else, if fulfilment were to be found?

The baby's full name was Peace Jenny Miranda, after her two grand-mothers. Peace Jenny Miranda Tucker.

'A big name for such a little creature,' Bella said.

But it was clear the baby would not be little for long; already she was growing: sideways as well as upwards.

'A bit older, she'll be quite sturdy,' Garth said.

'Not too sturdy, let's hope,' Bella said.

Peace had the voice to go with it, too: piercing, endlessly demand-ing. The voice of a fighter, Bella thought. One who would never know she was beaten. She told herself she was pleased although there were nights when, sleepless, she could barely endure the aggressive way the brat tugged at her already sore nipples.

Fortunately that time soon passed; Bella hoped she had her share of maternal fondness but, anxious to get out and about once more, had no desire to continue the messy and uncomfortable business of breastfeeding a moment longer than she must. Uncomfortable *and* restricting: because, let's face it, the baby was a tie: although she was careful to keep such thoughts to herself, for fear of upsetting her husband.

Garth treated the child with a sense of wonder that touched Bella's heart, but – like most men – didn't know how to handle her.

'It's easy,' Bella told him. 'You hold her like this. See?'

Yet somehow Peace always ended up hanging upside down in Garth's awkward arms.

'You're hopeless,' she told him, but spoke affectionately; at least he'd been willing to have a go.

Certainly he was fond of the child, which was what mattered. If he was disappointed that Peace was a girl he showed no sign of it. In any case, he soon had cause for renewed hope.

'I don't believe it!' Bella said. 'Nothing for five years, then two, one right behind the other.'

Because, sure enough, she was pregnant again. She was pleased, of course she was, but exasperated, too.

'It is so *restricting*,' she told Mitch the bull terrier. 'No sooner over it than the wretched business starts all over again.'

Mitch was a handy confidant; she could say nothing to Garth, who was over the moon and assumed she was, too.

'This time I shall have my baby at home,' she decided.

A week later Garth went for a ride.

'Where are you going?' Bella asked him.

'Nowhere in particular.'

'Don't be late. I've got barramundi for tea.'

She had been into Wyndham that morning. One of the blessings of the new road was this ability to drive into town when she had enough petrol and bring back fresh food, even saltwater fish, which would have been an unimaginable luxury in the old days.

She watched him spur away past the creek and into the scrub. He was riding faster than was safe in that country but he was the best rider Bella had ever known so his speed didn't worry her. Other considerations did. He had told her he was getting old. He was forty-five, hardly ancient in physical terms, but she knew that age was as much in the mind as anywhere else. Garth's father had died young and she thought he was capable of doing something crazy, just to prove he could still do it. Like riding off at sunset, knowing he would have to come home in the dark.

'Men,' she told the advancing shadows. 'Why do they always have to prove how tough they are?'

She heard a full-throated bellow from the bedroom. Peace was awake: hungry as always; demanding attention as always. At six months she was the spitting image of Garth, in attitude if not in looks.

'Two tyrants in one house,' Bella said. 'Heaven help me.'

Her nipples throbbed. They knew all about it.

An hour later Garth was still not back.

Bugs were banging against the outside of the windows as Bella went to the screen door and looked out. It was pitch dark, the bush rowdy with the sawing of cicadas. A half moon shone intermittently between the breeze-shivered leaves but under the trees its light would be almost non-existent. What was keeping him?

She went back into the kitchen. The fish was ready, the stove at just the right temperature, but the barramundi was delicate; cook it too soon and it would be like leather.

She told herself he would be back when he came, but it was no use. She poured herself a drink but didn't touch it; she would wait until Garth was home again.

She looked at her watch. An hour and a half now.

Her nerves twitched. Should she go and look for him? She remembered Colin riding off in a rage and Garth saying there was no point searching for him in the dark, yet she could not sit here indefinitely and do nothing.

'Another fifteen minutes,' she said to the empty room. 'Then I'll look for him, dark or not.'

The fifteen minutes passed. She could bear it no longer. She had just called Maisie to look after Peace when she heard a whicker and the soft thud of hooves.

Thank God!

Until she went out to greet him and realised the stallion had come back without its rider. No doubt about it now; Garth was missing.

It took her five minutes to saddle up and whistle for Garth's dog. She thrust the shirt that Garth had been wearing earlier under Blue's nose.

'Find the boss,' she said. 'Find him.'

She rode out, Blue questing ahead. It was impossible to ride fast; in the shadows the darkness was absolute and where the moonlight shone through the leaves the jumbled pattern of black and white confused rather than guided. Soon they were climbing. This was the way Garth usually came, to the bluff with its views to the distant hills. He had told her he had come here for days at a time after his first wife died. He had come after Colin's death, too.

As she climbed, the trees fell back. The ridge was a blaze of silver light. The Aborigines disliked coming out at night for fear of Bima, the spirit woman whose infidelity had brought death to the world. That was why Bella had not asked them to join her; she was confident Blue would find him, if he was there to be found. Anxiety gnawed, just the same, as they climbed. What would she do if...

'No,' she told the darkness, swallowing her fear. 'We shall have no ifs here.'

They were halfway up the ridge when Blue, circling on either side of the almost-invisible track, began to bark. Bella was out of the saddle in a wink and running to where the dog was baying on the edge of a patch of shadow. They had found Garth. He was conscious but unable to move.

'Thank God,' she said. 'How are you?'

'I've busted my bloody leg,' he said.

'Let me see.'

She felt with both hands. The thigh bone felt all right but when she explored below the knee...

'Bloody hell, woman!' Garth said, panting. 'You trying to kill me, or what?'

This was the second time she had crouched beside a man who had come off a horse.

'It's broken all right,' she said. 'I could feel the bone.'

'Now she tells me. What kept you so long, anyway?'

Garth was weak and in obvious pain, yet still managed a grin. Old not-to-be-beaten Garth. Bella was caught halfway between laughter and tears.

'Had to pretty myself up first,' she said. 'Have to look good for my old man.'

Such nonsense things to be saying to an injured man on a bare mountain. Such important things.

She had remembered to bring a flask of brandy with her. 'Have some of this.'

He swigged a healthy mouthful.

'Leave some for me,' Bella said.

'You're not the wounded hero,' Garth said.

And gulped another mouthful before she could snatch the flask back.

'Hero? Is that what you are?'

'Something like that.'

'A real hero would have crawled back. Saved me the trouble of coming out in the dark.'

'I'm not that heroic,' Garth said.

Although he did a pretty good job – not even a squeak as she levered him up. His arm draped around her shoulders, with Blue dancing anxiously about, she led him hopping up the slope to the horse waiting on the track.

How she got him into the saddle Bella never knew but somehow she did, then took the bridle and led horse and rider back down the hill. When they got to the homestead she told him she was driving him to the hospital in Wyndham.

'What's wrong with the Flying Doctor?'

'In the middle of the night? In any case,' she told him, 'they're only interested in serious cases.'

Garth was indignant. 'If your leg felt like mine you'd think it was serious enough.'

'Ah, but it doesn't, you see. I don't fall off my horse.'

She still didn't know how it had happened nor did she care. Her heart was dancing because she had found him and he was safe: that was what mattered. Or would be safe, once she got him to hospital.

She eased him into the ute.

'You stay there,' she told him. 'I'll check on Peace, but she should be right until morning. Then I'll be with you.'

'Waste of petrol,' Garth said. 'I'll be coming home again directly.'

The hospital had news for him. They kept him in a month, because the leg was slow to heal. They said Garth was the worst patient they'd ever had. Given a choice they'd have chucked him out weeks before, but until the leg came right he was going nowhere.

'You'll have to do the first muster of the Dry without me,' he said. 'Reckon you can manage?'

Some questions did not deserve an answer. Two weeks later she was back.

'How did it go?' Garth asked.

Like a dream would have been the truth but Bella was too wise to say that. 'It would have been much better with you.'

'No trouble from O'Malley?'

'He was keeping his eye out for us, especially along the Archer Ridge. He had his boys everywhere.'

'He say anything?'

'"I'm keeping my eye on you, Mrs Tucker…"'

'What did you do?'

'I fluttered my eyelashes at him. "I'm honoured," I told him.'

Garth was delighted. 'You never!'

'He was so horrified he rode off and left us to it. That wasn't the end of it, either. There were a hundred cleanskins in a draw. Could have been ours, or his. No way to know. So I waited until he was gone and then…'

'Yes?'

'We drove them down the hill into Miranda Downs.'

Garth said later it was that news, more than anything else, that put him on his feet again.

As the time drew near for the birth of her second child, Bella made her plans. Unmoved by Garth's protests, this one really would be born at home, with old Maisie doing the necessary.

'I am fit. I am strong. What could possibly go wrong?'

Nothing did. Whether having it at home made any difference was unlikely, but on the fourteenth of August 1946, two days after Bella's own birthday, the baby was born at Miranda Downs without incident and with little of the pain she had experienced before.

Bella would have liked to call him Garth-Charles: Garth for his father, Charles for her lost love, but she knew Garth would never permit his son to have a poncey, double-barrelled name. She compromised by calling him neither Garth nor Charles, but Richard. Garth didn't care; he was a boy and thriving; that was what mattered.

Even the breastfeeding seemed easier, this time round.

CHAPTER TWENTY-FIVE

Below the house a small stream zigzagged between a complication of tiny hillocks, marsh and dense bush until it reached Saurian Creek. The creek had been named by Garth's father for the crocodiles that had inhabited it when he had first arrived at the newly acquired Miranda Downs, back in the 1880s. The crocs were mostly gone now, although one occasionally ventured up from the Carlisle during the Wet, and that was enough for Bella to warn Peace not to play in the creek during the rainy months.

To five-year-old Peace, prohibition was another word for challenge, and challenges were not to be denied.

One day she sneaked out when no one was looking and wandered down to one of the little streams that flowed into the creek. She was not heavily into reading yet but liked looking at the illustrations in books, particularly children's How to Do It books which were just coming back on to the market after the war, and had come across one showing how to construct your own mud dam.

It wasn't much of a stream, not more than two feet wide, but it was gently flowing, with muddy banks and a sandy bed. It might have been designed for the purpose. Peace, crouching amid reeds and in no time up to her ears in mud, set to work. She used a flat stone to excavate a diversion, watching with fascination as the water wormed its way with increasing confidence along its new channel, creating tiny earth islands that were quickly inundated by the rising flood. She piled mud in a wall across the stream's main bed, blocked off the diversion and sat observing as the water returned to its proper course. She patched the odd leak that appeared in the mud wall. The level of the stream rose while Peace stared, enchanted by what she had achieved. The wall did not last long; the water pressure grew too great and within minutes it had been breached. Soon the whole structure had vanished but in Peace's mind it remained as an enduring source of wonder, because for those few minutes she had changed the face of the land.

It created in her a sense of purpose that, allied to her successful defiance of Mother's authority, brought an awareness of her own power that would remain with her always.

A year later, two weeks after her sixth birthday, Peace started at the school in Wyndham that had been set up to cater for the needs of the Outback kids. They stayed at various boarding houses around the town during the week, parents dropping them off first thing Monday and collecting them Friday afternoon. It was the first time most of the new pupils had been away from home and some were tearful and homesick but Peace had as much brass as a band and took it all in her stride.

Just as well, because from the first she fell foul of her teacher. Mrs Barker was well intentioned but had her ways, one of which was to assume that none of the new children could read or write. With many of the kids this was correct, but Peace could do both, an inconvenience that Mrs Barker seemed to think came close to insubordination. Certainly she had no intention of allowing Peace's unexpected literacy to change her routine, so for the first week, until Bella collected her on the Friday afternoon, Peace sat while Mrs Barker explained in excruciating detail the intricacies of a children's basic reader, page one of which contained in block capitals the words *PAT SAT IN A PIT*, with a coloured drawing showing a child, presumably Pat, and the sandpit in which he was sitting. Peace did not try to hide her boredom, an attitude that had her standing in the corner two days into her first week.

'It's stupid,' she told Bella when she picked her up on the Friday afternoon. 'I'm not going back.'

'Yes you are,' Bella told her.

It was an argument that Peace had no hope of winning but something happened in the second week that gave her hope that things might not be too bad after all. She made a friend.

Charlene Ludwig was as tough as teak, a year older than Peace. She had been brought up hard, and it showed. From her Peace learnt a number of useful tricks: how to steal, although never from her mates; how to lie without the lie showing in her face; how to eat her fear so that no one knew how scared she was.

'They must never see you're afraid,' Charlene counselled her.

One day they were confronted by Willy Brown and his mates, and Peace observed Charlene put her advice into practice. Willy was eight and big for his age, with bright red hair, a pale skin blotched with freckles and red-rimmed, piggy eyes. He was a bully, and had two followers very like him. They had a cocky way of strutting about, their scowls terrorising children smaller or weaker than themselves, and they thought they owned the world.

They watched as Peace and Charlene approached.

Both girls were carrying the little cases that were the standard issue at school. Peace was no softie but she was a realist; there were three boys, all older and stronger than they were, and it was hard to see how two girls could hope to get the better of them, but Charlene marched on without a pause. Willy stood waiting but Charlene did not hesitate. She walked right up to him as though he were not there at all. At the last moment Willy stepped in front of her, forcing her to stop. Peace, walking just behind her friend, saw that Willy was a good head taller than she was.

'Where you think you're goin'?' Willy said.

Charlene looked up at him. 'Wha'?'

'You stupid or somen?' Willy leant down and yelled, right into Charlene's face. 'I said where you think you're goin'?'

Exactly what Charlene had been waiting for. She did not speak but leant back on her heels, swung her hard case horizontally and caught Willy a tremendous clout above his eye.

Willy staggered back, hands to his face, blood welling between his fingers. Peace thought Charlene would take off but she did not. She stood her ground, the case swinging easily from her hand, and it was Willy who backed away: one step, a second, then turning and running. The mates ran with him. When they were at a safe distance they turned.

'I'll getcher fer that,' Willy yelled. 'See if I don't.'

Charlene knew better. 'Not him,' she said contemptuously. 'He's yellow. We'll have no more trouble from him.'

She was right. From that day on, Willy Brown kept out of their way. Charlene was a good teacher in other ways, too. She taught Peace not only how to look after herself but what was valuable in life and what was not. You stood by your mates, no matter what, and you never told the authorities anything.

Peace always reckoned she learnt more from Charlene Ludwig than she ever did from Mrs Barker.

CHAPTER TWENTY-SIX

It was a brilliant June day, just after Peace's seventh birthday, the last day of the school holidays, and Bella had been expecting Garth and Peace since mid-afternoon.

Tomorrow Bella would be dropping her off at the start of the new term and today, as a farewell treat, she had finally yielded to her daughter's pleading to go with the father she worshipped to collect cattle from a fenced stock camp five miles up the Tait River valley.

A mob of cleanskins had been brought in a week earlier for branding and tagging before being loaded for delivery to the meatworks. Some of the young bulls in particular would be as wild as tigers, as liable to charge as run the other way; getting them into the trucks might be a tricky business but Peace had been on at her for months and Garth had promised to keep an eye on her.

'She's only seven,' Bella said.

'If she's going to be a cowgirl,' Garth said, 'she has to start learning some time.'

Bella wasn't sure she wanted Peace to be a cowgirl, although she seemed a more likely candidate for life on the land than Richard, who showed signs of being studious by nature. But cattle and dust lay at the root of their life in the Pilbara and the child couldn't be protected from them forever.

Garth had recently picked up a high-axle jeep fitted with a bull bar in front of the radiator, so provided Peace stayed in the vehicle she should be safe enough.

'Just don't let her ride on the bar, okay?'

The hands balanced on the bar and jumped off when they needed to throw an animal for branding. It was a trick Peace would want to copy, but what was jake for a seasoned man was not for a seven-year-old.

'Stop fretting, Duchess.' Garth was fifty-two but still strong, and his blue eyes laughed at her. 'I'll look after her, no worries. We'll be home before you know it.'

With tea nearly ready, she left it to Mary to finish off and strolled up the track to meet the boys on their return. She enjoyed the walk. Her days were so full of things that had to be done that she barely had time to notice their passing. It was good to have time to breathe for a change, to think where she was in her life and what the future might hold for them all.

She loved her life on Miranda Downs: she had a good husband, two wonderful children and few financial worries. There were days when her heart swelled with gratitude at the blessings life had brought her. She still found herself missing Charles Hardy and knew she always would, but the intensity of her feelings was less than it had been once. There were times when she wondered what her life would have been like had things worked out differently but there were also weeks on end when she did not think of Charles at all.

There were other days, though, when restless Bella found herself needing more than she had. What that might be she had no idea, but knew only that she was thirty-three, there was a challenging world out there, and time was passing her by.

She had turned the renamed Tucker Meatworks into a highly profitable venture, but that was no more than an appetiser. It was not the end but the beginning: of what she was not sure.

She was a mile from the house when she saw the jeep. It was coming fast, bucking and lurching, and Bella knew the driver must have his foot flat on the accelerator. Something had to be wrong. Her breath froze in her chest.

The jeep skidded to a stop in a cloud of dust. Garth's haggard face stared out at her.

'What's happened?'

'Peace has had a fall. I'm going to radio the Flying Doctor.'

'What sort of fall?'

'Not good.'

Fear was one thing; having it confirmed was infinitely worse. Not Peace! It could not be!

'Where is she?'

'On the back seat.'

So she was. Bella flung herself into the vehicle.

'Get on with it, then!'

Garth slammed it into gear and roared away as Bella turned to look at her child. Peace was unconscious, her forehead a mass of blood. Crippled by fear, Bella turned to glare at Garth.

'Tell me what happened.'

'She fell, hit her head.'

The jeep was bucking as it screamed down the track. Garth would have them over if he wasn't careful, but Bella didn't care about that. The only thing that mattered was her child.

'Fell?' Bella had to yell to be heard above the engine's roar. 'How could she fall out of the jeep?'

'She wasn't in the jeep. She was on the bar.'

She had known it. Peace had been hurt, perhaps killed, by someone's stupidity. Her mind threw up every barrier against it, but it was no use. Terror remained, despite her efforts, and, with terror…
Rage, black and overwhelming.

'What was she doing on the bar? I told you –'

I shall kill whoever did this to her.

She was filled with a savagery she had not known she possessed, yet she meant every word.

With unnatural calm she said: 'Who was driving the jeep?'

'Ringer.'

A new hand, with a reputation as a tearaway.

Why was Ringer driving? Where were you when it happened?

Answers were needed but could wait; what mattered now was to get back to the house as fast as they could, radio for help and hope all would be well. Hope and pray.

Garth skidded to a stop outside the homestead door. They eased Peace out of the jeep, carried her indoors and put her on the settee. Garth began to gabble on the radio while Bella looked at her daughter.

The blood on her forehead came from a gash just above the hairline. Bella wanted so much to take Peace in her arms but did not dare. It was killing her to be so helpless. The child was breathing but how badly she had been hurt she had no way to know.

Garth got off the radio.

'Well?'

'They're sending an aircraft from Wyndham.'

'How long will it take?'

'They said they'll be here as soon as they can.'

They stared at each other, besieged by the ghosts of what might be. Bella could have screamed at him but did not: they had to support each other, not have a row that would serve no purpose.

'Tell me what happened.'

'I don't know. I had to give the boys a hand and I told Ringer to bring up the jeep. He must have let Peace ride on the bar. The next thing he'd hit a pothole and she was flung off.' He clenched his fists. 'He's finished here.'

Bella closed her eyes. 'Never mind Ringer! It's Peace we have to worry about.'

Richard was suddenly there.

'Why's Peace not moving? What's wrong with her head?'

'You get off out of it!' A sudden bellow from Garth. 'Don't come in here, okay?'

Bella went to the child at once. 'Come with me, darling.'

She took him out. He was in tears but Bella did what she could to console him.

'I wasn't doing anything –'

'I know you weren't. But Daddy's worried.'

'What's wrong with Peace?'

'She fell over but the doctor's coming.'

'Will she be all right?'

A smile was hard to find but Bella managed. 'She'll be fine.'

Pray to God.

The plane arrived: a two-seater Cessna, with barely enough room for the stretcher. Bella watched, Richard clutching her hand, as the men carried Peace to the plane and loaded her in.

'I must go with her,' Bella said.

'No chance,' the pilot said. 'No room.'

'Of course I must go.'

'See for yourself.'

It was true. It was impossible to get another adult in.

'But why such a small plane?'

'Only one available.'

'Where are you taking her?'

'Fitzroy Crossing.'

'Isn't Wyndham nearer?'

'No emergency department.'

She needed to be with her child, yet could not. It made despair a thousand times worse.

'How is she?' she asked, hoping for assurance.

'She's crook,' the orderly said. 'Hopefully she'll be okay. We'll let you know.'

They were gone, Bella feeling they had taken her heart with her.

She had to talk to Garth but not yet. Now she needed to be alone. She walked away from the house, going nowhere. Every joint ached; her mind's anguish had spilled into her body. Her open eyes saw only darkness. She crouched on the ground, away from everyone, her head on her knees as she rocked back and forth in a paroxysm of despair.

This must have been how Mumma felt when she packed off her only child to Ripon Grange, Bella thought. Although even Mumma had not had the terror of a possible death hanging over her.

There was a wind gusting in the trees. The branches creaked. The leaves hummed their dirge. A dirge for the dying?

Bella did not think she could bear it. Such promise to be destroyed. A life cut short by her stupidity. She had allowed Garth to over-persuade her. She had said no, the child was too young, it was unsafe... But she had let Peace and Garth talk her round. She knew that Garth, too, would be suffering but for the moment her heart had no room for any grief but her own.

Peace, her own dear Peace.

She could not even weep, her tears dried up by the flames of her remorse. She was alone and desperate. She was not a weak woman, yet she would willingly have died at that moment, had it been possible.

Here Maisie found her. She did not speak; words were futile. Instead she sat beside her for a while before taking Bella's head in her soft hands and cradling it to her breast. The two women sat silently, until at last the tears came.

'Okay, missus,' Maisie murmured over and over. 'It's okay, missus.'

Simple words to express comfort. They meant nothing. Yet later that night, when Garth came running to say that he had just heard on the radio that the child was out of danger, it was as though a promise had been fulfilled.

Bella looked at him, barely daring to hope.

'She'll be all right?'

'She'll be fine.'

More tears, then: the easing of anguish, Bella and Maisie weeping together, their arms about each other.

Bella thought she would never be able to repay her friend, who had come to her in her agony. Who had said it would be okay. Who, frightened of the night and its spirits, had nevertheless stayed with her through the long hours.

'Thank you,' she said, over and over again. 'Thank you. Thank you.'

And kissed her and went back with her to her place and waited until she had gone inside before returning to her own house more exhausted than ever before. She sat with her husband, sharing a drink with him before bed. Garth knew she had not been there for him but that did not matter. Neither had she blamed him as she might have done. He said nothing but helped her into bed and lay unmoving at her side. Until she turned and kissed him passionately, and tried to smile, and finally fell asleep with his arms about her.

It was a week before Peace was fit to come home. Bella had driven over to Fitzroy Crossing and stayed with her while she recovered. It had been a bad knock but the doctor said she would make a complete recovery.

'At that age kids bounce,' he said. 'Don't try it yourself.'

They drove back together, taking it easy. When they got home Peace hopped out of the car and looked around her with a pleased expression.

'When can I go on another muster?' she asked.

CHAPTER TWENTY-SEVEN

'Damn this bloody leg!' said Garth.

It still troubled him but Bella knew that was not the true reason for his bad temper. He was only fifty-two yet his body could no longer do all the things he demanded of it. It made him mad, and when Garth was mad he took it out on the whole world. Not that she let him get away with much.

'It's not my fault you came off.'

Eventually, when she'd had enough of his foul temper, Bella decided she must do something about it.

When petrol rationing had ended back in 1950 Garth had bought a Cessna 140 to replace the much-mourned Minnie. Now it was April 1953, with his birthday coming up.

'How are we going to celebrate?' Bella asked her husband.

'We're not.'

That she had expected but Bella was in the mood for adventure and would not let it go.

She kissed him. 'You'll be fifty-three. Of course we must celebrate.'

'I'm old and lame. Worn out, for God's sake. What's to celebrate about that?'

'The fact that you are still alive,' she said.

Again she kissed him. And a third time. They were in the bedroom, so the rest was easy.

'There you are,' she said later. She started to get dressed. 'Not bad for such an old man.'

'I dunno what got into you,' Garth said.

'You should,' she told him. 'Unless you're losing your memory, too.'

At least she didn't have to worry about falling pregnant. She loved her children with all her heart but without discussing it with her husband had decided after Richard's birth that two were enough. She had spoken to Maisie about it and Maisie, an authority in what she called women's business, had told her what she needed to do. So far it seemed to be working.

'Was that the celebration you had in mind?' he said.

'That was special,' she told him. 'Thank God it always is, but no, I was thinking of something different.'

'Like what?'

'Like an adventure.'

On the twelfth of April, the day before his birthday, they flew back to the Carlisle River, where in 1939 Bella had asked Garth to marry him and he had accepted. She had found enough space in the cockpit for two extra items: a tin containing a birthday cake, which Garth was supposed to know nothing about, and a collapsed inflatable dinghy, complete with paddles, about which he had complained vociferously from the moment he had discovered her real plans.

'Downstream in a rubber dinghy? When we know nothing about the river or the rapids or anything? Are you crazy?'

'It'll be fun,' Bella said.

'We may not be able to land,' Garth warned. 'We don't know what the country is like down there.'

They knew there were mountains; the Hamersley Range contained the highest peaks in Western Australia. Asbestos was mined

there, and there had been rumours of gold, but for the moment
they had no interest in the Hamersley. It was the unknown country
this side of the range that Bella wanted to explore.

They followed the river until they found a patch of level ground
on the bank east of the mountains. Here they camped overnight.
In the morning they inflated the dinghy, grabbed the paddles and
the folding trolley they would need to get the dinghy back to the
aircraft and took to the water.

At this point the river flowed fast, with many rocks and rapids
in the gorges, but they avoided the worst of them and made good
progress. The water was slate grey, with spectacular rock formations
along banks that rose so high overhead that all they could see of the
sky was a narrow strip of light far above their heads.

Garth watched Bella staring up at the passing cliffs. He thought
how young she looked. She'd had two children yet looked hardly
any older than when he'd married her thirteen years before. Somehow, by instinct or artifice, she always made their lovemaking a
feast of the unexpected, a never-ending source of joy. It wasn't that
they experimented with anything new, but it was the *way* she did
it that made the difference. It was not only in bed that she had this
effect on him, either; in so many ways she made him feel younger
than he was. Take this trip. If it had been up to him he would never
have done it, yet now he was enjoying it. She had added an extra
dimension to his life.

Bella frowned, and pointed up at the cliff. 'What's that red stuff?'

At this point a break in the eastern wall of the canyon allowed
the sun's rays to penetrate, and he saw a reddish-brown band in the
granite. It was several feet wide, dipping occasionally to water level
but for the most part running parallel with it. He stared in disbelief.
The band grew wider as the current carried them downstream. At
times it was one-third the height of the cliff, and continued as far
as he could see.

Garth sat back on his heels. His mouth was dry, his heart racing.
'It's hematite,' he croaked.

Bella remembered the rusty-coloured piece of rock on the table in Garth's mineral room. He had called that hematite and said it was the pride of his collection.

'It looks very pretty,' she had said.

'Never mind what it looks like,' he had said. 'It's what it contains that matters.'

Now he gripped her hand. 'There it is! I've found it at last!'

'Gold?'

'Iron.'

'Oh.'

It was hard to get excited about iron. Now if it had been gold... A hundred years earlier people had been picking nuggets off the ground, but nowadays riches were not so easily found.

Except that Garth *was* excited. He wriggled about so much she had to laugh.

'You'll have us swimming if you don't watch out!'

He subsided, yet excitement continued to froth. 'I knew it had to be here somewhere...'

He had told her so in Charters Towers.

'Well done,' she said indulgently.

She thought he was crazy to get so excited over something that – surely? – could not be that important. She'd read somewhere that iron was the most common mineral on earth. So what if they'd found more of it? She supposed it was a victory of sorts, like rustling O'Malley's cattle, but what did it mean? Their lives would go on as they always had, focused on cattle and dust. All the same, she was pleased for Garth's sake. He had always said the ore was there; the authorities had said it wasn't. It was gratifying to be proved right. She smiled and put her hand on his arm.

'Happy birthday, darling,' she said.

When they got back to Miranda Downs Garth went straight to his mineral table, which they had moved into what had been Bella's room. She gave him five minutes, then followed him. She found him turning his prized chunk of hematite in his hands and muttering to himself.

'Come and have a slice of birthday cake,' she said. 'Then you can tell me what all this means.'

But he could not control his excitement and the words burst out of him, with crumbs, before he was halfway through the cake they had never got around to eating on the Carlisle.

'I always knew it had to be there somewhere,' he said. 'The trick was finding it.'

'What we've seen today: is it a big find or not?' Bella was feeling her way.

Garth looked at her. 'We followed the river downstream for – what? – five miles?'

'About that.'

Certainly her feet had known all about it by the time they'd got back to the Cessna.

'And there was no sign of the seam petering out?'

Garth was tossing the hematite sample in his hand.

'It was getting wider,' she said.

'That's right.' He pondered. 'I think this could be really big. Huge.'

Bella had thought the find meant nothing but now she began to wonder. If it was indeed huge, it might put a different complexion on their discovery.

'When you say huge, what do you mean? Hundreds of tons? Thousands?'

He looked at her. 'Try millions.'

'Millions of tons of ore?' It was hard to comprehend. 'What's it worth?'

'No way to be sure until we know how far it goes. But I guess we'd be talking in the tens of millions.'

'Tens of millions of pounds?' Bella thought: This must be what it feels like to have a heart attack.

'Almost certainly.'

'Who owns it?'

'Whoever claims it.'

Now she was aroused, too: not by the simple joy of discovery or the prospect of riches, but by the challenge the find represented. Buying the meatworks had taught her that she had an unsuspected business flair. Development of a new mine would be on a vastly different scale but that made it even more exciting. She thought it was possible that no woman had ever done such a thing. No doubt the world would laugh at her for even thinking of it, but what a wonderful achievement it would be if she could prove the world wrong!

'What do we do about it?' she said.

She sensed the excitement go out of him. 'We can't do anything. Mining iron ore is prohibited. We can't even peg the claims.'

It was like being offered a lolly and having it snatched away again. 'I don't understand.'

'Iron is a strategic material. The federal government believes there's very little iron ore in Australia so no one's allowed to export it. The state government even forbids prospecting or the pegging of claims.'

'So what we saw today –'

'Stays where it is. We can do nothing about it.'

Bella was not a woman to be beaten so easily. 'I don't think I accept that,' she said.

'What do you have in mind?' Garth said.

'I think we should buy a house in Perth.'

Garth frowned. 'Why would we do that?'

'We'll need a place when the children go to school.'

'That won't be for a while yet.'

'Not so long,' Bella said. 'Peace will be eight in June. And land prices are rising. Besides…'

He looked at her cautiously. 'Besides what?'

'You've just told me this discovery could be worth tens of millions?'

'It would have to be assayed, to find out what the mineral content is. Then the area would need surveying –'

'But it would still be worth millions?'

'Definitely.'

'And the only thing standing between us and those millions is the law?'

'That's right.'

'And the laws are made by politicians?'

'Of course.'

'How do you feel about all that wealth lying there and being unable to do anything about it?'

'I hate it, of course –'

'Chews holes in your guts, does it?'

'It certainly does.'

'So we need to change the law.'

He was struggling to keep up but her agile brain was taking her further and further ahead of him.

'How do we do that?' he said.

'We spend time in Perth. We entertain, sweet-talk the pollies, help the ones who have influence –'

Garth was listening now, all right. The discovery had galvanised Bella. She had never been one to let the world go by, but now she was on fire. Finding the hematite had opened the door on depths that neither of them had suspected.

'We tell them there are huge deposits of iron in the state, how iron will make Western Australia the economic leader of the country. We say how the law is the only thing holding the state back. That, if only the government had the vision to change things –'

'So they repeal the law –'

'And we peg our claims,' said Bella.

'And then? We shall need equipment, transportation, development. We're talking huge investment here. Millions –'

'But at the end of it, it will still be profitable. Right?'

'Of course. Hugely profitable.'

'Then let's take it one step at a time. Besides, that's what banks are for, isn't it?'

CHAPTER TWENTY-EIGHT

Bella stared at the Chinese capital from her hotel window. Dusk was falling but arc lamps had been set up on the building sites and work was still proceeding at a furious pace, clouds of dust blowing everywhere on the gusting wind.

Yes, she thought as she remembered what she had said to Garth, that was exactly what banks were for. And to act as traps for the unwary.

Three days had passed since her meeting with Comrade Fang. They had visited the Summer Palace and the Forbidden City. They had ridden in a dragon boat; they had been to the Wall and climbed a section of it, but Bella was no tourist. Worried what other devilment Pete Bathurst might be plotting, she wanted to finish her business here and get back to Australia, but she was in Comrade Fang's hands. Every day Su-Ying warned her against impatience. Very well; she would wait as long as it took.

The phone rang.

'Hullo?'

A man's voice: sibilant, clipped, formal.

'Comrade Fang wishes resume discussion at nine this evening. It is convenient?'

Bella remembered the advice Su-Ying had given her. 'I regret that will not be possible. Please give Comrade Fang my apologies. May I suggest nine tomorrow morning?'

'One minute...'

Bella waited, phone pressed to her ear, watched leaves blowing on the autumn wind along the hotel drive, where lights on suspended wires were shining at intervals.

'Comrade Fang will expect you in his office at two-seventeen tomorrow afternoon,' the caller said.

The call was disconnected. Slowly Bella replaced the receiver.

Two seventeen tomorrow afternoon... The precision of the new schedule signalled Fang's displeasure at her rejection of his original proposal. She, too, was uneasy, but remembered Su-Ying's words.

'The Chinese are a very symbolic people. If you agree too easily, they will think you are weak. You must make them understand that discussions must be between equals. That way things will go better.'

Bella thought, I hope you know what you're talking about, daughter-in-law.

She closed her eyes and thought about the coming meeting. The first had meant nothing; a simple getting-to-know-you session. Tomorrow would be the one that mattered. She decided that tonight the three of them would have dinner together. Su-Ying would order the food and they would talk about the meeting. Talk very cautiously, she thought; the dining room, like the bedrooms and telephone, was almost certainly bugged. If they needed to discuss anything especially sensitive, they would go for a walk.

One thing they would not discuss at all was what they would be willing to accept and what they would not. Not because of possible eavesdroppers but because Bella, never the democrat in matters of business, would decide.

Bella ran a bath and eased herself gratefully into the warm water. No, she was not a democrat but knew how to appreciate the value of those around her, particularly the members of her family, because they, much more than Tucker Mining or Miranda Downs, were the true measure of the future. She stretched out luxuriously and thought about what she liked to consider her legacy.

Peace the mining engineer, bossy, belligerent, capable of being both wonderful and abominable as the mood took her. Staff feared her; Richard often resented her. Peace was a brilliant administrator but so far had shown little of the diplomacy that the top job required.

By contrast, Richard was a natural diplomat but lacked his sister's drive. To this day Bella doubted he would ever have proposed to his wife had Bella not pushed him into it.

That would have been a tragedy, because quite apart from how happy they had made one another Su-Ying – Chinese educated, former student at the University of Western Australia, her father once again a senior official in China's government – was a treasure, her slender body concealing a will of steel. Facing the prospect of what looked like make-or-break negotiations, her contribution during the next few days would be invaluable.

When Bella was dressed she picked up the phone and asked to be put through to her son's room.

'We are summoned to a meeting at the ministry,' she said. 'Two-seventeen tomorrow afternoon. I think we should have dinner together tonight and talk things over.'

Bella would decide, but getting other people's opinions never hurt.

The car was waiting before they had finished lunch. Siren howling, the driver got them to the ministry by two-fifteen; agitated officials scurried them into Comrade Fang's office on the tick of two-seventeen.

Where they were left to cool their heels for ten minutes.

More gamesmanship, Bella thought but said nothing; Su-Ying had warned her that this office, too, was almost certainly bugged.

When Comrade Fang arrived he brought a file of papers, an interpreter and a contemptuous expression. He did not speak but slammed the file down on the desk.

The Chinese are a very symbolic people, Su-Ying had said.

Comrade Fang's discourtesy, so different from their first meeting, was therefore part of the act. But to what end?

He spoke angrily. The interpreter said:

'Comrade Fang insist you explain how company intend to honour commitment to Chinese government.'

He glared as though he hated them with all his soul but as a child Bella had been intimidated by experts and was not to be terrified now.

'There is enough ore at the Carlisle Mine to satisfy all China's needs,' she said. 'Bulk carriers are available –'

Fang interrupted in a furious burst of Mandarin.

'Bulk carriers not issue,' the interpreter said. 'Chinese government demands you explain how Tucker Mining intends to deliver ore to carriers.'

'By rail. There is no other way it can be done.'

'And you have no rail link.'

'We had an understanding with BradMin –'

Comrade Fang was shouting, clenched fist pounding the surface of his desk, the interpreter's face expressionless as she translated.

'You have no agreement. Comrade Fang say you undertook delivery of twenty-five million tons of iron ore a year knowing you had no way to honour that undertaking. You deliberately concealed –'

Bella Tucker was no more to be shouted at than intimidated. 'The memorandum of understanding states very clearly that delivery is conditional upon the availability of a rail facility –'

'Which you do not have. Which you have never had.'

'That was why we were negotiating with BradMin –'

'Which owns only rail line that can convey ore from Carlisle Mine to coast.'

'At present that is correct,' Bella said.

'Our information is that BradMin not permit Tucker Mining to use that line.'

'Negotiations are proceeding. We have made a fresh offer –'

Fang shouted over her.

The interpreter said: 'Comrade Fang say BradMin not plan to give Tucker access to rail line. Never!'

'Never say never,' Bella said.

Fang stared at her for a full minute. Her stomach churning, Bella forced her face to remain tranquil as she returned his gaze.

Contemptuously he threw a few words at her and stood up.

'Comrade Fang say nothing more to discuss,' the interpreter said. 'Nothing!'

Fang walked out, leaving the interpreter to gather the papers off the desk and scurry after him.

'And now?' Richard said, after a moment's silence.

Bella remained calm. Comrade Fang had not said discussions were finished. Despite his posturing, a deal might still be possible to enable her to salvage the dream that had been part of her life for so long. She followed the instinct that over the years had seldom let her down.

'We shall return to the hotel,' she said. 'And wait.'

CHAPTER TWENTY-NINE

'Two hundred and fifty acres?' Garth said. 'I thought you wanted a house, not a farm.'

'I want to create a favourable impression,' said Bella.

'Two hundred and fifty acres of scrub and a weatherboard house,' Garth said. 'Some impression.'

'But I have plans,' Bella said.

She spent days with architects, landscape gardeners, engineers, interior designers. Plans were produced and rejected. More arrived, to be rejected in their turn or discussed, modified, set aside for further study. Budget estimates were prepared; accountants shook their heads dubiously.

The planning took a year but Bella revelled in the problems. One by one her will overcame them. Every day was full of excitement; she had never known such purpose and determination.

'This will be the finest estate in Western Australia,' she declared.

She even had a name for it: Desire.

Garth studied the drawings and shook his head. 'You are planning a palace,' he objected; the idea of so much luxury made him uncomfortable.

'We want the law changed. To do that, we have to impress the men who make the laws. Nothing impresses them like wealth.'

'The rate you're going, we're more likely to be bankrupt,' Garth said.

'All in a good cause,' she told him gaily. 'How many millions did you say were in the ground up there?'

'It's not ours, not yet.'

'That's why we're doing this. So that it becomes ours.'

That wasn't her only reason. She was recreating the identity in which she had grown up and whose home was Ripon Grange. She had rediscovered the world in which luxury was taken for granted.

'We shall be rich!' she said.

She had never given a thought to riches or power, but now the prospect beguiled her. Mumma had told her to be a woman who did things rather than have things done to her. Now, with good fortune and determination, she might be about to follow that advice.

Garth washed his hands of Desire, its walls beginning to rise out of the raw earth. 'I'm a cattle man and prospector,' he said. 'I'll never be smart enough for this place.'

In any case, there was more to be done up the Carlisle River. He had discovered that surveys of the area had already been carried out. The reports made dismal reading. 'They say there's nothing there.'

'We saw it, didn't we?' Bella said. 'What have they done? Flown over it.'

'They've also got experts and the latest scientific instruments.'

They took it up with the Canberra Bureau of Mineral Resources but had no joy there, either.

'They say we're talking through our hats,' Garth said when he got the bureau's reply. 'There've been several surveys, some by the government, others by mining companies, and none of them came up with anything. Their instruments showed no variation at all.'

'Are you saying we never saw what we saw?'

'I'm telling you what's in the letter.'

'What you need to do is go in with an expert and have a proper look. Then we'll know what's really there.'

Garth knew it made sense, yet to take into his Outback some scientist with a string of letters after his name... 'What the hell would he know?'

It went against every instinct and, when he heard the fee Saul Rich was demanding, he became even more hostile to the idea.

'What's he trying to do, buy the whole field?'

The way it turned out, things were not as bad as he had feared. Saul was an American but proved the sort of companion any man would choose to take on a trip into the Outback. A mining consultant, certainly, but also a human being with a keen eye for the beauties of the Australian bush. He was young, tough, resourceful, with a pragmatic approach to the law that endeared him to Garth at once.

Garth explained that what they were planning was, strictly speaking, against the spirit of the regulations imposed by the state government that prohibited prospecting. It didn't faze Saul one bit.

'It'll be a pleasure to disregard such a stupid rule,' he said. 'Almost a duty, one might say. In any case, who said anything about prospecting? We're out here, two friends innocently enjoying the scenery.'

He certainly loved what Garth was showing him. 'A great country,' he said. 'A man can breathe out here.'

'Don't you have open spaces in America?'

'Not where I come from.'

'And where is that?'

'New York City,' he said.

They had flown in on the Cessna, with every square inch taken up by the trappings of Saul's trade.

'You really need all this junk?'

'This is only half of it. I shall need you to go back for the rest.'

'How long do you expect us to stay out here?'

'For you, just as long as it takes to show me what you found.'

'I'm not paying you five thousand quid for that,' Garth said. 'I already know it.'

'Sure you do. That's just the start of it. You show me, then you get the hell out and leave me to do my job.'

'And if I want to stay?'

Saul shook his head. 'I don't work like that.'

'How do I know you'll be straight with me?'

'You don't,' Saul said. 'But that's the way it is.'

'Take it or leave it?'

'You got it. But there is one thing I shall want you to do when I've finished the ground work.'

'Which is?'

'I want you to rig a camera on the Cessna, then we'll fly over the area I've examined and take photographs.'

'How long's all this likely to take?'

'Could be two weeks, I guess. Maybe three. Assuming there's anything to see. Drop by in two weeks, I'll tell you if I've found anything.'

'It's there,' Garth said.

'We'll see,' Saul Rich said.

Garth fetched the rest of Saul's equipment.

'How's it going?' Bella asked.

'Bloody delivery boy, that's me,' Garth said.

Banished from his own mining site and driven mad by the frenzied comings and goings in Perth, Garth flew north. To see, as he put it, whether Miranda Downs was still there. It was and he even managed to squeeze in another muster before he headed south again.

Saul Rich had set up his camp ten miles from the original site and Garth had to circle for several minutes before he found a safe place to land. It made him mad. Safely on the ground at last, he marched purposefully towards Saul, who was watching him from fifty yards away. When he was halfway he began to shout. 'What the hell have you moved here for? For a minute I didn't think I'd be able to land at all.'

'Good afternoon to you, too,' Saul drawled. 'A great day, is it not?'

Garth succeeded in controlling his fury although both men knew it would take little to set him off again.

'I asked what you were doing here?'

'What you are paying me for. Seeing what lies under the ground.'

Garth became aware of a pattern of holes that Saul had drilled across the open ground, each with a small red flag flying from it.

'As far as this? It must be ten miles, at least.'

'It is twelve miles and a third. And I moved here because it is too far to walk from the original site.'

'You're not telling me you've found ore here as well.'

'No, sir. I am not telling you that. I am telling you nothing. But if you would care to come back in one week's time, I should be able to let you have my report. One week, Mr Tucker. Not a day before.'

'What's it looking like?'

Saul smiled and shook his head. 'One week, Mr Tucker.'

Garth could have hit him, except it would have served no purpose. Instead he eased his feelings by punching the fuselage as he climbed aboard.

Once he reached altitude he looked back. Saul Rich was walking purposefully from one flag to the next, completely oblivious to his recent visitor.

A week later, to the hour, Garth was back.

This time Saul had packed up his gear and was waiting for him. It was a hot, dry day with a light wind scouring veils of dust from the parched land. Garth helped Saul stow as much of his equipment as the plane would hold.

'Now I suppose you'll tell me I gotta come back for the rest of your junk,' Garth said.

'Yes sir, that is exactly what I am telling you.'

'Bloody hell!'

There was a mahogany box the size of a small briefcase that Saul would not relinquish, even when Garth tried to take it from him to put aboard the plane.

The consultant said nothing, even after they were strapped in again, the door closed and the aircraft taxiing.

That's it, then, Garth thought. He's found nothing. Five thousand quid down the gurgler and nothing to show for it.

He waited until the Cessna had gained altitude and was settled on its southerly course. Saul Rich scratched his neck, looked out of the window at the dust-veiled ground two thousand feet below and whistled softly to himself.

I was a fool to think I knew more than the experts, Garth thought. How could I, with all their experience and equipment?

He didn't want to hear what the consultant had to tell him but supposed he might as well get it over with. Then they could put all this nonsense behind them and get back to something he understood: cattle.

'I thought you wanted aerial photographs,' he said.

'I guess they won't be necessary, after all,' Saul said.

That was it, then.

'So tell me the worst.'

'I'll be sending you my formal report later,' the consultant said. 'When I get back to the office.'

'Give me the gist now.'

The plane yawed and lurched in an air pocket before steadying. The miles unwound below them. The empty land, smeared in dust, stretched away, vast and inscrutable.

'I'm not sure what to tell you,' Saul said.

Garth's nerves, already wound tight, quivered. He said: 'After three weeks you still don't know? What the hell am I paying you for?'

For a moment Rich did not speak. Instead he snapped open the lid of the mahogany box he was cradling in his lap. He took out a large test tube containing what looked like crumbly yellow cake.

'That's what I found. I took samples at one-hundred-foot intervals all over the area and everywhere came up with this.'

'What is it?'

'It's what they call marra mamba.'

'Not iron at all?'

'Oh yes, it's iron.'

Garth threw a quick squint at the contents of the tube.

'Looks like you could crumble that stuff between your fingers.'

'You could, indeed. Marra mamba is very soft.'

'Can you produce steel from it?'

Saul Rich whistled softly beneath his breath and again stared out
of the window. 'That is the hundred-dollar question,' he said.

'Stop playing games,' Garth snapped. 'Is it any good or isn't it?'

His impatience communicated itself to the controls. The plane
swayed and dipped before he brought it back to an even keel once
more.

'Most people will tell you that marra mamba is useless. The fool's
gold of the iron ore world, if you will.'

'Most people,' Garth repeated.

'Personally, I have my doubts. That was why I said I was not
sure.'

'How do we find out?'

'I shall take these samples to a laboratory. I know the people
there. They will carry out a spectrograph analysis –'

'Never mind all that,' Garth interrupted. 'Will it tell us whether
it's any good or not?'

'It'll tell us the mineral content of each sample, and the level of
impurities such as sulphur. By analysing these samples, taken right
across the field, we shall get a fair idea what we've got here.'

'And what we haven't,' Garth said grimly.

'Exactly. Say,' Saul said, his eyes once again fixed on the land
below them, the veils of glinting dust, the dried watercourses like
sinews against the brown, 'isn't that just the most wonderful view
you ever saw?'

* * *

It took a week for the lab report to come back. Saul Rich phoned with the news.

'I got the figures.'

'Well?'

'The analysis of the marra mamba cake samples shows results that are consistent right across the field, with no significant variation –'

Garth could have strangled him.

'What does it say?'

'Sixty-two per cent iron,' Saul said. His voice showed no excitement and Garth's heart sank.

'Sixty-two per cent?'

'That is correct. With far less sulphur than in normal hematite. And the field extends a long way. We would need an additional survey to find out how far.'

'Sixty-two per cent,' Garth repeated. 'Is that good news or bad?'

'If the government can be persuaded to change its policy,' Saul said, 'I would say you've enough iron ore there to supply the steel requirements of the entire world for a hundred years.'

CHAPTER THIRTY

From the age when she had been old enough to comprehend such things, Peace had worshipped her father. He was strong, handsome, altogether wonderful. She had known at the age of four that she would marry him when she grew up. If she could not be him, she could think of nothing better than that. When she learnt that marrying her father was not a proposition, she sulked for a week. In general, she had no time for girls, herself and Bella included. Girls were soft and soggy. Even Charlene Ludwig would have had no chance, one on one, against a boy with more brains than Willy Brown. By contrast boys were hard and tough, qualities that Peace admired above all others.

It was therefore ironical that, when Peace started at high school at the age of twelve, she attended an academy in Cottesloe that was focused on turning out young ladies with the attributes needed to become good wives and mothers, with social and domestic skills deemed more important than a more liberal education. As for science... Forget it.

Peace, who already knew precisely what she wanted from life, fitted into that environment like a vixen in a hen house. She bitched about it continuously: first to Richard and then to Mother. Richard was not in a position to do anything about her complaints but at least was a patient listener, as eleven-year-old boys went, and moaning to him made her feel better. Talking to Mother was a waste of time, of course, not because she couldn't do anything but because she wouldn't.

'You could be worse off,' Bella said. 'I had a governess and never went to school at all.'

Which didn't help Peace in the least.

'Maybe I should try that,' she said. 'Skip school altogether and go back home. Do a correspondence course, maybe.'

Home was neither Desire nor Perth but the vastness of the Pilbara, riding muster with Dad. But she spoke without hope, because she knew there was no chance of it. Nor was it really what she wanted: she wanted to be a geologist, which meant university. She would never make university by mustering cattle or even by correspondence.

'How did you make out?' she asked her mother. 'I mean, you're not exactly illiterate, are you?'

'I think they call it the university of life,' Bella said. 'Plus I've read a bit, of course.'

Which was the understatement of the year, because Bella was never without a book of some sort in her hip pocket, ranging from Robert Frost's poems to a *Layman's Guide to the Theory of Relativity*.

'I like to read, when I can find a peaceful moment,' she often said.

Peaceful moments were hard to find. Desire had already been years in the building but the project was so vast that it was still more construction site than house. Everywhere jackhammers clattered, drills snarled, dust rose in choking clouds. Fortunately they didn't have to put up with the racket for long. The day after Peace walked through the door, Richard went to stay with a school friend and mother and daughter went camping in the country south of Margaret River. It was nice, of course it was – there were trees there older than time – but it was a pity Garth was up north chasing cows: as far as Peace was concerned that was the better part of the family done and dusted.

There was nothing to be done; a week was not long enough to get up to the Pilbara and back.

'I am sorry he isn't here,' Peace said.

'He's sorry, too,' Bella said, 'but he said he couldn't get away; without cattle we'll have no income and without income we shall all be in the soup. He said he'd try to get down for the long holidays. Or maybe you could go up there.'

Even without him it was a great opportunity for mother and daughter – what was the phrase her class teacher Miss Aucutt had used only the other day? – to bond together, but somehow it only came off on the last day. Until then they had both been awkward with each other – yes, school was okay, once you got over the pointlessness of it; yes, she was playing hockey with the juniors and thought she had a good chance of being picked for the team when they went back; yes, the half-term tests so far had been easy, she'd come top in everything but art and history; and no, she'd made no particular friends.

'I swear to you, Mother, I'm in with a bunch of morons.'

Then, on the last day, Mother decided to start talking about her plans for the Carlisle Mine. 'What I'm telling you now is confidential,' Bella said. 'But I know I can trust you to keep it to yourself.'

Mother was not one for compliments and for her to say this made Peace feel good. For the first time she thought that when she was older and knew more they might even become a team.

Family was not a concept that had figured large in Peace's life until now – she was a loner, even on the hockey field inclined to do her own thing – but she thought this business of the mine might give her a whole new perspective about things.

'Will it make money?' she asked.

'If things work out, it should make a lot of money,' Bella said.

'That'll be nice.'

Although it was not the money that interested her so much as the mine itself.

'Will there be a job for me? When I leave school?'

'School and university,' Bella said. 'Yes, there will. I'm counting on you.'

That was a new concept, too; she had never thought of Mother relying on anyone in the world bar herself.

It made the idea of going back to school that much more meaningful. Even… exciting?

CHAPTER THIRTY-ONE

Eleven-year-old Richard glared at his friend Luke. 'You chicken, or what?'

Luke glared back. 'Course I'm not!

'Let's do it, then.'

The two boys lay in the long grass and stared through the fence at the paddock of watermelons. The farmer was an Italian, with a reputation. He owned two dogs; they also had a reputation. All three were said to be savage brutes that would show no mercy to melon-stealing boys.

But the melons were ripe, large and shiny, and at this hour of the morning, with the sun not yet over the horizon, there was no sign of either the Italian or his dogs.

Lying in the grass, Richard swallowed thirstily, already tasting the sweet flesh.

All they had to do was zip under the wire, grab a melon or two and zip back again. They couldn't take many, the melons were too big, but two each should be possible. One or maybe two to share and sell the others: there was always a market for juicy, ripe watermelons.

But the bottom strand of the fence was barbed.

'Get hooked on that,' Luke pointed out, 'those dogs will eat your guts. They'll tear you open and –'

'We won't get hooked.'

'Sez you.'

'Yeah!' said Richard.

'Yeah yourself!'

Richard lifted the wire as high as it would go. Which wasn't very high.

'I'll go first,' he said.

Luke had no problem with that. He held the wire and Richard squeezed under. So far so good.

Luke released the wire. It twanged loudly; Richard thought the farmer would certainly have heard it. His previous glare was nothing to this one. 'What you doing?'

'Sorry!'

Flat on his stomach, eyes everywhere, Richard inched over to the nearest row of melons. Close up, they looked huge. Getting them back would be a problem. One at a time would be the only way. He took out his knife and cut through the tough stem. If the farmer caught him now, he was dead.

He trundled his trophy back to the wire. Now there was another problem; the melon was too big to go under the wire.

'You'll have to chuck it over,' said Luke.

All right for him; he was safe on the other side of the fence, but Richard would have to stand up before he could throw the melon over, which meant putting himself into clear view of the farmer's house, a short distance up the hill. No choice; it was either that or lose the melon, and after all his efforts he wasn't going to do that.

He stood, held the melon in his hands and threw it up and over.

'Catch it!'

Too late; the melon fell with a thud, but at least they had it.

'You going back for the rest?' Luke asked.

But Richard had had enough for one day.

'I don't reckon the others are quite ripe.'

They both heard it at once: the savage baying of the dogs.

'Quick!'

Luke was hauling on the wire, lifting it as high as he could. Richard lay full length and began to squeeze himself under, but doing it when you had plenty of time was one thing; doing it in a rush, with the fear of death squeezing your heart, was another matter entirely.

'They're coming!' Luke squeaked. 'Coming fast!'

Richard's shirt snagged on the wire. Frantically he tore himself free. He left a bit of shirt behind, a bit of skin, too, but he was through, he was safe. Luke let the wire go in the faces of the two dogs that came racing up, all howl and sharp teeth. Not far behind them was the farmer, shouting and waving his stick.

'If he sees who we are he'll set the wallopers on us,' said Luke, who had heard the expression from his older brother.

The last thing Richard needed was the police coming round the house, asking about stolen watermelons.

'Let's get out of here!'

They were round the corner and out of sight when they realised they had left the melon behind. Richard made the best of it.

'We couldn't have run fast enough carrying it. He'd have seen us for sure.'

All the same...

'Maybe another day,' he said.

Yeah, right.

Richard had not given up his plans for making money. When the time came he reckoned the Melbourne Cup was the way to do it. He ran the idea past Dad, who said it was a mug's game.

'All right for the bookies. They make quids. But no one else.'

Richard decided in that case he'd be a bookie. He ran his own book, encouraging his classmates to put their sixpences and the occasional shilling on the horses of their choice.

'Ten to one on Baystone! A shilling will get you ten!'

With odds like that, the chances of Baystone winning had got to be... well, ten to one against. Right? Good odds, if you were a bookie.

The money flowed in. Everything was doing just great. And then...

Baystone won. The ten to one chance came in first. Its backers would have cleaned up, had Richard had the money to pay them. As it was he paid out every penny and was still left with dissatisfied customers. Might have had a couple of black eyes, too, if the previous year Dad hadn't sent him to learn a few tricks from a fairground pug with whom he'd had a scrap or two himself, in his young days.

So Richard escaped the worst of his Melbourne Cup venture. Not that it ended there. When Garth heard: 'What you going to do about it?'

'What can I do?'

'How much do you owe?'

Richard could always put a figure on things. 'Seven shillings and eightpence.'

'How you going to settle up?'

'I can't.'

'Don't give me that,' Dad said. 'Tuckers pay their debts, okay?'

'But how –?'

'I'll lend you the money.'

'Then I'll owe you instead.'

'Too right you will. Wash my car, and your mother's car, every week for four weeks, we'll be square. Right?'

'But that means I'll have washed eight cars for less than a shilling a time.'

Which was what Garth normally paid him. Another thing about Richard: he could do mental arithmetic quicker than anyone in his class.

'You'll be dudding me,' Richard protested.

Garth grinned at him: teeth.

'Call it my discount,' he said.

Who'd be a bookie?

It was Richard's first year at high school. There was a movie he wanted to see; Bella gave him the money. When he came back...

'What was it like?' Bella asked.

'It was great.'

'What was it about?'

'A missionary.'

That was a new one. Bella stared at him.

'And you found it interesting?'

'Yes.'

More than interesting; he had found it inspirational. Richard's instinct was already to keep his most important thoughts to himself but his mother was not easily fobbed off.

'Tell me about it.'

He suspected she was asking only to show how interested she was in him – she'd seen her play the same trick on Peace, asking questions about her hockey, for heaven's sake: a subject in which he was certain Mother had no interest whatsoever. But he was happy to humour her, if it made her feel better.

'It's about this woman who was a missionary in China. She helped the poor people and especially the children and when the Japanese soldiers invaded she managed to get the children to safety.'

Mother obviously thought it was a strange story to have excited his imagination. 'It was good, was it?'

'Ingrid Bergman was in it.'

No need to say more; Ingrid Bergman was fabulous and Richard, like every other teenage boy, was in love with her. But it was not Ingrid Bergman who caused the movie to remain in his mind. It was China. Despite his teenage fantasies about the Swedish film actress it was that vast, mysterious, impoverished country that was the real star of the film.

He found himself going to the library and looking up books on China's history, China's art, China's culture and civilisation. He understood exactly why Gladys Aylwood, the real-life missionary on whom the film had been based, had gone to China in the first place. In her shoes he believed he would have done the same.

He had discovered a mine of pure gold.

CHAPTER THIRTY-TWO

'Thank you,' Bella said. 'Thank you very much.'

Exultation eeled through her as she put down the phone. She walked to the French windows and stepped on to the terrace. Tiny clouds floated high up in an otherwise clear sky. A light breeze was blowing and the roses were in full flower.

'What a glorious day!' Bella said.

Glorious indeed. Still stunned by the telephone call, she walked to the edge of the terrace, placed both hands on the stone balustrade and breathed the scented air deeply into her lungs.

For seven years she had done everything she could to get the law against prospecting repealed. Seven years of bargaining, negotiating, bringing into play every ounce of charm she possessed. To snobs she had been the earl's daughter, to battlers the Akubra-hatted woman who mustered cattle in the far north. She had wooed the press, supported causes, donated to charities. She had wined and dined those who had, or might have, influence. She had made more promises than a dozen prime ministers.

There had been times when she had thought she was getting nowhere. Garth wanted her to wash her hands of the whole business and go back to ranching, but Bella would not have a bar of it. Excited by the challenge, she had discovered she was good at winning people over. She was enjoying herself too much to think of quitting.

The Pilbara and Miranda Downs would always be important to her. For most of her adult life they had been her home and her salvation. There she had won her husband and given birth to her children, and she would always be grateful for that. There, too, she had started her first business venture, and the success of the meatworks had given her a hint of how much more she was capable of doing. Life was a challenge and she was convinced she had the talents to meet it. She already knew that the world of business was not Garth's natural environment whereas for her it was oxygen in the blood. Striving to create a new industry gave her more satisfaction than anything she could have imagined.

She had found fulfilment in a pile of dust.

'There's a fortune waiting for someone to pick up,' she told her husband, 'and I intend that someone to be us.'

'Next thing, you'll be in politics,' Garth had grumbled.

Bella had smiled. She was in politics already, even if Garth didn't realise it.

Nor had it been all she had to cope with. There were the children, who needed her and whom she would not abandon even for the biggest mine on earth. There was Miranda Downs and the meatworks that provided their only income. There were endless plans of what they would have to do when the law was changed.

'If it ever is,' Garth said.

'When it is,' Bella said firmly, 'we shall need to be ready. We'll need a railway to get the ore to the coast. And a loading terminal for when it gets there.'

'You're talking mega-millions,' Garth objected.

He was right. Once the land was theirs, they would still need to wow the banks, overseas investors...

'We'll be dead before we see a return,' said Garth.

He might be right, but giving up had never been Bella's response to difficulties. None of it would be possible until the law changed but now – at last! – that phone call from a contact in the premier's office had informed her it was about to happen.

'The legislation to legalise prospecting becomes law tomorrow,' the contact had said.

'*Tomorrow?*'

She had hoped for more notice.

'Effective immediately.'

'And you have the numbers?'

When dealing with politicians she had learnt to dot the i's and cross the t's.

'In both houses.'

'So we can start pegging claims straight away?'

'From tomorrow.'

'Party time!'

Bella danced naked around the bedroom.

Where is your dignity? she asked herself, even as she laughed out loud. What happened to decorum? You're forty-one, not eighteen. You have two children in high school, a half-share in a cattle station twice the size of Lichtenstein, a highly profitable meatworks and now – at last – a half share in the iron ore mine that is going to make us rich.

Tonight they would party; tomorrow she and Garth would fly north and begin pegging the claims that Saul Rich had been helping them identify, surreptitiously because of the embargo, for the past seven years.

'Come and dance with me,' she cried to Garth, who was watching her from the king-size bed, but her husband shook his head and did not move. He was sixty years old – not such a great age – but his leg had never sorted itself out properly and his dancing days were done.

'I'll stick to watching,' he said.

'That's no fun,' she objected.

'It is for me. I like to see you waggle.'

The truth was she liked it, too, even if waggling was the main physical pleasure either of them had derived from their marriage for a year or two now; it was not only Garth's dancing days that were in decline. Yet she had never been tempted to take a lover.

She stopped dancing, her shoulders shiny with sweat, a trickle of moisture between her breasts. She sat beside her husband on the bed. 'Did you wonder whether this day would ever come?'

'Frequently.'

'Me, too.'

'You never showed it,' he said.

'Not even to myself.'

'Have a shower before you catch cold,' Garth said.

'Yes, sir.'

She came back swathed in a towelling wrap and rubbing her hair dry.

'Now the hard work starts,' she said. 'Banks, investment funds… They'll all want a slice of the pie. That's where you come in.'

'How so?' Garth wondered.

'Mining is men's business,' she said. 'The bankers think women are too frivolous to handle it.'

'Frivolous? You?' he said. 'On the other hand I have just seen you doing your wild dervish dance.'

'In the nude,' she pointed out.

'So maybe they are right.'

'And that is why you will have to deal with them,' Bella said.

'Let's get the damn things pegged first,' Garth said.

Next morning they left Perth and flew north. Below them, the featureless land stretched away into a green and brown infinity. Ahead lay the Carlisle River and a future filled with excitement, danger and the prospect of unimaginable wealth.

That evening, with Garth lying in his sleeping bag, Bella slipped a coat around her shoulders and sat on the ground outside the tent to watch the sunset. The fire upon which she had grilled their meat was burning low. She got up and added more wood to the embers. She watched until the flames licked up, then went and sat down again.

Losing power with every second, the sun slid down the western sky. To her left, the rounded outline of the Hamersley Range changed from russet and green to purple. It was still, not even a breath of wind to disturb the silence. Northwards, the land lost definition as the twilight came down. The first stars pricked out. She thought: I have been too busy. Not for years have I given myself time to look at the stars.

The thought made her sad and she wondered how much else she had missed of the things that made life worth living. She had promised the children she would take them overseas. It hadn't happened but this year she was determined it would. She had promised herself that she and Garth would explore at least part of the Outback together. They had done it only once – And look what happened when we did, she thought. Maybe next time we'll find emeralds.

The stars were brighter now, innumerable points of brilliant light throbbing amid the incomprehensible vastness of the universe.

She thought: I have done what I could with my life. I have accepted the challenges when they occurred. Now I am confronted by the greatest challenge of all.

It would not be easy; so much of what had to be done lay in unknown territory. Dealing with banks and overseas investors; the development and management of the mine; negotiating contracts with overseas buyers... To say nothing of handling competition that would no doubt do its damnedest to bring them down. What did they know about these things?

They would need advisers, men who not only knew what they were doing but could be trusted. A big ask. Was she was up to it?

I shall do the best I can, she thought. No one can do more.

She sat unmoving until it was completely dark and she was alone with the stars and shifting coals of the dying fire. To be alone out here in the Outback was already an adventure beyond anything she could have imagined in her childhood. By contrast, the smoky

sprawl of London, the view from the verandah of the Johnsons'
house in Charters Towers, even the snow-covered winter moors
of Yorkshire, were no more than an effete and fading memory.
Miranda Downs would always be home to her but this, the harsh-
ness of stone and emptiness, also had its place.

It was too much to hope they would be alone for long.

Halfway through the next morning they heard the sound of an
engine. Bella stood at Garth's shoulder and watched the light aircraft heading deep into the Hamersley Range. Within half an hour
there was a second, followed twenty minutes later by a third.

'Here come the vultures,' Garth said.

'There's a name written on the fuselage,' Bella said. 'Can you read
it?'

Even at sixty Garth had amazing eyesight. 'BradMin,' he said.
'Bradford Minerals.'

One of the biggest mining outfits in the world.

'Lucky there's enough for all of us,' Bella said.

All the same, with three aircraft already here, it was obvious Brad-
Min would soon have more boots on the ground than the Tuckers
could match.

'All the more reason to keep moving,' Bella said.

The arrival of high-powered competition was incentive enough
to get on with the back-breaking job of pegging and identifying
claims that might otherwise be filched from under their noses.

'Who's the boss of BradMin?' Bella asked, wiping the sweat from
her eyes and easing her back after three hours' non-stop work.

'Pete Bathurst,' Garth said. 'An American.'

'I remember him. Big man, big mouth. We need to catch up
with him as soon as we can.'

'Why?'

'They're pegging in the Hamersley so they'll need a rail link to
the coast, the same as us. Maybe we can come to an arrangement
with them to share the line.'

* * *

They finished pegging their claims in what Bella thought might be record time, in the unlikely event there were records for such things, but when they tried to arrange a meeting with Pete Bathurst they ran into problems.

'What is the nature of your enquiry?'

By her dulcet tones the young woman on the other end of the phone would no doubt have been a dab hand at a carol concert but Bella was not in the mood for herald angels, however sweetly they sang.

'To discuss matters of mutual interest.'

'In connection with?'

'The new Pilbara development.'

'And what is the nature of your interest?'

Enough!

'Just tell him the Tuckers rang. He'll know what it's about.'

'The Tuckers?' As one might speak of a small and insignificant creature. 'I see. And you are?'

'I am Mrs Tucker. Speaking on behalf of my husband.'

Garth was watching her. She flashed him a quick wink.

'*One* moment…'

'Thank you for landing me in it,' Garth said.

'My pleasure.'

Almost immediately the fluty-voiced lady was back. 'I am *so* sorry but Mr Bathurst is in a meeting.'

'When will he be free?'

'That I couldn't say.'

'Then I shall phone him tomorrow,' said Bella, jaw outthrust.

'He won't be in. He's flying to Houston first thing in the morning.'

'And will be back when?'

'Not for at least two weeks.'

'He's giving us the run-around,' said Garth when she told him.

'But why? It makes no sense when we can save him money on the railway.'

'To show us who's boss, I suppose.'

'He's not our boss. Never will be, either.'

'Maybe not. But I don't intend to hang around twiddling my thumbs while he plays silly buggers.'

'What do you plan to do?'

'Go home, of course. I've got a cattle station to run.' He gave her a sideways glance. 'You could come with me, if you like.'

Bella thought about that. Miranda Downs in mid-winter. It was the best time of year in the far north. The humidity would be down, the countryside after the rains green and lush… She could meet up with her friends, Maisie and the rest. There would be no crotalaria. They could do a muster. Thinking about it she could smell the clean, sharp smell of the bush. For a moment she wavered but only for a moment. Desire was now complete, as far as the building was concerned, but the grounds still had to be laid out and she was determined to be on hand to make sure they were done exactly in accordance with her vision. She had put it on hold while they had been staking their claims but now it was full steam ahead once again. It was out of the question for her to be away from it.

'I'd better stay here. But you go.'

Garth didn't need urging. Two days later he was heading north.

It didn't take long for Bella to regret letting him go. She knew he would have stayed had she asked but knew, too, that his heart was in Miranda Downs and always would be.

It was a worrying thought to take to her lonely bed each night. How would that commitment tie in with the development of the ore deposits along the Carlisle? Since her own focus had changed from Miranda Downs to the development of their mining interests with all that had entailed – the endless wowing of politicians and anyone else who might be of value, the building of their status-symbol house – she had sensed a divergence in their marriage where previously there had been none. She told herself she was imagining it, knew she was not. She told herself it was an inevitable conse-quence of having been married for twenty years, did not believe that either. She wanted passion, she wanted love, she wanted the comfort and tenderness of being together. Something would have to be done, and soon. As soon as they had had their meeting with

Pete Bathurst, as soon as they had reached some satisfactory accommodation regarding the rail link to the coast – an accommodation that would benefit them both – she would take steps to rectify the situation. Her marriage would be restored to what it had been and should still be; she was determined of that. And she would do it, what was more, without sacrificing either Miranda Downs or the mine.

It was a month before Bella and Garth finally got across the table from Pete Bathurst: Bathurst had been out of the country for three weeks and it was another week before Garth came back from the north.

'Looks like we got that whole goddamn area tied up between us,' Pete Bathurst said. He was indeed a big man, as Bella had said, more cliff than human, with teeth like gravestones in the rugged face, and she did not trust him at all. 'I'm glad you dropped by, folks. I got something I'd like to talk over with you all, if you're agreeable.'

'Tell us what's on your mind,' Garth said.

'I've been looking at the geological reports on the whole area and I can see trouble ahead for your claims,' Pete Bathurst said.

'Why is that?' Bella said.

'There's no shortage of ore,' he told her. 'But it looks like the deposits are horizontal.'

'Is that bad?' Garth asked.

'It'll involve massive extra costs.'

'How massive?' Bella asked.

'Hard to put a thumb on a figure. One hell of a lot, that I can guarantee.' He smiled at Bella, this man who with every word showed what he thought of a woman involving herself in a mining venture. 'It's not like going out to buy a dress, you know.'

'Is that right?' Bella gave him her most charming smile. 'And there I was thinking what a good dress-shop manager you'd make.'

Pete switched his smile to Garth. 'Hey, quite a little tiger you got there, right?'

'You'd better believe it,' Bella said. 'Explain what you're talking about.'

Pete scrubbed his red hair with a massive paw. 'Most mines work on vertical deposits, but from the geological scans it looks like the ones along the Carlisle are horizontal. That means special equipment. You're talking millions here. On top of that you've got the cost of the heavy haul railway and the port facilities to ship the ore out. Frankly, you'd be better to involve us. Soon as the leases are granted I can just about guarantee BradMin would be interested –'

'Why would they be interested?' Bella asked.

'Because it's their trade.'

'And because they can see a profit. Right?'

Pete hesitated. 'I guess.'

'So why should we give it away?'

'Like I said, BradMin has the expertise and you folks don't –'

'Expertise can be hired,' Bella said.

'He's talking a lot of sense,' said Garth.

'He's talking a lot of crap,' said Bella.

She used the word deliberately. It made Garth uneasy – a duchess wasn't supposed to talk like that – but Bella had always been a plain-speaking woman and had discovered, with her husband at least, that it helped her get her own way.

Not this time.

'They've got the capital and the expertise. They know what they're doing and we don't. They take responsibility for the operation and pay us a royalty. He's offering us a good deal,' Garth said.

'He pays us a royalty and BradMin keeps the profits, which could be in the hundreds of millions? That's a good deal?'

'We get twenty million a year, Bella. With nothing to do but spend it.'

Bella knew that the Garth she had married, the man who had rustled O'Malley's cattle from under his nose and laughed while he was doing it, would never have agreed to such an arrangement. But she reminded herself that Garth was sixty years old – not a young sixty, either – and the burden of such a challenge weighed heavily upon him. She didn't like the royalty option at all, would have preferred the excitement and challenge of going it alone with the possibility of a big pay-out at the end of it, but Garth wanted no more dramas in his life and she had to admit that the idea of twenty million a year for doing nothing had its attractions. Perhaps she should let him have his own way for once.

'He wants a longevity clause in the agreement,' Garth said.

'What does that mean?'

'He will want to renegotiate the deal in the event of my death. Or yours,' he added.

What difference could it make to the operation if either of them died? But such an arrangement would offer Bella a let-out. Heaven forbid that Garth should die but, if he did, she might end up running her own show, after all.

'Okay,' she said. 'If that's what he wants. But I want something, too. I want it in the contract that we must have access to the railway when it's built.'

'Why would we want that? If we're going to be on a royalties-only basis?'

'I've always believed in belts and braces: it seems only sensible, in case we ever want to renegotiate.'

'I can't imagine we ever shall,' Garth said.

'Nevertheless. And I still intend to keep an eye on what's going on. In case the time comes when I want to manage things for myself.'

'Planning to bury me already?' Garth asked.

'I hope you live forever. But just in case you don't –'

'You want to be prepared.'

'Got it in one.'

CHAPTER THIRTY-THREE

Bella knew two things.

She had promised her children they would go away together, as a family. Have a real holiday somewhere new. Now there was an added urgency because a holiday of the type she had in mind would help stall the drifting-apart that she had felt between her husband and herself. To achieve that she knew they would have to go somewhere special, where they had never been before.

The second thing she knew was that, if they didn't make it this year, it really was likely to end up as never, because next year the mining leases would be issued and after that there would be no chance of her getting away for the foreseeable future.

Bella was not prepared to settle for never, because she had given her word. To the family, what was more, and that was the defining factor. The mine was hugely important but at best would never be more than second in line because for Bella, brought up with all the benefits of wealth and position but no real family to share it with, her tiny group of loved ones was the one card in the pack that outtrumped them all. She had said they would go away somewhere exciting, and that was exactly what they would do. Together.

Garth – of course – was a stumbling block. He explained that he would have given his eye teeth to go with them but to his eternal regret was simply too busy to manage it. When that tactic failed he said he was too old, too tired, he would be a drag on the party, he would spoil their fun. It was them he was thinking of, he insisted. He could think of nothing he would rather do, but in the circumstances felt it only right to make the sacrifice.

Bella asked him to please forget his nonsense. 'You are coming with us,' she said. 'And that's the end of it.'

'Where are we going?' asked Peace, always one to get to the point of any discussion.

'To Africa,' Bella said.

She had read about it in a book, she said. Spoken to agents about it. Consulted a man at the South African consulate. They would fly to Johannesburg, then travel to the huge game reserve called the Kruger Park. They would spend a few days there before moving to a hutted camp high in the mountains.

'They say it is very beautiful. And there are caves with bushmen paintings.'

'Will there be animals?' asked Richard. 'Lions and things?'

'Yes.'

'And elephants and giraffe and zebra and –'

'Yes.'

'Is that all we're going to do?' Peace said. 'Spend time in the bush?'

To sixteen-year-old Peace the sophistication of city life rated higher than any game lodge you could name. As for the bush, what was so special? She had been *born* in the bush, for heaven's sake.

Bella could do nothing about it; Peace was in the middle of the adolescent rebellion against her mother that was natural for any teenager, especially one of Peace's temperament.

'We shall be spending three days in Cape Town and two in Durban before we fly out,' she said.

That would have to do her.

They were away a month. Bella brought back photographs for the family album: images of Garth and the children standing in front of a hippo pool; Garth inspecting an inquisitive giraffe; the silent vastness of elephants, grey and monumental; and, most precious of all, the mask of a black-maned lion, shot from inside the viewing vehicle, staring yellow-eyed into the lens from a circle of thorns. After dark that same day, under a swollen moon that painted the bush with conflicting patterns of silver and black, they heard for the first time a lion's spine-tingling roar.

They crouched in a bird hide overlooking a waterhole and watched a leopard come down to drink. It was sinuous, beautiful, full of menace. It drank its fill and departed, swarming up a tree with the speed and grace of a stream flowing uphill. It was gone; it might never have existed. Around them the brooding darkness of the bush was still. Yet they had seen it and the image would remain: of a confrontation from a time before memory, the primeval past come suddenly to life in front of them.

Bella's nerves crawled beneath her skin, yet she was delighted. *Somewhere exciting*, she had promised them. What could be more exciting than that?

They went into the Dragon Mountains or, in the Afrikaans language, the Drakensberg. The Injasuti camp was high up, with a stream running through it. The water flowed fast over rocks that shone white in the sunlight and at night Bella lay awake, listening to the stream, and it was a clean, cold sound.

There was a footbridge over the stream and a path that wound along a gorge. There was no one else at all. They followed the path, listening to the savage barking of baboons from the cliffs above them. They came to a rock shelter vibrant with bushman paintings and it was like stepping through a doorway into the past. Beyond the shelter the path climbed steeply between tormented turrets of stone. They surprised a pair of tiny klipspringer antelope, which fled from them across almost vertical cliffs; they came out on grassy uplands where in the distance they saw a browsing group of eland, mightiest of the antelope. From a cliff a black eagle surveyed them;

a lammergeyer circled; it was the Garden of Eden come to life around them.

Peace didn't have much to say for herself but fourteen-year-old Richard spent every night before bed writing up a diary of the things he had seen during the day.

'Did you know that if you see a hamerkop bird it's supposed to mean someone close to you has died?' he told Bella.

Trust Richard to come up with something like that.

'Did you know it's also called the lightning bird?'

'No, dear, I did not know that.'

Ignorant of the legends of the hamerkop she might be, but for Bella their time in Africa was both a wonder and delight: wonder that such places still existed in the world, delight that they had been able, as a family, to share it together.

Best of all was the opportunity to be as one, after so long a time, with Garth, her husband and her love. It had not happened immediately. For the first three days of their time in Africa they had been friendly, they had laughed and joked and made love, but it had been like a meeting of old friends with none of the magic or passion of the past. The exultation they had shared so recently, with Bella dancing naked in the bedroom, was no more than a wistful memory of good times that had passed them by.

I shall not accept it, Bella thought, because that is the essence and meaning of our lives. Yet passion was its own master. It was not something you could produce to order. It was there or it was not.

She thought, if the purpose of the trip has been to restore the magic in our relationship, it has failed.

That was the night of the lion, when magic had touched all their lives (even Peace had been impressed) yet had still failed to reignite the shared ecstasy of the past.

Perhaps I imagined it, thought Bella, knowing she had not.

Then came the day of the bushmen, the klipspringer, eland and lammergeyer.

Standing in the entrance of the rock shelter she studied the wall paintings of the prancing, stick-like figures, spears raised in endless flight across the silent distances of the past, the male figures in permanent erection, the women with breasts ballooning beneath their armpits, and felt herself roused. A visceral thrust of energy, deep in her core, stimulated not by the priapic images of a vanished race but by the sheer energy of the painting, the flying images of a past returned to live again in the present, so that time ceased and all were united in an endless Now.

Desire scorched her like a flame. Glancing sideways at Garth she saw him look at her and knew that the impact of the long-dead artist had stirred him also.

Richard was studying the details of the painting with big eyes. 'Cor!' he said.

While Peace, nose raised dismissively, pretended to do no such thing but did so anyway, on the sly.

Bella felt her own heat and Garth's. If it hadn't been for the children they would have lain down right there. They would have coupled before the stick-like figures racing eternally, before the images of eland and impala, with the mountain air cool on their hot bodies and the chatter of the mountain stream in their ears.

A baboon barked on the ridges above the cave; later they saw the living forms of the creatures depicted in the painting, and the magic of the day did not betray them but remained until their return to the hut. Then came their meal and Richard's endless prattle about the hamerkop, with Garth looking sideways at her and a tremble of excitement seething in Bella's belly, and she wondered how much the children sensed of the things that went on between their parents.

Richard probably not much, she thought, but Peace... She suspected that Peace was alert to the vibes and knew exactly what went on.

And so what? She thought it was a great pity that sex and shame had become so entangled by past prejudice. There was no shame in it; it was at the core of their relationship, respect and admiration and sharing and tenderness all engendered by the simple reality of the sexual union that was not simple at all but immensely complex and indescribably wonderful.

Wonderful was right. She couldn't wait to get Garth into the bedroom, couldn't wait to get her clothes off, couldn't wait...

And oh God, oh dear God, oh dear and wonderful God...

The best ever, amid the fleeing figures of the bushmen, the diamond-tailed lammergeyer, the massive stillness of the browsing eland. And Bella, returning from a distant place, ecstasy still in mouth and limbs, grateful nerve ends at peace at last.

'Thank God I have found you again,' she said.

'Had you lost me?'

'Not lost, exactly, but I felt we were drifting apart. I wouldn't want that.'

'Would you rather I stayed in Perth with you?'

'I wouldn't want that either, Garth. Miranda Downs is your life. I've always known that.'

Through the open window she heard the stream rushing in the darkness.

'I thought it was yours, too,' he said.

'In a way it still is. It is very precious to me. It's my home.'

'But the other is a challenge.'

'I think I can make it work, Garth. I really think I can.'

'But if BradMin runs it, as we agreed...'

'I can't see that lasting for long. I don't trust that man. He'll do us down if he can.'

'And you don't intend to let him.'

'I do not.'

Silence settled between them. The voice of the stream beyond the window was loud in the stillness of the room.

'Do you think it's natural?' she asked. 'To feel the way we do? To behave the way we do – like this, I mean? After so many years?'

'Does it feel unnatural to you?' Garth said.

'No. It feels right.'

'Exactly.'

'The thought that we might have lost it made my heart sore,' she said.

His hand moved. 'It does not feel sore,' he said.

'I said my heart. That is not my heart.'

'My mistake.'

His fingers moved a little, but only to caress. To take hold. 'Is that better?'

'That is much better,' she said.

While the beating of her heart stifled the chatter of the rushing stream.

'Being apart does not mean separation,' he said later.

'Then let us make sure it does not,' she said.

Later still, with Garth sleeping at her side, Bella contemplated how her plan had succeeded after all.

Africa has given me this, she thought. The true worth and essence of my life restored in the land of the lion, the fleeing figures of the naked, stick-like hunters.

Peace got her three days in Cape Town, with its majestic mountain and streets lined with oak trees and buildings dating back three hundred years to the earliest days of Dutch settlement, and two days in Durban, sandy beaches and surf rolling out of the eastern sea, yet to Bella the high point of their visit to Africa remained the time in the mountain hut with the stream rushing beyond the window, when her faith in her marriage had been restored. Strengthened and refreshed, she knew that with Garth beside her she was equal to any challenge the future might bring. The leases would be issued; battle – with the elements, the riches of the Pilbara, the unremitting rivalry of Pete Bathurst – would be rejoined. Refreshed by all that had happened, she could not wait.

Battle flags flying, Bella Tucker returned to the fray.

CHAPTER THIRTY-FOUR

At the end of the winter Garth came down from the Pilbara to stay with them for a spell.

One morning in the second week of September, a day when the promise of spring seemed finally to be coming to fruition, he walked out of the house and discovered a small boy washing his car.

He found Bella in the room she had turned into her office. 'There is a boy cleaning my car.'

'That'll be Andrew,' Bella said.

'Who is Andrew? And why is he cleaning my car?'

'He works for Richard.'

Garth stared. 'I beg your pardon?'

'We pay Richard to wash our cars every week. Two shillings a pop, right?'

Once it had been only a shilling but the year before Richard had negotiated a pay rise.

'And so?'

'He sub-contracts the work to two boys he knows at school. Pays them half, keeps the rest for himself.'

Garth was willing to be outraged. 'That's ridiculous.'

Bella smiled at him. 'Why is it ridiculous?'

'We don't pay him two bob a car for him to sit on his backside!'

'We pay him two bob a car to have two clean cars. And that's what we get.'

'But –'

'They call it delegation.'

Garth was unwilling to go along with that. 'I'll have a word with him.'

'Don't,' Bella said. 'He's doing exactly what we all do. Take the mine. Will we operate the machinery ourselves? Of course not. Will we load the rail wagons? Of course not. We'll employ other people to do that for us. That's what Richard is doing. It's not the only thing, either.'

'What do you mean?'

'Paper rounds,' Bella said.

'Lots of boys have paper rounds.'

'Yes, but Richard has three.'

Garth stared. 'How does he manage that?'

'The same way. He's cornered the market around here, so he sub-contracts them to other boys, pays them half, keeps the rest for himself.'

'At that rate he'll be rich before we are,' Garth said.

'Good on him if he is,' Bella said.

To Garth it was a new slant on his son, who he knew to be studious and reserved. Because of his mild ways they all tended to bully him a little; no harm in that, as long as it stayed in the family, although he had sometimes wondered how Richard would make out when he had to deal with the outside world. Now it seemed he need not worry; the boy had the makings of a tycoon.

It was a stinking hot day at the end of January 1963, the humidity way up, and at last, eighteen months after the leases had been granted, a new road had been cut joining the new mines with the coast. It was a roundabout route from Miranda Downs but, having cleared it with Pete Bathurst, Bella drove out there six weeks after the development started.

'This is where we'll be cutting the first terraces,' Rory McNab said.

'You're making good progress,' Bella said.

'Six months and we'll be ready to roll.'

Bella stood with him on an elevated section of what would eventually become the Bradford Gulliver Mine. Explosives had torn holes in the carapace of hard rock covering the ore deposits and giant earthmovers were beginning the mammoth task of opening up the soil. The air was thick with dust and the roar of machinery.

Pete Bathurst had been entertained by the notion that such a toothsome lady, as he described her, should wish to trouble her pretty little head with how a mine actually worked. 'It's filthy work,' he had said. 'Noisy work. Man's work.' His grin could have devoured her, had she permitted. 'I would have said there were better ways for a beautiful woman to keep herself amused.'

Oh, he was a detestable man.

'I like to see men grovelling in the dirt,' she said. 'It seems so appropriate.'

Which might have offended him, but Pete's skin would have shamed a hippopotamus.

Rory McNab was about thirty-five, with blond hair and steady eyes. He had a good body, too, which Bella appreciated. Altogether he was quite a change from Pete Bathurst and she took to him at once.

'They call me the mine development manager but it doesn't mean much,' he said. 'Not with the boss breathing down my neck all the time.'

'When are you starting on the railway?' Bella asked.

'Already started. The first bridges are in, and some of the culverts. They'll be shipping in track directly.'

'What about Carlisle? When do you begin work there?'

'I've no orders about Carlisle,' Mac said.

The works canteen was up and running. They sat at a table and drank coffee out of thick mugs.

'I knew a McNab in Charters Towers,' Bella said. 'He lent me two pounds when I desperately needed it. I paid him back but I owe him a lot more than that.'

'Runs a haulage outfit? He's my cousin. Good bloke, Paul.'

'He's a lovely man,' Bella said. 'How long have you been with BradMin?'

'Twelve years.'

'Good outfit?'

'It's big.'

They looked at each other.

'Hard boss?' Bella said.

'I don't mind that. It's other things.'

Bella sipped her coffee, staring out of the window as a giant earthmover ground past. 'You can feel the ground shake,' she said. 'How long before the ore starts flowing?'

'Like I said, six months, give or take. Maybe a year. Anything more precise than that, you'll have to ask Pete.' Mac gulped the last of his coffee. 'I only work here.'

They walked to Bella's car.

'That's a lovely piece of machinery,' Mac said.

Even below a thick film of dust, the maroon cellulose of the Bentley Continental glowed with an inner fire. Bella patted the bonnet. 'It is, indeed.'

She climbed in, waved to him merrily and drove away.

That, she thought, had been an interesting conversation. Rory McNab had not come across as a whinger yet that was what he had been doing, and to a stranger at that. No significance at the moment, perhaps, but some time in the future it might be useful to know.

Bella locked away the thought and drove back to Miranda Downs.

The road was uneven, potholes already showing in its gravel surface and rattling her teeth at anything approaching a reasonable speed. She thought it might be impassable in the Wet.

It was a long haul; there were times when she shared Mrs Johnson's views about the vastness of this country, especially when she had to get about in a hurry. As now: Perth was a lot further than Miranda Downs and she had an appointment there at the end of the week she did not intend to miss. It would mean leaving first thing in the morning. Drive to Derby, fly to Geraldton, finally on to Perth. It was a long and wearisome journey and she was not looking forward to it.

Our own airline, she thought. Wouldn't that be something?

Peace had finished school as captain of the hockey team and with a string of straight As to her credit, and on a hot morning in early February Bella and Garth went with her for her first day at the University of Western Australia, where she would be studying geology and business management.

'Wouldn't be a bad idea if someone in the family knew what was going on,' Garth said.

Bella tried to imagine how she would have felt in her daughter's place – the challenges of new disciplines and a new life, and she not yet eighteen – but if Peace felt nervous she showed no sign of it.

'I sometimes think she hasn't a nerve in her body,' Bella said as they drove home.

'And you such a shy creature yourself,' Garth said.

'I feel better for having gone with her, all the same,' Bella said. 'It shows we're interested.'

'If she's in any doubt about that she needs her head read,' said Garth.

Bella said nothing; she knew that Peace had always been closer to her father than herself.

'Either way, I'm sure she'll do very well,' said Garth.

'She'd better,' Bella said.

She had plans for Peace.

Ten days later, Garth and Bella were sitting in Owen Freeth's office. He was a lawyer and Garth had known him since university. They had been close mates at the time and had stayed in contact ever since. Now Garth wanted to appoint him to look after their affairs.

'Not just because I know him. He's a top bloke. I've asked around and everybody says so.'

'I've no objection,' Bella said. 'As long as he's good.'

He could certainly afford an impressive suite of offices: one of the smartest addresses in the city with extensive views of the Swan River from its tenth-floor windows. Bella supposed that must be a good sign.

Owen Freeth went well with his elegant offices. He was wearing a button-down shirt with maroon stripes and a fashionably broad tie. His massive cufflinks were chunks of gold with rubies inset in the metal. His manner was suave but Bella thought that his sharp eyes wouldn't miss much. Despite their closeness over the years he was clearly a very different animal from Garth but there was no harm in that, provided he knew what he was doing.

'We'll have twenty million coming in each year,' Garth said. 'So we thought you were the man to tell us how to handle it.'

'We have nothing at the moment,' Bella pointed out.

The agreement with BradMin stipulated that royalties would be paid only when the ore began to flow, and development of the Carlisle Mine had not begun. Bella would never have accepted such a deal but Garth had.

Owen leant back in his chair, tapping his teeth thoughtfully with a gold pencil, and began talking about tax shelters and government bonds. No doubt they had their place; twenty million – should it ever materialise – left plenty of room to move. But Bella had other ideas and interrupted him.

'I've a wish list here,' she said. She took out a piece of paper and laid it on the desk.

Owen raised his eyebrows; perhaps he was not used to clients interrupting him. 'And what do we have in mind?' he said.

She gave him a look; he had not called her dear lady, but it had been close. She read off the list.

'Real estate. A business or maybe two, not too large but with growth potential. And a cattle transporter.'

'A truck?' Owen Freeth was puzzled.

'An ocean freighter.'

'My dear lady, what on earth do you plan to do with that?'

'Ship live cattle.'

'Goodness me…' He lent back in his chair with a patient smile. 'And what gave you that idea?'

The extraordinary ideas some women have! Businesses and live cattle? Whatever next?

She read his thoughts and decided to put an end to them at once. 'We shall get on a lot better, Mr Freeth, if you do not patronise me.'

Garth frowned at her but she ignored him; it was important the lawyer understood where she was coming from. She held his eyes until she saw his expression change. He sat up in his chair with an apologetic cough. He adjusted his position behind his desk. 'My dear Mrs Tucker, that was not my intention, I assure you. Nevertheless I beg your pardon.'

'As long as we understand each other,' Bella said.

'Where do you propose to send the cattle?'

'Indonesia. They are desperate for protein and do not have adequate refrigeration, so frozen beef is not the answer. Also there are religious considerations.'

'You have contacts there?'

'I shall fly to Jakarta to make arrangements.'

Garth was looking at her like a mother hen who has hatched an eagle.

'I was going to tell you later,' she told him.

'And the businesses?' Owen asked.

'I am interested in two areas. Civil engineering and machine tools. With the mining development there will be a crying need for infrastructure and mining equipment.'

Owen Freeth was jotting notes with his gold pencil. 'And the real estate?'

'Commercial buildings in the best areas. The price of property will go through the roof once the mines come on stream.'

The lawyer's expression was very different from before. He spoke carefully. 'You have given this some thought.'

'Even a woman can think,' she said. 'Some women. Some men, too. Or so they say.' But smiled to soften her words. Now she had spelt things out to him, she fancied that she and the lawyer would get on very well.

Garth was put out that she had not discussed these strange notions with him before the meeting.

'I had thought we'd be running the mine ourselves,' she told him. 'Which would have left us no time for anything else. But you felt – quite correctly! – that it made more sense to leave it to the experts. So now we shall have the money and all the time in the world to do what we like with it. I thought I would like to try my hand at business. Nothing too ambitious, but I have a hunch I may be good at it.'

'Not me,' Garth said. 'I'll stick to cattle.'

'There is one thing I would like you to do, though.' It was important that Garth should not feel sidelined by developments. 'We need a financial director. Someone really clued up whom we can trust. I would like us to pick him – or her! – together.'

She saw that Garth was pleased although, being Garth, he had to start by dismissing the idea. 'What do I know about finance?'

'You know people.'

'Funny you should say that,' Garth said. 'I had Billy Gould on the phone only yesterday.'

'What did he want?'

She despised Billy Gould, a feeling that was unlikely to fade.

'Looking for a job. Perhaps he might do. As he's always telling me, he is almost family.'

'Oh, Garth, not Billy. I can't stand him. Neither can you. You know you can't. We need someone with proper skills and experience and Billy doesn't have them.'

'I feel I should help him if I can.'

'Tell you what… You still planning to prospect further along the Carlisle River?'

'Why not?' Garth said. 'We might come up with another treasure trove.'

Mustering cattle was fine; exploring the Outback was fine. Anything other than the nitty-gritty of business; even the idea of sitting in an office sucked the air out of Garth's lungs.

'Then why don't you take Billy with you? Let him carry the gear. If he does a good job we could maybe fit him in somewhere. Not as financial director but in some other role.'

'I am perfectly capable –'

'Of course you are. But you're the one wants him to work for us. Let's see how he likes doing some real work for a change.'

Together Bella and Garth appointed Martin Dexter, a forty-five-year-old accountant with experience in the industry and brilliant references, who they agreed would be perfect for the job. A month later Garth and Billy Gould headed north.

Garth had learnt some of the tricks of the trade during his time with Saul Rich, but his real reason for going into the Outback was to get away. His instinct would have been to return to Miranda Downs and continue where he had left off, the cattleman he would remain until he died, but he was reluctant to turn his back on the mining project on which Bella had set her heart. He remembered what she had said to him in Africa. Do that and he would be turning his back on Bella herself and that he did not want. He believed the difference in their ages might also have created a distance between them and was anxious not to make things worse.

He had taken Billy with him because Bella had suggested it, and within twenty-four hours was regretting it.

'I'd hoped for something better than this,' Billy said.

They had camped for the night and the fire, as always in the Outback, was creating a sense of isolation amid emptiness that Billy, a city slicker to his boots, did not appreciate.

'Feels like we could be the only people in the world,' he said, hunching as closely as he could to the flames: what spelt freedom for Garth meant terror for Billy Gould.

Terror, or maybe laziness, crippled him. He avoided giving a hand with the cooking, or the clearing up, or anything.

Garth was not the sort to keep quiet about it. 'You're as useful as a block of wood,' he said.

'I got a sore foot,' Billy explained sulkily, watching the darkness out of the corners of his eyes.

'You told me,' Garth said.

One thing was sure; he had not got it through carrying more than his share of the gear since Garth, at sixty-four, had been lugging most of it.

'I'd been thinking of something in the office,' said Billy. 'I understood you wanted a financial director.'

'We have a financial director,' Garth said.

'Not a member of the family, though, is he?'

'He knows what he's doing.'

'And that's what matters, isn't it?' Billy said. 'Skill and experience mean more to you than blood.'

Garth was tired of his endless bitching. 'Blood doesn't come into it. Your granddad and my father were partners, not brothers.'

'Doesn't mean a thing to you, the fact they dug up the dough to buy that cattle station for you. Doesn't mean a goddamn thing.'

Garth thought Billy was looking for a fight. His dad had bought Miranda Downs for himself, not for Garth, but he didn't intend to go on yapping about it. He was feeling out of sorts in any case, more tired than he would have expected, and beneath his shirt his chest was wet with sweat. Also he was sick of Billy Gould.

'This isn't working out,' he said. 'We'll go back in the morning.'

'Not as though we're finding anything,' Billy said.

They flew back to Perth. Garth had a moment of dizziness before they took off but once they were in the air everything was fine. He left Billy at a lodging house in town and went home. Not that Desire had ever been a real home to Garth. Bella was in her office. She smiled at him as he came in and kissed him on the cheek. He wished he were ten years younger, able to treat his wife as a woman deserved.

'I wasn't expecting you for days,' Bella said. She looked at him with concern. 'You're looking pale. Are you all right?'

'Sick of Billy, that's all.'

'No help?'

'A real dingo. Beef, beef all the time, and I ended up carrying most of the gear anyway.'

'At least you gave him a chance.' She went back to her desk. There were papers in neat piles and she seemed in complete command both of them and herself.

'I'll only be a sec,' she said, picking up a typewritten report. 'Grab a drink and pour one for me.'

Garth sipped his scotch, watching her and thinking how completely she had grown into this new and, to him, uncongenial environment.

She was a woman who never ceased to amaze him. The aristocratic governess he had first known had become a true woman of the Outback, yet he knew now what he should have recognised from the first, that the bush had never been enough for her. She had talked him into buying Galloway's meatworks; her adventurous spirit had taken them down the Carlisle River and led to their finding the ore; now she had reinvented herself again and become the consummate businesswoman.

It was like being married to a jack-in-a-box; you never knew what was going to pop up next. They'd shared days of passion and tenderness, grief and joy: Colin's death, the birth of their two children, Peace's accident, the discovery of the ore bodies and that trip to Africa. He had said it before and it was still true: she had given a new dimension to his life.

And now?

Now he was no longer sure of anything, or of their role in each other's future.

Bella said: 'I'm glad you're back early. It's always good to see you, of course, but this time there's another reason. The premier's giving a reception for some German bankers and we're invited.'

'What's it all about?'

'They are interested in mining investments.'

'So why are we invited?'

Bella clipped some papers neatly together and put them away in her desk drawer. 'He must think we could be significant players.'

Garth found it a strange concept.

'And are we?'

'Twenty million a year is hardly chickenfeed.'

'If we ever get it,' Garth said.

The function was held in one of the reception rooms of Parliament House. The Germans stood in a small group, smiling, formal and polite. There was a handful of politicians and about thirty people representing the mining industry.

'Quite a select group,' Bella said, nibbling a limp canapé.

An aide introduced one of the bankers. He was trim, in his middle forties, with greying blond hair and wearing a very good suit, dark grey, with a white shirt and silver tie.

He told them his name was Helmut Muller. Like the rest of the delegation he was looking for investment opportunities offering minimal exposure in this new and potentially most profitable business.

'What sort of money are you talking about?' Bella asked.

He gave her the sort of smile that reveals nothing. 'Perhaps two to three billion marks, but that would depend on the investment, its return and the degree of risk.'

Muller spoke very good English with only a trace of accent, but Bella sensed that Garth had not taken to the banker. Sure enough:

'There's no risk-free investment in mining,' Garth said. 'If you're looking for that you've wasted your trip.'

'I did not say risk-free,' Helmut corrected him. 'I said minimal risk.'

The two men smiled with closed lips and did not like each other at all, but Bella saw the banker as a potential source of capital and made much of him in the few minutes before they parted.

'I wonder you didn't kiss him,' Garth said crossly as they drove home.

'He could be useful,' Bella said. 'If we need more funds.'

'What's wrong with our own banks?'

'It doesn't hurt to keep our options open.'

'Too much of a smartarse,' Garth said.

'He was just being polite,' Bella said. 'Which is more than I can say for you.'

'It was his mates killed Colin,' Garth said. 'Don't forget that.'

'The war's been over eighteen years,' Bella said.

'You're saying I should forget my son?'

'Of course not. Neither you nor I will ever forget him. But it's time we moved on, Garth. Please?' She turned and put a hand lightly on his arm but his face, staring through the windscreen, remained stone.

'You'll be waiting a long time, if that's what you're hoping for,' he said.

She said no more. She knew the fact that Muller was German had nothing to do with it. What Garth resented was that the banker was in his forties and personable, whereas he was nearly sixty-three. She loved him, not with the helpless surrender of a first love but tenderly and sincerely, this man who had been her companion and friend for over twenty years. She still found him attractive but knew he had long doubted his ability to excite her as he once had. So when they got home and he took hold of her she knew it was not from simple desire but because of his need to show himself the banker's equal, even in that. She did not mind; on the contrary, she welcomed it because it was then that she felt truly united with her husband once again.

It was not the storm it would have been once – although Garth was still as strong as an ox, thank God – but tender and generous, deeply satisfying, and when they were done Bella had tears of enduring affection in her eyes.

CHAPTER THIRTY-FIVE

Garth Tucker had always liked to believe he was a down-to-earth man who worked hard, took his pleasure where he found it, swore like a trooper and didn't give a damn for any opinion but his own.

The truth was otherwise. Twenty-six years back he had hired Bella to sort out what he had called his tip of a house. Marrying her had not been part of the plan but that was the way things had worked out, because in the course of changing his house she had changed him. He no longer went in for the massive binges that had been a feature of his life in the pre-Bella days; he no longer shared his bed with any woman who came to hand; he had even moderated the war he had waged for so many years with his neighbour on Limerick Downs. When Colin had been killed he might have slipped back into his old ways but had not. He was a changed man and now, quarter of a century after Bella had first come to the Pilbara, he was not exactly old but certainly no longer a youth.

He decided to organise an outing to celebrate the anniversary. He laid his plans in secret, with not more than ten people in the know, but if Bella heard anything about it she didn't let on.

He had been teaching her to fly; she didn't have her licence yet but could manage the Cessna well enough, and he suggested they should take a spin together to give her a bit of practice. Nothing unusual in that; they flew together two or three times a week, but this time he proposed going a little further.

'We'll head south,' he said. 'I went there once, years ago. There is a lot of timber, and a valley with hills on either side and a river running down the middle.'

'It sounds wonderful,' Bella said.

It was even better than he had said: gorges and peaks eroded by the centuries, stately forests and a waterfall spouting a hundred feet into a valley shrouded in mist.

They put down on a level strip of ground, Bella handling the landing perfectly. They climbed out of the cockpit, Garth moving more stiffly than he would have done once, and it was like stepping into the past. Everything was old and watchful and still.

'It feels like we could turn round and see a dinosaur,' Bella whispered. It was a landscape where even whispers were an intrusion.

'Better hope not,' said no-nonsense Garth.

They sat within sight and sound of the waterfall and mulled over the past, the things they had hoped for and how they'd worked out. Garth talked about Colin and Bella reminisced about her childhood and the mother she had lost and mercifully found again.

'You didn't stay in contact after you came to Australia?'

'I tried, but the letter came back. It seemed she'd moved and I had no idea where. I'd have got a private detective to look for her but in those days I couldn't afford it. And afterwards there never seemed the time.'

They talked about their children and the hopes they had for them. Peace was doing well at university. It was early days but already she was making a name for herself in both sport and academics.

'Tough as hell, that one,' said Garth.

Bella smiled. 'You mean she's a chip off the old block.'

As for their second child... They agreed Richard would make a fortune quicker than any of them.

'Three paper rounds and that car-wash business,' Garth marvelled. 'Other boys doing the work and him creaming the profits! I can't imagine where he got that from.'

He did not notice Bella's smile at his remark, nor did he discuss the mine. The massive royalties – when they eventuated – would mean that Miranda Downs and by extension his own life would become little more than a sideshow in the funfair of the family's growing prosperity. To accept that was a hard ask for any man, let alone someone as proud as Garth Tucker, so he avoided the subject whenever he could and instead talked only of peaceful times, happy times, loving times, and the morning passed.

Garth, who always said he was the most unromantic of men, had smuggled aboard a picnic basket which Bella pretended not to have seen, so they had roast duck pate and huge steaks that Garth grilled on the fire he lit for the purpose, and shared a bottle of wine, Bella taking the barest sip because of having to fly them back, and eventually they packed up and returned to Perth at peace with each other and the world.

Safely home, Garth turned to his wife in their gigantic bedroom with its unparalleled view of the Swan River and gave her what he hoped was an evil grin. 'Now for the best part.'

She had expected it. Soon, eyes shut and hands clinging to his shoulders, she lay revelling in the rising momentum of their union, familiar yet always new, always wonderful, nerve ends beginning to plead for the release that was coming, coming now...

Until, in mid-thrust, Garth paused, gave a deep sigh and fell off her and lay unmoving.

For a moment Bella lay still, paralysed by shock. She could not believe what had happened. At sixty-three Garth was still a young man, still vigorous. It could not be serious. Could not. She did not panic. She scrambled to her feet, checked he was still breathing and rang for an ambulance. They said they would send someone at once.

She covered his inert body with a sheet. Garth was breathing more easily but still unconscious. It reminded her of the day of Peace's accident. It had scalded her, knowing there was nothing she could do; now, once again, inaction was a trial.

Garth had over-exerted himself. That was all. Nothing serious. Nothing permanent.

She pulled on her clothes, the ambulance came and Bella went with him. At the hospital the doctor said it was a heart attack.

'Is it bad?' Bella asked. 'He's still young, still strong...'

Of course he would be all right. He had to be all right. But her voice tailed off into uncertainty and the doctor, more honest than many, shook his head. 'It is very bad...'

Bella was back in the bedroom at Ripon Grange, the dust-brown curtains draping the windows, while Achilles Richmond waged his unsuccessful battle for life. She had told the doctor the truth; her husband, like the seventh earl, was a strong man, vigorous and vital. He was sixty-three, for God's sake, not eighty-three. Yet now, like his father before him, Garth lay in the hospital bed, a faded shadow of himself, and Bella knew in her heart if not her head that this was the end.

It took longer than she expected. Over the next twenty-four hours he seemed to rally. His colour improved. The damaged heart beat more strongly. The fluttering pulse grew steady. He hung on long enough for Bella to start thinking in terms of miracles, even when she knew it was foolish to do so. Then, quietly but remorselessly, the pulse and heartbeat faded, the colour turned to chalk, and Garth Tucker died.

Bella's thoughts rattled in the space left by her husband's dying. That was her first response: that Garth's death had created an emptiness impossible to fill. Perhaps that was nonsense; she hoped so. Even as her mind grappled with shock and grief she was planning what she must do.

Immediately after it had happened she'd tried to get hold of the children but had no luck. She had left messages for them at the university and at Richard's school. No doubt they would be arriving at the hospital very soon. The three of them would have to comfort each other. There would be the funeral to arrange, notices to put in the papers, accountants and lawyers to deal with. The will... No doubt there would be stacks of reporters looking for a story. No room for love in any of this. No room for grieving. Like so much else, death had been taken over by the system. Dear God, she thought, we dehumanise everything.

She would have to get up to Miranda Downs as soon as she could. That at least had not been dehumanised. There the red blood of compassion still flowed beneath the skin. She would put Tommy in charge. It would raise eyebrows, an Aborigine running the show, but she didn't care about that. Tommy would ensure the flow of cattle to the meatworks went on as before, and that was what mattered.

She could expect problems from BradMin; the terms of the agreement gave them the right to seek variations now Garth was dead. Pete Bathurst would shaft her if he could but she had one or two ideas on that subject and was not scared of him at all.

As for the rest of her life... The deals, both above and below the table, would continue unchecked; lawyers would send in their fees, bankers would shake their heads: in many ways her life would be unaffected. Yet that was only on the surface, because with Garth's death the foundations had shifted. Now, as never before, she was alone.

She had not realised until now how important it was to have someone share your bed: not just for sex but because only in that close relationship was true support and comfort to be found. For the first time in months she found herself wondering what her life would have been like had she married Charles Hardy. Certainly nothing like this. She regretted none of it – she would always remember Garth with love and affection – yet at that moment it would have been so wonderful to have the comfort of Charles's arms about her.

She shook herself to dismiss the thought, which in the circumstances seemed dangerously close to betrayal. She walked out of the hospital and looked at the sky pulsing with heat above the trees.

Peace, in particular, would be devastated. They would all be devastated. But the best way to remember Garth, she thought, was to go on with what they had been doing: to create a meaningful memorial to the man who had occupied her life for quarter of a century.

Bella set her jaw. I shall build something truly remarkable, she told herself. That is how I shall honour him, and myself. I shall create an empire.

Strength of body and will returned, yet when she got back to Desire it was all she could do to hold back her tears, because the man who had despised displays of emotion had prepared for her an unexpected gift to mark the anniversary of her arrival in the Pilbara.

She opened the cardboard box – no frills for Garth Tucker – and found a pair of antique silver candlesticks and a note.

You said once you liked Hester Bateman's work. I never gave you anything when the kids were born. I came across these at an antique dealer in Perth. He probably ripped me off but anyway, they're yours.

This man who'd had no time for romantic words or gestures. Tears were indeed very close but she bit them down.

News of his father's death left Richard feeling as though the skin had been ripped from his body.

They had never had much to say to each other. There had been times when he had felt Garth wished he had been more of the blood-and-guts person he was himself. Richard would have liked that, too, but he was not and there was no point fussing about it. He was as he was, as Father had been. Mother was the clever one, but Garth had the blood and bone of the land bred into him, and to be faced out of the blue with the reality that he was there no longer was hard to take.

The day after it happened he went down to the Swan River. There was comfort in that, to be alone with the water and the birds. He sat on the bank and let the silence soak into him. He closed his eyes, remembering.

Garth had been an in-your-face man, a true son of the land that had reared him. A man wedded not to books but to action, and glorious in his achievements. He had run a flourishing business, even in the depths of the depression and the war; he had done everything a man could for his family. A good man, therefore, who had found, out of all the women that rumour had attributed to him, the one woman who had been the right woman for him and their children. He had found her and held her close, and that had perhaps been his greatest achievement of all.

A moorhen squawked and rustled in the reeds. Richard opened his eyes and saw, far out in the stream, a flotilla of swans sailing majestically across the current.

He would remember him as Garth would have wished to be remembered: as a man larger than life, laughing, swearing, welded to his horse as he rode year after year to muster the cattle that were his – that at times were not his – robust and ribald, triumphant in victory and stoical in defeat, the flame of living a shining light to permeate all he did.

Richard had one final vision, diminishing now, ebbing gently like the strength from Father's sadly ruptured heart yet still vibrantly alive, a vision that he would hold close to his heart: the black-haired man on his black stallion, rearing like a figure out of heraldry, enshrined in a rainbow radiance of dust, the dust of the land across which in memory he would forever ride.

Peace's first response: it could not, must not, have happened. It was impossible. Later came anger.

Garth had been sixty-three, a relatively young man. A man like that, strong and vital, should have lived forever. And now, out of nowhere, to be suddenly dead? There had to be an explanation. Someone was to blame. She would find out the culprit and destroy him. How she would do it she neither knew nor cared.

Later, when she found out that there had been no explanation beyond the simple fact that, like his father, Garth had possessed a weak and ultimately defective heart within his strong body, she directed her anger furiously against the fate that had deprived her of the one being she had valued above all others.

With Garth's loss, Peace was on her own. No matter; she told herself she was tough enough to survive this or anything. She would devote her life to advancing the power and strength of the family as a monument to the heroic father she had lost. That would be her purpose and her justification.

Somehow Bella got on top of it all, with the help of Deborah Smith, the efficient young assistant she had taken on earlier in the year. Thank God for her, Bella thought. I would never have managed without her. As it was she still had to handle a lot herself. There were phone calls and letters without number. She accepted the regrets of people who had known him: members of the office and domestic staffs; business associates; casual acquaintances. Cattle men from the Pilbara sent telegrams. A handwritten note came from Pete Bathurst, saying that he looked forward to future co-operation with her. Whatever that might mean. Martin Dexter was especially considerate. The premier phoned, promising support for the bereaved widow.

'Most kind,' Bella said.

She said it until she was sick of saying it. She spoke calmly, showing her sorrow but with emotion well under control. She allowed people to see that life was for living; in Bella's future there would be no room for tears, and if people thought her cold it was too bad.

In the dark hours in the empty bed in the echoing house it was a different story. Then loneliness, grief and apprehension took her by the throat and she wept until she thought there could be no more tears left in the world.

Bella had known the children would be desolated and so they were.

Richard was withdrawn, face white, feelings locked away. Like her, he kept his grief hidden. For both of them, their tears burnt unseen.

Peace, as always, was different. Grief was a challenge to be taken by the throat. She had clear ideas what she wanted for her father's funeral: the sky and mourners alike dressed in black, the sombre sound of trumpets over a rain-pocked grave.

Bella felt for her but would not go along with her ideas. This was Garth's day, as that last day amid the forests of the south and upon the bed had been Garth's day, a time of fulfilment and celebration as well as grief. She was determined that the proceedings would reflect Garth's wishes as she believed they would have been.

She told herself that Garth would have turned the whole thing into a rodeo. Bull-riding was hardly a practical proposition but at least they could celebrate his life while mourning his passing.

For the funeral she chose not the cathedral, as Peace and no doubt the premier would have preferred, but a small church in the country.

'I wonder you don't just dig a hole and dump him in it,' said Peace, fighting to the death for the father whose memory, she thought, was being debased.

'If I thought that was what he'd want, I'd do it,' Bella said.

The tiny church had been constructed by convicts over a century before. It was a stone building and in the graveyard the tilting stones were pocked by lichen. The site was surrounded by trees, their white trunks soaring into clouds that released a doleful rain on the proceedings.

Peace defied her mother by wearing black, as did many of the congregation, but Bella stood out, subdued but distinctive: grey patterned skirt, white shirt and an emerald silk scarf that had been one of Garth's especial favourites.

So I throw defiance in the face of death, she thought. He was my husband and believed, as I do, that life is a constant festival. Death, also: because death is a part of life. In a reversal of the normal way of saying it, Bella knew that in the midst of death they were in life; it was entirely appropriate that Garth should have died in the celebration of physical and emotional love.

It was a packed church, which would have surprised him. Politicians, industrialists, friends and the merely curious filled every seat. Others crammed the porch or sat outside in the marquee that Bella, one eye on the weather, had arranged.

Her choice of music – the Toreador's March from Carmen, The Rolling Stones' version of 'Come On' which had recently gone to number twenty-one in the UK and had been one of Garth's favourites – raised surreptitious eyebrows, no doubt, but Garth would have been rocking in the aisle, and that was how Bella was determined the world would remember him.

There was no burial service; the body would be cremated and later Bella would inter the ashes at the lookout on Miranda Downs where Garth had more than once sought solace from the bush.

'Why do we have to do it like that?' Peace demanded.

'It was what he would have wanted,' Bella said.

'Are you sure it is not just what you want?'

'That, too,' Bella told her.

The wake, if that was what it was, took place in the church hall. Like the church, the hall was not grand but Bella had arranged for the most upmarket caterers in Perth to provide the food and drink. They have certainly done Garth proud, Bella thought as she looked around. Those who felt themselves cheated by the humble nature of the church could console themselves with roast beef – appropriate for a cattleman – ham off the bone, fresh-run salmon, crayfish and prawns.

For drinks... You name it.

Wealth created its own obligations; funeral or not, Garth would never have wanted anyone to go away hungry. Nor did they.

After the majority had gone, Bella went for a walk. Greatest and oldest of living things, the trees gathered close about her. Had worship come naturally to her, Bella would have worshipped now. As it was she followed the avenues of silence, the shadows of the forest. She was one with its presence, its breathing and unspeaking knowledge.

She would hold on to this moment. There would be difficulties ahead, times of frustration and even fear, but this memory would sustain her.

She would not forget.

CHAPTER THIRTY-SIX

Billy Gould phoned the next day. Bella hesitated but eventually took the call.

'I thought I might drop by for a chat,' he said.

'Chat about what, Billy?'

'This and that.'

'And there I was, thinking you were phoning to offer condolences. You did know that Garth has died?'

'It was in the paper,' Billy said. 'When can I come by?'

She thought she might as well get it over with.

'Tomorrow morning. Eight forty-five.'

'A bit early for me,' Billy said.

'Eight forty-five,' Bella said. 'I'll give you quarter of an hour. Don't be late.'

It was too much to hope for; it was almost five to nine when Deborah showed him in. Bella looked at her watch. 'You have five minutes,' she said.

'You want to live a little,' Billy told her. 'That way you'll live longer.' He took a chair in front of Bella's desk. He pulled out a pack of Marlboroughs and put one in his mouth.

'No smoking,' Bella said.

Billy thought about it but eventually put the cigarette back in the packet. 'Well, aren't you the tough one,' he said.

'Do you have anything to ask me or not?'

'When is the will being read?'

'Why would you want to know that?'

'Last time I saw him, Garth said he'd taken care of me in his will. So I was wondering what he left me.'

'I can answer you in one word,' Bella said. 'Nothing.'

He glared at her indignantly. 'That can't be right.'

'Deborah will give you my lawyer's address. You can speak to him about it.'

'Damn right I will.'

'Now, if there's nothing else…'

'Hang on… He promised me a job, too.'

'Strange he never mentioned it to me,' Bella said.

He smiled at her, a member of the exclusive male club to which she would never belong. 'A chat between mates, that's the way things get done in this world. Or didn't you know?'

'Perhaps. Nevertheless I am afraid we have no vacancies at this time.'

'That'd be right. Well, lady, let me tell you this –'

Bella picked up the phone. 'Mr Gould is just leaving. Ask Jake to come and escort him out.'

'Hang on a minute…'

Bella put down the phone. 'You are not mentioned in the will and there is no job. What part of that sentence don't you understand?'

He was on his feet, fists clenched. For a moment she thought he really might go for her, but she stared him down. 'What else could I expect?' he sneered. 'A harlot and now a thief. I'll be telling the world about you. I wonder whether your banker mates will be so keen to help you when they know about that?'

After he had left, slamming the door furiously behind him, Bella sat and thought for a while.

Garth's will had been simple enough. He had left Billy nothing. Apart from a few small cash bequests, he had left five per cent of his shares in the mine to his friend Owen Freeth — *for a lifelong friendship manfully endured* — and the remainder of his estate to Bella.

If Billy fancied his chances of getting anything out of her, he had another think coming. She picked up her private phone. Thanks to her remarkable memory, she did not need to check the enquiry agent's number.

'Gayle, good morning. There is an asbestos mine at Van Damm Siding owned by a man called Billy Gould. Some of the workers at the mine are supposedly suffering from health problems. I want you to do something for me.'

She spelt out what she wanted. When she was finished, she put down the phone. Her mouth was tight, her expression implacable.

Harlot and thief. Did Billy Gould really think he could say such things without a comeback?

CHAPTER THIRTY-SEVEN

There were a million things to do and it was two months before she headed north to Miranda Downs. For the first time she flew herself because one of the things she had done in that time was get her pilot's licence.

It was her first visit since Garth's death yet, seeing the familiar buildings, the waters of the creek shining in the evening sun, it was hard to believe she had been away. Any minute, surely, her husband would emerge to greet her. She couldn't help herself. She looked expectantly at the workshop, but its door remained closed: the world had truly changed. The logic of her new life meant she would be spending more time down south than here, yet this was still home, the one place where she could be the self she had been and not the super-efficient tycoon she was in the process of becoming.

For months now there had been mornings when she had looked in the mirror and seen a stranger.

Daughter of an English earl; hostess in a Townsville brothel; Garth Tucker's wife and lover; the Akubra-hatted woman mustering cattle, her body caked with dust and sweat; the mother of two wonderful children; now the businesswoman, owner of vast reserves of iron ore and a growing number of other businesses... How many

more metamorphoses could there be? How many more people were
hiding inside her skin?

The buildings were peaceful in the fading light. Two small children playing near the creek were called home by their mother.
A horse whinnied from the paddock and fell silent. All was still
beneath the gentle pressure of the growing dusk.

I must be sure I come back here often, Bella told herself. To
remind myself what is of value in this life and the person I really
am. Because, beneath all the manifestations of Bella Tucker, she
knew there remained one being with whom she could truly identify: the woman who had been wedded not only to Garth Tucker
but the land. That was the source of the various images of herself
that the world had seen over the years.

Now, surrounded by the familiar sights and sounds among which
she had spent so much of her life, the full sense of her loss struck
home and it was a cruel and bitter thing.

With an attempt at briskness, she told herself she had not come
here to be sorry for herself but for two important reasons. She
would deal with them first thing in the morning but now another
matter took precedence. She was tired after the long journey and
the mixed emotions of coming home churned in her mind and
heart, but there were obligations that must not be ignored.

She had brought fresh vegies with her, loaves of bread and a five-
kilo tin of apricot jam. Also half a dozen chooks, already dressed,
and three circles of linked sausages. Red meat she had not brought;
there was never any shortage of beef on a cattle station.

She was setting out the supplies on the kitchen table when Maisie,
Mary and the rest of the women turned up at the door. They talked
quietly as they worked but Garth's name was not spoken, because
that was the tradition.

They set up the barbecues in the yard outside the kitchen door,
piling dry wood in the trays and letting it burn into hot coals. Soon
the smell of grilling meat was sending signals to the rest of the
camp. Within minutes everyone had gathered. With the stars burning overhead, they sat on the ground and ate together.

Afterwards there was a repetition of the ceremony Bella remembered from the time of Colin's death, the men and women coming one after the other to farewell the man who many had known for most of their lives. Yet this time it was different, because to them Garth Tucker had *been* Miranda Downs, and in losing him they had lost something of themselves.

Here, too, death was not something to be hidden under a stone, as it was in white communities, but was as much a part of living as Garth himself had been, so after they had eaten, the men sat around and, without naming him, talked of a man whose exploits had already become legend. The endless war with O'Malley of Limerick Downs and the triumphs all had shared whenever they had successfully filched some of the Irishman's cattle. The time of the crocodile, when he had plunged fully clothed into the creek, risking his life to rescue a small child who might otherwise have been taken. So many stories, most of which Bella knew, others not. Slowly the tales became entwined with others from Aboriginal legend: Sun-Woman and Moon-Man, Purupriki and the flying foxes, Wuluwait the boatman of the dead. And all the time, while the stories unwound in the night air, Bella watched the firelight casting orange and red shadows on the faces of the listeners, heard the falsetto call of a distant mopoke and knew that this would be the place to which she would return at life's end, just as what remained of her husband's earthly being would finally be laid to rest there the next day.

Eventually all went off to bed. The quietly clicking coals had died to the faintest glimmer; even the smell of the meat had been absorbed by the moist and spicy scent of the bush, and Bella went into her empty house, lay upon her empty bed and waited to fall asleep. She remembered her first night at Ripon Grange and how as a six-year-old child she had lain in the darkness, rigid with fear, waiting wide-eyed for unknown creatures to devour her.

She had thought she might feel something of the same tonight, her present peopled by memories of her past life with Garth, but the simple ceremony and the stories of the people who were also her friends had calmed her mind, bringing a measure of peace that she had not felt since Garth's death.

Bella slept, and did not dream.

First thing the next morning she went through the books with Tommy. Everything was in order and she told him she was appointing him manager to run Miranda Downs for her.

Next, she spoke to Maisie. Once again, she was careful not to use Garth's name.

'I have brought the ashes with me,' she said. 'I shall bury them at the place that he loved. It would be his wish that his friends should be there to witness this but if it is against custom he would not wish it.'

Maisie said, 'Sometimes what you say is true. There is fear that the spirit of the dead one will attach itself to the living. But we have talked about this. This man was not of our kinship system nor was he Aboriginal. We therefore believe his spirit will not trouble those who watch. If it is your wish, we shall gladly attend the burying.'

Bella had been planning to ride up to the lookout but now, after Maisie's words, she walked instead, carrying the urn and the little trowel with which to dig, and all the camp walked behind her.

Up through the trees, the light first green and soft, then bright and dazzling as they came out into the sunlight and saw the bare ridge extending ahead of them with the turquoise sky beyond.

When they came to the place Bella knelt and dug the hole while the people stood in a circle about her.

'Be careful not to strike a rock,' old Maisie said, and Bella was.

Finally the hole was deep enough. She took the urn and lowered it into the hole and filled it in with soil from the pile she had dug. And so it ended. Bella stood. Far below the trees dreamt in the sunlight.

I had thought his life was over, she thought, but I was wrong. He is here still, in the sunlight and the trees, and the bush flowing like the tide until it comes at last to the sea. The land will hold him in its memory as it will hold me, when that day comes. An end and a beginning.

She turned to the people. 'Let us go down.'

That evening old Maisie came to see her at the house. 'You are going away.'

'Tomorrow. But part of me will remain and I shall come back.'

'That is good. Because this is your place, as it is for the man who died.'

They sat together, unspeaking, for a long time. Without ever saying so, Bella knew that Maisie had been one of Garth's women in the long ago but that did not matter. They were two women united by memory, and each comforted the other.

CHAPTER THIRTY-EIGHT

Bella flew south.

She made a refuelling stop in Geraldton, keeping a watchful eye on the petrol bowser until the aircraft's tanks were brimming, then went into the airport office and phoned ahead.

'Deborah… It's Bella. How's it going?'

'Mr Bathurst's office phoned yesterday. They say they need a meeting with you as soon as you get back. It sounds urgent.'

'I'm sure it does. Tell them four o'clock next Thursday afternoon, if they would care to drop by then.'

'I think they are expecting you to go to them, Mrs Tucker.'

'They want a meeting, they can come to us.'

'I'll let them know.'

'Anything else?'

'Gayle Hastings says she has the information you wanted.'

'Tell her I'll see her first thing tomorrow morning.'

'One more thing. We've had a registered letter from a firm of solicitors called Hoblyn, Smith.'

'I've never heard of them,' Bella said. 'What do they want?'

'You want me to open it?'

'You know a better way of finding out?'

A pause; a rustle of paper. Deborah said: 'It's to do with Billy Gould...'

That wretched man, Bella thought. 'Leave it on my desk,' she said. 'I'll look at it when I get in tomorrow.'

BradMin's treasurer Amos Bellamy was affronted. 'She expects us to go to her? Who does she think she is?'

'Take no notice. A woman on her own, with no hubby to hold her hand? She'll be lost,' Pete Bathurst said, grinning like a wolf. 'We'll get her royalty down by fifty per cent, no sweat.'

Two things Bella particularly liked about Gayle Hastings: she was always on the ball and never kept her waiting.

'Tell me what you've got,' Bella said.

Gayle told her.

'And they said they'd testify?'

'Like a shot, once they knew you were covering their legal costs.'

'Give me a spare copy of your report for Owen Freeth. I'll tell him what I want him to do.'

Bella had decided that the meeting with BradMin should take place not in her office but the adjoining boardroom. At four o'clock on Thursday afternoon – the hour she had stipulated – she studied the smiling faces of the three men as they were ushered into the room and took their places along one side of the long rectangular table that three years before Bella had had made from selected jarrah timber. They were BradMin's CEO Pete Bathurst, the company's legal counsel, Sinclair Smythe, and treasurer Amos Bellamy. Pete Bathurst was the one to worry about; the others would follow wherever he led. On her side of the table Bella was flanked by Owen Freeth, here to handle any legal problems, and financial director Martin Dexter. She waited while Deborah gave each man a folder containing the documents they were here to discuss.

It gave her an odd feeling to watch these men. They were all successful, experienced and ruthless and she knew without question that behind the pleasant smiles they had come here with one purpose only: to devour her as quickly and completely as they could. No doubt they thought that an inexperienced widow, recently bereaved, would be easy pickings.

When they had left Africa she had been full of confidence but then Garth had been beside her. Now she was alone, would it be a different story? That was something she was about to find out. She had sought advice from no one. Single-handed, she had made up her mind how she was going to conduct the meeting.

She remembered the first time she had been up on a horse. She had been seven years old and the ground had looked an awfully long way down. Now Bella did what she had done then. She took a deep breath, refusing to accept even the possibility of failure, and...

Got on with the job.

Deborah went out, shutting the door quietly behind her. Bella looked around the table. She gave them all a weak, tremulous smile. She said: 'I should like to thank you for breaking into your busy schedules to come here to discuss the decisions that we must take following my husband's death. I really appreciate it.'

'We were all real sorry to hear the news about Garth,' Pete said.

'Thank you.'

'Good man. Really. I liked him a lot.'

Pete putting on the sincere act was more than Bella could stomach. 'My husband's death has created a new situation,' she told them. 'Among other things, we have to review the agreement regarding the Carlisle Mine.'

Sinclair Smythe had a thin neck and looked like a gander. Now he seized his chance. He had brought his own papers, which he now proceeded to spread on the table in front of him.

'Indeed we must. Clause 11, sub-clause 3 (b), of the agreement specifically states that the terms have to be renegotiated in the event of the death of any of the parties. Which in turn means –'

'She knows what it means, Sinclair.'

Like Bella, Pete Bathurst had no patience with the reverence that overcame so many lawyers when they started talking about sub-clauses.

'We're here to discuss the rate of royalty,' said Amos Bellamy.

'Hey, straight for the jugular!' Pete said. He twinkled at Bella across the table. 'Trust the bean counters, right?'

Bella contrived a worried look. 'What do you have in mind?'

'I went to bat for you,' Pete said kindly. 'I know how tough things are for you at the moment. But my board feels...' He shook his head as sorrow overwhelmed him. He turned to his treasurer. 'Tell her, Amos.'

Amos was not as affected as Pete Bathurst. 'Given the increased risk factor the company has no choice but adjust the amount of the royalty. However, it wishes to be fair.'

'How much does the company have in mind?' Bella asked.

'Fifty per cent. Some board members thought that was too much but the majority favoured generosity.'

'Fifty per cent?' Bella repeated sadly. 'Is that all?'

'That is fifty per cent of your personal share. Your late husband's share naturally falls away altogether.'

'Five million instead of twenty,' Bella said.

'It's still a useful piece of change,' Pete said consolingly.

His expression said he felt her pain as keenly as she did. Poor little widow, out of her depth and alone in the world.

'Yes,' Bella said. 'I see...'

'Anything I can do to help,' he said sincerely. 'You have only to ask.' Such helplessness! Hey, Pete thought, we should have made it twenty-five per cent. Maybe it's not too late...

And Bella smiled. 'Let's nail one assumption straight away. On this side of the table we're not here to talk about the rate of royalty but the agreement itself.'

Watching them, Bella saw their expressions change, although Smythe still clung to his sub-clauses like a drowning man.

'In terms of our joint understanding —'

Pete Bathurst cut him off. 'What you got in mind, Bella?'

'Mr Smythe has said the agreement must be renegotiated but we are not sure we want to continue with it at all.'

Shoulders like a Patton tank, Pete Bathurst hunched forward in his chair. 'I don't get you.'

And Bella thought, I can do this. I really can do it. Euphoria threatened but she controlled it; for the moment, euphoria was the enemy. 'Let me spell it out,' she said quietly. 'The present arrangement is unsatisfactory —'

'In what way?'

She looked sideways at Martin Dexter. 'Tell him.'

'Because it says that no royalty is to be paid until the ore is produced,' Dexter said.

'And development has not yet started,' Bella said.

'The agreement does not specify a timetable,' Pete Bathurst said.

'But Mr Smythe has reminded us that Clause 11, sub-section 3 (b),' — such a whimsical smile! — 'requires us to renegotiate the terms, and that is what we intend to do.'

Pete's scowl had terrified many in his time but if it terrified Bella she did a fine job of hiding it.

'You're saying that instead of royalties you want a management agreement?'

'Depending on what you can offer us.'

Pete's look of concern was as convincing as the rest of the charade. 'It wouldn't be right if I didn't warn you of the risks. All development costs will be down to you, Bella. Every last penny. Frankly,' he said, 'I would be failing in my duty as Garth's friend if I allowed you to go ahead, risk losing everything. Know what I mean?'

'You are saying BradMin is not prepared to enter into a management contract for the development of the Carlisle Mine?'

'I'll put it to the board but quite frankly —'

'You're saying it's royalties or nothing?'

'It's you I'm thinking of,' he said.

Bella worked to reinstate her worried look. It was hard to believe she could get away with it twice but given Pete's attitude to women in business she thought it was worth a try.

I can do it, I really can... 'I'll let you know,' she said.

'Don't take too long,' he said. 'We got other irons in the fire, even if you don't.'

'He wants the profit,' Martin Dexter said.

'Don't we all,' Bella said.

'All the same, you have to accept,' Owen Freeth told her. 'What choice do you have?'

'Leave it with me,' Bella said. She had the Hoblyn, Smith letter with her. Now she handed it to him. 'In the meantime, do what you have to do with that.'

He glanced at it quickly, then nodded. 'It'll be a pleasure,' said Owen, no friend of Billy Gould.

Bella nodded at the both. 'Thank you, gentlemen.'

Martin said: 'You want me to –?'

'Thank you, Martin.' She walked back into her office and closed the door behind her. She sat at her desk, lifted the phone and asked Deborah to come in.

'I am going back to Miranda Downs,' Bella said.

'So soon?'

'Something's come up.'

'Must be important.'

'Could be,' Bella said. 'I want you to get this number for me.'

It took an hour; long-distance calls were always a problem. When at last she got through it was a horrible line – that, too, was no surprise – but through the interference she was just able to make out the voice of the individual she had wanted.

'Sounds like someone's frying bacon and eggs on the line,' she said. 'Can you hear me?'

'Just about. How can I help you?'

'I'd like to invite you to lunch,' Bella said. 'I have something I need to talk to you about.'

'Invite me? You astound me. Where are you?'

'In Perth.'

'Long way to come for lunch.'

'It's also not private enough,' she said. 'Miranda Downs is a better bet.'

'What do you want to talk about?'

At this stage Bella was unwilling to say more; if there were no interest in hearing what she had to say, there would be no meeting. However, if there were…

'I'll tell you when I see you.'

She could almost hear the thoughts clicking one after the other as she waited. But eventually:

'When would you like us to meet?'

'Shall we say twelve o'clock next Tuesday?'

She took great care over the preparations. She had her visitor down as a no-nonsense, practical person. That was what she was hoping, anyway, with flowers and silverware unlikely to be priorities. At the same time she wanted to send a message that Bella Tucker was a person worthy of trust and respect. That was fundamental; without it, no one could be expected to put themselves on the line in pursuit of a dream, and that was what Bella needed.

Bella got old Maisie to help her fire up the barbecue pit first thing in the morning and rig the wind-up spit over it. She'd ridden out with a rifle the previous evening. There were wild pig in the hills and she had bagged one as night came down over the forest. It was the right size: big enough to be worth eating but not a shoe-leather-tough giant. She'd lugged it back strapped behind her saddle, the mare all white eyes and snorting at the blood smell.

She was out of bed first thing and, as twelve o'clock approached, the smell of roasting pig, basted at regular intervals with honey, was enough to bring saliva into the mouth of the most fastidious. She'd brought red wine, beer and malt whisky, with some Coke on ice just in case. There was a mixed salad with spicy hoisin sauce, fresh crusty rolls with real butter, and huge potatoes roasting in the fire.

All she needed was her guest, who arrived precisely at the time they'd agreed, the ute bumping and bucking down the rutted track.

Bella was by the door as the vehicle braked to a halt. 'Welcome to Miranda Downs,' she said.

'Nice place you got here,' Rory McNab said as he climbed out.

'It suits me,' she said.

They shook hands and Bella liked the open way his eyes met hers. Insofar as it was possible to trust anyone in this life, she thought she could trust this man. It gave her a good feeling after all the nonsense she'd had from Pete Bathurst and the rest of his shabby crew.

She took Rory into the house and pointed him at the new bathroom that had been one of the last improvements they'd made before Garth's death.

'I'll have a cold beer waiting when you've freshened up,' she said.

'Sounds good.'

By the time he rejoined her she had cracked the tops off a couple of Amstels. 'Here's to us,' she said.

'Cheers.'

They drank straight from the bottle.

'You want wine with your lunch?'

Rory said he'd stick with the beer and did so, tipping down the first after his long and dusty drive but taking his time over the second.

He looked at his plate piled high with pork, well cooked but still juicy. 'This is what I call living,' said Rory.

After that neither of them had time for conversation; Bella had never known good food improved by chatter and was glad her visitor apparently thought the same.

Finally they were done. Rory leant back in his chair, squinted at the sunlight-paddled yard beyond the window, then turned to look at Bella across the table. 'So, why am I here?'

Bella drew a deep breath and explained what she wanted and why she thought he was the man for the job.

He heard her out without interrupting, then said: 'I have a senior position with one of the major players in the mining industry. You, on the other hand, are just starting up. You don't know, nor do I, whether you'll make a go of it or not. Explain to me why I should give up everything I have for a gamble like that?'

Bella said: 'Because it gives you the chance to do what you have always wanted but never done.'

'And that is?'

'To be in charge. To run your own show from the very beginning. To bring in a brand new mine.'

Silence, while he looked thoughtfully at her. 'You hardly know me, yet you read me like a book.'

'Because we are both alike. Because, like me, you're a number-one person, and nothing less will do.'

'If I work for you, I shall never be number one.'

'In the company, no. But at the mine, you will be in charge.'

'Solely?'

'My word on it,' Bella said.

'Would you do it, if you were me?'

'I'd kill for the chance,' she said.

'So would I,' he said.

Bella's heart skipped a beat. 'So you'll do it.'

'To develop my own mine? That I will, and gladly. And I swear to you, Mrs Tucker, you'll have no cause –'

She held up a hand. 'If I needed your oath you would not be the right man. But explain one thing to me. You have not mentioned money, or how I am going to raise the finance for the development. Pete Bathurst warned me the costs would be huge –'

'He was right. But I am sure you'll find a way round it.'

'Why do you think that?'

'Because you're willing to take on Pete Bathurst, something no one else I know would dare. Not only take him on; woman or not, I believe you are the only person I know with the balls to make it work. Pardon me for speaking so plainly.'

'I expect you always to speak plainly to me,' Bella said. 'And I shall do the same to you.'

'There's another reason, too,' Rory said. 'You're canny. I like that.'

'In what way am I canny?'

'Access to the BradMin railway. If you hadn't arranged that, Bathurst could have choked you before you'd even started.'

'It's only until 1984. But it seemed a sensible precaution. Without it, we were helpless.' She looked at him candidly. 'I am very glad we met each other. I think we'll do all right together.'

He nodded. 'Trusting each other is half the battle.'

'I believe it is,' Bella said.

'Pete won't take it lying down,' he warned. 'He'll do whatever it takes to destroy you. And a more ruthless bastard never walked.'

'Then we'll just have to be smarter than he is, shan't we?'

'Damn right.'

Back in Perth, Bella told Owen Freeth and Martin Dexter of her meeting with Rory McNab and how it had gone.

Owen was astonished.

'You mean he'll come to work for us? How did you manage that?'

'I offered something he's always wanted and he said yes.'

'How much will we have to pay him?' Martin asked.

'That wasn't discussed.'

Owen clearly thought this the most extraordinary thing of all. 'What kind of lunatic would agree to such a thing?'

'A lunatic of great ambition,' Bella said. 'And faith. In himself and in me.'

'You really propose to develop the mine independently from BradMin?' Owen asked.

'I do.'

'And what do you plan to use for money?'

'That is the next challenge,' Bella told him and laughed at his expression. 'Exciting, isn't it?' She turned to Martin Dexter. 'You have a valid passport?'

'Where are we going?'

'London,' she said. 'Tonight.'

She spoke to Deborah, who arranged two first-class return tickets and would spend the rest of that day and the next on the phone to the list of London bankers that Bella gave her.

'I don't care how you do it,' Bella told her. 'Make sure they're willing to see us when we get there. When it's all fixed, send me a telegram at the Ritz Hotel. And let me have a copy of the geological report that Saul Rich prepared when he did the initial survey.'

Rory McNab had told Bella he was sure she would find a way to raise the money. She had thought so, too, but the London bankers were an eye-opener. She had never met a group of people more courteous in their manners or ruthless in handling the stiletto with which, one after the other, they dispatched Bella Tucker and her as yet undeveloped mine to the Hades of broken dreams.

'I would not have believed it,' she told Martin in her suite overlooking Green Park. 'How can they be so blind?'

Yet they both knew why; none of them believed a woman capable of developing an iron ore mine in the Australian Outback. It was a fantastic notion and the bankers, serious men all, were not keen on fantasy.

'So what do we do now?' Martin Dexter wondered.

'I have one string left to my bow,' Bella told him. 'And we had both better hope it works.'

She gave instructions to the hotel switchboard. They were having lunch – smoked salmon sandwiches, a green salad on the side, Vichy water to drink – when the call came through.

'Helmut,' Bella said. '*Wie geht's?*'

'Thank you. I am very well. And you, too, I hope. It is a great pleasure to hear from you.' The German accent was as faint as she remembered, but Helmut Muller's voice was so clear that he might have been in the same room. 'What can I do for you?'

'I would like to come and talk to you.'

'You are in Frankfurt?'

'In London. But I am flying over.'

'When do you arrive?'

'Tomorrow morning.'

'One moment.' She could hear him turning the pages of his appointment book. 'Why don't you come to the office at twelve? We can have lunch in the directors' dining room and you can tell me what this is all about.'

'I look forward to it,' Bella said.

'Your husband is with you?'

'Unfortunately my husband died a few months ago.'

'I am sorry to hear it. Please accept my condolences. And I look forward to seeing you again tomorrow.'

They booked into the Méridien Parkhotel. Bella dressed with especial care; Helmut Muller had made no secret of his admiration back in Perth and Bella was prepared to trade on that, at least to a point, if it would get her what she wanted.

'Restrained but sexy,' Martin said. 'I like it. I gather you won't be wanting me to chaperone you?'

'Not this time.'

She rang reception to organise a cab. By the time she was downstairs it was waiting; one of the many benefits of a five-star hotel. She gave the driver the address and a few minutes later he dropped her off in front of what might have been the door of a private house, had it not been for the bronze plaque set in the wall beside it.

She pressed the doorbell and a minute later was admitted to a hallway with a black and white tiled floor and a variety of dark oil paintings on the walls. The man who had admitted her looked at her enquiringly.

'Mrs Arabella Tucker for Herr Doktor Helmut Muller,' Bella said.

She could not remember the last time she had used her full name but instinct said it might come in useful now.

The man murmured discreetly into a phone. He hung up and in very fair English said:

'The Herr Doktor's assistant will be with you very shortly.'

The assistant was young, blonde and classy-looking. Bella was unsurprised; no one who worked for Helmut Muller would be anything else.

She escorted Bella to a lift with an old-fashioned grille gate which took them swiftly to the fifth floor. Helmut was waiting at the door of his office and came at once to greet her as the lift gate clanged open.

'This is a most delightful surprise,' he said and led her into his office.

Bella looked around the room. Everything was understated but of top quality: mahogany desk and fitted bookshelves, quality prints upon the walls, lined silk curtains at the windows. Herr Doktor Muller fitted his background perfectly. He was as personable as Bella remembered and was wearing a light-grey woollen suit, white shirt and silver tie, with highly polished burgundy leather brogues on his feet. His fingernails were clean and well shaped and he wore no jewellery of any kind.

'You had a good flight?'

'You are staying at the Méridien Park? The historic wing, no doubt? Just so. An excellent choice.'

Inconsequential observations, while Bella was aware of his eyes studying her. Aware, too, that this was not only a formidable but a highly attractive man. It was the first time since Garth's death that she had been conscious of herself as a woman in the presence of a man.

'Shall we have luncheon?' Helmut said.

The directors' dining room had a series of screened alcoves around the walls with individual tables in each, where it was possible to talk without being overheard. The table linen was immaculate, the cutlery real silver.

Bella ordered a fillet of sole and a green salad, with a glass of Gerolsteiner to go with it. Helmut joined her with the Gerolsteiner but ordered a breaded veal cutlet.

'I cannot interest you in a glass of wine?'

Bella shook her head. 'I'll stick with the mineral water.'

His eyes signalled his pleasure at the company of this beautiful Australian woman yet he was not in the least uncouth about it and Bella found she was enjoying the attention. Nor did it get in the way of business. They finished eating and he ordered coffee, which arrived in a silver pot, with chocolate mints on the side.

'Tell me what this is all about,' Helmut Muller said. 'And how I can help you.'

He listened attentively while Bella explained.

'You wish to develop the mine yourself?'

'That is my intention, yes.'

'And you have head-hunted this mine development manager from BradMin? This will not make you popular with Mr Bathurst, I think.'

'I can live with that.'

'Even so, he could be a dangerous enemy.' He drank coffee, pondering. 'Have you spoken to any other bankers?'

'In London, yes.'

A raised eyebrow questioned her. 'And?'

'They found it hard to envisage a woman developing an iron-ore mine in northern Australia.'

'With a pick and shovel, *ja*?' He laughed lightly. 'I suspect you would do that, too, if necessary. Do you have figures for me?' he asked. 'Any information at all?'

'I have the geologist's report, including estimates of mineral reserves. Also our projected capital needs, including development costs and plant requirements, based on estimates produced by the mine development manager.'

'It will be very helpful if our experts can examine these documents. On a confidential basis, of course.'

'I have them in my briefcase,' Bella said. 'Also I have my financial director with me and he will be able to give you any additional information you require.'

'That will also be very helpful. How long are you planning to stay in Frankfurt?'

As long as it took was the honest answer but Bella did not want to tell him that. Instead she said: 'I want to get back as quickly as I can.'

'If you can let us have those reports and make your financial director available to us, I should be able to give you an answer within three days.'

CHAPTER THIRTY-NINE

It was a long three days. The weather remained fine. She prowled the city. She drank coffee beneath the trees in the Wiesenhütten-platz; she visited the art gallery and museum; she read English language newspapers on the hotel terrace; she strolled in the summer garden and dawdled over lunch in Le Parc restaurant. Slowly the time passed.

On the evening of the third day Helmut Muller phoned and invited her to come and see him. She could not tell whether it was good news or not, so her heart was in her throat as the lift carried her to the fifth floor.

'Let me tell you at once,' Helmut said, 'that some of my directors were at first inclined to share the view of the English bankers. However, those of us who feel differently were able to persuade them to our point of view. I therefore believe we shall be in a position to assist you.'

Bella opened her mouth to speak but Helmut raised his hand.

'However…' he said. 'There are conditions.'

'Which are?'

'One. We shall be prepared to fund fifty per cent of the projected development costs subject to your obtaining backing for the remainder from banks in Australia. Two. You have told us that Mr McNab has not yet joined you. The loan will be subject to confirmation that he has started work. Three. We shall require monthly reports both from Mr McNab and a suitably qualified independent mining surveyor regarding progress of the development. Are these terms acceptable to you?'

'Yes,' Bella said.

'When do you plan to return to Australia?' Helmut asked.

'Tomorrow. Provided we can get a flight.'

'In the meantime my office will prepare the necessary documentation. Would you like us also to make the arrangements for your return journey?'

'That would be most kind.'

'There is one further condition upon which I must insist,' he said.

Bella's heart sank. 'What condition is that?'

His smile was like sunshine through clouds. 'That you have dinner with me tonight.'

'My goodness,' Bella told him, 'are you telling me I must cancel all my prior engagements?'

'I am. No compromise will be permitted.'

'Then I have no choice, do I?'

'Absolutely not.' He looked at her curiously. 'Do you really have prior engagements?'

'No,' she said, 'I do not.'

They went to Weidemann, on Kelsterbacher Strasse, and ate traditional French cuisine and drank a bottle of burgundy. Afterwards he drove her back to the hotel, parked and suggested that the evening might be best concluded by his coming upstairs with her.

She looked at him. This was a very attractive man. When he made the suggestion she had felt her body react with something like an electric shock. Also he was a man she could not afford to offend. She told herself there could be no harm in combining business with what she was certain would be a great deal of pleasure. She licked her lips. She said: 'I don't think so.'

His expression showed nothing; it was impossible to know what he had expected, or whether her refusal had caused offence.

'You are a widow,' he said. 'Without commitments?'

'The trouble is I do not feel like a widow,' she said.

'It is perhaps too soon after your husband's death?' he suggested.

She seized gratefully on his words. 'I am sure that must be the reason. I have had a lovely evening and I can assure you I find you a most attractive man, but you are right. I am not yet ready for another relationship.'

'I understand,' he said. 'I respect you for taking such a position. You are a woman of principle. You have no idea how refreshing that is. In this business we encounter endless liars and con-artists. That is why you are getting your loan, because I have informed my co-directors that I regard you as a woman of integrity.'

'Thank you,' Bella said. 'I like to believe you are right.'

'And of course there may be another time,' he said.

'I shall look forward to it,' she said.

She leant forward and kissed him on the cheek. She got out of the car and stood as he lifted his hand to her and drove slowly away.

She closed her eyes and drew an uncertain breath. She went up to her room, closed and locked the door and lay fully clothed upon the bed. She wondered how she would have been feeling at this minute had she answered him differently. She wondered what she was feeling now. Regret? Relief? She could not be sure. At least he did not seem to have taken offence. And, as he had said, there might always be another time.

Now everything seemed to happen at once.

They flew back to Australia and two days after their arrival Owen Freeth arranged for a consortium of bankers and their advisers to meet Bella and Martin Dexter at his office.

Speaking on Bella's behalf, Owen set out the situation and the fact that Mrs Tucker intended to develop the Carlisle Mine on her own account.

Bella saw that the bankers were not happy with that idea.

'A woman miner?' one of them said, and rubbed a dubious chin. 'That's a new one.'

The man was a director of the Western Pacific Bank, and his reservations were obviously shared by others around the table.

'Almost a contradiction in terms,' another banker said.

'We understood that you and your late husband had a royalty agreement with BradMin,' said a third. 'You receive royalties and BradMin provides the expertise. That, if I may say so, seems a more sensible arrangement.'

'Much more sensible,' agreed number two.

'Under the agreement which lapsed with my husband's death we would receive a royalty on the ore extracted. Which in practice meant we were getting nothing because BradMin has not begun production. Also it meant that, should they ever get around to doing so, they would pay the royalty but keep the profits. This does not seem to me to be an equitable arrangement.'

'How much profit are we projecting here?'

This from one of the advisers, an eager little ferret of a man.

'Between one hundred and one hundred and fifty million dollars a year,' Bella said.

The magic of those figures cast a spell of shocked silence about the room.

'So you can see why I am anxious to keep those profits for myself,' she said.

'These figures are impressive, no doubt, but hypothetical,' said number two banker, who clearly opposed the whole concept. 'Credibility in business is all-important.' He spoke as though explaining the two times tables to a five-year-old. 'A woman running a mining operation does not possess it. The market will not like it. It will tend to regard it with considerable scepticism. Certainly not one for large-scale investment.'

'It is fortunate that not everyone shares that view,' Bella said. 'I have here a letter of intent from the German Investment Trust Bank of Frankfurt. You may recall that Mr Muller, one of their directors, was out here recently looking for investments offering both security and a high level of return. Now it seems he has found one.'

This put a different complexion on things. The Germans had an excellent name in banking circles and the German Investment Trust Bank was one of the best regarded of all. The letter of intent was passed from one pair of hands to the next, and all of sudden smiles took the place of frowns.

'I am offering you an opportunity to participate in a profitable new industry,' Bella told them. 'But I need a quick decision and, if you feel you would rather not become involved in an operation where a woman is CEO, I shall of course make other arrangements.'

They scrambled hastily for cover. *Of course* they had never been opposed to a woman CEO. Perish the thought! It was simply a question of market acceptance and credibility.

'You have forty-eight hours, gentlemen, to come up with a yes or a no,' Bella told them.

More protests but less assured now.

Such short notice... A decision might not be possible...

'Forty-eight hours,' she repeated. She stood up. 'You will no doubt wish to get back to your offices as quickly as you can. Mr Dexter will be available over the next two days for telephone consultation, should you require further information.'

Meek as sheep, they filed out. Bella watched them sardonically, waiting until the door was safely closed behind them.

'Gotcha,' she said.

The telephone rang and was picked up. A man's voice spoke gruffly.

'McNab...'

'We've got the funding,' Bella said. 'When can you start?'

It was the briefest of conversations. She put the phone down and drew a deep breath. Martin Dexter was watching her from the other side of the room but for a moment she did not speak. She got

up, walked slowly to the window and looked out. The sun was shining and in the rose garden the flowers were coming out. At the base
of the hill the Swan River was a crooked sword, shining between
the trees.

Another three months, Bella thought, and the family would be
together for Christmas. Now Garth was gone the children were her
only family and she was looking forward to doing things with them.
Which was not to deny the importance of the mine. Every time she
thought about that her heart went into overdrive. It was small wonder; she was committed now, prey to conflicting emotions of exhilaration and terror. Exhilaration, because it was exciting to live on
the edge, to challenge her destiny; terror, because she was putting
everything – not only her assets but her and the children's future –
into the hazard. The banks would require every asset she possessed
as security. Even Miranda Downs would be pledged. If she failed...

The thought made her feel sick but her expression showed nothing as she turned to face Martin Dexter across the room. 'He has
to give three months' notice. He starts with us in January,' she said.

'Pete Bathurst is going to love us.'

'Pete Bathurst can take a hike,' Bella said.

'So you've got the money and the man. Seems to me congratulations are in order,' Martin said.

'A bit early for that. I may end up ruining us all.'

'I don't believe that and neither do you.'

'Don't be so sure. If you see me hobbling it's because I've got my
toes crossed as well as my fingers.'

'I wondered if I might invite you to have dinner with me,' Martin said. 'To celebrate.'

Bella had always told herself she would never get involved with
a member of her staff. What she had said to Helmut Muller was
also true; it was too soon after Garth's death to think of another
relationship. But Martin was a friend as well as a senior member of
her team and having dinner with him – to celebrate, as he had said –
was hardly getting involved.

'I would like that,' she said.

They went to Thomas Kettle's Place, a new restaurant in Perth that Bella did not know. She had dressed up moderately for the occasion and she was pleased to see Martin had done the same in a tailored turquoise shirt, grey pants and highly polished black shoes.

'I hardly recognise you without a suit,' she said.

'The hidden me,' he said.

'It suits you,' she said.

They both ordered the duck, with a bottle of Margaret River cabernet merlot to go with it.

'One stipulation,' she said. 'No shop.'

After the complexities of mining finance it was pleasant to talk instead of other things: the poetry of Dylan Thomas, a visit Martin had paid to South-East Asia the previous year, Bella's trip to Africa with the family in 1961.

It made for a pleasant evening but when Martin suggested doing it again Bella was non-committal. One meal together was not a relationship but repeating it too soon might make it so.

'Let's see how we go,' she said.

CHAPTER FORTY

Four days later Pete Bathurst came into his office and found an envelope, sealed but unstamped, lying on his desk. It was addressed to him and marked private and confidential. He opened it. His neck went dull red as he read it. He threw open the door and was down the corridor, face like the wrath of God. He threw open the door to Sinclair Smythe's office without knocking or apology. Sinclair was studying a document. He looked up enquiringly as Pete stormed in, one finger marking the place he had reached.

'McNab has resigned,' Pete said.

Sinclair pulled a pad towards him and jotted a note before he answered. 'Is it so important?' he wondered. 'Since you keep pretty close control of things yourself?'

'McNab is on the ground,' Pete said. 'I monitor what's going on but you must have somebody there to keep an eye on the day-to-day operations. Particularly with communications so bad.'

'Does he say why he's resigned?'

'He doesn't need to. He's a mining engineer. He's not going to work in a cake shop, is he?'

'I am not sure I take your meaning,' Sinclair said. There were times when he found Pete Bathurst's boorishness hard to swallow.

'I mean he's going to work for another mining company. No prizes for guessing which one.'

'Why should we care what he does after he's left us?'

Bathurst's big hands were clenching and unclenching as he looked at his treasurer. 'It matters if he's gone to work for that damn Tucker woman.'

'Is it likely? Leave a company like this for a tuppenny-halfpenny outfit like Tuckers?'

'Not such a tuppenny-halfpenny outfit, once she's up and running. She's got twice the ore reserves we have!'

'Maybe she has. But she'll have a job raising the finance. I was talking to Murchison in London. He tells me the London banks have all turned her down. Assuming that is correct, she will have to agree to our terms, won't she? What other choice does she have?'

'If McNab is going to work for her she's raised the dough somewhere,' Bathurst said.

'I'll make enquiries,' Sinclair said. 'See what I can find out.'

'While you're at it, check that agreement we had with the Tuckers. See if there's any way we can stop her breaking loose from us, if she's foolish enough to try.'

'I can tell you now. There is nothing we can do. We worded it so that we could walk away from her, if it suited us to do so.'

'Instead of which she walks away from us,' Pete said grimly.

'We don't know that for sure. But if she does there is nothing we can do to stop her.'

'Except break her back. You think I'll let a two-bit woman run rings around us? I'll be the laughing-stock of the industry!'

'All this is supposition –'

'If she's talked McNab into working for her, it's a declaration of war. And I fight wars to win. Whatever it takes.'

CHAPTER FORTY-ONE

'You need to tie up markets for this stuff,' Rory McNab told Bella.

It was the tail end of 1964 and the Carlisle Mine would soon be open for business. Only limited amounts of ore would be produced to begin with but it would be a start while they waited for the rest of the development to come on stream. They stood under the concrete-roofed observation shelter and watched, mufflers over their ears, as the exploding charges stripped the overburden from the area Rory had chosen for the mine's first development. Clouds of dust erupted skywards. Within two weeks they would start installing the huge surface miners. The special design needed to suit the horizontal nature of the deposits had caused significant delays and cost over-runs, but Rory had assured Bella they would be in production eight weeks after installation began.

'And the rest of the equipment?'

Work had been in progress for months on the screening, crushing and de-sanding plants.

'Another month and they'll be ready, too.'

'You're right,' Bella told him. 'Time I went on my travels.'

'Shouldn't be hard,' Rory told her. 'Japan's crying out for the stuff.'

It certainly was. Martin Dexter, ever mindful of the pennies, had suggested that everything could be arranged at long range, but Bella had always been a believer in personal contact.

'This is the first time we've dealt with them. Face to face will be best.'

'If you're going you'd better go now,' Martin warned her. 'Or you won't be back for Christmas.'

'I mustn't miss that. This could be one of our last Christmases together as a family. My God, Martin, I'm getting old.'

'You certainly don't look it.'

It was so nice to get compliments; it made looking in the mirror less of an ordeal. But I am still forty-five, she thought. Maybe not ancient but not a kid any more, either.

She lived on the phone for the next two days and then flew out. She told Martin she did not expect to be away long, nor was she. Ten days later she was back.

'Tokyo, Wakayama, Nagoya and finally Nagasaki,' she said. 'I am utterly exhausted.'

But was not; she was radiant because she had won contracts with three of Japan's major steel companies. The trip had been a huge success.

'Deliveries to begin three months from the date of signature,' she warned. 'We'll need to get our skates on. And won't Pete Bathurst be mad we've beaten him to it!'

She had Christmas with her children, as planned. She took them hiking in the forests around Cape Leeuwin, on the far side of the Blackwood River, where she and Peace had gone once before. It was a lovely time. Even Peace lived up to her name for once. Bella wondered whether the boyfriend she mentioned, ever so casually, might have something to do with that but there was no way to be sure; Peace had never been one for confidences.

After the holiday, they all got on with their lives.

CHAPTER FORTY-TWO

Peace had taken up with Ian Lassiter three months after Garth's death.

She thought afterwards she had done it to fill the gap left by her father's loss. If that was the case it was a mistake because never in a million years would Ian measure up to the man she had revered above all others. Ian was caring, considerate, patient and, above all, respectful of authority. A gentle soul with qualities that were supposed to be pluses in any relationship. Garth had been a larger-than-life man whose personality had dominated everyone he had known with the exception of his wife; Peace had never been able to make up her mind whether she resented or admired her mother for that. Both, probably. And perhaps that had been another reason why she had taken up with Ian: because of the qualities possessed by neither of her parents nor, in truth, by herself. He was a shoulder to cry on and would no more have rustled his neighbour's cattle than jump off a cliff.

Within twelve months Peace had known they were going nowhere but they remained an item — more friends than lovers — until Peace's final year, when she used her need to study as an excuse to break off with him.

It was an uncomfortable parting but Peace, having made her decision, stuck to it and it was soon over. She could have had any number of other boys, had she wanted them – she knew she was no beauty, but there was something about her that drew them to her like a suction pump – but she had set her sights on a post-graduate course at the Camborne School, which meant getting good grades in her finals. Socialising was out.

For six months she worked eighteen hours a day without distractions and came away with a first class honours degree and an air ticket to London.

Mother came to the graduation. They caught up on each other's news and were good mates together and Peace wished with all her heart that darling Dad had been with her.

They talked about the mine. Things were coming along nicely, Bella said. The Japanese contracts were on track. Pete Bathurst was still trying to cause trouble but so far Bella had managed to fend him off.

'What kind of reserves does the mine have?' Peace asked.

'Unlimited.'

'There is no such thing as unlimited reserves,' Peace said.

'Scientifically speaking, maybe not.'

'What other way is there to speak about mining?'

Bella ignored that. 'There is enough to keep us going until you come back from Camborne. Then you have my permission to be as scientific as you like.'

There was a graduation ball that night. Peace was going with a friend. No doubt he would want to grope her before the evening was over, probably try to talk her into bed, too. Since the advent of the pill girls had been expected to play along with these casual adventures but Peace and no one else was in charge of her life. Maybe she would and maybe she wouldn't. The chances were she wouldn't. By the end of August she would be in the UK and wanted no complications in her life. If he didn't like it, tough.

She had found that a measure of physical activity helped her to think. Concentrating on her studies, she had dropped out of hockey a few months back. Instead, after Mother had left, she wandered down to the squash complex, found an empty court and smacked a ball around for a while.

She moved automatically, paying no real attention to what she was doing. As she sent the ball crashing about the walls, she thought about the Carlisle Mine.

She had read Saul Rich's original report. He had thought the reserves of high-grade ore were huge. What a challenge it would be if he proved to be right. She had a vision of a development like a mighty city, of terraces and mountains. Machines the size of multistorey buildings crawled along the terraces, creating and exploiting them; mountains of ore were loaded in a controlled frenzy of endless activity into rail trucks, bulk carriers, the gaping maws of blast furnaces. Transformed into shining rivers of steel, then into pipes and beams and bars and bolts without number, into sheets of plate, the ore from Carlisle would transform the world.

The land would be ripped open by the machinery and changed thereby, as it would be changed by the men and women who would help in the development, their energies as much a contribution to the new structures as the ore torn from the reluctant earth. The wilderness would be destroyed in the mining areas but elsewhere much would remain, although in ever diminishing quantities. There was sadness in that thought, a dichotomy between seeking to preserve what was good and holy while utilising the earth's resources for the improvement of humanity. It was a contradiction to which she suspected no one knew the answer, yet the excitement of the development rang in her mind like the ripple explosions of charges shattering rock, and she knew no regrets.

CHAPTER FORTY-THREE

University was behind her at last. It was seven o'clock in the morning and Peace was in her bedroom in Desire, getting ready for her first day at the office.

During her time at university she had stayed in shared accommodation close to campus. Now she had eight months before she was due at Camborne and she and her mother had agreed it made sense for her to fill in the time by doing some work for the company. Bella had provided her with one of the guest suites – a living room and bathroom to go with the bedroom and its own separate entrance – so Peace had no gripe about the accommodation, but all the same she was glad she wouldn't be staying here long. She was proud of her down-to-earth attitude to life and Desire was way too grand for her, but the main problem was that the suite, like the house, was not hers but her mother's, the furniture was her mother's, even her privacy was in her mother's gift, which she could take away whenever she chose.

She had forgotten what an overpowering place Desire was. Even living here was a challenge; every inch proclaimed power and wealth. No wonder Dad had preferred the rough-and-tumble of Miranda Downs. Now that was a real, no-nonsense home; Desire

was a showplace, very tasteful, no doubt, and the treasures it contained were marvellous, but a constant reminder of Bella's personality and the certainty that one day there would be a falling-out
between them. That was guaranteed; Peace had to work because she
could not imagine life without it, and she had to be number one.
The problem was that in the Tucker empire Mother was already
number one, and there was no room at the top for anyone else. Also
there was the fact that Bella was only forty-six and the last person
on earth to hand over authority to anyone.

For the moment it didn't matter; Peace would soon be gone in
any case. Even when she came back from the UK she wouldn't have
the experience to run the company – but that time would come.
She would work hard, she would learn. She would give Mother
until she was sixty. If she wasn't willing to hand over then, Peace
would move on: it was that simple.

That was assuming she came back at all. With her qualifications
she would be able to land a job anywhere in the world: Africa, the
USA, even Brazil. She had no particular preference as long as she
was free, eventually, to do her own thing.

There was not much chance of that in Australia, at least to begin
with. Bella would expect her to join the company and working *for*
and not working *with* was the way things worked with Mother.
Peace had only been back from uni twenty-four hours yet Mother
was already bossing her about. Of all things, about what she should
wear.

'On site it'll obviously be industrial boots and overalls, but your
first day you'll be in the office. A business suit might be best,' Bella
had said. 'Something plain but stylish. You're going to work, not
taking part in a fashion parade.'

Peace didn't have a suit and had no plans to buy one; she hated
business suits. You needed class legs to get away with that style
and hers were nothing special. Instead she had decided on tailored
slacks, a lightweight blouse in blue with a hint of bust, shoes with
three-quarter heels. Blue suited her colouring and she suspected

that, even without class legs, a hint of femininity would not hurt, even in the mining industry.

If Mother didn't like it, too bad.

Her heels clicked on the marble floor as she walked through the vast reception room – like a museum, she thought – and went into the dining room. There was coffee perking on a side table, orange juice in a crystal jug. Chafing dishes contained eggs Florentine, bacon and mushrooms. There was no one about or any sign of Mother.

Peace checked her watch. Seven-fifteen. Better get moving, old lady, she thought. The new girl's arrived.

A young woman, not above sixteen, appeared at the kitchen door.

'Have you seen my mother this morning?' Peace asked.

'She's in her office upstairs. You'll have to catch her sooner than this, you want to speak to her. She left a message, though. She's not to be disturbed, but you're to go to the office, soon as you're ready. When you get there, speak to Martin.'

'Martin?'

'Martin Dexter. The financial director. She said he'll see you right.'

Peace was so surprised that the girl managed to escape before she had a chance to ask her anything else. Clearly the competition had started already, and she hadn't even got to the office.

CHAPTER FORTY-FOUR

Richard Tucker — tall and slender, dark hair a tangle across his fore-head — came bounding down the steps of the commerce faculty at the university. There was a lecture on commercial law and if he didn't get a move on he would be late. The lecturer had just stood up as Richard pushed his way into a row near the back of the hall. He found he was sitting next to an Asian girl of about his own age, whom he had never seen before. An older man was sitting on her far side, another Asian, who looked at him disapprovingly.

'Just in time,' Richard said cheerfully.

The girl did not answer.

There was an intermission halfway through the lecture; only then did Richard take proper note of his neighbour and for the first time saw that she was beautiful.

He said: 'There's tea and coffee in the corridor if you'd like a cup.'

The girl looked at him but did not speak.

Her companion leant forwards. 'Miss Lee appreciates your offer but regrets she is unable to accept.'

Richard was taken aback. 'Perhaps Miss Lee can decide that for herself.'

He looked enquiringly at the girl.

'Thank you,' she said. 'I am grateful for your offer –'

'The answer is no,' the man said.

'Answer is no,' Miss Lee said.

Denied her company, he went out and had a coffee by himself. Had it not been for the man's intervention he would not have given the girl another thought but now remembered her remarkable looks and wondered who she was. Richard had an acquaintance in the office. After the lecture he asked him about her.

'Name's Lee. Just arrived from China. Father's some big shot in Beijing.'

Which would explain why she was so closely guarded.

'I've always been interested in China,' said Richard. 'Art, ceramics, stuff like that.'

The acquaintance grinned. 'And of course you wouldn't happen to fancy her, too, would you?'

'Looks like that, it wouldn't be hard,' Richard said.

Two weeks passed before he saw the girl again. The same man was with her so he kept away but several days later he saw her sitting by herself at the end of a row.

He could see no sign of the man so during the interval he changed seats. The one next to her was occupied but the one behind was not, so he sat there. It gave him the chance to look at her properly for the first time.

Black, glossy hair fastened by clips above the ears. Ivory-coloured, smooth-textured skin. An inexplicable radiance. He could not see her hands but was sure the fingers would be long and elegant; everything about her breathed elegance. She was exotic, too, excitingly so.

He thought: We have barely spoken and already I am drawn to her.

It was a foolish reaction yet he did not feel a fool. He felt brave.

The lecture reached its dusty conclusion and the ranks of students surged up the gangways to the exits. He waited until the Chinese girl stood and turned to leave before stepping into the gangway in front of her. She was dressed like the other women students, in blue jeans and white T-shirt. Her figure was slight, but good. For a moment they faced each other while the rest of the students surged past them.

An island of silence, he thought. Simply by standing there she has silenced the mindless noises of the mob.

She looked at him gravely, and he thought: She knew I was there all the time. He was filled with elation, thinking how she could have brushed past him but had not. He looked at the oval face almost painful in its symmetry, the almond-shaped eyes beneath finely drawn eyebrows, and she was everything he had remembered or imagined or desired. He felt his heart turn over.

That is it, he thought, I have heard of it but never thought to experience it. I felt my heart turn over.

'We spoke briefly once before,' he said. 'You may have forgotten.'

'Not forget,' she said.

'I offered you a cup of coffee. On that occasion you refused. Perhaps you would like one now?'

'No.'

'Something else, perhaps?'

'No.'

'Tell me,' he said, 'do you say no to everything?'

'No.'

He was convinced there was a smile and a challenge in the dark eyes. Daring him to do... What? He felt the breath tighten in his chest. 'I would like to see more of you. If that is possible.'

He waited for her to say no again, but she did not.

'We both student here. We see each other often. Yes?'

The accent was a challenge to him as the language clearly was to her, but it was enough, for the moment, that she had spoken. That she had not said no.

'Of course we shall.' He spoke slowly and clearly, watching to see her response. 'Here, in the lecture hall. And outside it.'

They walked side by side to the exit but, before reaching it, she moved away from him, creating space between them. Richard walked into the sunlight and saw at the foot of the steps an illegally parked car. Waiting beside it was the man who had been with her before.

He stopped and stood watching her back as she walked on down the steps. The man opened the car door and she got in. The door closed. At the last moment he thought she might have looked back at him but the movement of her head, if that was what it had been, had been so brief that he could not be sure. The man got behind the wheel and the car drove away.

He had let her go yet she had not left him. He would see her again, because she had spoken to him. The man would have wanted her to walk away from him but she had not. She had spoken. Only a few words but that did not matter. She had spoken and he would see her again.

Surrounded by a chattering crowd of students, Lee Su-Ying walked down the long flight of steps towards the waiting car. She was thinking about the young man who had just spoken to her. She wondered who he was. She wondered why she should care, but there had been something about him...

A strange western boy in a strange western country. Tall, with a kind face. Su-Ying knew she must be very careful. She was in Australia to learn so that when she returned home she would be better able to serve the Party and the People. She was not here to make friends.

At their last meeting Father had stressed what an honour was being paid to her and the family by her being entrusted with this mission.

'Remember what you are.'

What, not *Who*. The Great Helmsman had taught that the individual did not matter. The individual did not exist. Only the Party mattered. The Party and the People.

'Every day you will repeat that to yourself,' Father had instructed her. 'Lee Su-Ying does not exist. There is only the Party and the People. Be on your guard at all times. You will be surrounded by class enemies. Make friends with none of them.'

Walking down the steps beside her, a woman student, blonde hair flying, was laughing amid a crowd of boys. Laughing, joking, all happy together. Students of her own age, having a good time. She saw Su-Ying and gave her a big smile. Happy...

You will be surrounded by class enemies.

She caught herself before she could smile back.

Lee Su-Ying does not exist.

It was a hard rule to understand. She was aware of the stone steps beneath her feet, the laughter of the students, so how could she not exist?

She had another thought also. Surely a degree of friendship was necessary if she were to understand these foreigners? What had Chairman Mao said? *Let a hundred flowers blossom and a hundred schools of thought contend...* Without getting to know them how could understanding be possible? Without understanding how could knowledge be possible? Without knowledge what value would her learning have?

Such confusion... I am too young, she thought. I do not even understand myself. How can I understand westerners with their different thoughts and ways?

That boy is still watching me, Su-Ying thought. I can feel his eyes on me but I shall not look back. It would be unthinkable to look back.

She reached the car, the driver waiting, engine running, door open. She stepped into the car and the driver closed the door. As he did so she risked a sideways glance. He was there, as she had suspected, standing motionless at the top of the steps. She remembered how he had looked at her after the lecture, with all the students pressing up the auditorium steps around them. She remembered how for a moment they had seemed to be alone amid the crowd.

Perhaps she could learn from this boy? If she was very, very careful?

It took Richard a long time to coax the relationship beyond that first stage but eventually he succeeded, because he wanted it. He knew now that he had wanted it from the first moment he saw her. There was another thing, too: with the passing weeks he became more and more convinced that she wanted it, too.

Slowly she was becoming integrated into the student body, mixing and making friends. Girl friends, mostly, but with her looks it would have been too much to hope that some of the boys would not be after her too. Richard watched apprehensively, asking himself what he had to offer this wonderful, beautiful, exotic woman with whom he now knew himself in love. It was hopeless, of course. She was from China, her father a senior man in the Party. As students among other students, friendship might be possible, but a closer relationship was out of the question.

She had told him that Comrade Minister Deng believed that China needed the west to develop its own potential. That was why she was in the commerce faculty, to study western business methods and improve her English. What she learnt she would take home with her and use for the benefit of China.

'What does your mother think about that?' he asked.

'My mother died when I am small,' she said. 'In any case make no difference. We are taught individual not important. Obedience to Party everything.'

He knew he must not become too attached to her; their lives were set on separate paths. But knowing and accepting were two different things.

'There is Chinese fable,' she told him. 'Spinning maiden and cowherd.'

'Tell me,' he said.

'They live in night sky, are permitted to meet once each year. They cross a bridge of stars and are with each other for a single night.'

'And the rest of the time?'

'They wait for that one night.'

'You are saying that you are the maiden and I the cowherd,' Richard said.

'Except that in our case there is no bridge,' she said.

He had found out her full name. It had taken a long time to get it out of her.

'What is secret about anyone's name?' he had asked in exasperation.

'No secret.'

Lee Su-Ying: the sounds were unfamiliar yet fitted comfortably in his mouth.

'And that is what people call you?'

'My name is Lee,' she said. 'Miss Lee. My father and close friends call me Su-Ying.'

'May I use that name?'

She studied him, her expression so grave that he almost withdrew his request. Yet did not, sensing it might be important. At last she nodded. 'You may call me that.'

They were seeing more of each other now, regularly with other students but sometimes by themselves, too. It was surprising how much they had in common. Not in everything: his jokes were a problem. He sensed her feeling around the edges of his offerings, attempting to decipher them but seldom succeeding. It might have irritated him but did not; it endeared her to him more than ever.

I shall hold her hand. I shall explain everything to her and she will understand.

He was besotted yet said nothing, afraid he might frighten her off. They never met off campus. Control over her seemed more relaxed than at the beginning, the watchers less in evidence, but still there were limits. Always there was the waiting car, the watching man. Having coffee in the students' cafeteria, he asked her about it.

'What harm can it do? Go to the movies? Go dancing? Do all the things other couples do?'

She stirred her coffee thoughtfully, not looking at him. 'I know it is difficult for you to understand but it is impossible,' she said.

Her fluency with English had increased beyond belief. The accent was still there but she had learnt to use the tenses that did not exist in Chinese, and all the other phrases that had baffled her at first. Her conversation was no longer stilted. Richard liked to think that the relaxation in her speech was increasingly mirrored in their relationship.

At a nearby table a girl was shrieking at a boy who was shouting back. His attention focused on Su-Ying's lovely face, Richard shut out the distraction. 'For heaven's sake, why not?'

'That man is my father's friend. He sends weekly reports to Beijing.'

Richard was aghast. 'He spies on you?'

'It is not spying! He protect me. He is right to keep my father informed. How else is Father to know?'

'Does he know about us?'

She shook her head emphatically. 'If Father thought I had become friends with a westerner, he would summon me home at once.'

'And you would go?'

'What else should I do?'

'It is your life, after all.'

'I serve the Party, and my father. Their wishes, not mine. Anything else would be unthinkable.'

'You are with me now,' Richard said. 'Is this what the Party wishes? Is this what your father wishes?'

'My father would be distressed.' She looked troubled. 'I am a most unfilial daughter.'

'But the right to decide does matter. The individual does matter.'

'You are wrong. The individual does not matter at all.'

Yet she was still seeing him, although she knew her father would disapprove. The spinning maiden and the cowherd… Perhaps the bridge between them might be found, after all.

* * *

Su-Ying stood at her bedroom window and stared out at the walled garden at the rear of the house. It was July 1966, winter in Australia. The plants looked drab, there were no flowers and the sky was grey.

The colours matched her mood because she could no longer pretend Richard Tucker meant nothing to her. She had known him for eighteen months and had let herself get fond of him, which was very dangerous. She did not love him – she was the Party's instrument to be directed as the Party wished, and there could be no question of that - but from the first he had been comfort in a strange land.

I wish to remain his friend, she thought. But it is not easy because I know he feels more for me than he should.

Her dilemma about Richard was made worse by the bad rumours coming out of China. There had been nothing so far in her father's letters, which arrived punctually every month, reminding her of her duty to Chairman Mao and to the Party, but the Chinese businessman in whose house she was billeted had been hearing stories for two months now of schools being closed, of teachers being attacked and even murdered. Bands of students, waving Chairman Mao's *Little Red Book* and calling themselves Red Guards, were said to be spreading mayhem through the countryside. And now *The People's Daily* newspaper was full of criticism of former President Liu.

The whole country was in turmoil. What could it mean?

She was increasingly scared for her father. If Liu Shao-Qi could be attacked in such a way no one was safe.

It was mid-August and he thought they had become close. They were not lovers – they had never even kissed – but Richard was in love. What was to be done?

There was nothing to be done.

He had got into the habit of meeting Su-Ying every morning at the students' cafeteria where she had first told him that the individual did not count. They met; they talked. Students' talk, mainly, although once or twice Su-Ying mentioned unrest brewing in China.

'Nothing serious, surely?'

'No need for concern,' she said brightly. 'The Party is in complete control.'

She *was* concerned, whatever she might pretend, but Richard knew she would never say anything critical of events in China, even to him.

Today she was late. Richard sat at their usual table. Through the window he could see the grounds sloping down to the river. It was a fine day at winter's end, the sky clear and the temperature likely to rise to twenty-five degrees. What he would like to do was cut classes, take a boat and picnic basket and explore upriver with Su-Ying beside him. He would like to do that and all the other things his friends did with their girls. He would like to take her to movies, the theatre, concerts. He would like to take her to bed. He knew there was no chance of any of these things.

With her, he was happy. Apart, doubts came crowding. What was he doing, longing to possess what he could never have? The most he could hope for was half a relationship: and not the better half, either. There was no chance of intimacy or even tenderness, because they were never alone long enough for tenderness to be possible. He had invited her to his room only once.

'To listen to music,' he had said. 'To be together.'

To be alone. To hold hands. To kiss. To touch.

It was natural, wasn't it?

It might have been rape, the way she reacted to his suggestion, and he saw nothing of her for a week. There were times when their different cultures were a trial, indeed. He looked at his watch. It was getting late. He had plenty of work to do. After five minutes he assumed she wasn't coming and headed back to his room.

For three days he saw nothing of her. On the fourth she was there, acting and speaking as though everything was normal, but he had read the papers, saw the strain in her face and knew that things were very far from normal. He did something he had never done before. He leant across the table and covered her hand with his. She flinched but did not withdraw her hand.

'Tell me what is troubling you.'

She would not look at him. 'It is nothing.'

'I do not believe you.' Richard took the newspaper that lay folded beside his cup. He opened it and showed it to her.

'Page two,' he said. 'Middle column.'

He watched as she read the news report that he had read several times.

Several million so-called Red Guards gathered yesterday in Beijing's Tiananmen Square. Chairman Mao addressed several mass meetings, calling for an end to revisionism. This is widely interpreted as an attack on certain prominent officials, former president Liu Shao-Qi and leading Party member Deng Xiao-Ping among them. Observers believe these attacks are likely to continue and intensify.

Su-Ying put down the paper. Her lips were white; she was staring not at him but at something Richard could not see.

'Deng Xiao-Ping?' he said. 'Could this be dangerous for your father?'

'I do not believe this story.' Her eyes told a different story. 'I love Chairman Mao,' she whispered.

In the early spring of 1967 Su-Ying was walking on the beach. The sun was shining, the sea blue. All should have been harmony in her world but was not.

She was not alone. The previous year control over her movements had been relaxed but now she was once again being watched. The comrades who had come with her from China had been replaced by others, more prison guards than protectors, who answered none of her questions and seldom spoke except to each other. Now they walked ten yards behind her as she paced the sand. She knew she was their prisoner in all but name and felt increasingly adrift, alone and helpless.

One by one, her beliefs had been destroyed.

She had been taught that Australia, like all western countries, was starving. She had believed it unquestioningly; now she knew it was a lie.

She had been taught that westerners hated the Chinese and were envious of China's living standards. That was a double lie. There was no hatred and Australia's living standards were much higher than those in China.

She had been sent here to gain knowledge for China's benefit. What use was that now that China had descended into an anarchy where violence was commonplace, rape and murder encouraged, schools and universities closed and in which nothing and no one was safe?

Brought up from childhood to revere Chairman Mao, she had told Richard that she loved the Great Helmsman. Maybe once that had been true; not now. Whatever good things he had done in the past, she believed that Mao Ze-Dong had become a monster.

Deprived of faith, she had fulfilled her father's parting words. She no longer knew who she was. Lee Su-Ying did not exist.

Waves edged with foam ran up the tawny beach and retreated and she could hear the sand grating as it was sucked in and out. Gulls sailed overhead, white wings curved to capture the wind. The sunlight on the wind-flecked sea was dazzling; the soft sand made walking hard but she went on. There were standing rocks twenty feet high at the end of the beach and she was determined to reach them. If her escorts hated her for making them walk so far under the hot sun the feeling was entirely mutual. Lies had destroyed the old Lee Su-Ying but with each step along the steeply shelving beach she became more determined that a new Su-Ying would take her place, one loyal to the values of the past but less gullible than before. From now on, she thought, scepticism will be my guide.

She reached the end of the beach. The rocks were stinging with heat when she placed her hands on them. Her body was a lather of sweat beneath her clothes and there was no shade. The sand shimmered and she could feel her temples swelling beneath the impact of the light. She turned and walked back past the two men, ignoring them as they ignored her. They had their orders. If they were told to follow her they would; if they were told to kill her they would. That was the level to which the new China had reduced them: all three of them were things, without will or individual significance.

She feared for her father under this new system. She thought his faith in the omniscience of the Party and the perfectibility of man could not survive, as hers had not. But there was a difference. She was young enough to remake herself; she feared that he was not. If the Red Guards did not destroy him he might destroy himself.

She feared for herself, too. *The People's Daily* had quoted Madam Mao as saying that those who worked with foreigners were enemies of the people. Where did that leave her? If they could force her back to China she might find herself another victim of the madhouse that the country had become. Banishment, rape, murder... None of these things was impossible.

Only one person had shown her unfailing respect, support and loyalty. She knew that Richard Tucker loved her, would protect and cherish her if he could. She also knew there was nothing he could do. He was Australian and she Chinese, separated not only by race but by civilisation and beliefs. He had a mother, a sister who might regard her as an enemy. Whichever way she looked she could see no refuge. She was adrift, alone and helpless.

It was over a year since the troubles had begun. Formerly they had been seeing each other every day; now it was once a week. Whenever he saw her Richard asked about her father.

'Still all right,' she said.

Her face was wan; the tension was draining her. She no longer proclaimed her love for the Chairman, yet still he could not reach her.

'Can nothing be done?'

'Nothing.'

Only wait anxiously for news. Which in some ways was the worst punishment of all.

He felt for her so much.

'I would shed my blood for you.' Never would he have believed he could have expressed his feelings so openly, yet now he could say no less. 'You know that, don't you?'

Even after saying such a thing... She looked at him silently, her drawn face showing nothing, her eyes showing nothing... Still he could not reach her.

'There have been developments,' Su-Ying said.

'Where?'

'Here. And in China.'

She told him that the man who had been entrusted with her care, the Australia-based businessman who was also her father's friend, had been replaced.

'He has been ordered back to China to answer charges.'

'Obviously he won't go.'

'He has already gone.'

'And in China?'

'*The People's Daily* has reported that Comrade Deng has been sent for re-education to an engineering works.'

Her father's mentor and, until now, his protector. No need to ask the implications: they were written clearly on her face.

It was terrible to be so helpless.

In November 1967 she received news that her father had been dismissed. He had been sent to the countryside, to labour in the fields.

For the first time she came sobbing into Richard's arms, head resting on his chest.

'They are calling him a class traitor,' she sobbed.

Richard told himself he would kill whoever had caused her such pain. Such a stupid thing to think. He was powerless; they were both powerless. Yet that was not the worst thing she had to tell him.

'This is goodbye,' she said.

He stared; he could not have heard correctly.

'I have been ordered back to Beijing.'

He said: 'You must not go.'

'The plane leaves tonight.'

Richard stared at her questioningly. 'Plane? China has no diplomatic representation here.'

'Commercial flight to Hong Kong,' she said. 'Then on to Beijing.'

'I want you to listen to me,' Richard said. 'Listen to me well.'

He made her sit in her usual chair, pressing gently on her shoulders until she did so. 'Wait here while I get us some coffee.'

He went to the counter to order, turned and saw her halfway to the door. In two strides he had caught her.

'Sit down!' he said. 'I want you to hear me out. If you feel you must go after that, I won't stop you.'

More tears now, her unquestioning belief in the Party and its chairman destroyed, but Richard felt better than he had for weeks. He had seen the faintest possibility of helping her and that prospect sent adrenaline racing through his blood.

'Will you sit down and wait for me?'

He held her by both arms and all his body was shaking with the vehemence of his feelings.

Eventually she nodded.

'Say it.'

'I will wait.'

They went back to their table. Unbidden, she sat down, head bowed. He did not think she would try to leave again. He ordered the coffee, carried the mugs back to the table. He was conscious of eyes watching him – many of the students knew something of her problems – but nobody spoke.

He sat down and took her hands in his. 'Look at me,' he said.

She did so, eyes swimming with tears.

'What will happen to you if you go back to China?'

'My father has been banished because of his connection with Minister Deng. I think I shall probably be banished, too. If I am lucky.'

'And if you are not?'

She bit her lip. 'Anything.'

'Anything? Prison? Rape? Murder?'

She sat with bowed head. Tears were falling on her hands and she did not speak.

Now the vision that Richard had discerned became reality. It was very simple, now he had found the courage to speak the words. 'I will not allow it.'

'How can you prevent it?'

'You will come with me,' he said. 'It will give you time to decide what you need to do.'

'Come where?'

'I shall take you north.'

She shook her head, unable to grasp what he was saying.

'I cannot –'

'You have your passport?' he asked.

'No passport. But I have a letter of identification that I was given before I left China. With my photograph.'

'How did you get here?'

'By car. The men who have been guarding me came with me. They are waiting for me now. They didn't want me to come at all but I could not leave without saying goodbye.'

'It is not goodbye,' said Richard. 'But thank you anyway.'

'I said I had to fetch some personal papers. I must get back or they will come looking for me –'

Panic was building.

Richard tightened his grip on her hands. 'You're going nowhere except with me.'

'I must get my clothes, personal things –'

'If you go back, they'll make sure you're on that plane. Is that what you want?'

'But –'

Is that what you want?

'No,' she whispered, her face tragic. 'The way things are in China at the moment, I would be frightened to go.' Suddenly she froze. 'There is one of them,' she whispered.

Richard did not turn his head.

'Where?'

'In the doorway.'

'Alone?'

'Yes.'

Which meant the other man must have stayed with the car. Or so Richard hoped.

'Has he seen you?'

'Not yet.'

The cafeteria was not big enough to hide anyone for long.

'Keep your head down,' he said.

He walked over to the group of students whose eyes had followed him sympathetically ten minutes before. He spoke to them in a low voice for a few minutes, then went back to Su-Ying.

'What is happening?' she asked in a frightened voice.

'Wait,' he said. 'Be ready to move when I say so.'

He sat, blood pulsing in his ears. The group of students edged casually towards the door where the Chinese man was turning his head this way and that, trying to see where Su-Ying was.

Suddenly the students turned on each another, shouting and barging, throwing punches… Inevitably innocent bystanders were caught in the fray. Within moments the group, Chinese man and all, had swept out through the cafeteria door, which banged shut behind them.

'Now!' Richard said.

He leapt to his feet, Su-Ying beside him. In seconds they were across the room and out the second door by the kitchen before anyone could stop them.

'Run!' he shouted.

Run they did: down the grass slope and on to the footbridge that spanned the river and led to the students' car park on the far side.

They were halfway across the bridge when they heard a yell and, turning, saw the second man racing down the slope behind them.

'Come on!'

They raced across the car park to Richard's car, parked – thank God! – close to the exit. Doors banged as they flung themselves into the seats and Richard took off, aiming for the road, when the man appeared directly in front of them, screaming incoherently and brandishing a –

'A gun?' Richard was incredulous; more, he was outraged. 'You don't wave guns around in this country, mate!'

He rammed his foot down on the accelerator and drove straight at him. Su-Ying screamed, hands covering her eyes; at the last moment the gunman threw himself sideways; the car cleared the exit and turned down the road in a screech of tyres.

'Welcome to the wild west,' yelled Richard, grinning, adrenaline levels through the roof. 'We'll show the bastards!'

They reached the highway and headed north. As promised.

Now she was over the initial excitement Su-Ying was as limp as rags.

'Where are you taking me?'

'My family's got a cattle station in the Pilbara called Miranda Downs. My mother spends most of her time in Perth these days but she's up there at the moment. She's looking forward to meeting you.'

'She's expecting us? How does she know we're coming?'

'It'll be our little surprise for her.'

'Then how can she be looking forward…?'

But gave up. The hows and whys could wait. For the moment, she saw, Richard was beyond explaining anything.

Richard laughed; he felt he could spend the rest of his life doing nothing else. Why not? He had got Su-Ying away from the men who were trying to kidnap her; he had defied a gunman and got away with it; after months of frustration he had finally done something decisive. Most important of all, he had beside him the woman he adored above all others. Why shouldn't he laugh?

And laughed again, to prove it.

They stopped overnight in Geraldton, two hundred and sixty miles north, so Su-Ying could buy clothes.

'Underclothes, at least,' she said. 'And something to wear when I meet your mother.'

'You have money?'

'Oh. They would not let me have any,' she said.

'Take this.'

He gave her some; it was lucky he had some to give.

While she was in the dress shop, Richard phoned Bella at Miranda Downs. 'Where are you?'

'In Geraldton.'

'Coming to see me? How nice! Any reason in particular?'

'I have a girl with me.'

'That Chinese girl you've been telling me about? The one whose father is caught up in this Cultural Revolution business?'

'Yes.'

'How exciting! Anything I should know?'

Richard smiled into the receiver. Matchmaking mother... That was a new role.

'I'll explain when I see you.'

'It's too late to get down there today. The plane will pick you up in the morning.'

Su-Ying wanted it to be all very righteous.

'Of course I must have a room to myself,' she said. 'What will the world think if we spend the night in the same room?'

Richard would not have a bar of it. 'And if those men track us here and come after you in the night?'

'How will they be able to do that?'

'I don't know. But it's not a risk I'm willing to take.'

She wasn't happy about it but Richard refused to give way.

'I promise not to lay a finger on you, but I'm not leaving you unprotected overnight.'

In the end he got his way, sharing a room but with separate beds and not even a good-night peck on the cheek to speed them to dreamland.

* * *

The plane arrived at midday. They stood outside the airport buildings, Su-Ying in a sky-blue dress patterned with yellow flowers. The Cessna taxied to a stop and Richard stared in astonishment as Bella climbed down from the cockpit and came running towards them, her face one big smile and her arms open wide to hug her son.

'How wonderful to see you! And looking so well, too!'

She turned to Su-Ying, taking her hands in her own. 'I am so pleased to meet you.'

'Since when have you been able to fly?' Richard asked.

'Your father taught me years ago. I neglected it until recently, then I thought how handy it would be for nipping around between Miranda Downs, the mine and the new loading terminal we're building near Port Hedland, so decided to get myself taught all over again. After I'd done that it seemed sensible to change your father's plane for a more modern one.' She threw out her hand. 'Allow me to introduce my new toy,' she said. 'Your father called his first plane Minnie. This is Minnie Mark II. Faster, more economical and with a range of seventeen hundred miles. Plus loads of new safety features, most of which I do not understand.'

'Do not believe a word she says,' Richard told Su-Ying. 'If there's one feature on that crate she doesn't understand I shall be very much surprised.'

'You underestimate my ignorance of things technical,' Bella said. 'And don't call her a crate: she'll be offended. Well, hop aboard,' she said briskly. 'We need to get moving if we want to be home before dark. What a pretty dress,' she said to Su-Ying.

CHAPTER FORTY-FIVE

While they waited for Comrade Fang's summons Bella, Richard and Su-Ying made use of the car he had kindly provided.

They had visited what remained of the ancient summer palace outside the city. They had taken a trip on the lake in a dragon boat. They had admired the marble vessel, constructed by order of the Concubine Empress Tzu-Hsi, that lay securely berthed alongside the bank. They had lunched at a restaurant recommended by the hotel.

'Do you remember any of this?' Bella asked Su-Ying.

Su-Ying shook her head. 'So much has changed.'

'But not the Summer Palace.'

'I never went there,' Su-Ying said. 'I remember my father took me once to the grave house of one of the Ming emperors.'

But that, she had discovered, had been vandalised during the Cultural Revolution.

Safely back at the hotel, Bella looked out through her window. Everywhere the darkness was broken by the glare of arc lamps from construction sites and she wondered at how things had changed since Mao's time. There would have been no shortage of seemingly insurmountable problems in those years yet somehow they had overcome them. It is nothing short of a miracle, she thought. It was an inspiration to her because China's troubles, although incomparably greater, seemed in some ways to mirror her own. She had certainly known testing times in the battles she had waged to defend her company and her legacy from the predatory assaults of Brad-Min and its CEO.

Pete Bathurst, she thought. Now there's a piece of work.

Bella lay on her bed and revisited the first days of the Carlisle Mine and a few of the landmines that Pete Bathurst had sown in her path in the years following Garth's death.

On her return from Japan in 1964 she had told Rory McNab they would need to get their skates on to fulfil the contracts she had won in Japan. She had also said that Pete Bathurst would be fit to be tied that she had got into the Japanese market ahead of him.

She had been right on both counts.

China might now be the gateway to the future – whether to catastrophe or triumph remained to be seen – but back then they had indeed got their skates on. Then as now the problems had seemed insurmountable but somehow Rory McNab had found his way around them, working twelve and sometimes fifteen hours a day and motivating his workforce to do the same. Even a week before the first delivery deadline Bella would not have bet her life on their meeting it yet somehow they had and for the first few years of operation the Japanese contracts had kept them afloat.

As for Pete Bathurst… He had indeed been fit to be tied. He had done everything he could to bring Tuckers down, but Bella had a spy in BradMin's offices and that had helped. She heard how Pete Bathurst had instructed Sinclair Smythe to find a way to challenge Bella's decision to break away from BradMin, and how Smythe had told him there were no legal grounds for objection.

'Keep trying, anyway. Any woman can be made to panic,' Pete had said. 'All we gotta do is find the right button to press.'

Smythe had sent Bella the letter, as instructed, and Bella, forewarned, had handed it to Owen Freeth. Owen had contacted

Sinclair to point out the flaws in his argument, flaws that the courts would be certain to confirm, and that had been that.

Pete had then tried to charge Bella an extra levy for track maintenance; that had got nowhere, either.

Finally he had come up with another plan that he hoped would cause Bella at least some inconvenience. He sicked Billy Gould on her.

Bella stared at the hand-delivered letter that had arrived that morning. So Billy Gould still fancied his chances of overturning Garth's will, did he? They would see about that.

She had more than enough to occupy her mind without Billy's nonsense and would normally have passed it to Owen to sort out, but the lawyer was travelling interstate and she had no intention of leaving it until he got back. She picked up the phone.

'Deborah, bring me that report Gayle Hastings did on the asbestos poisoning at Van Damm Siding.'

Deborah brought the report. Bella read it carefully, then phoned Billy Gould's lawyer.

'My legal adviser is away,' she said.

'How very convenient for you.'

The sassy voice of a man who expected her to settle rather than put up with the expense and inconvenience of a court action. A man she would derive great pleasure from disappointing.

'You are right,' she said. 'If he were here I would feel obliged at least to listen to his advice but since he isn't I can speak freely. I have three things to say to you. One. Your client will shortly be involved in a number of civil suits relating to serious injury incurred by a number of his former employees. The charge will be negligence and the damages substantial. Two. I have no intention, now or at any time, of settling any claims Mr Gould may think he has against my late husband's estate. Three, if you want to go ahead, be my guest. But a word to the wise: make sure of your fee first.'

A prolonged silence greeted her words. When the lawyer eventually spoke, it was in a very different tone. 'I shall take my client's instructions.'

You do that, mister, thought Bella savagely as she slammed down the phone. One question remained. That lawyer would never have agreed to act unless his fee was guaranteed. Gayle had told her that Billy's asbestos mine was on the rocks – he had even been forced to dispose of his sugar interests to cover its losses – and Gayle had discovered no other sources of income. So who was paying the lawyer?

Who would be interested in helping Billy Gould? Or, perhaps more relevantly, in hurting her? She could think of only one candidate.

Again she lifted the phone. 'Can you talk?'

Two hours later...

'Thank you for coming back to me so quickly, Tania. Yes, I guessed Pete was behind it but it's always good to have confirmation. If you want to drop in this evening, I'll let you have your money. Of course in cash. Everything as usual.'

She put down the phone and sat unmoving. Another bimbo de luxe from Pete's past, still employed by BradMin, boiling with resentment and only too willing to spill the beans. You'd think he'd have the brains to keep his prick out of the payroll, she thought, but some men never learn. Rory McNab had said a more ruthless bastard than Pete Bathurst never walked. Well, that was all right; she could be pretty ruthless herself.

Lying on her bed in the Beijing hotel, Bella sighed. So it had continued to this day. It was why she was here now: problems created by Pete Bathurst.

Given Comrade Fang's tirade at their last meeting, it looked as though the wretched man might have beaten her at last. If Beijing refused to back her, there was no more she could do. But let Beijing's own triumphant record be her inspiration. She had been waging war all her life: against the countess, the Johnsons, the

Cockatoo Club. More recently against sexist prejudice, the banks and the politicians. The Chinese would not have brought her here simply to dump her. No, the field was still hers, the battle not yet over.

Give up now, against a thug like Pete Bathurst? Not in a million years, she thought. On the contrary: if things worked out as she still hoped she would make it her business to destroy him.

Thank God I am a fighter, Bella thought.

There was a knock on the door. Bella looked up from the bleakness of her thoughts. 'Come in.'

It was Su-Ying.

'I wish they would make up their minds,' Bella said. 'This waiting is bad for the nerves.'

'That is why they do it,' her daughter-in-law said. 'To wear you down. It is the Chinese way.'

'I know, and they won't succeed. But it's not easy. What can I do for you anyway?' she asked.

'I came to ask your permission to visit my father.'

'You don't need my permission. Of course you may visit him, if you wish. Why not?'

'No reason why not. And it is my filial duty.'

'I understand.' Bella smiled. 'Perhaps you can persuade him to put in a word for us.'

'That would be most improper,' Su-Ying said.

'I know.'

'It might even be counter-productive.'

'Indeed it might.'

'I can only do my best,' Su-Ying said.

'No one can do more,' Bella said.

After Su-Ying had left, Bella thought what an asset she had proved to the family. What was even more remarkable was the way she had herself recognised that potential from the first. Why, if it had not been for her, Su-Ying might never have become a member of the family at all.

CHAPTER FORTY-SIX

Mother and son were alone in the tarted-up version of Miranda Downs. As Richard chose to call it.

'Don't you like it?' Bella asked.

'Of course I like it. But it takes a bit of getting used to. I would never have known the place,' he said. 'Air-conditioned, too!'

'Kerosene generators,' Bella explained. 'They gulp it down like drunks but they're worth it. You know how hot and humid it gets here in the Wet.'

It wasn't just the air-conditioning. Bookshelves were fitted around two of the living room walls – extra books spilling everywhere – and the furniture had been replaced. Large, welcoming armchairs were upholstered in grey cloth, with red, blue and yellow cushions in a silky material. A seven-foot settee ran under the picture window.

'They're Swedish but very comfortable. Try them.'

Between the bookshelves were good reproductions of paintings by Braque, Matisse and Picasso.

'I can't believe it,' Richard said. 'Sophisticated but welcoming.'

'It was one of the first things I said to your father, that a living room should be for living. For expanding your perceptions, if you feel like it. Or stretching out, if that's what you fancy.'

'Nobody would expect this sort of thing in the Pilbara.'

'Perth has made you a townie,' Bella said tartly. 'This is the Out-back, not the Stone Age.'

'I wonder what Dad would have made of it.'

'In theory he'd have been all in favour, but when it came to the point he liked things to stay the same.'

'Not like you,' Richard said.

'Not at all like me. What did Robert Frost say about promises and having far to go before I sleep? That's me.'

'Promises to whom?'

'To myself. And the future. Where's Su-Ying?'

'Having a bath.'

The bathroom, too, was new. It was still the only one, but suited more to a five-star hotel than the Miranda Downs he remembered from the past.

'Tell me what's going on,' Bella said.

Richard spelt out everything that had happened and how he had persuaded Su-Ying not to return to China.

'Very wise, the way things are over there,' Bella said. 'Although I'm not sure how long we can hang on to her.'

'What do you mean?'

'She's presumably on a diplomatic passport. All they have to do is cancel the passport and tip off the immigration people in Perth.'

'Surely they wouldn't kick her out?'

'That's exactly what they would do,' Bella said.

'What do we do about it?'

'I would say that depends on you.' She looked at her son thought-fully. 'I admire your wanting to help her. But how much do you really care for her? Not as a victim but as a human being?'

On the lawn outside the living room a parliament of crows had gathered, cawing and gabbing. Richard stood at the window watching them, then turned. 'I love her with all my heart,' he said.

'Love her now or love her forever?'

He looked at her, the ghost of a smile in his blue eyes. Softly he quoted:

'*Till a' the seas gang dry, my love, and the rocks melt in the sun.*'

'Robert Burns,' she said with pleasure. 'Or close. Very civilised. But never mind Robert Burns. How does Richard feel about it?'

'I love her, Ma. I'll love her till I die. I think sometimes I loved her before I met her.'

'That is the true feeling,' Bella said.

She was delighted that he had found such a precious thing so early in life, yet felt a familiar pang as she remembered what was past in her own life and should be forgotten yet still, over thirty years later, was not.

'What do you propose to do about it?' she asked him.

He looked at her uncertainly.

'How far are you prepared to go to stop them sending her back?'

'You're saying I should hide her?'

She could have shaken him. 'How long would you get away with that? Talk sense, boy! Are you willing to marry her?'

'If it would help.'

'There are times I despair of you,' his mother said. 'It's not a question of help. Do you want to marry her or don't you?'

'Like a shot. If she'll have me.'

'Even though she may be using you to protect herself?'

He did not hesitate. 'Even then.'

'It could lead you into a vale of tears,' Bella warned him.

'I'd risk it. But, if I do, does it mean she can stay here?'

'I doubt they'd forcibly deport a woman married to an Australian citizen.'

'Maybe I should discuss it with her.'

'Don't discuss it with her! Ask her! Ask her outright!'

For the first time he hesitated. 'What if she says no?'

'That is the risk you take,' Bella said.

He had thought it would be difficult or impossible, but when it came to the point it had nothing to do with race or culture or politics or what his friends might think. Only one thing mattered.

This was the woman he loved. She was beauty and peace, respect and honour. She had become his life.

They were alone, not entirely by chance. The evening sky was red behind the trees and a light breeze kept the mosquitoes away. Richard led Su-Ying down to the creek, where the water gleamed red with ink-black shadows in the dying light. He had thought to tell her about the water lilies that flowered here in early summer, the crocodile that made a periodic appearance and that some of the old women claimed had magical powers. He had thought they might hear the soft drone of a didgeridoo singing the night.

He said none of these things and, apart from a sleepy flutter of birds, the night was silent.

They stood at the water's edge. He took her gently and turned her to face him, seeing the last of the light reflecting in her dark eyes. She stood unresisting, all woman, all beauty, all mystery. For the second time since he had known her, his heart turned over.

He said, very softly: 'Darling Su-Ying, I love you with all my heart. Will you marry me?'

He saw her smile.

'Of course,' she said.

Not hard at all, when you came down to it. She had not told him that she loved him but that, he told himself, would come.

The way Bella was dancing around, she might have been eighteen again.

'Excellent!' she said. 'Wonderful! I am delighted.' She kissed Su-Ying. 'I am very happy to welcome you into our family as my new daughter. But we'd better waste no time making it official, in case your friends try to snatch you away from us.'

That was true, Su-Ying thought. Although from what she had seen she suspected there would be few people capable of snatching anything away from Bella Tucker against her will.

'There's a registry office in Derby,' Bella said. 'I suggest you get married there.'

'Derby's too far,' Richard objected.

'I'll fly you over,' Bella said. 'I intend to be there, anyway.' She smiled at Su-Ying. 'I'm bossy, as you'll find out, but I promise this is one occasion when I shan't interfere. All the same, if there's anything I can do to help, just ask.'

'I need a dress to get married in,' Su-Ying said. 'Quite a few other things. But I have no money.'

She felt ashamed of having to confess it but Bella dismissed it at once.

'That's easily fixed.'

She went to the phone. 'Mr Timms, please... Bella Tucker... Good morning, Keith. I need a favour.'

She explained briskly what she wanted; listened less than patiently to the bank manager's protests.

'I know all that. But she needs to draw on it immediately. Not later than tomorrow. The paperwork can be arranged later. Opening deposit? Transfer ten thousand from the number one account. That's right. Ten thousand. And let your Derby branch know, right? She'll be taking out cash tomorrow. Is that clear? Everything in order? Splendid. And she'll come in to fill in the forms. When? Very soon.'

She hung up and turned to Su-Ying, smiling. 'Fixed,' she said.

A whirlwind would be calmer. Su-Ying was perturbed. 'How do I repay you?'

The smile broadened. 'Call it a down-payment on your wedding present.'

They flew to Derby the next morning and spent the afternoon getting kitted out. White brocade for the bride, dark blue for the bridegroom's mother: they admired themselves enormously in the shop's mirror, then went next door.

'I want you to show us some of your finest lingerie,' Bella said, with just a touch of Ripon Grange in her manner. 'The best you have. If you please. Not for me, for this lady here. Miss Lee is doing me the honour of becoming my daughter-in-law tomorrow.'

Bras were brought out and displayed.

'I like that one,' Bella said.

'Very pretty,' Su-Ying said.

'Why don't you try it on?' Bella said.

She came back to report it fitted perfectly.

'But I don't know how much it is.'

A price was mentioned.

'Too much,' Su-Ying said.

'We'll take it,' Bella said.

'Maybe we should ask for a discount.'

'Maybe we shouldn't.'

Bella, who had promised not to interfere, seemed to have taken charge.

'And the knickers to go with it. What is your hip size?' she asked Su-Ying.

'Too expensive,' Su-Ying said as they left the shop.

It wasn't as though anyone would see them on her. Except her husband, of course. Even he might not. She would prefer to undress in the bathroom; it would be less embarrassing that way. But perhaps Richard might have other ideas. What did she know about men and their ideas? Not for the first time, she wondered if she had been wise to go through with all this; she couldn't imagine her father's reaction, when he heard. His daughter married to a foreigner in a foreign country, among foreigners? He would be horrified. Yet what choice did she have? It would be madness to go back, and if this was the way to avoid it... She was very fond of Richard. She liked him very much. As for love... She was not sure what that was. She tried out the words, in Chinese and in English.

Wo ai nee. I love you.

It was no use; she could not bring herself to say it, not yet. She thought he might have expected her to do so but she had not.

Wo ai nee, she told herself again. I will say it only when I mean it. And then, heaven permitting, it will be forever. She had been brought up to regard religion as superstition, but now she addressed her supplication to the goddess of mercy.

'Lady Guan Yin, help me to love my husband.'

* * *

The ceremony was formal and brief. A few words from the registrar; signatures – their own and witnesses' – on a paper; it was done.

Another in a series of events in a life that, for Su-Ying, had become surreal.

'You are free now,' Bella said. 'They can't force you to go back.'

They – mother-in-law, husband and herself – went to the hotel where they would spend the night; they had a meal in the downstairs dining room. It was naturally a western meal but the students' cafeteria had trained Su-Ying, to some extent, and she managed to gulp it down. And later came the time to be alone with her husband, whom she liked very much, the time of the dimming of the lights and so by degrees to the moment when for the first time she felt her body possessed by another being. Afterwards she lay, wide-eyed in the darkness, and wondered what the future would bring.

Bella, alone in her room in the same hotel, remembered how things had been between Garth and herself. For the first time in many years she wondered how she would have felt had she and Charles ever made love and felt a fleeting regret they never had.

Darling Charles, she thought. How much I missed you in those days. How much I miss you still. She had thought, after Garth died, she might write to him. As an old friend, no more. But it was useless. She was not an old friend and Charles was a married man. What point was there in resurrecting a past that she should have buried years ago?

Once again she ordered herself to think of him no more, knowing it would do no good. She had learnt to control every other aspect of her life but not this. Her feelings for Charles would remain forever.

CHAPTER FORTY-SEVEN

Su-Ying woke at dawn. Even before memory returned she sensed an unfamiliar warmth in her bed. She opened her eyes. The ceiling above her, the picture on the wall... Even in the half-light they were unfamiliar. She turned her head to stare at the sleeping man, his dark hair spread upon the pillow. The man who was now her husband.

There was pain in her loins, the small of her back. Again she stared at the ceiling as she tried to piece together the events that had led her to this: the flight from terror; the journey north to an unknown place in an unknown land, surrounded by unknown people; the proposal of marriage that would have been unthinkable only one day before but that had become her only refuge; and now this. Her body was the property of a foreigner whose background and beliefs were as different from hers as it was possible to be. A lifetime commitment: to this?

It could not be; it was.

Mother-in-law had told her she was free but how was that possible? She was a married woman and must defer to her husband. That was not freedom. She was a prisoner behind doors labelled custom, law and possession. That was not freedom. She believed she would never be free again. She had turned her back on all that mattered to her: the father who had given her life; Comrade Minister Deng; even China itself. In a moment of panic she had thrown away home, loyalty and culture. For what? This land was not hers. This way of living was not hers.

How could she live with the shame of what she had done?

She was desperate to escape but there was nowhere to run. This man and this country were now her destiny. This, now, was her home.

She had never felt lonelier in her life.

She had no idea what her husband would require of her, this first day of their marriage. Would he expect her to be there when he woke? To bring him tea? Last night, after lovemaking, she had washed them both. It had been her duty yet she had sensed he had not expected it, had perhaps even been embarrassed by it. How could she be a good wife if she did not know what was expected of her?

She could not bear to stay where she was a moment longer. Moving cautiously so as not to waken her husband, she edged from beneath the covers. The air was cool on her body as she took clean clothes from the wardrobe. She washed and dressed in the bathroom: underclothes her mother-in-law had chosen for her, the usual white shirt and jeans. She opened the bedroom door and went down the stairs. Behind the hotel a lawn sloped to the river. The grass was cool beneath her bare feet. She sat on a bench beside the water. Swans preened their black plumage on an island in midstream. One swam over to investigate, its red eyes inspecting her from a cautious distance. She had nothing to give it, nor did she know whether feeding the big birds was allowed. Reeds lined the bank but she did not know their name. She knew nothing about anything.

There were shreds of pink cloud overhead, the silence of a world waiting for the sun. She breathed the cool air deeply into her lungs. From trees on the far bank came a kookaburra's raucous cackle.

That was a bird she knew. She drew courage from the sound. At least it was a beginning.

'Soon I shall know more.' Saying it out loud made her feel better. 'The future is a challenge but I shall face it bravely. I shall learn what I must do. I shall come to love my husband. I shall survive,' Su-Ying told the swan.

If the bird had any thoughts on the subject it kept them to itself. Soon, inspection finished, it sailed majestically away.

She got up and walked back across the lawn to the hotel.

Two days later, in the evening, Richard and Su-Ying arrived back at Miranda Downs. The next morning they were both up early.

'Want to go for a walk?' she said.

'Sure.'

'Do you have a gun?'

He stared. 'Why should I need a gun?'

'We might see a wild pig.'

'They are deep in the forest. They don't come down here.'

They hadn't gone far before he looked at her. 'What's the matter?'

'Nothing's the matter.'

'You're on edge. I can feel it. What's the problem?'

'The men who were going to take me back to China,' she said. 'Your mother says they will do nothing to a woman married to an Australian but she does not know these people. They take their orders from Beijing and care nothing for anyone else.'

He saw that she was frightened.

'They'll never track you up here. But we'll go back if you prefer.'

'Better we should,' she said.

She hoped he was right but every day she woke to fear. To guilt, also, that she had chosen the west over China. Who was she to make such a decision? She saw that Richard did not understand why she was troubled so tried to explain to him.

'For centuries family and land have been two most important things in Chinese society. Without them, hard to believe I exist at all.'

'I can't do anything about the land,' Richard said. 'But this is your family now and all of us are glad that is so.'

She hoped he meant it. She didn't mind her mother-in-law being in charge – that had been the Chinese way for centuries – but how Bella felt about having a Chinese daughter-in-law it was impossible to know.

As for her husband… She liked and respected him, this man who was so considerate outside the bed, so masterful in it. But love… So far Lady Guan Yin had not answered her prayers, although she still hoped she might.

In the meantime she remained on her guard, fearing the men from Beijing would not give up so easily, and was careful not to stray far from the house.

One day Bella came into the living room and found Su-Ying on hands and knees, washing the floor with a damp cloth and bucket of water. She was barefoot, wearing her usual jeans and T-shirt, and got up at once, standing with head bowed, the damp cloth clutched in her hand.

'There's no need for you to do that,' Bella said.

'I was trying to help,' Su-Ying said. 'I apologise if you feel I should not do this but it is not right that I should sit here all day and do nothing.'

'I am sorry,' Bella said. 'I took it for granted that as a newly married bride you would have plenty to occupy your mind without needing to do anything else. I know I found it so.'

'I beg your pardon if I have done wrong,' Su-Ying said.

Bella saw how defensive she was. She had been on her guard since she first got here. If I want to break through Su-Ying's defences, Bella thought, now is the time to do it.

'You have done nothing wrong,' she said. 'It is I who should apologise to you.'

Su-Ying's body tautened like a wire under strain. 'You are my mother-in-law. Why you apologise to me?'

'Because I have underestimated how difficult it must be for you. An unfamiliar house in the middle of nowhere, people you don't

know and ways of behaving that are strange to you: I have not done
enough to help you. I feel particularly bad about it, because you
have done so much to help Richard.'

It was the wrong thing to say. Su-Ying shook her head emphatically. 'He has done so much for me, you mean. Had it not been for
him –'

'You would have been sent back to China. That is true, and I'm
not pretending that isn't important, but never doubt you have given
him a lot, too.'

'I have given him nothing.'

'You have changed his life,' Bella said.

Through the open window, screened against flies, came the rusty
cry of a red-tailed cockatoo. Su-Ying opened her mouth but at the
last moment changed her mind and said nothing.

'His father was a strong man. His sister is also strong. So, in my
way, am I.' She smiled almost apologetically. 'We are a family of
strong people. Richard is more intellectual than the rest of us. More
sensitive. He has grown up surrounded by people more assertive
than he is. I do not say more able but more inclined to throw their
weight about. Perhaps we bullied him occasionally. And he allowed
it, which may be why we did it.'

The almond eyes watched her. Su-Ying said: 'He is a man who
walks his own path. He is like bamboo, bending in the wind, but
inside he is strong, as bamboo is strong. He allowed it, mother-in-
law, because it didn't matter to him.'

Bella stared at her daughter-in-law. 'You believe that?'

'I have come recently to believe that is so,' Su-Ying said.

There was a pride in her voice that was new and Bella knew
instinctively that Su-Ying was right. Richard had the same inner
strength as she did. Yet it had taken her son's wife to see what his
mother had not, and the realisation made her respect her daughter-
in-law more than ever.

'If he was strong before, you have made him stronger. Perhaps,
in helping you escape from those men, he discovered he could take
on the world physically as well as mentally. I do not know how it

happened, nor does it matter, but it has. So you see you have done a lot for him, too. And I have been neglectful in not saying so before. In not welcoming you as I should into this family. Of which you are now a valued member.'

'I thought, perhaps, you were unsure. A foreigner…'

'Do you think I care where you come from? Your mother bore you the same way as mine. Do you think I care that your eyes are a different shape?'

'Some people might.'

'I am not some people,' Bella said. 'I am pleased and proud you are my daughter-in-law.'

'I am honoured,' Su-Ying said.

It could have been only a formal acknowledgement of Bella's words, but Bella knew better.

'Do you know how to ride a horse?' she asked.

Su-Ying shook her head.

'People who live in this part of the world have to know how to ride. It is a basic requirement. Take that bucket outside and I shall teach you.'

'I am not sure about horses,' Su-Ying said dubiously.

'You will come to love them,' Bella told her.

In bed that night Su-Ying told Richard about the conversation.

'She says she will teach me to ride a horse,' she said.

'Pity the poor horse,' he said.

Having learnt something of her husband's ways, she knew he had been thinking of doing a little riding himself, although horses had nothing to do with it. She was therefore unsurprised when, with a familiarity that was becoming habitual, he cupped her breast in his hand.

A week later Bella announced she had to go back to Perth; there were business decisions concerning the mine that could not be delayed. As to whether Richard and his wife chose to come with her or remain at Miranda Downs, she left it to them.

'I don't know whether you would feel safe in Perth,' she told Su-Ying.

'Once I would not,' Su-Ying said. 'But now I think you are right. I am married to an Australian and I do not think they will trouble me.'

'Then will you come?'

'We shall come with you,' Su-Ying said.

'I am fatally attractive to strong-willed women,' Richard mourned, rolling his eyes. 'They cluster about me like bees.'

Richard was delighted that Su-Ying had spoken without checking with him first; even a week before she would not have done it but since talking with Mother she had become a new woman, truly part of the family. All the same, he wondered how she would take to life in Perth. Desire, even more than Miranda Downs, was Bella's home ground and he was afraid Su-Ying might find it hard to adapt to her mother-in-law's vast mansion.

He soon discovered he need not have worried. Su-Ying informed him that in China it was normal for several generations of the same family to live under one roof. She was deferential to Bella. She was cautious about interfering in household affairs but showed independence in small ways, supervising the washing and ironing of their clothes and making sure their meals were served at the right times. But the greatest difference was in their private life.

Her beautiful body smelt of flowers; its deceptive fragility had excited him from the first, bringing him a pleasure beyond anything he had ever known. Now there was a new development.

'*Laukong*,' she crooned. Balanced on his thighs, she lifted his hands and pressed them to her breasts. '*Laukong, laukong...*'

'What are you saying?'

'Husband.'

'So what do I call you?'

'You may call me *taitai*, if you wish.'

'Meaning?'

'Respected wife. If you wish to honour me with that name.'

'I respect you very much,' he said. 'Why not? I love you.'

'It is a pillow name,' she warned him.

He understood what she was telling him: the face of passion was not to be revealed to others or, outside the bed, even to each other.

It did not trouble him; being married to Lee Su-Ying was an excitement in itself, an adventure seemingly without end. He had loved her almost from their first meeting. He had known virtually nothing about her then; there was much he did not know about her now. He didn't mind; her mystery added to her enchantment.

Certain things he knew by instinct. She was strong-willed and brave; she was a thousand-generation Han Chinese and always would be: married to the king of England she would still have been as Chinese as the Great Wall. She was reed-slender and as strong as tempered steel. If anyone could make a successful transition from the life she had known to this new life, Su-Ying was the woman to do it.

He thought, this gift she has given me. I am a truly happy man.

It was the use of Chinese words in their lovemaking that led Su-Ying to her first public show of initiative. Had she said such a thing to Richard he would have told her she was making no sense so she did not say it. This did not bother her; she knew his understanding of her was becoming greater by the day but was still too superficial to uncover the subtleties of her thoughts and feelings.

Takes Chinese to know Chinese, she thought, but in truth it was very simple. She had promised herself she would say she loved him only when it was true. Now that time was close. Calling him husband, and in Chinese at that, was a first step; the rest would follow very soon. That certainty gave her the self-confidence to take an initiative that she would have found impossible only weeks before.

She went to Bella and explained what she had in mind.

'Why not?' Bella said. 'I'm not sure we'll find what you're looking for, but we can try.'

They drove into the city. They stayed together; Su-Ying might have told Bella she was no longer afraid of being kidnapped but it was as well to be sure. She found what she was looking for not far from the docks.

That night, chin defiant, she served up the first Chinese food ever put on the table at Desire.

She sat back and observed them. Richard, fascinated by all things Chinese, had experimented before but Bella approached it with barely concealed apprehension.

She studied the first dish: a bowl of thick soup. 'What is this?'

'This fish maw soup.'

'Fish maw?'

'Fish maw is bladder of fish.'

Bella sipped cautiously; then again. Her eyes lit up. 'It's delicious!'

When they came to the fish course, the sauce brought tears to Bella's eyes.

'Spicy,' Su-Ying said happily.

'You can say that again,' Bella said.

All in all it was a huge success.

'We must do this more often,' Bella said.

'Happy you like,' Su-Ying said.

The success of the meal gave her the confidence to come up with her next suggestion.

'Chairman Mao is very old man,' she said one evening.

She and Bella had been out riding together – Bella had insisted she keep up with her lessons – and, while Su-Ying would never make a champion jockey, she managed well enough. Now, bathed and rested, she and Bella were sitting in the upstairs gallery watching the night come down across the vastness of the land that lay to the east. An empty land full of promise, rendered more mysterious by the gathering darkness.

'Many Chinese people respect him very much,' Su-Ying said. 'But not all; the Cultural Revolution has held China back. When he dies there will be many changes. China will modernise. There will be a huge demand for western resources.'

'Such as?'

'Such as copper. Coal. Iron ore.'

Bella slanted a glance at her. 'You think so?'

'I am sure of it.'

'China might want these things,' Bella said, 'but how will it pay for them?'

'The money will be found. My respectful opinion is that this will offer fantastical opportunity, most truly, and company should be ready to take full advantage.'

'How does it do that?'

'Very simple. Richard took classes at university so already speaks some Chinese. Very important he becomes fluent. This will be very useful in negotiating contracts for us in the future.'

Bella noted Su-Ying's use of *us*. 'You are as confident of China's future as that?'

'After Chairman Mao's death, my hope is that Minister Deng will be restored to power. Then I am confident, yes.'

'Minister Deng and your father?'

'I hope so, yes.'

'Have you spoken to Richard about this?'

'Better I speak to Mother-in-law first,' Su-Ying said.

'And who will teach him?'

'I shall.'

A month later Su-Ying made another suggestion.

'I am troubled,' she said.

Bella had been working in her office downstairs; now, late in the afternoon, she had joined her daughter-in-law for tea – arranged by Su-Ying. Once again they sat in the gallery in what Bella was beginning to call their favourite roosting place. The skies were dark; lightning prowled in spasmodic bursts of violet light along the horizon and they watched the rain sweeping in grey sheets across the land.

'Why are you troubled?' Bella asked.

'Richard took me away to prevent my being sent back to China.'

Bella sipped her tea. Jasmine tea, obtained from the same back-street shop where Su-Ying bought all her Chinese supplies.

Keep going like this, she thought, I shall end up as Chinese as she is. Although when she checked in the mirror her eyes were as round as ever.

'So?' she asked.

'So he never write exams,' Su-Ying said.

'The rector of the university is a friend of mine. I have spoken to him and explained the circumstances. Richard will be able to write the exams next year.'

'Then he must work.'

It was true that much of the time Richard had his nose in non-accounting books – his current favourite was Sun Tzu's *The Art of War* – but Bella was unconcerned.

'I think you will find he'll be more than capable of passing his exams when the time comes. And in the meantime he is helping Martin Dexter in the office, as you know. Martin speaks very highly of him.'

'It is not enough to pass,' Su-Ying said. 'He must be the best.'

Well, hullo, Bella thought. Quite the little slave driver.

But she thought none the less of her daughter-in-law for that. To be the best was what she had always wanted for herself.

Four months later her positive feelings about her daughter-in-law were reinforced when Su-Ying announced that she was with child.

The next generation already, Bella thought happily. Now all we need is positive news from Peace. But she knew from their correspondence that for the moment at least her daughter's life had an entirely different focus.

CHAPTER FORTY-EIGHT

The Cornish summer was at its peak. The previous month Peace Tucker had graduated from Camborne with the Macalister gold medal. She would soon be moving on – she had already had an approach from the States – but it was not about honours or America that she was thinking now.

Peace and Greg Terblanche had been an item for six months. She'd had plenty of casual friends since she had been in England, including a couple of lovers, but no serious relationships. At first she had thought Greg might change that. After the frustrating time she'd had with Ian Lassiter, too gentle and accommodating for a woman in love with the tough masculinity of her father, it had been a pleasure to be with a real man who knew what real men wanted.

Greg Terblanche was Mr Testosterone himself but unfortunately had turned out to be not only tough but rough. He hadn't hit her – I'd fillet any man who tried that, Peace thought – but she had discovered that what he really wanted was a sexual doormat, and Peace Tucker was nobody's doormat. So the relationship was dead or at least dying; more and more she was finding it hard to remember what had drawn her to him in the first place.

'I have family business in Yorkshire,' Peace said. 'But I think I'd better go alone.'

She had written to tell Bella she planned to see her grandfather before she left England and Bella had given the suggestion her blessing.

I am sure he will be delighted to see you, she had written. *And you might ask him about his neighbour, Charles Hardy, while you're there. He used to be a friend of mine. We haven't been in touch for over thirty years, but I shall be interested to know if he and his wife are well. And look up Grandma Jenny, too, if you can find her.*

Peace had phoned the Grange in advance and was expected. All the same, her nerves were jumping as she sat in the vast drawing room and waited.

How did you deal with an earl? Would he be welcoming? Polite but distant, or wondering, audibly, why this stranger had come to bother him?

She looked at the room, its furnishings discreetly worn yet still elegant, with what she suspected would be good paintings of rural scenes hanging on the walls. It was hard to imagine her mother, at home in the rough and tumble of Miranda Downs, being brought up in such an environment.

The door opened. The man who came in was tall and wraith-thin, walking tentatively with the aid of a stick. She had known Grandfather must be old but had not expected to find him decrepit. She stood and walked towards him. He permitted her to come to him, smiling gently with his hands folded on his stick. She had thought she might recognise a faded version of her mother or even herself in the earl's features, but there was no sign of either of them.

'So you are my granddaughter,' he said. 'It is a pleasure to meet you. Even if a little late in the day.'

He smiled and Peace caught a glimpse of the young man he must have been, and how, more than fifty years before, he had succeeded in charming the bait-digger's daughter. Gracious was the only word to describe him. She guessed he would speak to his tenants in exactly that tone of voice but it didn't matter because here, at last, was one half of the roots that only now she realised she had missed so much.

'We shall sit down and take some tea,' he said in his amiable, lordly way. 'I wonder if I might trouble you to ring the bell? Age is such a nuisance. And how is your mother?'

'She is very well.'

'And prospering?'

'Certainly.'

'Unfortunately the countess is away. She will be sorry to have missed you.'

The tea came, with slices of Dundee cake of which the earl told her he was particularly fond. 'You have no objection to Dundee cake?'

'On the contrary.' But felt awkward even as she said it, trapped in a period drama to which she could not relate.

If Bella had stayed, she thought, would she, too, be apologising to visitors about Dundee cake? She could not imagine it; it was impossible to visualise Bella in this over-civilised environment. She would have suffocated, as would Peace herself. Perhaps it was as well Bella had walked out when she had. Not that it excused the way the countess had behaved.

'My mother is planning to name a port after you,' she told him.

'I am not sure I understand.'

'We are developing an iron-ore mine. We need a port for the vessels that will take the ore to the countries buying it.'

'And your mother intends to name it after me?'

'Port Anthony.'

He brushed cake crumbs from his lips. 'I am not sure I deserve the honour. I have always felt guilty that I did not give her more support when she was living here.'

And so he should, thought Peace. Even now he spoke of her more as a slight acquaintance than his daughter. She remembered her mother telling her of those early days, and how ineffectual he had been. Not that Bella had ever held it against him. All her resentment had been directed at the countess. It still was; if the opportunity came to pay Charlotte Richmond back for the malicious things she'd done, Peace was sure Mother would grab it with both hands. Good on her, Peace thought, and to hell with the bloody countess.

'My mother asked me to enquire about a friend of hers,' Peace said. 'Charles Hardy and his wife. Are they still alive?'

'Charles? Oh, very much so. I don't get out much nowadays,' the earl explained, 'but the last I heard he was in excellent health. Yes, Charles and your mother were very close, at one time. But there's no wife.'

'Is she dead?'

'He never married. Quite the confirmed bachelor, Charles Hardy.'

'My mother heard he had married your sister-in-law.'

'My wife would have liked to arrange it, but it never happened. Your mother must have misunderstood the situation.'

That bloody countess, Peace thought. Mother would never have misunderstood anything like that. The bitch must have lied. And jumped the gun, too, putting that false announcement in the paper.

The question was what, if anything, she should do about it. She played with the idea of going to see him herself but there was no point. Also she disliked the idea of Mother having been close to anyone but Father. She would tell her about it, of course; what she chose to do would be her business.

Grandma Jenny was a different matter. Having seen one grandparent, Peace was determined to find the other one. It took some doing but eventually she tracked her down to a small house in Whitstable.

It had a green-painted door and a white doorstep, and stood in a little court off the main street. A boy cycled past, whistling, as Peace rang the bell.

She heard the shuffle of feet, the rattle of a chain, and the door opened a crack. A woman's face, pale and hollow-eyed, peered out

'Mrs Such?'

'Yes?'

'I'm your granddaughter,' Peace said.

And the old lady, staring, let out a small shriek.

'My dear life!'

As though she had seen a ghost.

Peace was horrified. She had expected surprise, perhaps even pleasure, but not this. 'I'm sorry if I startled you. I should have warned you but there was no way.'

The old lady had opened the door now but was swaying in the doorway, her face whiter than ever.

'Please... Let me help you.'

Peace stepped hastily across the threshold and took her grandmother by the arm. Beneath the frayed cardigan the bones were as thin as sticks. The front door opened directly into the sitting room; she led the old lady to an armchair and sat her down in it, while Grandma Jenny continued to stare at her in wonderment.

'My dear life,' she repeated in a pale voice.

Does she know who I am? Peace thought. Or has her mind gone? 'Peace Tucker,' she said. 'Your granddaughter from Australia.'

'You give me such a shock,' Grandma said. At least she was smiling, now, if only tentatively.

'I'm sorry,' Peace said again. 'Can I get you anything?'

'Don' matter. I'm over it now. I'll make us both a nice cup of tea directly.' But she was shaking her head slowly, still looking at Peace with an expression of wonderment. 'An' what brings you to the old country?' she asked.

'I've been studying over here. I shall be leaving soon but wanted to see you before I left.'

'That's nice.'

'I had a job finding you.'

'You would. Mr Such sold 'is boat ever so long ago,' Grandma told her. 'Fishing's a young man's trade, so 'e decided we should move into town and we been 'ere ever since.'

She insisted on getting them tea, despite the effort it obviously took her, for Grandma Jenny, although not as frail as the earl, was sick.

'Cancer,' she explained. 'I've had it on and off for years but this time I reckon it'll see the finish of me.'

It might have been a cold in the head, the way she spoke.

'You should have let Mother know,' Peace said. 'Maybe she could have arranged something.'

'No address. Then there was the war, no way to know whether letters got through or not. I was never much for writing,' Jenny said. 'Besides, I didn't want to bother her. My generation, we sorted out our own problems. Nothing to be done, anyway. This thing gets its claws in you, sooner or later that's it. Not complainin', mind. I've 'ad a good life. I'm glad you come, though, afore it's too late. How is your mother?'

'She's fine. Active as ever.'

'Maybe I'll write her a letter now,' Jenny said. 'Just a few lines. Hold on a sec and you can take it with you.' She smiled. 'Save the cost of a stamp.'

Five minutes later she brought back the sealed envelope.

'Give it to her direct, won't you? Can't have no one else readin' our secrets, can we?'

She cackled, seemingly recovered from her shock, although every so often her eyes slid back, frowning, to examine Peace afresh.

Peace had not definitely decided to return to Australia at all, at least not immediately, but one look at Grandma's anxious expression and she thought that maybe she should. 'I'll put it straight into her hands.'

'That's right, dear. So tell me about yourself.'

They talked: about Peace's plans, about Australia.

'And you,' Jenny said. 'Not married yet?'

'Not yet.'

'You still got time,' she said consolingly.

Peace mentioned Charles Hardy.

'She was that keen on 'im,' Jenny said. 'I didn't know nuffin about him until just afore she went to Australia but I reckon it hit 'er 'ard when they split up: although maybe I shouldn't say so, seein' 'e's not your dad. I blame that woman,' she said fiercely. 'A right evil bitch, that one. I loved 'er 'usband,' she said. 'You never saw a more handsome man when I first met him. Just afore the First War, that was. The Tankerton girls reckoned I must have bewitched 'im.' She smiled reminiscently. 'Maybe I did. But if I did, 'e done the same to me.' She looked up at the clock on the wall and was suddenly on her feet. 'Look at the time! I don't like to seem unfriendly, dear, but I'm going to shoo you aht now. Mr Such'll be 'ome directly and I got to get his tea ready. Don't like to be kept waiting for 'is tea, Mr Such. Never mind, 'e loves me, an' that's all any woman can ask, ain't that so? Pity you won't get the chance to meet 'im, but there it is.'

She was obviously determined to get Peace out of the house as soon as possible. It was strange: Perhaps she doesn't want me to meet her husband, Peace thought, although she couldn't imagine why, but if that was her plan it failed, because Luke Such turned up half an hour earlier than expected.

Peace met him and smiled and said how nice. He was stronger looking than his wife, his hair grey but still brown in patches, his squat build and square shoulders as solid as a rock. He had nothing to say for himself but that didn't matter: Peace had seen the person she had come to visit. She made sure she had the old lady's letter and took the train back to London.

Two weeks later, having said goodbye both to England and Greg Terblanche, she was back in Perth.

CHAPTER FORTY-NINE

'I promise you,' Bella said. 'I had no idea.'

Jenny's letter lay on the table between them. Whether she was talking to herself or her daughter, Peace could not tell. Bella's face was deathly white; the contents of the letter had clearly shocked her to the core. It was a notion that Peace found astonishing.

Lower lip caught between her teeth, Bella took up the letter and read it a second time. When she was finished she sighed heavily and held it out to Peace. 'Read it,' she said.

Peace took it, her eyes still fixed on Bella's face. Mother had always been such a cold fish, never showing any real emotions; privately Peace had sometimes wondered whether she had any emotions to express. Now her reaction to the letter revealed she might not be so bulletproof, after all.

Peace began to read. Halfway through she sat back in her chair and stared at her mother before continuing to read.

I wasn't sure I should tell you because I wasn't ever certain, but now I've met my granddaughter I know I won't rest easy until I do. The fact is, my darling girl, the earl is not your father. When I got news he'd been killed in the war nothing seemed to matter no more, so when Luke Such wanted to comfort me I let him, only it went further than I meant it

*to. Then straight away Anthony come back after all and I was that glad
to have him home I never even thought the baby I was having could
be anyone else's. I suppose I should have thought it odd that with all
the times we was together I only fell pregnant once but it never entered
my mind. Then, when your Peace turned up, I took one look and there
was no doubt. She's got Luke's looks, the spitting image, which means I
have lied to you, to Anthony and to my husband. I feel that bad about
it but there's nothing to be done. I know it'll come as a shock but I hope
you can forgive me, because I swear to you, Bella my love, that I never
knew.*

Peace put the letter down. Eyes wide, she stared at her mother,
each woman as flabbergasted as the other.

'Surely she can't be right?' Peace said.

'It's like finding a stranger hiding inside your skin,' Bella said.
'But she must be right. She would never have written that letter
otherwise.'

'Then that man I saw in Yorkshire wasn't my grandfather at all.'

'Apparently not. Until this minute I've never thought of him as
anything but my father but the truth is after I went to the Grange
I was always closer to my grandfather anyway. The man I thought
was my grandfather. Frankly I don't care if he was or wasn't: he'll
always be Grandpapa to me.'

Bella was gobsmacked; there was no other word for it. She thought:
I shall always be a stranger to myself now. She lifted her hand and
stared at it, seeing each vein separate and distinct, the skin taut and
white over each knuckle. Her hand. No one else's: hers. Yet in her
head, where this newly discovered stranger lived, there was only
turmoil. How could Mumma have done this to her? It was one
thing to keep her secret when she was unsure of the truth. But why
let it out now?

The truth was that Mumma had turned her back on the truth
because she had not wanted to believe.

Bella thought, it worked out all right for you, though, didn't
it? Without the lie, there would have been no Ripon Grange, no

Miranda Downs, no anything. Bella – *this* Bella – wouldn't exist.
Yet she still had the same body, the same blood and heart and brain.
Nothing had changed.

Everything had changed.

Why had Mumma done it?

Because of the shock of seeing Luke Such in her granddaughter's
face. And because she was dying.

Oh God!

Unknowingly, Bella had clenched her hands. Now she straight-
ened her fingers. Mumma was dying; whether she should have kept
her secret or not, that was what mattered. Mumma was dying.

Bella looked at her daughter. 'There is one thing I must do.'

'What's that?'

'Whoever my father was, Grandma Jenny is my mother. I shall
go and see her again before she dies.'

'And Charles Hardy?' Peace asked, greatly daring.

Bella's expression gave nothing away.

'We shall have to see about Charles Hardy,' she said.

She flew to Singapore, Singapore to Bangkok, finally to London.
Even first class it was an exhausting business. Deborah had arranged
a hire car to meet her but by the time the Daimler dropped her at
the Ritz Bella felt as though she had just gone through a dust storm
with five hundred of the wildest cattle on Miranda Downs. Fortunately she had never found jetlag a problem; she slept the clock
round and the following day, with autumnal London cool and wet,
with fallen leaves blowing in the street, she arranged for a hire car
to drive her to Whitstable.

She had Jenny's address and found the house without difficulty.
It turned out worse than anything she could have imagined.

A strange woman opened the door.

'What do you want?'

No nonsense was written all over her but Bella could have handled a regiment like her.

'Mrs Such, please.'

'Mrs Such ain't receivin' visitors.'

'She'll receive me,' Bella said.

'You from the welfare?'

'I'm her daughter.'

It was less than a month since Peace had seen Jenny but it was obvious she had gone steeply downhill in the interval. She lay in bed and looked like death. Her face was grey: a skull stripped by suffering.

The shock made Bella gulp. For a second she swayed, then took hold of herself. 'Hullo, Mumma.'

Jenny looked at her daughter, unspeaking, then held up her arms. Bella held her, Jenny so wasted that it was like holding nothing at all. Bella was a woman who never allowed the world to see her feelings but now the tears ran down her face.

'You'd best get a chair,' said Jenny.

Even to say that had exhausted her. She lay for a minute, eyes closed, breath harsh, then looked at the child who had returned to her across so many years and miles. A ghost of a smile. 'You read me letter?'

'Peace gave it to me.'

'Come as a shock, I daresay.'

The biggest shock of my life. But now was not the time to say so. 'It didn't bother me, if that's what you're asking. I was a bastard before, I'm a bastard now, so what's new?'

'I 'ope,' Jenny whispered, 'that you don't plan... to mention it to your dad?'

The effort to speak was painful to see.

'Not to Luke, not to the earl,' Bella said. 'It's our business, no one else's.'

'That's good.'

'Don't talk,' Bella said. 'You don't have to talk.'

'Not good fer much.'

Her words were barely audible. Yet, while breath remained, Jenny was determined to have her say and Bella recognised herself in her mother's determination not to admit defeat.

'You plannin' on seein' the earl while you're 'ere?'

'Probably not.'

Especially now. But that Bella would not say. 'I was closer to Grandpapa than I was to him.'

''E was a lovely man when I first knew 'im.' Jenny's eyes were closed again; it was difficult to know whether she was talking to Bella or herself, yet from somewhere she seemed to have gathered new strength. 'The war mucked 'im up. 'E weren't never the same afterwards.'

Her eyes opened. A skeletal hand rested on Bella's arm.

'Your 'ubby's dead, too, I 'ear.'

'Almost six years ago.'

'Footloose and fancy free, that's you.' Jenny smiled wanly. She drew a shaky breath. 'What about that Charles 'ardy you was so keen on?'

'What about him?'

'Not good for a woman to live alone,' Jenny whispered. 'Maybe you should look 'im up, while you're over 'ere?'

Bella shook her head. 'I doubt we'd have anything to say to each other after all this time.'

'One way to find out. Satisfy your curiosity, like.'

Jenny's mouth sagged. Strength had run out. Intelligence still glowed in the faded eyes but words were beyond her. A thread of saliva ran from the corner of her mouth.

'She needs to rest,' said the woman who had let her in.

'I'll come and see you again,' Bella said to the dying woman. 'Tomorrow.'

She walked heavily to the door.

'Do we know how long?' she asked the woman.

'Nurse said could be any time.'

'And you are?'

'Mrs Nunes. A neighbour. I keeps an eye on 'er while 'er 'ubby's out.'

All the years of childhood travelled with Bella on the journey back to London. She thought about Mumma and Charles Hardy.

She had also thought about him during the flight. The news that he had never married had hit her like a fist. Now, her wits scrambled like a dozen eggs, she did not know what to do for the best. The best for Charles Hardy; the best for her.

She ached to see him yet Bella, who was seldom afraid, was afraid now. The centre of Charles's life was here, in England; hers was in Australia. Neither would wish to change that, even if they could. She remembered England with affection but it was still the past, and so was Charles. It would be better to retain her memories of the boy he had been rather than the middle-aged man he had become. The boy and girl who had been so much in love no longer existed; by not seeing him, she could keep her memory of that love alive, but if they met she might not have even that.

No, she would stay in London, visit Mumma every day, do what she could to comfort her. And wait.

The car dropped her at the Ritz. She had examined herself in her handbag mirror during the drive. Her eyes were pink and slightly swollen, but nothing that anyone would notice.

She walked into the lobby and stopped at the concierge's desk. 'Any messages?'

'Two, Mrs Tucker.'

She looked at the slips. Perth had been on the phone. Twice. The messages were marked most urgent. She looked at her Longines.

Three o'clock. That would make it ten at night in Perth. Too bad. If it were that urgent they would be expecting her call.

The lift took her up. She walked down the corridor, went into her suite and picked up the phone. 'Perth, Western Australia,' she said, and gave the number.

The suite was furnished in the Ritz's signature colours of blue, peach, pink and yellow. The drapes were luxurious, the antique furniture ivory dressed with gold, the chandelier fine crystal. It was a very comfortable suite. While she waited she looked out at Green Park. The traffic went up and down Piccadilly and she wondered what the calls were about.

The phone rang. She picked it up. Deborah might have been in the same room.

'Martin is in Sydney about that new banking facility and I can't get hold of him,' Deborah said. 'So I thought I'd best phone you.'

'What's the problem?'

'Mr Bathurst's office has been on the phone twice today. They say it's urgent.'

That was Pete Bathurst all over: wait until she's out of town, then put on the screws.

'What does he want?'

'Some problem about the terminal.'

'That was settled before I left!' Dealing with Pete Bathurst was like picking your way through a pit full of vipers. 'Let Martin handle it when he gets back from Sydney.'

'They asked specifically for you.'

She was the decision-maker, after all.

'In that case they'll have to wait.' She hesitated. 'I don't think it'll be long.'

'I get the impression they think you're stalling.'

'If he wants a doctor's certificate,' Bella blazed, 'tell him I'll arrange it.'

Fuming, she slammed down the phone.

Her own mother, for God's sake! Surely even Pete Bathurst could understand that? Although there had been times when she had asked herself whether Pete had ever had a mother.

The next day she drove back to Whitstable. There was no change in Mumma's condition but this time she met Luke Such. His likeness to Peace was unmistakable. So Jenny had been right; Bella was definitely his daughter. She looked at him but felt nothing. The fact that he had impregnated her mother – by accident, you might say – did not make him her true father. As she had told Peace, that was Anthony Richmond. And Grandpapa was even more her family, because he had been the one who had truly cared for her.

Luke was a stranger in every way. A good man, no doubt, but – like most men – useless when it came to sickness. He had survived shipwreck and storm, for years had dragged a living from a hostile sea, yet now he was as much use as a bull in a milking parlour. He stood around, getting in the way and looking anxious yet doing nothing, until Bella could have screamed at him. The only reason she did not was Jenny and the obvious affection that existed between the dying woman and the ineffectual man. Luke might be useless but he was there, and ultimately that was what mattered.

'Sometimes I 'as to get out,' he told Bella. 'Library, mostly. It's hard to watch when it's someone you care for. When I can't take no more, I ask Mrs Nunes to come in. She's always willin'. Good woman, that. I wouldn't leave her with just anyone.'

Two days passed. Jenny did not speak. Her eyes remained closed. She breathed, but that was all. One evening, as Bella was getting ready to head back to the Ritz, the breathing stopped.

It was a quiet funeral at the local church. Bella wasn't sure what Mumma would have thought about a church service but Luke wanted it. She felt sad but not devastated; life had separated them too long for that. Now Luke was the one to be consoled. For the first time Bella felt something for him. It made her feel better about him, and herself.

'Will you stay here?' she asked him.

He looked about him as though at a strange and stricken world. 'I reckon.'

But he was lost and she thought it would not be long before he followed his wife to the grave.

Three days after the funeral, she flew back to Australia. She did what she could to put England and the past behind her. Instead she thought about Pete Bathurst.

Trust him to make more trouble.

CHAPTER FIFTY

Bella got home at six in the evening after flying halfway around the world. She had a hollow ache in her stomach whenever she thought of Jenny – you only have one mother, after all – but she was in bed by nine-thirty and slept well, as she always did. By eight the following morning she was in her office and in conference with Owen and Martin. The subject of the discussion, as far too often in Bella's view, was Pete Bathurst and his latest objections.

'What is that wretched man on about now?' she said.

This time it was the exact terms upon which BradMin would be willing to allow Tucker Mining to use their loading terminal just outside Port Hedland.

'Owen and I spent the best part of three days with Sinclair Smythe, getting that sorted out,' said Martin Dexter crossly.

'With BradMin nothing is ever sorted out until Bathurst has given it his okay. Quite often not even then,' Bella said.

As always it ended with her having to get together with Pete Bathurst and thrash everything out yet again. It was a tense meeting. It was seldom anything else; Pete had never forgiven Bella for opening up her own mine and thus depriving him of the potential for huge profits, or for poaching his mine development manager.

Possibly even for having found the Carlisle deposits in the first place. Every time she sat across the table from him he did his best to give her a hard time, but Bella knew how to be patient. She would get her own back one day but not yet; she needed BradMin's facilities to fulfil the contracts she had with the Nippon Steel and Blast Furnace Company.

They got things sorted in the end, but she knew it would not be long before he dreamt up another excuse to harass her some more. So it proved. The next time he was fussing about the rail link and how the maintenance costs were to be shared in view of the increase in traffic on the line, and the matter came up the very day Su-Ying went into hospital to have her baby.

When Richard had been born Bella had ensured that it happened at Miranda Downs with old Maisie to help her and not a doctor in sight but when it came to her first grandchild only hospital and the best gynie in Western Australia would do. Bella had intended to be on hand to witness the birth but the way Pete Bathurst dragged things out she could almost believe he had heard about Su-Ying's baby and was doing it deliberately to spite her.

'I wouldn't put it past him, the bastard,' she fumed to Martin Dexter when they finally got away. She flung the Bentley through the traffic towards the hospital. 'Get some decent cash flow under our belts and we'll build our own loading dock and rail link.'

'We're already close to our limit with the banks,' Martin said.

'At least it'll get Bathurst off our backs. And if we can pay for them out of profits, everyone will be happy.'

They screeched into the hospital car park, almost collecting an ambulance on the way, and drew to a stop in front of the main entrance. Within seconds Bella was out of the car and heading for the doors.

'Find somewhere to park it,' she told Martin over her shoulder.

Even financial directors had to play chauffeur, with Bella calling the shots.

She knew where the maternity ward was. She took a lift to the third floor and stopped at the reception desk.

'Mrs Tucker?' she said.

Lethargically the nurse examined a list.

'Who's asking?' she wondered.

'Mrs Tucker's mother-in-law.'

'The patient is in post-natal. If you care to wait, Sister will be with you shortly.'

'I am asking you,' Bella said. 'Has she had the baby or not?'

'She would hardly be in post-natal if she hadn't,' said the nurse, happy to put this pushy woman in her place.

'So what is it?'

'It is a boy.'

'And they are both well?'

'I believe so.'

Bella smiled at her: a fearful sight.

'And you would have heard, I take it.'

'Sister will be able to put you in the picture when she comes through,' said the nurse, impervious to sarcasm.

Bella looked around the waiting room, then opened the glass-panelled door and stepped out onto a railed verandah overlooking a small but pleasant garden.

My first grandchild, she thought. She supposed the thought should make her feel old but it did not. The birth invigorated her, filling her with barely suppressed exultation. She had no shortage of challenges in her life but this was the most potent of them all.

Before today, she thought, I was thinking simply in terms of the children and myself. Now I have moved beyond that, into the third generation. It will be up to me to build an empire worthy of the dynasty that will be my true legacy to the world.

Excitement frothed like champagne in her blood. She couldn't wait.

The nurse was talking in the room behind her.

'I believe your wife has stepped out onto the verandah.'

Wife?

Bella turned and saw Martin Dexter standing in the doorway.

'It's a boy,' she said, deliberately ignoring the nurse's remark. 'Mother and child both doing well.'

'Congratulations.'

'Thank you.'

'You heard what she said?'

'I did.'

Bella did not in the least mind the nurse's misunderstanding.

'Calls for a celebration,' he said. 'Drinks on me.'

Of course it was no secret that Martin fancied her or at least the status that a relationship with her would provide. She had let him take her out to dinner that one time. She had enjoyed herself but had made up her mind that she would not repeat it. Martin was a valued subordinate and a friend but that was as far as it went. There were times when she ached for a man's company and he was undeniably attractive, but having an affair with her financial director would make life too complicated, with the near certainty of problems down the track.

'Good idea,' she said. 'We'll have drinks in the boardroom with the others. I'll get Deborah to organise it.'

CHAPTER FIFTY-ONE

A month later Peace came into Bella's office very early one morning.

Bella looked up from the memorandum she had been reading. Other papers were stacked in a neat pile in her in-tray awaiting her attention.

'Are you busy?' Peace said.

Bella gave her a rueful smile. 'The paperwork is ever with us,' she said. 'But it can wait. I've just ordered some coffee. Sit down and have a cup with me.'

She looked thoughtfully at her daughter as she poured the coffee. She knew why she was here but would say nothing; it was up to Peace to start the ball rolling.

'I have decided to move on,' Peace said abruptly.

'I am sorry to hear that, dear.'

Bella had known for a long time it was inevitable. She would be sorry to see Peace go but knew it would be for the best and had no intention of fighting her about it.

Rory McNab was doing a brilliant job for the company. He was going nowhere which meant there was no opening for Peace in the only place she was willing to accept: at the top of the tree.

Also working in another organisation might give her the breadth of experience that she currently lacked.

'Have you decided where you're going?'

'Vancouver. Canadian Shield has offered me a position.'

Peace threw out the words as though daring her mother to challenge her decision but Bella had no intention of doing that.

'I think it's an excellent idea,' she said. 'When are you planning to leave?'

'Next month, if that's okay with you.'

'That will be fine. I always assumed you would want to go somewhere else to widen your experience. I shall be sorry to see you go, of course, but it won't be forever and when you come back you'll be even more valuable to the company than you are now.'

'If there's a place for me,' Peace said.

'There will always be a place for you,' Bella said. 'In the company and in my heart.'

Although there were times Bella could have shaken her. Peace was brilliant at her job and had huge potential but one besetting sin: she was always trying to fly before she could walk. Bella knew Peace had been hoping she would move Rory McNab sideways to make room for her but that was something Bella would never do. Rory, too, was brilliant. She had another reason, as well. To Bella loyalty was sacrosanct, a sacrament she would not defile for Peace or anyone else.

'This group has huge potential,' she said. 'Not only in iron. I am quite sure that in a few years' time we'll be able to offer you a top job worthy of your talent.'

Later, after Peace had gone, Bella sat looking into space, the waiting papers lying disregarded on her desk, and asked herself why she and Peace had never been able to have a relaxed, friendly conversation with one another, as mother and daughter should. It shouldn't be like that, she thought, but the fact was she had always found it easier to get on with her Chinese daughter-in-law than her own child, and that was a sad thing. Maybe it was her fault, but somehow there had always been a prickly hedge between them.

Perhaps a few years apart would benefit them both.

CHAPTER FIFTY-TWO

Two weeks before Christmas 1972, Bella held a meeting with Owen Freeth and Martin Dexter to discuss floating Tuckers shares on the market.

Owen was against it. 'I cannot see the benefit of diluting your control of the group.'

'We need the money,' Bella said. 'It's that simple.'

Owen was almost seventy now and had lost some of his edge but Bella had no plans to ease him out; she felt for him the indulgent kindness she might have had for an old dog – a bit slow, a bit stiff in the joints – but whose innate loyalty could not be denied. To humour him she set out the arguments again.

'We need more capital to exploit the Japanese market. Opening up new areas will cost us a bomb. We'll need another crushing plant, more earthmoving equipment, new roads, an extension to the rail link, more heavy-axle wagons, another stand-by locomotive... Do you know how much these things cost?'

To say nothing of the terminal she was determined to have. She had her eye on a suitable site, had already had confidential discussions with the premier and had sounded out the principal landowners across whose property the rail link would run. It would mean millions in additional costs.

'The banks will lend us the money,' Owen said. 'Iron ore is flavour of the month with the banks.'

Bella raised an eyebrow at Martin Dexter. 'What do you think?'

'I prefer outside capital, if we can get it without sacrificing control. We are too much in the banks' hands already.'

Two diametrically opposed views, but that was fine.

'Thank you for your input,' she said, smiling as she dismissed them. 'You've given me a lot to think about.'

The truth was that Bella had already made her decision and their opinions didn't matter, but she liked to test the strength of her thinking by bouncing the pros and cons off those she trusted. It was also politic to let them think they had greater influence than they did.

What was sure was that the company had to get massive amounts of new capital from somewhere. With the present price of ore, increased Japanese trade would generate enough profit, even after state royalties, to recoup most of the development costs, but she had studied Martin's projections of the up-front investment that was needed and it was enormous.

In the longer term she also wanted Tuckers to have its own railway. Once they had that they would be free of BradMin at last, but for the moment she thought it wiser to keep that idea to herself.

There was another consideration, too, which she had not discussed with them. Iron ore was an international commodity, which meant that any problems on the international scene would impact on the trade. Helmut Muller had pointed this out when she had last seen him in Frankfurt and had offered her the use of his various contacts around the globe.

'Successful business needs reliable information,' he had said. 'And reliable information means ears to the ground around the world.'

Spies, in other words, complete with encoded messages and a secret telegraphic address.

Quite the James Bond, Bella thought.

And now one of her Middle East spies had sent a report warning of rising Arab unrest at the USA's continuing support for Israel.

'We expect a strong response in 1973. Possibly even an oil embargo.'

If that happened, there would be an international sell-off of shares and iron ore prices would go through the floor.

If Tuckers were to raise market capital, it had to be soon or it might be too late.

The listing was a huge success. With the issue ten times over-subscribed (it was not only the banks that regarded iron ore as flavour of the month) even Owen Freeth with his inheritance from Garth had few complaints. Not that he would admit it.

'A nice nest egg for when you retire,' Bella said.

'What goes up can also go down,' Owen said snootily. 'In any case I am like you. We are not the sort to retire before we must. And then it's likely to be feet first.'

No matter; with the money from the subscription she was able to give Rory McNab the go-ahead for the development of the new areas. For several months the work continued on schedule but then the forebodings of Bella's spy were realised, and in spades.

On the sixth of October Syria and Egypt launched a surprise assault on Israel. Supported by military aid from the United States, Israel's response was immediate, and devastating. Within days both Egypt and Syria were in full retreat, the United States pledged further aid and on the twentieth of October the Arab oil producers announced an oil embargo against the USA and its allies.

The effect on the international economy was as catastrophic as Bella had foreseen. The price of iron ore collapsed. Tuckers were no longer looking at fabulous profits; instead they would be lucky to break even.

'What goes up can also come down,' Owen reminded her.

'And in this case what comes down will also go up again,' she said.

She believed it absolutely. The market would revive. Now was the time to invest in the future.

She sent Owen to enter into agreements with the landowners; she sat down again with the state premier. It took months, but in the end she had her way. Development at Port Anthony began. They would build a spur to connect the port with BradMin's railway. Even with the additional capital, finances were stretched well beyond the limit of what was prudent but, confident in her star, Bella did not care. She was living dangerously and loving it.

CHAPTER FIFTY-THREE

The runway lights appeared on schedule, standing out amid the thin cluster of lights of the town. They were a welcome sight in what until a few minutes ago had been the unrelieved darkness of the land beneath the Cessna's wings.

It was 7 December 1975 and Bella was on her way to inspect the on-going construction at the Port Anthony terminal south of Port Hedland. She had radioed the airstrip half an hour ago to confirm the lights would be switched on. The next few minutes would be tricky, even so; it was the first time she had attempted a landing in the dark but there was a first time for everything and tonight, she told herself, was the night.

She throttled back, checking altitude, wind speed and direction, trim… Slowly the runway rose to meet her. Throttle back a little, the engine noise quieter now… Careful not to stall… Recheck the alignment… Down and still down… The lights rushing to meet her… The wheels touched, tyres screaming, hands busy on the controls, slowing now, taxiing now, everything under control…

Whew!

There was a brick shack on one side of the runway. Bella parked in front of it and switched off. Silence came rushing as the engine died.

A man in overalls greeted her as, suddenly weary, Bella climbed down.

'Welcome to Port Hedland,' he said.

He was young, cheerful and bare-headed, the breeze lifting the blond hair on his head. A physique that even an old woman could appreciate.

'Sorry to keep you late,' Bella said as she shook his hand.

'With BradMin's terminal outside town and your Port Anthony coming up twenty-five kilometres down the coast, we get traffic at all hours. Very different from the old days,' he said.

They walked side by side towards the building. There was a light breeze and overhead the sky was bright with stars.

'Your vehicle is waiting to run you into town,' the young man said.

'When the Port Anthony landing strip is operational we won't have to trouble you any more,' Bella told him. 'Okay to leave my plane where it is?'

'She'll be right,' he said. 'There's a cyclone out there somewhere, but it's well off-shore and tracking west. We're not expecting trouble.'

The driver of the Land Cruiser was also young. This is a country for young men, Bella thought. His name was Frederick and, unlike the man who had greeted her, was taciturn and scrawny: no heart-throbs there. He took her overnight bag and tossed it into the back of the cruiser without a word. He drove her into town and dropped her at the motel, where a room had been reserved.

The motel was a low building, the walls yellow, and Bella thought that in daylight it would have a view of the sea. She breathed in the tropical smell of the coast, a mixture of salt, coral and rot, fecund with birth and rebirth. The night was still and she could hear the sound of waves in the darkness. She went indoors and booked in. She ate sparsely in the empty dining room and within the hour was asleep.

In the morning she stood on the balcony outside her room and looked at the view. There were palm trees along the shore, their long fronds hanging limply. The sky was clear, the calm sea the colour of slate. It was seven-thirty, the heat already oppressive, and the air was still.

She was eating breakfast when the cruiser arrived. She downed a second cup of coffee, went out and climbed in beside the driver.

'Not much wind today,' she said.

'Bad weather out there somewhere,' Frederick said.

'Not too bad, I hope.'

He grunted but said no more. They drove west along the coast road, the sea visible at intervals between clumps of vegetation.

The site manager, whose name was Steve, told Bella how things were going.

'About two-thirds finished,' he said. 'The deepwater jetty is almost ready, similarly the rail link and access road. We still have to complete the wharf, admin block and loading plant, but she should be up and running in a couple of months.'

'I want photographs,' Bella said. 'Pictures of everything here.'

'You want pretty pictures for your office,' Steve said, 'I'd wait until she's finished.'

'I shall, when it's ready. But I also want some today. To show how far we've got.'

'You're the boss,' Steve said.

They walked along the jetty, which ran quarter of a mile into deep water. A tug was anchored a hundred yards further off-shore. A team of men was laying rails down the middle of the jetty, while others welded guardrails along either side.

She reached the end and looked back at the shore.

'Long way,' she said.

'Bulk carriers need deep water,' Steve said.

She stared at the steel piles disappearing below the surface. Still no wind but the sea was surging against the structure, stirring uneasy bursts of foam a foot or two into the air.

She watched the water for a minute before turning and walking back with Steve towards the shore.

'The airstrip manager was saying there's a cyclone out there somewhere,' she said.

'They've even given it a name,' Steve said. 'Joan is well off-shore. They estimate it's tracking at about five kilometres an hour along the coast.'

'That's slow,' Bella said.

'That's its speed across the water. Cyclones spin around their centre much faster than their land speed. Sixty, eighty miles an hour, sometimes more. But those piles are built to last. We're not expecting trouble.'

'And if Joan turns inland?'

He grinned. 'That would be different. But it won't. The barometer hasn't shifted for a week.'

Yet Bella felt uneasy. She knew the marine architects who had designed the jetty had factored in the details of every cyclone along this coast for the past forty years, yet there was something about the sullen surge of the slate-grey sea that did not feel right.

A yellow earthmover ground past as Bella left the jetty and walked to the caravan being used as a site office. The caravan was large, with a bathroom and three bedrooms, and Steve said he slept in it when he was not working.

'You're not married?'

Not that it mattered but it was something to say, and she always liked to get close to her staff if she could.

He shook his head, grinning. 'Still playing the field, that's me.'

There were power cables lying on the ground and the caravan was air-conditioned.

'What happens to this if a cyclone hits?'

'Concrete base. Deep anchors. Heavy duty cables.'

'So she's safe?'

'As houses.'

Bella had a cup of coffee with Steve and studied the plans of the development. Afterwards she got him to escort her around the site; she was determined to see every inch of what had been completed and all that remained to be done. Teams of men were working everywhere. She could see they were making good progress and was pleased.

'Where do they stay when they're not working?' she asked Steve.

'Port Hedland. We've got trucks to run them to and fro.'

Bella took dozens of photographs. It was twelve o'clock and she was dripping with sweat by the time she finished.

'What I would give for a breath of fresh air,' she told Steve when they got back to the caravan.

'You can shower here if you like,' he said.

'I need a change of clothes,' she said. 'I'll get Frederick to run me back to the motel.'

After she had showered and changed she felt much better. She gave her hair a thorough brush and put on a dab of lipstick; being the boss lady meant looking the part, as well as acting it. Satisfied with her appearance, she went and ate lunch in the dining room.

She had told no one why she was here, but the banks were getting nervous and wanted a progress report on how things were going.

Had it not been for the Arab oil embargo they would have been all right. They could have funded the development out of profits but revenue had collapsed along with the iron-ore price. Prices had just begun to pick up again but she had learnt that banks to whom you owed money were like children, in constant need of reassurance, so she had flown up herself, knowing that a personal report, backed by photographs, would carry more weight than the normal surveyor's assessment. Not that she planned to say that to Steve; confidence was a fragile plant, easily damaged.

She finished her lunch – fillet of barramundi and salad – and had signed the bill and walked outside just as the Land Cruiser turned into the forecourt of the motel. As she walked towards the vehicle a breath of wind touched the back of her neck. She turned to taste it, feeling it cool on her face.

Frederick had got out to open the door for her and now looked at her, puzzled by her sudden movement.

'The wind,' she said. 'First time I've felt it all day.'

He frowned and turned to face it. It was very light, the merest breath, but it was unmistakable and blowing steadily from the west, the direction in which Steve had told her the hidden cyclone lay in ambush.

'Sea breeze,' Frederick said confidently. 'It'll pass.'

Bella wasn't so sure. 'I want you to run me up to the airstrip,' she said. 'I need to be sure my plane is well anchored.'

She had got what she came for and could have flown out, but the weather didn't feel right, whatever people were saying, so she decided to stay put.

There was an aluminium hangar behind the brick airport building, also a tractor that the airstrip manager used to manoeuvre Minnie into shelter. He came out again and closed and locked the sliding doors.

'Lucky no one was using it. She'll be safe there,' he said.

Bella went back to Port Anthony. There was nothing she could do when she got there but went anyway. There was little wind, yet she remained uneasy. All along the port road the vegetation was being lifted and flattened, pressed by an invisible hand.

'Stop here,' she said to Frederick.

She walked through the scrub and stared at the ocean. The water was still a uniform grey, broken only by a succession of long, black swells that rose, one after the other, to break sullenly along the shore. Here she could taste the wind. It was still light, the ocean calm, yet the air felt heavy, the horizon had closed in and it was no longer possible to distinguish sky from sea. She walked back to the vehicle amid a sudden rattle of rain that ceased as quickly as it had begun, and the drops were hard enough to sting.

'Let's get on,' she said.

Frederick drove fast along the rutted gravel road, yet Bella could not escape the apprehension that had gripped her.

Sea breeze, he had told her. *It'll pass.*

She did not believe it.

They passed a succession of vehicles heading the other way and when they arrived at Port Anthony she found that work had ceased. Steve had pulled all the work gangs off the site and sent them to safety. The heavy plant had been driven into a park a quarter of a mile from the shore and secured by metal hawsers to steel pickets driven deep into the ground. The tug had motored further out to sea and had all three anchors down: more than enough, Steve said, to withstand anything the elements could throw at it. The tug crew was now with the rest of the team, heading to Port Hedland.

'You'd better get back, too,' she told Frederick.

'How will you manage?'

'I shall stay here,' she said.

His expression said she was crazy; maybe she was. She smiled at him.

'Get moving,' she said. 'I'll be fine.'

He didn't need telling twice.

She watched the cruiser until it disappeared, then turned and walked to the caravan. The air was beginning to move. Somewhere it had picked up weight; it certainly no longer felt like a breeze.

More like a load of concrete, Bella thought.

The caravan was anchored securely to its base; while she'd been having lunch cyclone shutters had been bolted across the windows and door, the glass crisscrossed with sticky tape. Except for the lighting, all power had been switched off. Everything that could be done had been done.

Steve was beside her.

'The site's evacuated?' Bella asked him.

'Except for us.'

'And we are going nowhere,' Bella said.

All afternoon the westerly wind increased. The radio was issuing cyclone warnings yet the barometer remained steady at 29.8 inches.

'I've never heard of cyclonic winds holding steady from one quarter,' Steve said. 'They always back and veer. How can it be a cyclone? And the barometer's as steady as a rock!'

Bella hoped he was right but felt as though spiders were burrowing beneath her skin. The humidity was overwhelming and, with power to the air conditioner switched off, she was once again drenched with sweat. She had never been so uncomfortable.

She had intended to stay in the office but was too restless to do so. She walked down the roadway that ran along the almost-completed wharf and examined the turntable where the locomotives would turn before making their return journey to the mine.

The wind was stronger now, tugging the hair on her head, the rain squalls more frequent. She went back to the caravan and bolted the door behind her. She sat down, not knowing what to do with herself, and listened to the structure creaking in the wind.

She did what she did so often in moments of stress, when her body screamed for action which for some reason circumstances prevented: she let her thoughts travel back to other, earlier, times when she had been subjected to intense pressure. The dull thud of Charles being thrown from his horse in the gathering darkness of the Yorkshire dales. The nerve-screaming tension of Charters Towers, knowing that Johnson was watching her in the darkness of her bedroom. Cowering on Townsville beach, waiting to be recaptured by Mr Henry's thugs. The agony of waiting, after Peace's accident, to hear whether she was alive or dead.

She doubted whether the worst of cyclones could compare with the trauma of those moments.

'Living in this part of the world, I suppose this is routine to you,' she said to Steve.

'A cyclone is never routine,' Steve said.

For the third time since Bella had come back from the wharf, he got up and checked the barometer: 29.8 and steady.

'The barometer hasn't moved,' he said.

Yet Steve, too, couldn't sit still.

'Tell me about cyclones,' Bella said. 'What are they?'

'They're tropical storms that revolve around a central vortex. The whole system moves very slowly but the winds at the centre are huge. They are what do the damage.'

'But you think this may not be a cyclone at all. Despite the radio warnings?'

'The winds are too steady.'

'You'd better be right,' Bella told him. 'Because, if you're not…'

'If I'm not right, what does it mean?'

'It means the whole system must be tracking straight at us.'

'God help us if you're right,' he said.

'God helps those who help themselves,' Bella said. 'Why don't you radio Port Hedland, ask them what the weather's doing there?'

Steve spoke briefly on the radio then put down the microphone and stared at her. His mouth was working and he spoke as though there was no spit in his mouth.

'Wind gusting southeast to southwest. Speeds up to thirty knots and rising.'

Being locked inside the caravan was suddenly intolerable.

'Let's see what's happening outside.'

Bella pushed open the door. It took some doing but finally she forced her way out against what was now a gale. She let the door blow shut behind her and stood with her back pressed against the van, the wind probing every part of her body. Out at sea, the black swells had disintegrated, the waves breaking all ways at once. Towards the horizon the sky had turned black and the wind was still blowing without variation from the west.

The weather out there, cyclone or not, was heading this way. Slowly, perhaps, but it was coming.

She went back indoors, the wind sending papers flying from the desk. Steve was looking at the barometer. He turned towards her and she saw that his lips were as grey as his cheeks.

'29.3,' he whispered.

The barometer had dropped half an inch in an hour.

Bella could smell the beginnings of panic on him. 'You know what I would like?' she said. 'A nice cup of tea. Shall I make us one?'

Whether it was the tea or Bella herself she never knew, but his face grew still as he got a grip on himself. 'I never thought I'd see the day,' he said with the shadow of a smile. 'Bella Tucker making me a cup of tea in a cyclone.'

Because there could no longer be any doubt: a cyclone it was, and heading this way.

The caravan shuddered under a gust of wind.

Bella handed him a mug of tea. 'What can we expect?' she said quietly.

'There are no rules,' Steve said. 'We'll survive or we won't. No way to tell.'

'That's cheerful,' Bella said.

'It's honest,' Steve said.

There were times when honesty could be a burden but Bella said nothing. As Steve had said, they would survive or they would not. Ultimately nothing else mattered.

Again the caravan shook as a second strong gust buffeted it. Behind their protective shutters the windows rattled.

'It's coming,' Bella said.

'This is nothing,' Steve said. 'They'll get much more serious later.'

'What will?'

'The wind gusts. Cyclones spawn them. A Chinese sailor told me they have the same thing off the South China coast. He said there they call them *tai-feng*. It means strong winds, but apparently they think of them as devil winds.'

'Good name for them,' Bella said.

They listened to the rising voice of the gale.

'There is still time for you to evacuate before they arrive,' Bella said. 'If you've got a vehicle.' She would not hold him here against his will.

But Steve shook his head. 'My four-wheel drive is in a shed behind the building but it's too risky. There's no cover between here and Port Hedland and only the one road. Get caught in the open and we'd have no chance.'

'So we have to sweat it out?'

It made Bella feel better, knowing there was no choice; not that she'd planned to leave, anyway.

'You got it,' Steve said.

Slowly night-time swallowed the land. Across the sea, darkness merged with the approaching storm and became one. Bella had been out for a final look before it grew too dark to see anything. Now she came back in for the last time and shut and locked the door behind her.

'What's it like out there?' Steve said.

'The wind is a lot stronger.'

'From what direction?'

'Still from the west,' Bella said.

An hour later the first devil wind came screaming out of the darkness. Later they learned that when it fell on the tug, it ripped the three heavy anchors out of the sea bed as though they were made of paper. Lifted on the crest of a giant wave, the tug was flung against the jetty. The steel piles, each as thick as a man's body, bent like plasticine. Bows jammed in the wreckage, the tug became a battering ram, every wave driving it deeper into the jetty's wounded flank. Hull ripped by the broken girders, the vessel began to drown.

A second devil wind struck. It flung another wave, twelve feet high, against the almost-completed wharf, wrecking it in seconds and washing away the foundations, leaving what remained dangling in mid-air. Seconds and one wave later, the buckled wharf disappeared in a maelstrom of boiling surf. The trees along the rail tracks snapped like matchsticks. The winds screamed their triumph as they tore loose the rail turntable and flung five hundred tons of metal plate whirling through the air. It missed the roof of the caravan by a foot and ripped off the radio aerial before crashing into the shed at the rear, demolishing both the shed and the vehicle it contained.

Inside the caravan Bella and Steve cowered in a corner of the smallest bedroom. Speech and even thought were impossible. The violence of the wind stunned every sense. Even memory was gone, leaving nothing but a bottomless pit of terror. Into which they fell, endlessly.

The storm continued to rage. The caravan quaked on its foundations; any minute the roof might lift, or one or more of the window shutters break loose. The windows would burst inwards, showering them with stiletto blades of broken glass. If they survived that, the wind would blow the structure apart in seconds and the storm would finish the job.

Facing what now seemed certain death, Bella grew calm. Courage returned. Steve's body was trembling uncontrollably, his eyes screwed tight, but for her fear had no place. They would live or not, and there was nothing they could do. Fear had no place.

At that moment the lights went out. Steve moaned. 'The generator must have been knocked out.'

'Do you have a torch?'

Steve did not answer; perhaps he had not heard her above the bellow of the wind. The darkness made the storm seem ten times more violent than before. Clearly audible above the wind came a deep-throated rumble, like the charge of a thousand locomotives. Bella thought it must be a tidal wave, but it was not. The roar passed above the roof and faded into the distance, heading inland.

Silence returned. The absence of sound was almost as terrifying as the storm itself.

Bella had lost all sense of time. She knew it must still be night, yet now a silver glow showed around the door and in the cracks between the shutters. It grew steadily stronger.

Steve opened his eyes, staring in bewilderment.

'What the...?'

Bella stood. She moved awkwardly, knees stiff. She was fifty-six years old and felt eighty. She took a deep breath. Get your act together, for God's sake. She walked purposefully to the door and pulled back the bolts. She opened the door – no wind resistance now – and looked out.

The air was still: not simply free of movement but as though it had congealed. She stared incredulously at the scene before her.

The moon was shining, the sky cloudless. In the silver light she saw the wreckage of the jetty, the remains of the tug, half-submerged, funnel and most of the superstructure gone, jammed in the twisted girders. A major part of the beach had disappeared. It was hard to see what had happened to the railway, but it looked as though most of that had gone, too. The trees had broken off short; the stumps glowed white in the moonlight. Despite the damage, the overwhelming impression was of silence, while off-shore the sea had gone mad, waves rising in peaks of foam that broke again and again over the remains of the jetty. Far out, forming a circle that shone with an unearthly glow in the moonlight, pillars of cloud rose tens of thousands of feet into the air.

She wanted to believe the storm was gone, yet knew it was not. Here, at what remained of Port Anthony, they were at the bottom of a vast tunnel of silence and indescribable menace. They were in the eye of the storm, the clouds not stationary but edging closer with every second.

Bella went back inside the van and closed and locked the door. Steve was staring at her.

'We are in the eye,' she said.

'When the wind comes back it'll blow from the opposite direction,' Steve said.

'As strongly?'

'Maybe even stronger.'

'In that case we'd best make sure the windows at the back of the van are secure,' Bella said. 'And let's get on with it. We don't have much time.'

Steve had found a torch and they checked as thoroughly as they could. One of the shutters had worked loose and needed to be jammed tight.

'You have a hammer?'

Bella watched as Steve drove strong pieces of wood beneath the shutter to hold it in place, then closed the window and threw the bolts. Hopefully it would hold.

He was just in time; before he secured the shutter Bella had a moment to see, clearly visible in the moonlight, a whirling dust cloud moving inexorably towards them across the land. Bushes, ripped out of the earth, spun upwards and disappeared. First came a band of rain; Bella heard it drumming on the ground above the eerie hooting of the wind. It crashed on the roof in an explosion of sound and all visibility was gone. A second later and yet another devil wind fell upon them, the caravan shaking and groaning but still, miraculously, holding firm.

Bella mustered every ounce of her resolve. Endurance was the only weapon she had left. She lifted her chin. Inside her head she shouted her defiance at the storm.

I shall survive!

As once again the devil winds fell screaming upon them.

The sun rose, shedding a watery yellow light upon a shattered landscape.

Bella opened the van door – at least it would still open. Unable to comprehend that she was still alive, she stared out at devastation.

For all practical purposes, Port Anthony was gone. The jetty was in ruins. Where the wharf had been was now a gaping void, the rail tracks twisted and buckled, the remains of the turntable hurled two hundred yards from its mounting by the unimaginable force of the wind. The heavy dozers, parked in the hollow a quarter of a mile from the jetty, had been reduced to junk. Only the caravan, secured by massive bolts to its concrete base, had survived.

Steve stood behind her, staring over her shoulder at the destruction.

'What now?' he said in a shaken voice.

Bella closed her eyes, drew a deep breath and once again, as so often in her life, summoned the resources of her will. She turned to him, taking both his hands in hers.

'We start again,' she said.

* * *

She spent the next three days assessing the damage. It was both extensive and severe. The storm that had devastated Port Anthony spared Port Hedland. A few roofs were missing, buildings near the water's edge had been flooded, but the port and loading terminal were largely untouched, Bella's aircraft unscathed in its hangar. Inland, the Carlisle and Bradford Gulliver mines had been less fortunate, with massive damage to plant and installations. Repairs would take a vast amount of time and capital. To make matters worse, until they had been completed, cash flow would be nil.

For all her determination and cheerful words, Bella knew she was in the fight of her life. It was all very well to *say* start again. But what with?

CHAPTER FIFTY-FOUR

It was no good. Whichever way Bella looked at them, the books would not balance.

'It's the cyclone. The rebuilding costs have almost wiped us out,' Martin said.

It was true, and costs were three times what they had been originally. The contractors blamed it on the disruption caused by the cyclone. Perhaps they were right, but that didn't help when the insurance companies were refusing to pay more than a fraction of the replacement costs. And it had not been only the port; the rail link and crushing plant had been destroyed by the floods that had followed the cyclone, and for these the insurers, relying on a cloudy definition of what flooding the policy covered, had refused to pay anything at all. The Japanese, struggling with a downturn in their economy, had deferred further orders of ore. Cash inflow was more or less non-existent.

'While it goes out like water down the sink,' Bella said. 'It is kind of you to blame the cyclone, but the fact is I made a wrong call, going ahead with the redevelopment before the market had recovered.'

'You hoped to beat BradMin to the punch,' said Martin.

'In the meantime we are the ones on the canvas,' she said. Interest payments alone looked likely to wipe them out. 'Perhaps we should consider selling some of our other assets?'

'We can't do that,' Martin said.

'The Wyndham meatworks. I'd be sorry to see it go, it was my first business venture, but we can't afford to be sentimental. Surely that would help?'

'Sentimentality has nothing to do with it,' he said. 'When I said we can't sell, I meant it literally. The meatworks are pledged to the bank, like everything else you own. In a sense they're no longer yours, as long as the loans are outstanding. No, my dear,' – it was the first time he had ever called her that – 'it will have to be an increase in revenue or nothing.'

'Then I'd better get over to Japan as soon as I can, see what I can do.'

Perhaps she could talk her friend Mr Nakasumi into giving them a new order. Even a few million tons might give the banks renewed confidence.

'We need to do something,' Martin Dexter said. 'Halliburton is a worried man.'

With the bank's directors on his back, it was small wonder.

BradMin, too, was suffering, with talk of several thousand layoffs world wide, but BradMin had been in the game for years and had reserves that Bella could only dream about.

'We are in trouble,' Owen Freeth said. 'Mainly through your own stubbornness.'

Sometimes he talked to Bella like a stern parent. It exasperated her, particularly since in her heart she feared he might be right, so she went to Japan to see what could be done. She was away ten days, came back with a long face.

'They're suffering, too,' she told Martin at the airport. 'I used all the magic I have on them but could only get a few dribs and drabs.'

Three million tons was better than a kick in the face but would not get them far. As the bank's general manager, face like a wet week, pointed out.

'I don't know what the board will say,' Halliburton told her.

'Asia needs infrastructure,' Bella said. 'If we can only hang in there, the market is bound to recover.'

'Eventually, no doubt,' Halliburton said. 'The question is when. And in the meantime, Bella, you really have to do something.'

Like what?

'I suppose I could sell Desire, if I really had to...'

But she could not, because Desire, like the meatworks and everything else, was also pledged to the bank.

Somehow they hung on, thanks in part to the banks, in part to unexpected orders from Australian steel companies. An order arrived out of the blue from India's Tata Steel. Enough, at the year's end, to turn a small profit. But with interest payments eating up income, as Bella put it, like a fox devouring carrion, it was never enough and on the market the price of Tuckers stock remained resolutely in the doldrums.

CHAPTER FIFTY-FIVE

In the third week of October 1976 Bella received a letter from
Germany.

I am writing to you privately, Helmut Muller wrote, *because I am
concerned at the situation regarding Tucker Mining. I remain confident in you both as business woman and human being and would
regret it very much if you were forced to liquidate the company. I therefore would like to offer you a personal and interest-free loan of two
million Australian dollars in the hope that this may help the company
survive. I only wish it could be more.*

'It is a princely offer,' Martin Dexter said.

'A pity I can't accept it,' Bella said. 'It's not enough to dig us out
of the hole and I refuse to let him waste his money.'

'Are you sure we can afford such noble gestures?'

'Afford it or not, that's the way it's going to be,' Bella said.

Martin said no more but his expression spoke for him. It said
that when Bella spoke in that tone, further discussion was futile.

Damn right, Bella thought. Although she too said nothing.

Later she saddled up and rode as far as the land would permit. It
seemed crazy to be on the edge of ruin – Owen Freeth would have

DUST OF·THE LAND   443

said over the edge – yet still have such a house and estate. No doubt Martin was right to say it was the bank's property and not hers, yet she still had the use of it. Might as well take advantage of it while she could.

At the limit of the land she turned back and headed towards the rise from which she could look across the surrounding countryside. At the summit she reined in, looking down at the big house, white as icing sugar in the sunlight, and beyond it to the grey haze of the land that extended as far as she could see. Two hundred and fifty acres were hers, at least for the moment, but there seemed no chance of their remaining so much longer. Helmut Muller's offer had introduced a new element that she both welcomed and resented. She could not allow a friend – for this was the gesture of a true friend – to lose money on a venture that was certain to fail. The ore was there, but with no market the company could not go on. No, she thought, let it go. At least that way I shall be spared yet another obligation I cannot meet.

It was the right decision yet she rode back to the house with a sense of doom in her heart. Helmut's offer had been made with the best of intentions, but she wished he had never made it.

Somehow they clung on into the New Year, living from hand to mouth and fending off the banks with optimistic assurances in which she no longer believed, until Bella awoke to a summer day in early February, radiant with the promise of heat, and knew that things could go on no longer.

She told Martin of her decision.

'You will tell the Stock Exchange?' he said.

'We've no choice.'

'There'll be no going back if you do.'

'I'll be committing a criminal offence if I don't. Isn't there something in the law about trading when insolvent?'

'We are not insolvent.'

'But I see no possibility of any other outcome. Do you?'

He said nothing, his silence as eloquent as words.

She sighed and looked around the office of which she had been
so proud. The decision had drained her; she felt she could barely
stand but forced herself to walk to the window and look out at the
estate that, once she had phoned the Exchange, would not even
nominally be hers.

'How long will it take?'

'After you tell the Stock Exchange? Not long. The banks will
soon hear, of course –'

'I do not intend the banks to hear from anyone but me.'

'That'll be a fun conversation,' Martin said.

'It is important that we do things the right way.'

'Even in these circumstances?'

'Especially in these circumstances.'

'There is one possibility you have not considered.'

His voice reflected the hesitation he felt in saying it. She stared
at him.

'What is that?'

'Doing a deal with BradMin.'

'I'd sooner go broke,' she said. She wanted nothing to do with
BradMin.

'Think of yourself for a change,' Martin urged her.

Temptation was a razor, cutting deep. Yes, a deal was possible.
BradMin would get the mineral rights, the banks would be paid out
and Bella would keep most, maybe all, her assets. Miranda Downs
would be saved, for herself and the children. They would no longer
be mega-rich, perhaps, but they would still make a more than adequate living from the cattle station and meatworks, as they always
had until that fatal trip down the Carlisle. They would be safe.

But at what price?

'What about the unsecured creditors? The shareholders? The
ordinary people who put their savings into Tuckers because they
trusted us? What about them?'

Martin shrugged. 'That's the risk investors take. Some you win,
some you lose.'

Indeed they did. But if she rigged things so that she came out all right while others lost everything… She was responsible for the company and its investors. Not legally, but morally. To preserve her own assets while those who had trusted her lost theirs would be wrong.

'I'll not do it,' she said.

She watched a BMW coupe drive in and park at the side of the house. The driver got out and hurried towards the main entrance.

Su-Ying coming here at this time of day? Bella thought. And in such a hurry, too? Dear God, not more trouble. Please…

She turned towards the door of her office, hearing the clatter of stiletto heels as her daughter-in-law came down the corridor. The door was thrown open. Su-Ying's face, normally ivory-pale, was flushed. She saw Martin but ignored him: Martin and Richard had never got on and Su-Ying's loyalty, as always, lay with her husband.

'I have very interesting news,' she said to Bella.

She waited; what she had to say was obviously for Bella's ears alone.

'We've finished here, in any case,' Bella said.

'You want me to speak to the Stock Exchange?' Martin asked.

About to say yes, Bella hesitated. 'Leave it a bit,' she said.

She waited until Martin had left the room, then smiled and gestured to the other chair facing her desk.

'Sit down and tell me about this interesting news.'

Su-Ying's world had changed dramatically in recent years. First had come the realisation that she had fallen in love with her husband. She could not have said how it had happened, only that it had.

'*Wo ai nee*. I love you.'

She had said it for the first time the night when she later believed Adam had been conceived. Now to say it repeatedly in the throes of passion had become as natural to her as breathing.

Adam's birth had also affected her very much. She had taken it for granted she would love her son but the delight she felt in him had far outstripped her expectations. Love for her husband and then her son had added a new and wonderful dimension to her life.

There had been other changes, too.

Australia and China had set up diplomatic relations in 1972. To begin with she had kept away from the Chinese consulate in Perth, knowing that the staff there would be hostile to the daughter of a man purged during the Cultural Revolution. But last year had seen the death of the Great Monster, as she had come to think of him, and at once things in China had begun to change.

In Perth, the Chinese consul-general was replaced, along with most of his staff. In China many of those wrongly imprisoned were released. Deng and Su-Ying's father were restored to favour. Little by little, Deng gained control of the reins of power. Secure from the dangers of the past, Su-Ying visited the consulate regularly to find out what was going on in China and hear what news there might be of her father.

She told herself repeatedly she was happy in her life, yet China would always own a portion of her heart and there were days when she missed it very much.

Now, unexpectedly, there was a phone call that the following morning sent her first to the consulate and then to her mother-in-law's house.

'I have had a letter from my father,' Su-Ying said.

'That's nice,' Bella said. 'Tell me about it.'

The family was on the edge of disaster but Bella had always believed it was important to empathise with other people's news. 'How is your father?' she asked.

'He is well. Thank you. But that is not why I am troubling you.'

Bella smiled; she had long grown used to Su-Ying's formal way of addressing her.

'So what do you have to tell me?'

'I have taken the liberty of translating his letter. I hope you will excuse any errors in my English, which I am ashamed to say is still very poor.'

'Your English is very good,' Bella said.

She took the folded piece of paper that Su-Ying was offering her. She opened it and studied it silently for several minutes. Eventually she looked up, staring at her daughter-in-law across the desk.

'This is what he said?'

'As I said, my English –'

'Never mind that. This is the meaning of his message? Exactly, without any additions?'

'It is exact,' Su-Ying said.

'You are anxious to see the company survive its present difficulties. That is as it should be. But it would be understandable if your concern led you to read more into your father's words than he intended,' Bella said.

'It is exact,' Su-Ying said.

'I see. I shall think about it and get back to you. Do you have any objection to my showing it to Owen and Martin?'

'None,' Su-Ying said.

'Have you discussed it with Richard?'

'I have spoken to no one. I brought it straight here.'

'No one in the consulate?'

'The envelope was sealed. No one else has seen it.'

'Keep it to yourself for the moment. I may decide to call a board meeting later today. If I do, we can talk about it then.'

After Su-Ying had gone, Bella read the letter again, then put it down on the desk as she thought what it might mean.

Probably nothing, she told herself. There had been so many false hopes, so many starts and stops, that she was reluctant to think positively about this latest development. She would not allow herself to be poisoned yet again by failed hope.

'She has probably placed an over-optimistic interpretation on her father's words,' Bella said aloud.

Yet she had learnt a lot about Su-Ying since she had joined the family and knew it was not like her to make such a mistake.

She picked up the phone.

'Deborah,' she said. 'Get hold of Owen and Martin and say I need to talk to them. As soon as they can get here.'

At three o'clock that afternoon Bella told the Tuckers board that China, the secretive land that for so long had maintained barriers against the outside world, was planning to enter into a phase of sustained economic development for which it would require effectively unlimited quantities of high-grade iron ore.

'We must tell the bank,' Martin Dexter said.

'Not yet,' Bella said. 'We have nothing to show them but hope, and that is not a commodity that carries weight with the banks. What we need is something in writing.'

'From China? How do you propose to get that?'

'By going there.'

'Will they let you in?'

'Su-Ying will arrange that with her father. I have complete faith she can do it. If she cannot, that letter is meaningless, and why should her father waste his time writing meaningless letters?'

'The only way to find out is to ask,' Martin said.

'Exactly,' Bella said. 'And that is what I propose to do.'

'Assuming they want to go ahead,' Martin said, 'there is one thing we need to find out first.'

'Which is?'

'How they plan to pay. The last I heard China was broke.'

'Well,' Bella said, 'we all know how that feels, don't we?'

Bella spoke to Su-Ying, who contacted the Chinese consulate, who contacted her father. Within a week everything had been arranged. Bella would visit China as an honoured guest of the People's Republic.

CHAPTER FIFTY-SIX

There were no scheduled flights between Australia and China but the consulate, now totally compliant, arranged an embassy plane. The plane was old and uncomfortable but at least it got her there. On the fifteenth of February Bella was in a bitterly cold Beijing: the first significant miner from Australia to be admitted to the new China.

There were receptions, applause, flowers presented by smiling girls as delicate as flowers. Half-blinded by camera flashguns, Bella found herself the symbol of the ties a newly emergent country wished to forge with the outside world. Modernisation had been adopted as an official policy. Huge overseas loans had been arranged with European banks. Teams from Germany and Japan would build new steel complexes. There were plans to build power stations and railways, open oil and gas fields… All of which would require steel. Billions of tons of steel. It was a new world. Liberation!

Officials pressed Bella to tell them what Tuckers could supply, and when. There would be other suppliers in both Australia and Brazil but, as the first to respond to China's needs, they assured her that Bella and her company would have a place of honour in China's plans. When would she be able to start deliveries?

It was the salvation she had been seeking. Memoranda of understanding were prepared. She knew she would have to ask the banks – again! – for additional funding but, with official Chinese documents to confirm the agreements, it would be on an altogether different basis than before.

It was a feeling that should have filled her with delight but did not. After so long, the prospect of wealth seemed fraudulent, an exercise in self-deception. Bella was fifty-seven years old and things had gone wrong so often in the past that she could not believe her troubles were finally over. Experience had taught her that disaster always appeared when you least expected it; it was impossible to imagine anything else.

Yet reality seemed determined to prove her wrong. From threatening to lop off her head, commercially speaking, the banks now could not do enough for her. Anxious shareholders were soothed, ruined infrastructure replaced. A year later, with the loaded wagons pouring in a continuous stream along the repaired railway, Port Anthony was functioning at full capacity.

Bella stood on the wharf with Mr Hong and watched the first bulk carrier pulling out into the Timor Sea on its way to China.

'A great day for your company,' the Chinese consul said.

'Indeed it is,' Bella said. 'And for China. A very great day for us all.'

She would never tempt providence by saying it aloud but it really did look as though the bad times were behind them and that from now on full steam ahead would be the order of the day.

A year later Rory McNab came to her and said he was planning to get married.

'Congratulations!'

'Thanks. But there's a problem. My fiancée's from New South Wales.'

'Why is that a problem?'

'Her folks have farmed there for over a century and she doesn't want to move west.'

'Sit down,' Bella said. 'I've an idea that might interest you.'

He did so, looking cautiously at her across her desk.

'Have you been happy with us?' Bella asked.

'Very.'

'All things being equal, would you want to stay with us?'

'Of course. But –'

'I am currently negotiating with the New South Wales government for a permit to develop a coal mine northwest of Sydney. According to the survey reports the reserves in that area are phenomenal. If I get the go-ahead, which I anticipate I shall, I shall need a mine development manager to bring the mine on stream. Would you be interested?'

'You'd better believe it,' Rory said.

'Good. I'll give you all the documentation. Go through it carefully. Then I want you to fly over there, have a look on the ground and see what you think. If you're happy we'll draw up your new contract.'

'If it comes off this will be the second mine I've brought in for Tuckers,' he said. 'At one time I thought I would never do one.'

'That was why you came to work for me,' Bella said.

'And I've never regretted it. But who'll take my place at Carlisle? With all the new expansion we've been discussing you'll need someone who knows what they're doing to handle it.'

'I believe I have the ideal person,' Bella said.

A week later, after Rory had given the New South Wales project his okay, Bella rang Canada.

'I've got a job for you, if you're interested. Take over Carlisle.'

'Run it as I think fit?'

Even now she was on her guard.

'Absolutely,' Bella said. 'And a seat on the board to go with it.'

'I have to give three months' notice.'

'But you'll take the job?'

'You'd better believe it.'

Exactly what Rory had said. It must be an in-phrase, Bella thought.

She told Martin. 'So we get to keep Rory. And Peace will be coming back to run Carlisle.'

'A good day's work,' Martin said.

Bella smiled happily. 'You'd better believe it.'

CHAPTER FIFTY-SEVEN

They had just finished the normal weekly board meeting.

Bella had been heading back to her office when Peace asked for a word. It was a week before the party that Richard had christened Triple B – Bella's Birthday Bash – and with that on top of everything else Bella was up to her eyes. She sighed but made sure Peace did not see her do so. There were times when she found Peace's relentless energy exhausting and at today's meeting she had been particularly difficult, trying to get her own way in everything as usual. On the other hand she had done an excellent job since she had come back from Canada. And she was her daughter, after all.

She looked at her watch. 'I can let you have five minutes. I can't spare any more, I'm afraid. I've another meeting.'

There were days when Bella's life seemed to be nothing but meetings: financial report meetings, mine development meetings, the latest review of track and rolling stock maintenance, the inevitable BradMin problem meetings... No end to it.

'Five minutes will be enough,' Peace said.

They went into Bella's office and sat down.

'How can I help you?' Bella asked.

'I think we should make Angus a director,' Peace said.

Angus Duthie was a property developer with whom Peace had been living off and on ever since she came back from Canada. Now Bella sighed in earnest. She hated saying no to Peace, who took everything so personally, but could not see she had any choice.

'I'm not sure that now is the right time,' she said.

Bella had mixed feelings about Angus. He was amiable enough but she was drawn to men who travelled under a black flag and she could see no sign of either skulls or crossbones in Angus's life. Nevertheless she was willing to tolerate him because of his calming influence on her fiery daughter. If she ever decided to expand the group's property interests he might prove useful but making him a director now would in her judgement be a step too far.

'Su-Ying is a director,' Peace said. 'Why not Angus?'

'Angus is not a member of the family.'

She picked up a draft report and began to skim through it, jotting comments in the margin as she went.

'So what?'

Bella wished Peace would realise that pushing too hard was almost always counter-productive but that was a lesson her impulsive daughter had never learnt.

'Neither is Martin Dexter,' Peace said.

'He has skills we need.'

Bella picked up the phone that connected her with Deborah's office. 'Spare me a minute?'

'Angus also has skills,' Peace said.

'But none we need at the moment. Maybe one of these days we shall. Then we'll see.'

Deborah opened the door.

Bella held out the report. 'Tell Peter to have another go at this. I've made some suggestions.'

When Bella issued instructions she always called them suggestions but they remained instructions nonetheless.

Deborah took the papers and went out, closing the door behind her.

'That's another point,' Peace said. 'With the China business sewn up maybe we should start looking at the future.'

Bella had known from the first that the business of Angus was a smokescreen; what Peace really wanted to talk about was her future within the group. Yet even now she couldn't come right out and say it.

'The China business, as you call it, is a million miles from being sewn up. They are asking us for more production all the time. We're already at twenty-five million tons a year. As we've just been discussing, they are now talking of doubling it, with all that means in new infrastructure, capital costs...'

Yet such talk was also a smokescreen, because Peace's concerns were legitimate. She was ambitious, enormously talented and wanted to know if she was heir apparent or not. She would never be satisfied with less, but there was a problem. With better people skills she would make a wonderful CEO down the track but she was always rubbing people up the wrong way. Bella imagined her negotiating with the Chinese government and shuddered.

She would hate to lose her all over again, not only because Peace was her daughter but because of her ability, but Peace would never be satisfied with anything less than the number-one spot and without more finesse she would be a disaster. Of course responsibility did strange things to people. Look at her. She had never thought of herself as a tycoon but that was how the world saw her and she supposed that was what she had become. Did Peace have the potential to grow into the job if it was hers? Bella did not know.

'You're right,' she said. 'We must look at these things. But I'm up to my ears with China at the moment. I don't have the time or energy to concentrate on anything else.'

Peace was not fobbed off so easily. 'When will you have time?'

Bella stared straight at her. 'As soon as I have something to say on the subject, I'll say it,' she said.

* * *

Driving back into Perth that evening, Angus at the wheel, Peace was still spitting.

'Typical Mother!' she said. 'Never a straight answer to anything! Well, she needn't think I'm waiting forever. If she doesn't come to a decision soon I shall move on.'

'I don't see the problem. You say she's promised to review the situation when she can.'

'Are you taking her side?'

'You know better than that,' Angus said.

All this was foolishness. He was five years older than she was and had learnt the value of patience; with patience you could achieve a lot. He had been working on Peace ever since he met her and hadn't got her to the altar yet. But he would; all it took was time.

'Why can't she just tell me?' Peace said. 'One way or the other? At least that way I'd know.'

'Maybe she doesn't know herself.'

A car overtook them, horn blaring. Angus let it go; road rage was not a feature of his life.

Peace put her hand on his thigh.

'There are times when I think I don't deserve you,' she said.

'There are times when I agree with you,' he said.

He thought with any luck there might be a passionate night ahead. Peace was a firecracker in bed, whereas he was patience personified. It was a good mix.

Richard and Su-Ying were sitting at ease, enjoying the warmth of the heater and having a nightcap on the enclosed verandah of their bungalow overlooking the river.

'Peace was in a foul mood today,' Richard said.

'She wants to take charge of the company,' Su-Ying said. 'And she hates to wait.'

He sipped his whisky, the ice clinking in the glass, and watched the stream of car lights pouring down the road beyond the river.

'I don't think it's that. She knows Mother's going nowhere at the moment. But she would like to believe she'll get it all in the end.'

'Would you object if she did?' Su-Ying asked.

Richard finished his drink and debated whether to have another one.

'I don't think I would,' he said.

Su-Ying frowned. She had always wanted him to be number one when Bella decided to stand down, but Richard had never been a pushy man. 'Don't you want to be the top man?'

'I was thinking of something quite different,' he said.

He decided one more drink would do no harm. He tipped the bottle, added ice.

'What is that?' Su-Ying asked.

'China.'

He raised his glass to the light, admiring the amber glow of the liquor. He sipped slowly and put the glass on the table.

'You were thinking of *China*?' Su-Ying stared.

'I've always fancied the idea of building up our own business from the beginning.'

'And?'

'I speak Chinese. You are Chinese. It occurred to me there might be money to be made in China. Not at the moment, but maybe in a few years.'

'We would live in China?'

He smiled at her; did she really think he had not known about her longing to return to her homeland?

'I doubt we'd make much money out of a China business if we weren't there to run it,' he said.

'What sort of business?'

'Consumer goods for export. Your father's an important man. He might want to get involved himself. Through a proxy, maybe.'

'You have Chinese thoughts,' Su-Ying said approvingly.

'So you're always telling me. With low labour costs, I don't see how we could go wrong.'

'What about the boys' education? Adam is due to go to university in three years' time. And James will be going to high school two years after that.'

'That would certainly be a factor. It won't happen for several years, in any case. It may not happen at all. But that's the way my mind's working at the moment.' He laughed. 'With your family connections, we'd be multi-millionaires in no time. But not a word to anybody else, okay?'

'Of course.' Su-Ying looked at him with love in her eyes. 'Let's go to bed,' she said.

CHAPTER FIFTY-EIGHT

Bella remembered telling herself how disaster always appeared when you least expected it. How right she had been. They'd had seven years' grace and now everything was on the edge of falling apart yet again.

Ten days earlier Peace had been barracking for Angus Duthie to be given a seat on the board; now it was possible there might not be a board for him to sit on. Despair consumed her; she was looking into the jaws of failure and hating it.

It was the nearest she had ever come to self-pity. Such an ugly emotion; resolutely she turned her back on it. She sat at the bedside table in her hotel room and busied herself with plans that, without funding, would prove of no more substance than a dawn mist, dissolving at the first touch of the sun.

She was summoned to the ministry. She took Richard and Su-Ying with her. They might as well face the firing squad together. They sat in a plain reception room adjacent to Comrade Fang's office and waited. Spartan furniture, a linoleum-covered floor. No T'ang reproductions on these walls. No view across Tiananmen Square to the complacently smiling portrait of the Great Helmsman. No windows at all.

After an hour's wait an official entered the room: a stern-faced young woman who read a prepared text from a paper in her hand.

They would be advised of the official response in due course but in the meantime there was no need to delay them further. An embassy plane would be flying to Canberra in two days' time. Arrangements would be made for them to travel on it.

It was over. They had done everything they could and failed. Pete Bathurst, aided by the unknown traitor, had won.

The next two days dragged their leaden feet across Bella's life. Despair was a new emotion but she could think of no way to escape the trap.

They were told the car was waiting. They went down, as to a funeral. They got in. The driver turned right at the main road, not left, which would have taken them to the airport. Su-Ying spoke sharply to him. Where were they going?

He did not reply.

After five minutes she turned to Bella. 'At first I thought maybe there had been an accident, or roadworks. But that is not the reason. He is taking us into town.'

'Where are we going?'

'It has to be to the ministry. Where else?'

'Comrade Fang must have decided to hand us the formal rejection himself. That is what it is,' Bella said.

She was determined to deny the flicker of hope that had stirred in her heart. What if...? She would not allow herself to think it. To have her hopes raised, only to be dashed again... She did not think she could bear that.

She sat staring out of the car window, seeing not the lines of low buildings with the Chinese script in red or gold flourishes above each door, not the modern buildings rising, like China itself, from the lethargy of the past, but the stages of the sixty-five-year life that had brought her here. All had been for nothing. Unless...

Again hope seethed; again, sternly, she forced it down.

I will be sorry to lose the Monet, she thought. Yet what difference could that make? What mattered was the memory of Garth's life, in celebration of which, in gratitude and loneliness, she had bought it in the first place. A good buy it was, too, she thought with a flicker of her old spirit, worth a lot more now than she had paid for it. Not that it made any difference; like the Hester Bateman candlesticks, Soong vase and everything else, it was about to be swallowed up by debts that could be counted in their millions. All would be gone.

Su-Ying had been right. The car drew up before the entrance to the ministry. A uniformed man opened the door. Smiling. Deferential. Bella looked at him, senses alert. They were led inside. Not, this time, to the comfortless waiting room but to Comrade Fang's office. With smiles and gestures they were invited to sit. Across the square, the afternoon sunlight gilded the Chairman's smile.

They waited, not daring to speak or look at each other.

Five minutes later Comrade Fang came into the room. He had two aides but no interpreter. He went and sat behind his desk; then he studied his three visitors in turn before addressing his remarks exclusively to Bella.

'Our information is that BradMin has no plans to give Tucker access to their rail line.' His English was as close to perfect as made no difference. 'Never! Yes or no?'

'Never say never,' Bella said.

Comrade Fang sat back in his chair. He smiled amicably, all antagonism banished from the discussion. 'We shall have coffee,' he said.

Bella's breath eased out softly. This amiability, so unexpected after the hostility of their previous meeting: what did it mean? Nothing had changed. Without a rail link, the ore from Carlisle could not be delivered. Bella knew it; the Chinese knew it; Pete Bathurst knew it. She was over a barrel and without help Tucker Mining and all her dreams were finished. Now it seemed a deal might be in the offing, after all. At what price? But did price matter? If she wanted to survive she would have to agree to whatever terms they demanded.

'Coffee would be most welcome,' she said.

When the refreshments arrived they proved to be a great deal more than coffee.

'Dim sum,' Comrade Fang announced proudly.

Dim sum consisted of a variety of savoury dumplings, served hot. They were exquisitely prepared and presented in paper-thin dough wrappings. Prawns, so delicate as to be almost transparent; scallops; abalone in sticky rice; pork ribs in plum sauce...

Comrade Fang pointed them out one by one, explaining their contents with such pride that he might have prepared them himself.

'Please,' he said.

Chopsticks and individual plates had been provided. Once again Bella had reason to be grateful to her daughter-in-law, who had schooled her in the use of chopsticks. She leant forwards and selected a prawn dumpling, which she chewed with relish.

'The food is excellent,' she said.

'Very ordinary,' Fang said.

They ate contentedly for a while.

'Mrs Tucker enjoyed her visit to the Summer Palace?' Fang enquired.

'Very much.'

'The original was most beautiful,' he told her. 'People say it was one of the wonders of the world. So sad it was destroyed.'

Comrade Fang was reminding her how it had been vandalised by the British, almost a century before.

'So much destruction,' Bella said, shaking her head. 'So many buildings lost, all over Asia. So many temples that can never be replaced.'

Because the Chinese, too, had destroyed many sacred sites during their subjugation of Tibet in the 1940s and 1950s. And in China, too, during the Cultural Revolution.

Fang turned suddenly to Su-Ying and spoke to her in Chinese. She answered him in the same tongue, then turned to Bella.

'He asks me to convey his best wishes to my father, who he said has been a much-respected member of the Party for many years. I told him I was grateful for his kind words and I would be honoured to do so.' Again she spoke in Chinese, smiling at Comrade Fang as she did so. Once more she translated. 'I explain to Comrade Fang that the Lees and Tuckers are now related. All of us are grateful to him for the honour he pays Father, which we share.'

Bella looked thoughtfully at the two Chinese; there were undercurrents here she did not understand; no doubt Su-Ying would tell her later what it was all about.

The empty plates were removed. Back to business, Bella thought.

'If BradMin's rail link is unavailable, how does Tucker propose to ship its ore to the coast?'

'As I said, negotiations are under way –'

Fang shook his head slowly. 'BradMin has no plans to grant access. Why should they, after all? Tucker Mining is their competitor.'

'If they won't agree, the only way is for another railway to be built.'

'That would be a very costly process.'

'Indeed it would.' Bella turned to Richard. 'Explain the financial implications to Comrade Fang.'

Richard spoke at length. When he had finished Fang's hooded eyes were almost round. 'So many millions...'

'A railway capable of carrying heavy-axle wagons loaded with ore cannot be constructed for less,' Richard said.

'But a link to the existing railway...'

'Would be much less. Of course. That was what we had originally planned. But if, as you say, BradMin will not permit access –'

'I said BradMin has no plans to grant access. Plans can be changed.'

Aha, Bella thought. For the first time she did not reject the hope that now flooded her. 'Why should they change?' she said. 'As you pointed out, Tuckers are their competitors.'

Fang did not answer the question. 'Why does Tucker not build its own railway? Then BradMin's objections become irrelevant.'

'Money,' Richard said.

'Will the banks not help?'

Richard shrugged, smiling.

'But, if money can be found…'

'The railway can be built,' Richard said.

'And China gets its ore,' Bella said.

'The question is,' Fang said softly, 'what would Tuckers be willing to pay for such assistance?'

They had come to it at last.

'We shall be interested to hear Comrade Fang's thoughts on that subject,' Bella said.

Fang walked across the room and studied one of the T'ang reproductions. With his back still turned to them, he said:

'Fifty-one per cent.'

Bella's heart thudded against her ribs.

'Please explain.'

Fang returned briskly to his desk and sat down.

'China is willing to build a rail link connecting the Carlisle Mine to the coast. We shall provide money, engineers and labour. A loan, you understand. The value is to be agreed later and set off against payment for future ore deliveries. You agree?'

'In principle,' Bella said.

Wait, she warned herself. Hear the conditions first. There were bound to be conditions. But please, she prayed, *please* let them be something I can accept.

Her nerves at full stretch, she focused on what Fang was now saying.

'China does not need Tucker,' Fang said. 'China can buy all its ore from BradMin. But Tucker needs China.' He smiled. Like a shark, Bella thought. 'Not so?'

'It is not in China's interests to give BradMin a monopoly.'

Fang mimed astonishment. 'No monopoly. There are other suppliers, even without Tucker. Brazil –'

'Too far. Freight costs –'

'Which bigger bulk carriers will reduce. So no monopoly. Hah?'

Bella said nothing.

'To help Tucker, there has to be a reason. Invest in something China owns, very good. If not, very foolish.'

Bella's mouth was dry. 'Meaning?'

'You give fifty-one per cent Tucker shares, China provides rail link. Plenty of profit for everyone. Everyone happy. Good deal, hah?'

Take it, Bella told herself. Forty-nine per cent of something is a lot better than a hundred per cent of nothing. Take it, girl, and you'll be off the hook.

And you'll have lost control of your company. Lost your dream.

She sensed Richard and Su-Ying watching her, awaiting her decision.

What choice did she have? At the beginning of the meeting she had told herself she would have to accept whatever terms they offered. She opened her mouth to agree. She said:

'No.'

'Good deal for everyone,' Fang said. 'For you, very good. You keep forty-nine per cent, plenty of profit for everyone, banks happy, everyone happy, no further worries for you –'

'No,' she said fiercely. 'No! A thousand times no!'

She was prepared to stand up, walk away, accept the consequences, to hell with the banks…

To her astonishment, Fang chuckled. 'Australian government not permit foreigner company to own over fifty per cent, anyway,' he said.

He opened the folder that until that moment had remained untouched on his desk. He took out a paper that Bella recognised as the memorandum of agreement she had negotiated during her first visit to China.

'*Initial supply*,' Fang read aloud, '*twenty-five million tons of iron ore per annum, mineral content guaranteed at not less than sixty per cent, delivered on shore at Baoshan Steel in Shanghai, at spot price ruling at date of delivery.*' He looked at Bella across the desk. 'If China is to invest in a rail link on Tuckers's behalf, these terms will need to be renegotiated.'

'I understand,' Bella said.

'Spot price less ten per cent, five years,' Fang said.

'Less five per cent, seven years,' Bella said.

'Seven per cent five years, six per cent five more years.'

'Five per cent five years, four per cent another five.'

'*Ayoh!*' Fang said. 'Why so unreasonable? Rail link save Tucker, otherwise bankrupt. Hah?'

Bella shook her head, waiting.

Fang said: 'Five five, four another five, three another five. Yes?'

'Five five, four five, three three,' Bella said.

Fang turned to his aides. 'Leave us.'

They left the room; he looked at Richard and Su-Ying. 'Give us a few minutes,' Bella said to them.

They also left. The door closed behind them.

'You buy land, yes?' Fang said. 'Hundred acres Perth, hundred acres Sydney, hundred acres Brisbane. Good land, property development land. You can?'

'In whose name? Yours?'

'Give details later. Can do this?'

'I can. But who pays?'

'You will be paid,' Fang said. 'You can do this for me?'

Perhaps it was against Chinese law to buy land overseas. Well, Bella thought, that was none of her business. 'Let me have details of what you want and the name you want on the deeds, I shall arrange it for you,' she said.

'Very good,' he said. 'I shall let you have that information before you leave.'

'And the contract for the ore?'

'That, too.'

'I shall need my lawyer to check it,' Bella said. 'Important that everything is legal, don't you agree?'

'Of course.'

'And construction of the railway?'

'Will begin as soon as the contract is signed.'

My God, she thought, I've done it. I've really done it. She could have thrown her arms in the air, screamed aloud, danced naked on Comrade Fang's desk.

She did none of these things. She nodded. 'A pleasure to do business with you.'

Su-Ying sat with her husband in the dreary little room they had used before.

I believe we have done it, she thought. Ever since Fang mentioned my father, I was confident all would be well. I swore I would not speak to him about the rail link and of course I did. He said BradMin was strong, Tuckers weak, that it was foolish to side with the weak against the strong. I told him the truth, that I did it for China. For my husband, too, but first of all for China. Which was the reason he sent me to Australia in the first place.

Yes, I am convinced we have won. But when Mother-in-law tells me I shall pretend astonishment. I shall congratulate her on her cleverness. Bella will never know the truth, because it is better she should believe that she arranged everything herself. As for Fang... Of course he would want a sweetener. That is normal and will cost us nothing. I am sure Mother-in-law will agree and not pretend to be too righteous. Because she is wise, too, and understands the way of the world. Perhaps in an earlier life she was Chinese also?

Richard and Su-Ying were full of questions when she left Fang's office but Bella would say nothing until they were safely in the hotel. Even then, mindful of possible eavesdroppers, she was guarded in what she told them.

'We have a deal,' she said. 'I'll tell you about it later.'

She booked a call to Peace and waited.

When it came through she heard the hollow echo that was the sign that someone was listening, as with all telephone calls made by foreigners in China. Well, let them. She had nothing to hide, as far as China was concerned. Australia might be a different story, but she doubted anyone here would care about that.

'How are things back home?' she asked.

'Still hanging in there.' It was hard to hear Peace's words through the interference on the line. 'And you?'

This was the moment. Someone in Australia was trying to destroy the company. Perhaps she could help Gayle Hastings identify who that someone was. She would lay a false trail and see where it took them.

'I'm fine.' She spoke in a deliberately sombre voice. 'But things are not good here. I don't want to say too much on the phone but you understand what I'm telling you.'

'Is it definite?'

'Nothing is ever definite in China,' she said. 'But that's how things look at the moment.'

That evening Mr Fang sent her an envelope containing a piece of paper. On it was written in western script a name, with two numbers: the name in which the Australian land purchases were to be registered and the access code and number of the Swiss bank account from which would come the funds to pay for the deals.

It took two more days to complete the paperwork. Owen Freeth would check everything when they got back to Perth, but Bella had gone over every inch of the documents and was satisfied, so the lawyer's approval should be little more than a formality. For all practical purposes, it was a done deal.

A good deal it was, too. Bella's relief was indescribable. The consular jet had barely taken off from Beijing airport before she leant back in her seat, closed her eyes and was at once swimming. Afterwards she could not have said whether she slept or not, but certainly she was disconnected from present reality. The hum of the jet engines transported her not merely in space but in time, becoming the gutsy snarl of the Tiger Moth as it carried her from Miranda Downs on her first trip to the Carlisle River. Miranda Downs...

What had Garth said to her? *Just before you fall into the Timor Sea, stop. I've got a cattle station there.* Not only a cattle station but a way of life utterly different from anything she had known before.

'My life has been one of endless change,' she told herself.

And there those changes were: a kaleidoscope of images playing out behind her closed eyelids, ever changing yet the same, all playing their part in the evolution of the woman she now was. A thrush sang from the topmost branch of the apple tree beneath the Yorkshire moors; Miss Hunnicut's spiteful eyes sought fault; mobs of cattle stampeded, their horned heads tossing in an explosion of dust; Garth's astounded voice said: 'It looks like hematite.'

Like hematite, like hematite…

The voice faded as sleep came welling out of the tensions of recent days. There was another image, too, faint and gone almost before it had formed. Bella Tucker, neat and precise as always, lips closed and limbs tidy in the reclining seat, slept.

When she awoke two hours later she felt refreshed, yet for a while did not open her eyes as her mind revisited the image that had evaded her earlier. Charles Hardy smiled, his handsome face as young and vibrant as she had last seen it nearly fifty years before, sending the familiar pang through her heart.

'Charles…'

Bella spoke his name very softly to herself. Garth had been very dear to her. She had never been disloyal or unfaithful to him but Charles Hardy had been the love of her life.

Bella opened her eyes and saw Su-Ying reading in her seat. A treasure, that girl, she thought. She was gentle and delicate as only an Oriental could be, yet also down to earth, more worldly even than Peace at her most bellicose. A real treasure.

Su-Ying, eyes focused unseeing on the page in front of her, was thinking how the family had been so nearly destroyed and of her conversation with her father in the apartment in the senior officials' enclave guarded by soldiers off a side street near Tiananmen Square.

His sufferings during the Cultural Revolution had aged him but he was still vital, very much in charge of himself and those he dealt with.

'This marriage of yours,' he said. 'It has made you happy?'

'Very happy.'

He grunted. 'And you have two sons?'

'Yes.'

'That is good.' He stared at her severely. 'You know I would have forbidden it had I been in a position to do so?'

From the moment she had known she was coming to Beijing Su-Ying had expected the question and had prepared her answer.

'I would have welcomed Father's wise advice. But since I had to make my own decisions I did what I thought was best for China.'

'In what way was it best for China?'

'What benefit was there for China in my coming back to work in the fields as a peasant? You sent me to Australia to learn what I could about western ways and western people. By staying there I have learnt many things. I am a director of a large iron ore mining company –'

'Which we hold in our hand and can crush whenever we wish.'

'I do not believe it would be in China's interests to do this,' Su-Ying said.

Her father glared. 'Your opinion is neither sought nor wanted. We in China will make our own decisions.'

'Of course. Forgive me. I was simply offering my humble opinion –'

'You say you have learnt much. In what way does that benefit China? With you in Australia?'

'Because I believe I shall be coming back to China.'

He stared at her. 'Explain.'

She did so. When she had finished he pondered silently for a while. When he spoke his tone had changed.

'To rescue the Tuckers from their problems is very simple,' he said. 'It also means nothing. It is necessary to kill the snake or it will strike again. I shall contact Comrade Hong in Perth. He has excellent sources of information and will soon discover the identity of the snake.'

'Could I respectfully ask Father to instruct him to pass any information to Mother-in-law's agent?'

'You wish to remain out of it?'

'It would be best.'

'That is wise. You have the name of this agent?'

'I do.'

This would ensure that Mother-in-law never discovered the source of the information. It was not necessary for her to know everything, Su-Ying thought. In the family's interests they should all be concerned to resolve these problems. It did not matter how it was done; the results were what mattered.

CHAPTER FIFTY-NINE

Early on the morning of the third of September, three days before Bella Tucker was expected back from China, Pete Bathurst received a phone call on his private line.

'Yeah?'

'Pete? It's me.'

A grim smile as he recognised his caller's voice. 'About time, too, if I may say so…'

'She only phoned last night.'

'And what did she say?'

'She thinks the Chinese aren't going to play.'

Good news; the best. Pete's grin widened. 'I can't imagine how she ever thought they might,' he said.

'If you're desperate enough –'

Hands on the jackpot at last, Pete was uninterested in speculation.

'Which leaves the million-dollar question. What are you going to do about it?'

The same day, Gayle Hastings's assistant Belinda informed her there was a man on the line who said his name was Low.

Gayle knew no one called Low. 'Did he say what it's about?'

'He said it was confidential.'

It was the nature of Gayle's business to receive messages from many sources, not all of them willing to be identified.

'Put him on,' she said.

The caller had an accent Gayle thought might be Chinese.

'I have some information for you,' Mr Low said.

'One moment.'

Gayle switched on the recording machine she had connected to her telephone.

'What information is this?' she said.

She listened attentively while the tape unwound silently in the machine. It was not a long message but undeniably dynamite.

He finished.

Oh dear, Gayle thought. She made it a rule never to get personally involved in her clients' affairs, but Bella was not only a client but someone she admired – a friend, even. 'You have proof of this?' she asked.

Photographs, Mr Low said. And a telephone intercept.

Illegal, of course, but commonplace in the enquiry business.

'I shall need to see it all.'

'That might be possible,' Mr Low said.

'Proof is essential, if you want me to take it further.'

'It will be provided,' Mr Low said.

A click; Mr Low was gone. Slowly Gayle replaced the receiver.

Poor Bella, she thought. The information would devastate her.

It had been a night flight, yet in Bella's heart the sun had been shining all the way. Hours after the reprieve, she was still dizzy with relief. Not that anyone would have known by looking at her.

'Welcome home.' The immigration officer handed back her passport. 'Good flight?'

She smiled radiantly at him. 'The best.'

From Canberra they flew to Perth. It was cool but sunny when they arrived: a sparkling day. She stood at the entrance to the domestic terminal and drew the fresh air deeply into her lungs.

474 J. H. FLETCHER

Clear skies and bright colours: she looked around her with delight; at that moment she could have gobbled up the world.

She had phoned Deborah from Canberra and she was there to meet them. The sun shone on the brilliantly polished Bentley as Bella got into the front passenger seat, leaving the others to climb into the back.

Deborah looked at her. 'You wouldn't sooner drive?'

'Not today, dear.'

They headed for the city and the home it seemed she would no longer have to sell. It was an intoxicating thought.

As they drove she saw Deborah casting covert glances at her. She would be dying to know what had happened in Beijing but would have to wait; the board had to be told before anyone else.

'Any news for me?' she asked gaily.

'Gayle Hastings says she has something urgent to discuss with you.'

Bella took the car phone from its mount and tapped out Gayle's private number.

'I'm just driving in from the airport. Deborah says you've something to tell me.'

'Not over the phone.'

'Very well. My office. Half an hour.'

She hung up. Gayle had sounded troubled but Bella was unconcerned. Nothing could touch her now.

An hour later, having heard Gayle Hastings out, Bella sat and stared at her informant.

Nothing could touch her now, she had thought. She should have known better. She felt sick to the heart. Betrayal…

'You are sure of this?'

'I have seen the evidence.'

Of course she had; Gayle was a professional.

'Very well,' Bella said.

How weary she felt. Nor had Gayle finished. She took out a pocket recording machine and laid it on the desk.

'You need to listen to this,' she said.

Bella took a deep breath, but courage was one quality she had never lacked. She nodded.

Gayle leant forwards and switched on the machine. There was a faint hiss as the tape began to revolve.

'About time too, if I may say so...'

No mistaking that voice. Nor the one that replied.

'She only phoned last night.'

Bella stiffened but sat unmoving until the tape was finished. It was hard to look at Gayle but she made herself do it.

'Is that everything?'

'That's it.' Gayle hesitated. 'I'm sorry, Bella...'

'For doing your job? I asked you to find out who was behind it. Now you have.'

She knew she sounded cold but it couldn't be helped; there was no other way to hide her pain. To soften her response she smiled, stiff-lipped. 'I'll take it from here,' she said. 'And thank you, Gayle. You will let me have your account, of course. I appreciate your help.'

Alone in her office she sat looking into emptiness.

How could it have happened? Ambition? The need to run the show? The company was going down, so a future had to be found elsewhere? Any or all the above?

Did it matter which it was? Regardless of reasons, betrayal had only one face.

All their figures, cash-flow projections, correspondence with the banks... Bathurst had seen them all. He had known how close they were to bankruptcy, had thought that shutting them out of the railway would provide the tipping point. He must have imagined that Christmas had come twice. Pay back Bella, eliminate Tuckers and pick up the China business, all in one neat package. It had nearly worked, but he had never expected China to jump the way it had. Had she?

'Never doubted it for a moment,' Bella said aloud.

If it was a lie, there was no one to hear it but her.

Deborah came hurrying with a cup of coffee and a thick folder
in which, Bella knew, would be sheaves of correspondence and telephone messages awaiting her attention. Bella opened the file and
began to work her way methodically through the contents, scrib-
bling notes to inform Deborah what had to be done in each case.

Tell him no. But nicely.

Arrange a meeting for early next week.

Tell the vice-chancellor I'll be pleased to talk to his students.

Work was therapy. Work, ultimately, was all there was.

In half an hour she cleared much of the backlog. Now for it, she
thought. She picked up the phone.

'Get Mr Bathurst for me.'

She smiled savagely as she waited, fingers tapping the desk. The
phone rang.

'Good trip?' Pete asked jovially. 'Hot in Beijing?'

Let him enjoy himself, Bella thought. It won't be for long. 'On
the contrary. There was quite a frost.'

'Too cold for comfort is what I hear.'

Laughter bubbled derisively and Bella felt good, knowing this
despicable man was about to topple off a cliff and didn't even
realise it.

'I coulda told you you'd be wasting your time,' Pete told her.
Another snort of laughter. 'By the way, if you're looking for a job,
I'm not hiring.'

'Is that just me? Or does it include members of my board?'

A moment's silence. Then: 'What's that supposed to mean?'

Bella ignored the question. 'Have you heard from the Chinese
consulate yet?'

He was suddenly cautious. 'Why should I be hearing from them?'

'I'm sure they'll explain. I need to see you, in any case.'

'We've nothing to discuss –'

'Think of the telephone conversation you had with a member
of my board,' she said. 'Two nights ago, wasn't it? You want me to
quote it to you?'

'I dunno what you're getting at, Bella –'

'Here, in my office, three o'clock this afternoon.'

'I got meetings –'

'Reschedule them,' she told him crisply. 'Or Bradford Gulliver will be hearing from me. And the media. We're talking photographs, Pete. Tapes. Industrial espionage is so bad for a company's image, don't you think? I don't imagine Mr Gulliver will be very pleased.'

'Now wait a minute –'

'Three o'clock, Pete. Don't be late.'

And hung up before he could protest further. Bella spoke again to Deborah.

'I want you to phone Owen Freeth,' she said. 'Tell him I need to meet with him as soon as he can make it.'

'Today?' guessed Deborah.

'Preferably last night,' Bella said.

She returned to her messages.

Banker Halliburton had left several, asking her to phone him as a matter of the greatest urgency. Poor Halliburton… Even in Deborah's scribble his anxiety shone through. Another one scared for his job, Bella thought. No wonder; if Tucker Mining went down, the bank would lose millions. Never mind; she would get around to easing his fears in due course.

Once again she asked Deborah to come in. 'Where's Peace?'

'A meeting at John Ingram's office. She expects to be out all day.'

Ingram was the mining surveyor they used for some of their work, his office on the other side of town.

'Get hold of her. Tell her I want to see her. Tell the rest of the board, too.' Bella's blue eyes were as cold as the Arctic. 'Say I'm convening a meeting in one hour. I don't care what they're doing. Just get them here.'

Deborah saw the light of battle in Bella's eyes.

'You'll have a full house,' she said.

'We'll use the boardroom,' Bella said.

* * *

Bella sat in her usual place at the head of the table and looked at the faces of those she had long considered her family and friends. But every group, it seemed, must have its Judas.

She began by briefing them on the success of the Beijing trip and what it would mean for the future of the group and themselves.

'Does this mean the company is secure after all?' Martin Dexter asked.

She had spoken to Halliburton and made numerous phone calls to representatives of the overseas investors. In all cases the response had been ecstatic.

'The answer is yes.'

Even in this company she would not say what she had come to believe: that soon they would be not only secure but extremely rich.

Now she came to the final and most difficult part of the meeting. One of her basic rules had always been that betrayal brought punishment, immediate and merciless, as Billy Gould had been punished. When she had first sniffed treachery in the present case she had sworn retribution, but now she discovered something new.

Well, she thought, it was never too late to learn, even about oneself. Perhaps about oneself most of all.

'I have strong feelings for all of you,' she said. 'Both professionally and personally. We could never have achieved what we have except as a team. We have had differences from time to time, but that is to be expected. All of us thought the company was finished, but it was not. We have lived through bad times together, as a family should. Now we shall enjoy our prosperity together, as a family should. Because that is how I think of everyone around this table. You are my family and I love you. And to love, as I am sure you all know, is to forgive.'

Her eyes were burning torches as once again they moved from one listener to the next, and no one spoke.

She had thought to drive home the lesson, to talk about rumours she had heard, about the past being a closed book, but had decided to say none of it. What she had said was enough; it would send a message to the guilty and to add to it would cause finger-pointing

That she would not tolerate. Not only was it distasteful; it would weaken the company. And the company, now and as far into the future as any of them could envisage, had by its success and ability to bring prosperity not only to the family but to the state, the country and the world, become the unifying purpose of their lives.

Pete Bathurst was fifteen minutes late but Bella had expected no less. The miracle was he had come at all; it showed how worried he must be. Two other things: he was in a fury, and he had come alone. He was not even in the chair to which Bella, with elaborate courtesy, directed him before he was snarling.

'How the hell you managed it I shall never know,' he said.

'Managed what?' she said. 'The new arrangements with China or how I discovered your ham-fisted attempt to bankrupt my company?'

'I had the Chinese consul on the phone not half an hour after you rang me.'

'I believe I mentioned you'd be hearing from him,' Bella said.

'Damn right I heard.'

He ground his teeth; Bella had heard the expression a hundred times but this was the first time she had ever observed it in practice.

'And what did he say?'

'He asked me – as a favour, mark you! – to permit Tuckers access to my railroad. While alternative arrangements acceptable to all parties were being negotiated. Whatever that's supposed to mean.'

'Just that, I imagine. They are asking for a temporary arrangement while they work out suitable alternatives.'

'A temporary arrangement involving my railroad?' He pounded his huge fist on Bella's desk. 'Why in hell's name should I agree to that?'

'Why, indeed?' Bella said. 'As you say, it is BradMin's railway. You have every right to refuse.'

'And kiss goodbye to any new contracts from the Chinese government!'

'I know,' said Bella, expression concerned, heart exultant. 'It puts you in a difficult position, doesn't it? As you say, a request from that source is really an order. So what did you say?'

'I said I'd get back to them.'

'Mature consideration is always the best,' she agreed. 'But I wouldn't keep them waiting too long. My experience is they don't like it.'

'I might still say no,' he said. 'Hell, they still have to buy the ore from somewhere. They need us as much as we need them. And I gotta real problem with being shoved around by –'

'By a woman?' Bella enquired sweetly. 'A bunch of little yellow men? Or both?'

It gave her such delight to see the bully boy squirming.

'And of course there is always that other matter,' she said.

'Other matter?'

As though it would have slipped his mind, even for a moment.

For all her exultation over the railway she had never forgotten how he had plotted to destroy her business and herself. She would not have objected had he used proper business methods but the way he had gone about it had been despicable. Even, possibly, criminal.

She looked at him and saw – what was the expression? – a cat on a hot tin roof. She had no intention of making things easy for him. She smiled pleasantly and let him stew.

Eventually Bathurst said: 'If I agree to let Tuckers use our railroad...'

'Yes?'

'You mentioned something about photographs...'

That was why he was so anxious. It was not the risk of losing the contracts; as he had said, China needed them, too. It was not even the use of the railway; all he would lose over that was face. No, what had him scared was what she might be planning to do about the industrial espionage. A scandal like that could destroy his career. *That* was why he was sitting across from her now.

She smiled sweetly at him. 'You want to see those photographs? Is that what you're saying?'

She had them ready; she pushed the folder across the desk.

'I have copies,' she said casually.

He studied them, then looked at her. 'These prove nothing.'

'A senior member of my company visiting your home, late at night? Not once but several times? If you say it means nothing then of course I believe you. But I wonder how Mr Gulliver would view it? And of course there is the audio tape.'

Silence. Eventually he said: 'What are you planning?'

'Nothing.'

He had not expected that.

'Provided you give us unfettered access to your railway. But I shall keep them, in case you are tempted to try any more tricks in the future.'

'What's to stop you sending them to Houston anyway?'

'That is what you would have done, isn't it?' Bella did not hide her contempt. 'But my word is good. You behave yourself, this information stays with me.'

'We'll have to renegotiate the terms for using the railroad,' Pete said fiercely.

'I don't think so.'

They watched each other. Eventually he lifted his hands in surrender. 'I guess I'm over a barrel.'

'I believe you are,' Bella said.

She had won, and they both knew it.

He could do nothing against her, now or in the future, and they knew that, too. For all his bluster, she had tamed him at last.

CHAPTER SIXTY

Within the month, the authorities squared, Chinese engineers were on the ground and work on the railway had begun. BradMin's track had taken four years to lay; the Chinese estimated eighteen months. And there were enough iron ore reserves to supply even China's needs for fifty years. Betrayal left a lingering hurt but Bella was tough enough to survive that, as she had survived so much else in her life. The future, she told herself, was bright.

When the news broke, Tuckers shares went through the roof. From being a millionaire, Bella was looking at billions. Not only Bella; a month later, she had a phone call.

'Helmut! What a nice surprise!'

'Not as nice as the surprise you have given us. The way you pulled off your China negotiations was more like a miracle.'

'Miracles are stock in trade in the mining business.'

'So it seems.'

'Why are you calling?'

'Are you planning to visit Europe in the near future?'

Bella had been considering exactly that. The China contracts signed, Pete Bathurst tamed, the traitor warned, the business seemed secure beyond possibility of failure. Now, at last, she would have the time to branch out into other fields. Off-shore gas was one possibility, that clean energy project another. There would be funds for university chairs, medical research... She would need to get hold of the federal ministers, discuss what tax concessions might be available. All was wonderful, but how much better if she could share these exciting prospects with someone else.

Strange how Martin Dexter had once been a possibility for that role. Thank God I was wise enough to trust my instinct on that one, she thought. What a mistake it would have been. But there were other possibilities, were there not?

'Visit Europe?' she repeated. 'Why do you ask?'

'Some of our institutional investors would like to meet you. Give you a banquet, perhaps, as a token of gratitude. You have certainly earned it. And to discuss any further investment possibilities you might have in mind.'

'That would be delightful,' Bella said.

'On a more personal level,' Helmut said, 'I would like to see you, also. Very much.'

'*Ich auch*,' she said. Me too.

After she had rung off she sat for a while, thinking, imagining... She had a hard job keeping the smile off her face.

You are old, she thought. You should be propped in a corner with a bundle of knitting, not contemplating an affair with a rich and attractive man.

Oh yes? she thought. And who says so?

She flew to Frankfurt. Helmut met her with roses, his most charming smile and a chauffeur-driven Mercedes half a mile long. He had taken the most expensive suite in the Fleming's de Luxe for her. He was wonderful company – considerate, courteous, attentive at all times. As promised, he had arranged for her to meet the investors who were in the process of making several fortunes out of the Tucker empire. In every way but one her visit was a resounding success.

On the personal level the chemistry, when they came to it, wasn't there. She liked and respected him. He was an admirable man but kissing him was like kissing a doorpost. They did their best but both realised it was hopeless. They parted friends, and friends they would remain all their lives. They parted nonetheless.

She had been unsure what to do after Frankfurt. She had thought she might go to Copenhagen, to meet the alternative energy experts. She had considered Rome, a city she had always wanted to visit. In the event she flew to London.

She told herself she had one reason.

Shortly before leaving Germany she had received news from her London agent. She had known that the Earl of Clapham, her supposed father, had died at the age of ninety, four years before. Now she learnt that the countess, well into her eighties, had been reduced to living in straitened financial circumstances; her brother, true to character, had placed her money in a number of investments that, for one reason or another, had failed. Now he was living in luxury in Morocco, his actions under review by the fraud squad, while Charlotte Richmond, dowager Countess of Clapham, was enduring comparative penury in a small suite of rooms at Ripon Grange. And with no opportunity to appeal to the charity of the next earl because, with no cousins to inherit, the title – after three hundred and twenty-four years – was extinct.

Bella intended to go and see her because Bella, mindful of the way the countess had treated her in the past, had a plan.

When she arrived, her first impression was of neglect. The gate-keeper's lodge was empty, the blinds down in the windows. The gates were open, the wrought iron scarred with rust. The grounds, which Bella remembered as one of the glories of the Grange, were overgrown.

Her chauffeur-driven car stopped at the foot of the entrance steps. The massive front doors were closed. By the look of them they were seldom anything else, but Bella had phoned ahead and was not to be put off by appearances.

She climbed the steps – mossy, with rank grasses in the cracks – and rang the bell. While she waited, she looked out at the view.

Much had changed in forty-seven years but that had not. The verdant countryside stretched away to the moors that, now as then, dominated all.

The door opened and she turned. Once it would have been a liveried footman; now a slatternly dressed woman in bedroom slippers stared at her.

'Yes?'

'I have an appointment with the countess.'

'Best come in, then.'

Bella stepped inside; the door closed behind her. Shadows were everywhere; she doubted whether the entrance hall, once immaculate, had seen a broom or duster in years.

The woman trudged ahead of Bella towards the stairs.

'Countess keeps to her room. None too nimble, these days,' she said over her shoulder. 'Can't mind the last time she were downstairs.'

Charlotte was wearing a grey shawl and was hunched over a miserable fire. She had never been a beauty. Now her face was heavily lined and the knuckles of her hands swollen with arthritis, but the malignant fire that Bella remembered still flickered in the dark eyes.

She looked Bella up and down. 'You're back, then. What brings you to these parts?'

'I came to see you.'

'I can't imagine why. We never had any time for each other when you were here and I don't suppose you feel any more kindly disposed towards me now.'

'Perhaps not,' Bella said. 'But I am here anyway.'

'Why? To gloat?'

Driving to the Grange Bella had asked herself the same question. The countess had treated her abominably. As a child Bella had been helpless and she had taken full advantage, but now the boot was on the other foot. Bella was rich beyond dreams of avarice whereas the countess was a heap of impecunious bones in a moth-eaten chair. Yes, Bella thought, perhaps she had come to gloat.

If so, the sight of her old enemy changed her mind. There was nothing here but an old woman fallen on bad times, and what was there to gloat about in that?

'I just came to see you,' she said. 'You are part of my life, after all.'

'Revisiting the past? I wish you joy of it, in that case.'

Whatever else the countess had lost, the spirit was still there.

Bella's plan had been to wound the old woman's pride, the one area that still mattered to her. She had planned to offer her an allowance, knowing it would put acid in her soul, knowing she could not afford to say no. But now, seeing Charlotte as she had become, Bella changed her mind. It was all so long ago and she discovered she had no longer had an appetite for revenge.

If I do that, she thought, how am I different from her? I must be getting old myself. Ancient or saintly. What a choice.

She would pay the allowance but anonymously, to help salve the old woman's pride.

They had nothing to say to each other and within fifteen minutes she left her, and the Grange. The door closed upon the past.

'Where to?' the driver said.

Bella drew a deep breath. 'Branksome Hall,' she said.

Unlike her visit to Ripon Grange, she had not phoned ahead. Until this instant she had not known she would be going there. She was unexpected; there might be no one at home. She sat in the back of the Daimler, eyes closed, heart beating a hundred miles a minute. When she opened her eyes the car was just turning into the long driveway leading to the house.

The day had turned gloomy, the dark line of the moors hidden by cloud. Looking over the driver's shoulder, she saw that the lights were shining through what had been the library windows and remembered her youthful fantasy of riding beside her husband up the driveway to home.

Her life had certainly worked out very differently, she thought. More challenging, in some ways more fulfilling. Certainly she had scored a deeper line upon the page of fate than would have happened had she stayed at Branksome Hall. Yet she had wanted that more than anything. She couldn't have had a better husband, for all their faults the children were an unfailing joy, yet she felt sad that she had missed out on the one thing that had meant so much to her. Now, watching the house drawing closer, she had time to feel panic. I am such a fool, she thought. An old woman, seeking the lost romance of her past: what else could that bring but disaster? Far better to have kept the unsullied memories of golden youth…

Yet she was here and this time, stubborn as ever, she would not turn away.

She was admitted into the hallway she remembered so well. It was shiny with polish and bright with flowers. A woman's hand?

For a moment Bella was paralysed with doubt. Had her information been wrong? Had Charles married the countess's sister, after all? Someone else?

A woman came smiling from a back room. She was plump, about fifty, with a wedding ring on her finger.

'Mrs Tucker? Mrs Tucker from Australia?'

'Yes,' Bella said.

'What a pleasant surprise! I am Mrs Hardy,' the woman said. 'We have been reading such a lot about you in the papers recently.'

Bella's lips were numb as she struggled for a smile.

You fool, she thought. 'Why should that be?' she said.

'The iron-ore magnate? You are famous, I assure you. Especially to those of us who read the financial pages. And of course Charles has never forgotten you.'

'How long have you been married?' Bella asked.

'Married?' The woman stared; then her expression changed and she laughed. 'I am so sorry! How foolish of me… I am not married to Charles,' she explained, 'but to Charles's cousin.'

Bella blinked, licking dry lips.

'Charles never married anybody. The family always blamed you for that, you know.'

'I had no say in it, one way or the other,' Bella said.

Dizzy with relief, she did not know what to do with her hands.

'He's with his estate manager,' Mrs Hardy said. 'But he won't mind being disturbed. In fact I think he will be delighted to be disturbed.'

She led the way into the drawing room.

'Please have a seat,' said Mrs Hardy, the cousin's wife. 'I shall go and dig him out.'

Excitement, fear, embarrassment... Bella could not keep up with her emotions. She sat and listened to the thunder of her heart. This is going to be a disaster, she thought. We shall look at each other and there will be no spark, nothing. All my memories and dreams will be ash. I was a fool to come.

And Charles came. Eyes closed, she did not see him arrive, yet she knew. She looked up and there he was. For a moment she saw no change in him. He was as he had been almost half a century before. Then she saw that he had indeed changed, as she had. What else could she expect? Yet it was not so. He had not changed; she had not changed, and the world was as it had been half a lifetime ago.

She had been frightened, on the edge of panic but, as they smiled at each other, it was as though they had never been apart and she felt nothing but joy. Because she knew, with astonishment and something close to reverence, that she had come home.

CHAPTER SIXTY-ONE

That night Bella lay in her hotel bedroom and contemplated the challenges, so joyous yet perplexing, that had emerged that day to complicate her life.

Was she mad, to consider sharing what remained of her future with Charles Hardy? Was Charles mad, for sharing the same dream?

What would the children say? Bella had always marched to the beat of her own drum, but their views should be considered, too.

Peace would think, and say, that she had lost her marbles, but Peace believed in nothing she could not touch. That was her strength and weakness. Richard would be more philosophical, more inclined than his sister to let Bella live her own life.

Her own instincts shouted yes, but in this situation could they be trusted? After so many years, was it really possible to recreate the fire that had consumed them in those long-lost days?

What about the business? Should one of the children take over? And, if so, which one? She had thought about that during the journey from Australia and believed she had come up with the answer, but she would ponder some more before making a final decision.

What about her other plans: the universities and medical schools, research into alternative energy, bringing water to a parched land? What about Branksome Hall?

Could the impracticability of a love, so long denied, overcome the practical challenges of life?

Bella remembered Miranda Downs, the cinnamon dust incandescent in the sunlight as she, Garth and the boys fought to subdue the wild cattle amid the placidly circling coaches. She remembered the Carlisle Mine and the detonation of the charges used to bring the precious ore into the light. Dust again, in grey clouds this time.

The vastness of space and sky, sunlight, droughts and floods, the billowing dust that for her had come to represent the land itself. The dust of the land, like the cattle and freight wagons transporting the precious ore to the coast.

She thought: I cannot turn my back on it. No more can Charles walk away from the hundreds of years of his own history. Two aging lovers chained to the opposite ends of the earth: how could a life together be achieved? It was hopeless. Impossible.

Yet perhaps not. I have always enjoyed life's challenges, Bella told herself. To venture. To win. Mostly to win. Sometimes, of course, we lose. Because Judas is always with us.

But that is love, is it not? A challenge. Taking a step into the unknown. To venture. Hopefully to win.

I have to believe, or all these years I have been nourishing a delusion. I must have faith that the promises we made to each other, half a lifetime ago, will be fulfilled.

What else is life?

AUTHOR'S NOTES

Because of the imagined shortage of iron ore in Australia, prospecting or pegging claims was prohibited in Western Australia until the change of legislation in 1960.

Previous aerial surveys carried out by the authorities failed to identify the huge deposits of iron ore that in fact exist in that state.

Marra mamba ore was at one time regarded as of little value, an assessment that is now discredited.

On-going sales of ore to China continue to be of major importance to the Australian economy.

A dispute between two major mining companies resulted in the duplication of railways connecting the mining areas with the coast, where loading terminals have been developed for the shipment of ore.

Ore prices were significantly depressed by the 1973 Arab oil embargo.

Cyclone Joan struck the Pilbara coast on the date and in the manner described in the narrative.

The Tucker family and its adventures are entirely fictitious and have no connection with anyone actually involved in the industry or elsewhere.

ABOUT THE AUTHOR

J.H. Fletcher is the prize-winning author of fifteen novels, published to both critical and popular acclaim in Australia, Germany and the UK, as well as numerous short stories and plays for radio and television. He was educated in England and France and travelled and worked in Europe, Asia and Africa before emigrating to Australia in 1991. Home is now a house on the edge of the Western Tier Mountains in northern Tasmania.

ACKNOWLEDGEMENTS

Every book bears the name of its author but in reality its production is very much a team effort. I should therefore like to acknowledge with heartfelt thanks the contribution of all those who have been involved in creating *Dust of the Land*. I should like to make especial mention of Drew Keys and his extremely valuable suggestions and of Sue Brockhoff and her marvellous team at Harlequin.